# CHRISTINE'S

# CURSE

# GUY THOMSON

LONGCROSS PRESS

ISBN    978-99959-54-03-1

# CHRISTINE'S

# CURSE

Acknowledgements

I would like to express my heartfelt thanks to the many people who have given me their time, assistance and encouragement with this project: in particular, but in no particular order, Lizzy Hamill-Stewart, Maggie Wilkinson, Cheryl Meade, Jean-Paul Ciantar, Andrew and Annabel Murray, Dee Kemp, Georgina Board, Henry von Blumenthal, Hamish MacDonald, Nick Barker and Jon Thurley, all of whom who have helped in the typing, editing, or suggestion of material for this book.

Extra special thanks must go to my sister, Anne Dundas, for typing and re-typing time and time again the original manuscript; to Mark James, who acted as my main editor and filth filter; to John Graham, of adcreative.co.uk for his advice and input with regards the cover design; and to Mike O'Leary, who in effect sponsored me through this venture.

Finally, I am duty-bound to acknowledge the numerous television, radio and other media sources from whom I openly admit to having lifted the scatological collage of ideas that has gone to form the mosaic that is this book. If I am accused of plagiarism, I stand guilty. If any order has come out of the chaos, does it really matter?

CONTENTS

| | | |
|---|---|---|
| Chapter 1 | 1986 | 1 |
| Chapter 2 | And God Created Schtoink | 7 |
| Chapter 3 | On the Road | 31 |
| Chapter 4 | Crystal | 43 |
| Chapter 5 | Things Look Up | 53 |
| Chapter 6 | Roxanne | 67 |
| Chapter 7 | On the Rock ' n' Roll | 87 |
| Chapter 8 | India | 91 |
| Chapter 9 | Back to Life: Back to Reality | 101 |
| Chapter 10 | The Chipmunks | 125 |
| Chapter 11 | Losing It | 161 |
| Chapter 12 | Bombing Badly | 179 |
| Chapter 13 | Things Look Down | 193 |
| Chapter 14 | Slime and Punishment | 205 |

# Chapter 1: 1986

With the benefit of hindsight, and had I known where events were going to lead me, I might not have been in such a hurry to get back to what I *then* considered to be civilisation. There has been some good, of course. Since entering this abattoir of notoriety, this misanthropic tomb that is now my home, I've had plenty of time to reflect on my side of things. If there was ever a side to what I initially jokingly, and then with increasing alarm, referred to as "Christine's Curse". Whether the whole episode was an accident waiting to happen or things would have turned out as they did regardless, I suppose I'll never know. Somehow, I doubt it. It was a mistake and thus, by its very nature, it's almost pointless trying to speculate about the likelihood of it happening under different circumstances. One thing led to another and random incidents that occurred over the ensuing half-dozen years, which seemed unfocused and unconnected at the time, now appear as perfectly logical stepping stones to the *grande finale*.

Coming back was a matter of chance. I wouldn't have returned if I hadn't had a job to go to. It was a fluke that one happened to crop up when I was home on a visit to London. Till then I had spent most of my working life in various locations around the globe in the service of The Pan Asian Banking System Limited. I subsequently discovered trying to find a livelihood in the UK a struggle. Most prospective employers I approached regarded the Pan Asian as a colonial anomaly, which at the time it was. As was I, in a short, fat middle class sort of way.

Despite the late stage of the century, British banks were still unadventurous about hiring outsiders. To do them justice, I recognised that I was difficult to place. The Pan Asian had always played on this as a means of keeping their expatriate staff and made a point of teaching them a lot about the Pan Asian but not much about actual banking. But the pay was OK and tax free. Accommodation and flights home were all part of the deal, but I found that after ten years of being shunted from one country to the next without referral, I'd had enough. I wanted to have some control over where I lived, at least. I had become an over-privileged dogsbody without a kennel I could call a home. There were other factors that suggested that it would be prudent to leave the company sooner rather than later. I eventually became bored with watching the other emigrant pondlife filling their faces every night - all you can eat for ten dinars - at whichever hotel, motel or Holiday Inn I happened to be staying in.  Another airport, another queue.  Blah. Blah. Blah. I decided when the opportunity arose to throw my anchor down back home in England.

My chance came with the advent of the new style of foreign banks in London which, compared to their British counterparts, were positively flamboyant about their hiring procedure. I gained an introduction with one such organisation, Parker Barrow Brothers and for no apparent reason was promptly offered a job. I went back to the Far East to work out my notice and gather my bags.

I left Asia two months later on a Friday, and started working in a mildly disorientated fashion for my newly adopted masters in London the following Monday as an elderly sales trainee. The work was different from what I had been used to. The unfamiliar, unstructured dealing environment was in stark contrast to the praefectorial regime that had prevailed at The Pan Asian. The day would start with the early morning meetings, conducted in small conference rooms with thirty or so people packed in cheek by jowl, as the key traders spewed their jargon. The microcosm of CMOs, MBOs and LBOs, Fanny Maes, Ginny Maes and Freddie Macs had me completely fooled for the first few weeks, but once the vernacular was under control it was easier to confront the other technicalities. The hours were long and involved a certain type of concentration. Ignorance or a lack of awareness of a particular issue prompted instant derision. A chance question, or an ill-chosen remark could lead to hooplas of ridicule and rain dances of scorn around the unfortunate perpetrator.

Ostensibly everyone worked for the same company, but a dog-eat-dog mentality prevailed between the various sections and the individuals within. The sales force fought amongst themselves for commission or recognition while being heckled by the traders. The commercial paper people deluded themselves into thinking that they were superior to the floating-rate note team who in turn regarded themselves as a cut above the bond players. It was a seal colony of braying alpha males, grunting females and mewling pups. Essex aristocrats battled with preening Continentals while the Americans vied with each other to be the most professionally hip. Away from the front line, the managers hid in their glass menageries and counted the profits before awarding themselves their next pay rise, apparently unaware of the chaos going on outside. It was, as a company, in its own self-congratulatory way, a healthy example of a firm at war with itself.

I sat at one end of the perimeter desk that circumnavigated the main chamber. My slot had the usual bank of information terminals *de rigueur* of dealing rooms, and a visual display telephone where the numbers were dialled by touching the screen, faith healer style. On my left was a bookish-looking woman who initially helped me to settle in. On my right was a snooty French girl who spent most of the day talking to the Japanese woman who sat on her other side. There were a lot of women around. I nicknamed the French girl, for my private use, "Project 2000" because I reckoned that it would take me till the year 2000 to get into her pants. If I was incredibly lucky. That was in 1986 and I was still in my twenties. Just. From my position there was a good view of the room and most of the other dealing sections. The rest of the sales force was stationed on the outer desk. In the middle the traders sat like débutantes, poised as if to decline a dance, occasionally barking prices in grandiloquent glottal stops while the sales and settlements people milled around them like prospective suitors.

After a few weeks I became brainwashed by the constant exchange of information, prices, yields, spreads and announcements that had to be digested and then regurgitated down the telephone. The job somehow took a disproportionate chunk out of the day. No sooner would I return home and put my head on my pillow than it was time to get up and go back to work. I started to hallucinate about markets and rates. I dreamt I was a bond spinning round and round in an endless pirouette, turning gracefully from one currency to another, while being serenely pitched from switch to swap in gentle locations around the globe.

On the surface the London office was a replica of any of its Wall Street cousins. Men hurried about their business in striped shirts and braces, carrying bagels and styrofoam coffee, all adding to the cosy club-like fug. But beneath the surface there was a malevolent undercurrent of being beholden to the Head Office mandarins in New York. They were the ones who called the shots on who was hired or fired, the size of the budgets and pay-outs and so on.

As a career it struck me fairly early on that there wasn't much direction. Markets went up and markets went down. People got excited and then went back to sleep. Perhaps the deals and turnover grew larger with time and experience, but it was an odd sort of life, staring at screens all day and then going home to watch television at night. The money was good, which was why people did it. Not that I saw much of it, but there were plenty who did. They'd had it all their short little lives. Money was their birthright and to protect it there was a form of one-upmanship, thinly disguised between gritted teeth as comradely joshing.

I was in no position to criticise. I had been a beneficiary of the cavalier hiring technique of taking on anyone who happened to walk through the door, but as time went by I noticed one or two things were amiss. The clients - the banks, the institutions, the insurance companies and pension funds - were all getting stuffed. Not the whole time, but a lot of it which meant in turn that their customers - the pensioners, the insurance and annuity scheme holders, taxpayers and the average man in the street - were getting ripped off too. The system was too big to question; it would have been as futile as a corporal in the Waffen SS questioning the ethics of using torture as a means of interrogation. But something had to give. The money had to come from somewhere.

This so-called service industry had become a shooting gallery. The clients had become the targets. They were slowly being picked off by snipers. Half a point here, an eighth of a point there. By the time the money had eventually found a home it had changed hands six or seven times with everyone taking his or her slice along the way. Furthermore, if the hapless customers wanted to sell their investments, suddenly nobody wanted to know. Invariably the market would only buy at such a discount that it was hardly worth selling. This was put down to "illiquidity", but in most instances it was just a euphemism for greed.

At least I overcame the mysteries behind the earnest but uninformative tombstones in the financial press with banks of banks and brokers listed in diminishing typeset. Previously I had been stumped by such pronouncements as "First City Bank Corp $200,000,000 Revolving Note Facility", with the inevitable disclaimer at the top: "This notice appears by way of record only", as if the battle had already been won. I had tried to avoid such financial voodoo, but I now was obliged to be fully conversant with what it was all about in double-quick time. Euromoney. Eurobonds. Eurotrash. A lexicon of buzzwords had spawned a multi-billion dollar industry of hype. An élite of semiprecious Gucci-shod prospectors arose from the anarchy of optimism and became lords of all they surveyed.

A spirit of abandon took over as the planet had its last really big party before settling down to the serious business of properly choking itself to death once and for all. London had become a multicultural mishmash of dissociated tribes in the time I'd been away. The good-natured lethargy of Callaghan's Britain had, under the auspices of one wilful woman, been replaced by a very different zeitgeist. A confusing world of plastic kettles, filofaxes and mobile telephones had erupted in my absence. The absurdity of Docklands; the artlessness of Gilbert and George; kissagrams, stripograms and shop assistants wearing badges saying "Hi! I'm Allen. How can I help?" Even television, technology's laxative for the masses and already mediocre by design, had descended into a detritus of priggish situation comedies and idiotic quiz shows with the occasional series on impending environmental doom thrown in for good measure. And I had forgotten how *cold* the place could get.

I slipped into a routine and became like any other ant on the hill. The usual pattern of eat-excrete-work-relax-sleep, eat-excrete-work-relax-sleep became more homogenous with each passing day. Every morning I grudgingly bought a pink newspaper I didn't want to read, complete with pictures of tight-lipped businessmen in book-lined offices looking importantly down their demilunettes, while I fought with some killer supplement on "The Netherlands" or "Vehicle Fleet Management" that was about to spill onto the pavement

I took my place solemnly on the platform each day, standing in wait with my fellow travellers to join the can of human tuna that would sweep us off to the dark satanic mills of the City. Hurry - you'll miss your train. Busy. Busy. Busy. Strap-hanging dwarf! All wrapped up like tiny school children but now carrying briefcases in place of satchels, or shiny gym bags to ward off latent middle age. Too late! There's no going back! The cold underground stations flashed by. I changed their names for my own amusement: Glue Road, Embitterment, King's Cross (I'm livid), Groin Park, Tower Hell, Monument (for Blank).

At the office the institutional cancers of company cars, expense accounts and corporate hospitality had mushroomed in the general Archerisation of the economy. Yet in the quest for betterment, a little of the nation's soul had disappeared. The 'got-a-problem-build-a-shopping-centre' mentality had started to rob this green and pleasant land of its magic. Something once faded and flawed, but nonetheless precious, had become brittle and coarse. The streets in each town were now identical. The shops had been slaughtered by the malls and the franchises, bringing a not-so-cute conformity to town and village alike. Emporia vied with one another between the Burger Clones and McToilets, each with its own faddish niche; one for socks, one for ties, one for underpants, one for expensive chocolates and so on. There was even one, bless it, for body lotions that hadn't been tested on furry animals, although judging from their happy little presentation baskets, the ecological costs of so much plastic and padding far outweighed any gains achieved by restricting animal misery.

A contagious glow of complacency had spread across this populace. Two-a-penny entrepreneurs manifested themselves overnight, became shining stars and then collapsed like disgraced supernovas. Residential developments with names such as 'Blazer Court' and 'Cravat Square' broke out like cankers around the country in doll's house perfection to shelter their upwardly mobile occupants.

I stared at this new republic of precocity and began to wonder if I'd made a dreadful mistake coming back.

# Chapter 2: And God Created Schtoink

Back to base. At around the same time that everything else was going haywire, my own psychic gyroscope started to wobble badly out of kilter. It was only by making some hastily needed alterations in procedure that I managed to slip by unnoticed and pass myself off as a normal member of society.

Events were not enhanced for me by the fact that I was going through a period of emotional post-traumatic shock. I had been struck in an unprotected area by a woman whom I had originally met and seduced along my travels with The Pan Asian. Then she had been a willing pupil for my guile, but my role as Svengali became a thing of the past once we had both relocated to the relative discretion of London. After a series of rows, threats and bounced cheques, I limped away from the smouldering wreck of what had been an intense relationship, outclassed and out-gunned by the very person who'd once been my protégée. In the space of two years I'd made a monster out of Christine Hale. By the end I had lost all control. I tried to appease her, like the professorial creator in the white lab coat attending to some last minute surgical adjustments in an attempt to contain the damage, but it was too late. All that remained was the hissing serpent of mutual deceit which, but for my trance-like fascination, should have been left well alone. And with it, although I didn't know it at first, this strange and unaccountable hex that was to haunt me for the coming years.

In the end Christine left me for a knitting catalogue android and we never spoke as sweethearts again. As I lay at Christine's feet and gave my last display of drunken fawning, she looked at me and emitted an aura of such withering contempt that it transcended all parameters of normal human loathing. I gazed back at her spoilt child-queen face - Nefertiti chewing gum - and a part of my inmost mind became cauterised, or perhaps more accurately warped, forever. I vowed never to put myself in such a position again, but the moment had passed to save me from the faltering despair and sense of futility that I had been accorded.

I returned to alcohol with a vengeance and began my lonely but faithful affair with the bottle. I fluctuated between a state of delirium and regret for most of the first year back. I tried to dull the angst by throwing myself into a series of futile relationships and, for all I know broke the occasional heart along the way, as I tried to cast the devils from my head. Most encounters were little more than bizarre one night stands with unfortunate drink-gorged slatterns probably as desperate for company as I, on occasions mercifully too infrequent to warrant self-doubt or remorse.

I persevered nonetheless with my phallus of fallacious attachments, more due to opportunity than any conscious decision to build a bile silo to house my resentment. I kept my sights low in order to find an emotional foothold. I looked to the office for kicks and worked my way through various loveless liaisons, refurbishing my confidence with low quality trade while I adjusted technique and method in preparation for better things. I still used every opportunity to get close to 'Project 2000' at work but she was no Anglophile. To her all Englishmen were fools and I was no exception, but it passed the time. The more important females within the company were either hard-bitten Sloanes or Americans who kept themselves for the bigger fish. But despite my quick succession of shoot-to-kill relationships my parting with Christine always smarted.

Then one morning that summer a new girl walked into the office who looked as if she'd been made by angels. We didn't work in the same department but she came into mine every so often on various errands. She had the fresh radiance and impish bounce of adolescence, but otherwise I'd never seen anyone quite like her. She had clear light brown skin, large coal-black eyes, a thick hazelnut mane and slender arms leading to delicate hands with long Thai dancer-style fingers. To add to the biological helix she also had the faintest dusting of facial hair, which rather than being hideous merely softened the distinction of her features. Although her colouring was Mediterranean, her appearance was too exotic to be European. It was most confusing and I couldn't take my eyes off her.

I started to make spurious journeys on false pretexts to her department and indulged in weighty debate with her section head on matters that could just as easily have been resolved by a phone call. A few days passed before I casually asked Karen - they're always called Karen - one of the VDU vamps who worked near me, to make some enquiries about who or what this new girl was.

Karen possessed an unquenchable thirst for office gossip and readily agreed to the task set, but I was taken aback the next day when she excitedly waved an upward thumb at me. I couldn't think of anything that we'd discussed in the course of business that warranted such enthusiasm and at that point had no idea that she had moved so quickly with her investigations. It turned out that the new girl's name was Yasmin. Yasmin Simpson. She was half-Iranian, half-Finnish. No wonder I hadn't been able to place her. How exciting! To consort with a savage! She was only twenty-one but had already been married to a British guy whom she'd subsequently divorced, which explained the bathos of her last name with the exotic nature of her first. Started young, I thought to myself. She had no boyfriend and was new to London. Perfect.

Suddenly Karen dropped the bomb; Yasmin Simpson, apparently, thought I was rather nice. I nearly fell off my chair. Little pervy-looking me with my watery alcoholic eyes and drink veins! The happy coincidence of mutual attraction didn't happen to me every day. Normally I had to pester girls with the conversational equivalent of chocolates and flowers for weeks before they even knew I existed. I went into a state of shock as all my Christmases rolled into one. I'd died and gone to Heaven! I thanked Karen for her good work and mentally canonised her before passing back into a daze. I recovered my senses and asked Karen what I was supposed to do next, but she'd sorted all that out. She'd arranged for a group from the office to meet for a drink after work at the end of the week and why didn't I just happen drop by? Karen said she would make sure that Yasmin was there and on track.

I continued my macho posturing in Yasmin's department for the next two days. When the anointed evening came I made my way to the designated bar, half-elated, half-dog-tired with apprehension. Yasmin was tucked away in a corner and I had to make facile conversation with a couple of traders before I was able to position myself close to her.

"Karen says you're giving your hands a holiday and going after that foreign piece of schtoink over there, Mallet," one of the traders said, leering at me.

'Schtoink' was in-house traderspeak for any unattached member of the female staff under thirty.                                 'Mallet' was me, James Mallet, unattached member of the male staff, now over thirty.

"So?" I replied, acting tough. "I've always fancied a bit of chocolate on my popsicle. Besides they're all pink inside and there's nothing wrong with a bit of 'strange' now and then, eh lads?"

It took an act of superhuman bravery for me to make my first advance on Yasmin. My heart started to race. My mouth went dry and my bottom puckered as I gathered the courage to speak to her. In the subterranean semi-darkness of the bar Yasmin seemed even more sexually inaccessible. Long legs. Short skirt. Black stockings. Make-up. Mouth. Youth. All I was, was a stuffed shirt in a suit. Talk about an unfair advantage! Yet, by dint of ritual, I was supposed to take the lead.

Eventually, with startling inventiveness, I turned to her and said "Hello". A foolproof way to start a conversation, with a zero option for the recipient. She parried, predictably, with an identical response. I was left with the conversational ball back in my court again and at a loss as how to play it.

"I'm James Mallet," I said, offering a much wiped but still damp hand.

"Hi! I'm Yasmin Simpson," she said, as she accepted my clammy paw into her perfect, sweatless mitt.

Small talk that came to me so naturally in normal situations now deserted me in my hour of need. Short of saying "Do you come here often?" I was forced to switch onto conversational autopilot and go for other social banalities just as crass.

"So you've just joined us?" I enquired, aware too late that I was being absurdly condescending in using the word 'us'.

"Yeah. I joined a few weeks ago," she replied, neutrally. I detected a nasal lisp despite the lack of shibboleths in her reply.

"What were you doing before?" I asked hurriedly to compensate for her lack of colloquial co-operation.

"I worked for an egg cup factory in Alton."

"Alton?!" I exclaimed, clutching joyously at a contrived straw of coincidence. "My parents practically live next door in Farnham!"

After that it was convivial plain sailing and we talked easily until it was time to leave and go our separate ways.

For the next week Yasmin and I cheerfully smiled and acknowledged each other in the corridor whenever our paths crossed. One day I managed to catch her on her own by the photocopier and after a brief chat suggested that we should get together for another drink after work sometime. She greeted the invitation with interest, if not rapture. I barged on regardless and asked her if she was free for a 'quick one' after work that Friday. The outer limits of my audacity had been well and truly tested, but I tried to make light of it and pass myself off as a natural groover. To my relief she said she was free. The ancient and noble art of trying it on had actually worked!

The rest of the week passed agreeably. I had a sugary feeling that I was about to receive a present. For sheer elation, there was nothing quite like the scent of an affair in the air. It was almost better than sex itself. It was better than a holiday or a promotion, not that I'd experienced either for a while. But the dark and sinister clouds of emotional precision bombing brought me back to earth and I turned my thoughts to the job in hand. I tried to think of a suitable venue. There was nowhere quiet or wildly romantic near work that struck the right chord. The idea of sitting in a bar with fifty million other Friday night City revellers was too appalling to contemplate, and at the same time I couldn't visualise travelling together to somewhere quieter. If we ever managed to find a taxi we'd be stuck in a jam for eternity and the Underground was hardly the most intimate place to strike up our first unaccompanied conversation. I decided, perhaps unfairly, to take a short cut across the rule book. I thought of an excuse whereby I would be obliged to put off meeting her directly after work, and instead would suggest meeting later, at some pre-determined location. What better place than my flat?

That Friday morning I took Yasmin to one side and told her that I'd been called to see a client after work. She registered a small flicker of disappointment, probably more out of general irritation than pique at not seeing me. It was then that I put it to her:

"But I could see you later."

"Like where?" she retorted, indignantly.

"Well I know this sounds idiotic, but I think it's the only way we can connect: I'll be through with seeing this client by about seven, so why don't you boogie on down to my part of town around then? We could meet *chez moi* and then go to supper around the corner."

Careful, Mallet, I thought to myself, you're sailing close to the wind and could be blown onto the rocks at any moment. There was a second's hesitation before Yasmin's expression recorded a confused realisation of the implications of my suggestion.

"But where do you live? And what am I going to do in between?"

Thrust, parry, step back.

"I'm really sorry Yasmin, but it's the only opportunity I've got to see this client. It would be on a Friday, wouldn't it? I mean I'm actually just off Alphabet Street... it's about half an hour down the line from here. You can be on a train home by ten." I paused briefly and assessed the chances of calling her bluff by offering her an escape route. I decided to risk it.

"What the heck... perhaps it's best if we made it another time?"

Yasmin looked dejected by my supposed attempt to flake out of the evening and my subsequent *volte-face* of leaving the initiative to her. I carried on quickly before she had time to collect her thoughts.

"Mind you, if you don't mind joining the others for a drink after work, all you have to do is get on the District or Circle for a dozen stops and you're there."

I hoped by sounding casual that any reluctance on Yasmin's part would automatically make her appear guilty of jumping to profane conclusions.

"Well, OK, but..."

"I'll draw you a map... it's too simple. There's a good little restaurant around the corner from where I live. I mean I wouldn't blame you if you think it's too much of a drag... I don't know about you, but apart from seeing this wretched customer, I'll be slightly at a loose end for the rest of the evening. I'm really sorry about mucking the whole thing up..." I said, trying to look miserable.

From improper suggestion to little boy lost in under thirty seconds! Either out of exasperation or by dint of attrition, she acquiesced. I drew a map of where I lived on a piece of photocopy paper. *About sevenish*, Mr Devenish?

Glorious! Poor thing. Little did she realise what she was letting herself in for. I was delighted at the prospect of playing on my home turf. It gave me time to have a leisurely bath and change into my 'Get Luckies' - a pair of frayed, yellow-fronted underpants that for some mysterious reason had in the past, had a talismanic effect in assisting me with my seduction objectives.

When I got back I booked a suitably friendly, medium-spend restaurant nearby and thought of some things that we could talk about. I rehearsed a few lines of conversation while I was in the bath and gently made myself pretty.

Seven o'clock came and with it Yasmin, looking as if she was about to climb the guillotine. My flat was a friendly little place, as slaughter houses went, and I did everything in my power to put her at ease. After a couple of drinks the ice was broken and the conversation was more or less on auto by the time we left for the restaurant. It was a warm evening and the distance to the restaurant was an easy walk. I took her via a particularly pretty backwater with leafy side streets, past some knicker-sheddingly affluent-looking houses.

The restaurant was lively but intimate. I steered us towards three courses and spun things out to make sure Yasmin would miss her last train. I quizzed her gently about her ex-husband, her past, her divorce, love, pain and the whole damn thing and in the process managed, I hoped, to present a caring, protective image of myself. For her part, Yasmin didn't seem massively intelligent, but intelligence was not what I was looking for that evening. She was nice enough but bland. Very much in the Wimbledon courtesy car driver mould. It was difficult to imagine that she had been old and wise enough to have held down a marriage, but then again she hadn't. She laughed bewilderedly at my jokes and it seemed almost cruel to take things a stage further. Then I thought of the times I'd been crushed, and quashed any pangs of conscience.

Over coffee it seemed perfectly natural, if nauseating, that we should hold hands across the table. Alcohol and ambience had by now got the better of us. I was practically on the point of washing my socks in Yasmin's pants when the bill came. The magic was temporarily broken. Yasmin came down to earth with a bump and looked at her watch.

"Shit!" she yelped. "It's eleven... how on earth am I going to get home?"

"Don't worry angel," I said reassuringly. "It's Friday. I'll get you a taxi."

"To Alton?! But it's miles away."

"So what? I'll pay. It's only money," I said casually, praying that she'd stop panicking and settle down. "Worse things have happened at sea. I'm sure we'll both live. It's been such a nice evening. There's a gypsy cab company near me that does the airport run at odd hours for twenty quid, and Alton's not much further. It'd be a pity to spoil it by getting into a flap," I added cryptically, safe in the knowledge that any *double entendre* would go undetected.

Yasmin was tense despite my assurances, but fortunately at that moment the *maitre d'* came to scoop up my credit card.

"Would *madame-monsieur* accept *un digestif* compliments of the 'ouse?"

I couldn't for the life of me think why we would want a biscuit after such a complete meal, but decided to nod my assent rather than appear ungrateful.

"Cognac? Courvoisier? Grand Marnier?" he asked, to my relief. As a distraction it not only took the heat off the moment but added to the illusion of my charmed, perfumed existence, where courtly restaurateurs proffered complimentary drinks wherever I happened to flounce.

After we had knocked back the drinks, I signed the credit card slip with an ostentatious lack of fuss. We made our way back to my flat. The evening was cooler. It seemed an innocent move to slip my arm insulatingly around Yasmin. After a few hesitant moments she reciprocated.

We stopped to cross another tree-lined, dimly lit street that I had unnecessarily steered us down. I turned Yasmin round in my arms and softly kissed her on the mouth. I could feel her melt and, for a brief moment, I felt like Burt Lancaster with Deborah Kerr in the surf. We started slowly with a few tentative, exploratory nibbles before going for the full multi-wash tumble spin. The inside of her mouth was refreshingly cool and had an unusual, slightly metallic taste redolent, I imagined at the time, of rusting carburettors.

We continued home, holding each other closely. When we got back to the flat I poured some more drinks. As a token gesture, to prove I was as good as my word, I went through the motions of calling a cab company. I dialled seven of the eight digits, put the phone down and repeated the process.

"Damn... busy... give it a couple of minutes."

I sat next to Yasmin on the sofa, clinked my glass against hers and cornily toasted our good fortune at having met each other. I shifted closer and fenced her into a supine position. We went into another tonsil-bashing exchange of tongues but this time I had the luxury of the sofa to press her against. My erection was undeterred by her disappointingly small breasts. I had just manoeuvred myself on top of her when, as if suddenly coming to my senses, I jumped up and cried, "Must get you a cab!"

Yasmin was temporarily relieved by my display of decency and fair play. I dialled seven digits again.

"Bugger it. They're still engaged."

I reluctantly put the phone down and asked, "Do you know any cab companies?" knowing that as an out-of-towner, she probably wouldn't.

"Not really," she answered, hesitantly.

"Well, we'd better get a black cab on the street then."

"To Alton?!" she exclaimed again more.

"Well, what else? I mean without being a jerk, you're more than welcome to spend the night. I'll have the sofa and you can have the bed or the other way round. And I've got a spare toothbrush. We're both grown-ups and it's Friday, so quite frankly what's the rush? You're better off, and safer, staying here rather than doing anything too ambitious at this time of night."

Yasmin shivered a little and contemplated her predicament. Slowly, reluctantly, she gave in. I gently resumed our tongue tasting and casually explored her thigh without encountering any resistance or suspicion. My alarm system went off again: steady, Mallet, don't freak her out at this stage of the evening. I decided to sell her another dummy.

I jumped off the sofa huffily and cried, "This must stop... it's getting far too heavy."

I could see that Yasmin was again grateful for my sense of decorum. I went to get her a toothbrush and suggested that she had first go with the bathroom while I made up the sofa.

I got some spare blankets out and fussed around. Yasmin brushed her teeth and came out of the bathroom. I showed her the gallery bedroom. The flat had formerly been the drawing room of a large house and had been adapted to provide a bedroom above the bathroom and kitchen, which overlooked the living area.

I brushed my teeth and got into my makeshift lair downstairs. I switched off the light and called out "goodnight" to Yasmin. All was still for five minutes. I racked my brain for excuses to jump into bed with her. I knew sleep would be impossible unless my scrotal urges were satisfied.

"Yasmin?" I said quietly. "Are you still awake?"

"Yes," she replied, timidly.

"You couldn't throw down my alarm clock, could you? I've got to get up at sparrow's fart and I know I'll never wake up without it."

As she switched on her bed-side light I said hastily, "Actually don't throw it down. Knowing my luck I'll drop it and there'll be tears."

I darted nimbly up the stairs - Capulet to her Montague - and was at her side before she had time to think.

I took the alarm clock and smiling pleasantly said, "Are you all right up here?"

"Yes," she said weakly, looking pathetically like a trapped rabbit. I switched off the light and bent down, supposedly to give her a quick goodnight kiss. I let it linger into a proper French job and put the alarm clock down. I pulled her into my arms. There was no resistance as I slid under the duvet. I felt her all over and slipped one hand deftly between her legs. I cupped the front of her panties and stroked the spider's legs that sprouted out from either side of her gusset.

"No, James... not on our first date," she whimpered, but her condition belied her objection.

"What's the difference, cupcake?" I retaliated.

Yasmin, bless her, was too confused to put up a fight. I continued to fondle and massage her groin as I nonchalantly slipped off her briefs. Within seconds I had my kecks off and was practically in her before she knew what was happening.

"James, you can't... James, you mustn't. Not the first time... please. I've never been with anyone else apart from my husband."

It was too late. I was in and there to stay. She groaned and slowly relaxed.

"Alright, but you must use a thingie."

What did she want? A baby with a plastic head? I just happened to have a couple of hundred 'thingies' in my bedside table drawer. With the speed of a pro I skinned up and quickly resumed activity before she had any second thoughts.

It was a glorious reward for such faultless planning and I entered her from every position I could think of before magnanimously exploding like a fire-extinguisher into my vulcanised antimacassar. She was like a rag doll by the end of it, but no sooner had I finished than I wanted to do it all again. I wasn't much good for anything, but when I got going I could fuck like a Kennedy. I threw her around the bed, thrusting gently one moment and then ramming like a crazed jackhammer the next, far into her abdomen, crashing the cul-de-sac of her uterus to pulp.

It was devoid of love or feeling; just pure used and abused licensed rape. Four assaults were enough for one night. I could have gone for a couple more but I was beginning to get bored and besides, I reasoned to myself, she'd be there in the morning to get my restaurant's worth.

I woke up early. The sun was shining agreeably through the curtains. I felt at peace with the world and my recently decanted scrotum. Christine Hale could eat her heart out. I imagined myself as the bare-chested stud from an after-shave advertisement, rather than a nasty piece of work who had taken advantage of some defenceless soul whom I probably wouldn't want to see again anyway.

I turned round and looked at Yasmin's dormant, vacant face. My gaze drifted towards her pubic enclosure. It looked like a black cat with its throat slit. The duvet twitched as my bladder-gorged erection reared its ugly head. Something bad had died on my tongue overnight. My mouth tasted like the bottom of an invalid's chair, but we weren't going to kiss if I could help it. Yasmin woke up with a start. A look of puzzlement crossed her vacuous features. She was beginning to look less intelligent with each passing sunbeam.

"Morning, nutkin," I said, brushing my lips past the tingly bit at the back of her neck.

"What happened?" she asked, stupefied.

"I don't know, but it was good," I murmured, not wanting any post-coital resentment at this juncture. "Don't worry angel tits, everything's OK; this is just the beginning."

I reached for a contraceptive and gently rolled her on top of me. The position made her involuntarily open her legs, removing the need to crowbar them apart. As before, I was in her before she could think to blink. I started to rock gradually in a comforting see-saw motion. I felt her begin to move in tandem and cancelled my fears of any morning-after reluctance.

As a session it wasn't quite up to the splendour of our earlier performance. It lacked the previous evening's marinated euphoria and thrill of the kill. Now I had to resort to Indo-European fantasy to get my genitals up to their maximum state of anger. The Cages... Bombay... sold into child slavery... for a few rupees she was my slaveling. I could do what I liked with her; I was her god. Her great big affluent, effluent white god and she was an anonymous minnow in a sea of a billion that I could throw away like a used Kleenex when I was finished.

Actually it didn't turn out like that. I was nice to her. I had to be as I saw her every day at work. We went out a few of times, but beyond the bedroom we had little to say to each other. The relationship evolved no further than a private one-to-one affair of going to the cinema or eating suppers in front of the television. I became bored and yet I grew accustomed to her following me around. She was the one person I had any control over and as such I took my responsibilities seriously. That didn't mean I didn't look at other women or ask them out, but I didn't rub it in Yasmin's face either. There was no point in keeping a dog just to be cruel to it. However I put the relationship to sleep after a few months when I thought it was time for a change. As an office perk, Yasmin had definitely been worthwhile, but when she stopped letting me put my fingers up her bum there seemed little purpose in continuing. Fortunately, she was transferred to another department after a while and I was able to get on with life without her dark, hooded stare burning into me.

The next office freebie came in the dull no-man's-land between Christmas and New Year. I had volunteered for extra office duties knowing there would be nothing to do. When the time came I was the only person in the dealing room. My sole function was to pick up the phone and say that we were closed. It was on one such morning, as I was recovering from some Yuletide excess, that I saw by the coffee machine a dazzling apparition of extraordinary beauty. I wanted to own it and take it to a cheap restaurant immediately. The apparition saw me, smiled politely and moved in the direction of the dealing room. How could anything be *so* cute? I dashed to the loo to check for eye bogeys and smoothed down the ruffles in my hair. I peeked back onto the dealing floor. There it was, radiating angelically at the other end of the room - near my desk! I went back to the loo to give myself another inspection and washed my face. Why was I feeling so cruddy, today of all days? Why had fate chosen this moment to make my face look like a bloodhound? I returned to my desk and answered a few calls, loud enough for the apparition to hear, using my most authoritative telephone voice. After half an hour I got up to make another cup of coffee and, heart in mouth, addressed the apparition for the first time.

"Can I get you a cup of something?"

"Oh, no thanks."

Her reply was made of silk.

I gulped and grabbed wildly at a conversational gambit in an attempt to get some momentum going.

"I haven't seen you around here before."

"No, I'm just temping. I'm supposed to report to Mr Castle, but he hasn't turned up yet so I'm just twiddling my thumbs."

Mr 'Bouncy' Castle, who had a minor claim to nobility, was the Managing Director that the American management had hired in a mistaken attempt to give the company a bit of class. He was known within the firm as 'the discount viscount'.

"Oh well, join the club. It's nice there's someone else around to twiddle with," I twaddled, anaemically, as I groped for something to keep the conversation alive.

"Do you always temp?" I asked, in what could have been taken as a rather patronising tone.

"Oh no. I used to work for Barclays in Chiswick but they made a whole lot of us redundant about six months ago. I've been looking for a permanent position ever since, but so far no go."

"Are you interested in trying to get back into banking?" I said, briefly catching sight of a pane, if not an entire window of opportunity, worth exploiting.

"Well it's what I know, I suppose," she said, looking at the ground forlornly.

"What side did you work on?"

"A rather naff side, I'm afraid: credit card retrieval."

We chatted in this fashion for a few minutes until the phone started to go at my desk giving me another chance to demonstrate my importance and problem solving abilities. I toyed with the idea of suggesting lunch with her as there still was no-one around, but I couldn't quite summon up the courage and I knew I wasn't in sufficient control to pull it off naturally.

I frigged around for the rest of the morning, trying to dream up the best method of attack. I felt at such a physical disadvantage compared to her composure that I contemplated abandoning the project altogether and leaving with my ego untested but intact via the back door. Mr Castle eventually turned up and the apparition became his keep.

By mid-afternoon I'd had enough of doing nothing and was about to go home when the apparition rematerialised from Mr Castle's office.

"Well, I'm off then," I said, as I put on my coat. "So goodbye and good luck with your job hunt."

"Bye," she said, looking up briefly to smile. "Nice talking to you. Have a happy New Year!"

I walked away wondering feebly about wasted opportunities and cursing myself for being so gutless. What if this was the woman of my life that I was turning my back on? I would probably never see her again or have the privacy in which to exploit an opening. If she happened to come back and temp another day when everyone was back at work, I would pale into insignificance. I wasn't exactly the most macho man in the dealing room, and in terms of rank I was on a par with the tea lady. I turned on my heels and went back.

"Listen," I said. "I've had a thought. By the way, I haven't introduced myself - I'm James Mallet," and then added importantly, "Retail Desk," as if it was a big deal.

"Rebecca Huxtable," she returned, and offered her hand. Yech, what a name!

"Good to meet you, Rebecca," I said, giving her paw an assuasive squeeze. "What I was thinking was, maybe, that I could be some sort of help to you if you really want to get back into banking. Why don't you take my card and I'll ask around to see what's available? If you want, give me a call next week and we'll see if there's any point in taking things a stage further."

"Oh, that's really kind of you," Rebecca responded coyly, as she took my card.

Good stuff, Mallet; keep it cooking.

"OK," I said, trying to keep my face from smiling, "I'm serious about looking out for something for you. I know what it's like being on the outside looking in, so don't be shy. Give me a call sometime next week, because if you're temping all over town I won't know how to get hold of you."

With that we said our farewells properly. I left feeling that I had at least exercised some gumption , even if I'd left the next move totally at the mercy of her initiative.

I had no particular plans for New Year's Eve and no one to share them with if I had. At the last minute Ahmed Nabil, an Americanised Jordanian friend from work invited me to a party. I didn't know his crowd but as he lived only a mile away and the television for the evening was rubbish, I thought it would be a good opportunity to get out of the flat.

I had the best part of a bottle of wine to get me in the mood before I left and arrived mildly pissed at Ahmed's at ten. There was a group of young American males in repro track gear drinking Budweisers from tins, talking about the tequila slammers they'd had the night before. They were a cheerful bunch but I wasn't on their wavelength and felt isolated. There were a few girls standing around dressed in similar collegiate style, with suede jackets bearing the names of American football teams emblazoned across them. I hit the vodka punch and spoke to a sheepish English couple for a while.

At eleven, in an attempt to enliven proceedings, Ahmed turned the music up several dozen decibels and announced:

" Yo everybody! Let' s dance!"

Some of the men seized the few women present and started to wriggle self-consciously near the loudspeakers. It was an Elvis record. Those who knew how to rock 'n' roll, did. Those who didn't attempted to twist exaggeratedly, as if treading out cigarettes without the benefit of shoes. I abstained. Dancing on carpets wasn't my thing, and I didn't know anyone to dance with anyway.

Mercifully, at eleven-thirty a stream of revellers from another party arrived to catch the midnight hoopla. Among them, for some reason, was Fenella Fellon looking as mellow as a cello, who I had on occasion worshipped from a distance. She was rich, beautiful and well connected. I stopped talking to the English couple and helped myself to another drink. I made my way to a lavatory and examined myself in the mirror. I looked like the fat one from 'The Likely Lads'. I checked my teeth for bits and had a pee.

I pulled the chain, ran the taps without washing my hands and put on a baseball hat that some inebriate had left by the basin. Perfect! Fenella Fellon, here I come!

By then there were only a few minutes till midnight. I chugged back my drink and helped myself to another. Someone had turned on the TV for the countdown to midnight. I positioned myself as close as was decently possibly to Fenella. The Americans were whipping themselves into a frenzy.

"Twenty... nineteen... eighteen..."

I looked around. It wasn't turning out to be such a bad evening after all, except that I was beginning to feel violently drunk.

"... fifteen... fourteen... thirteen..."

The room started to spin. I took a large sip to steady myself. I was getting too old for this game.

"... ten... nine... eight..."

The Americans hit new heights of hysteria. It was as if they were heralding the Second Coming.

"... four... three... two... one... *Happy New Year everybody*!"

Baseball hats were thrown into the air and everyone started kissing everyone else. I lunged for Fenella, elbowing a youth out of my way in the process.

"Hi, Fenella!" I gasped, excitedly.

She gave me a demure sideways glance.

"It's me... James Mallet."

She looked confused, but not unwelcoming.

Then I remembered the baseball hat. I took it off.

"See... James... you know, Annabel Dribble's friend... we met... late December... back in '63 – ha ha!"

She looked at me blankly.

"Forget it," I sighed, feeling miserable.

Suddenly she sprang to life.

"I remember...Vivvy von Steinbeck's do at the Dorchester last year... sorry, the year before last now?"

"That's it!" I said, having never been near the Dorchester let alone Vivvy von Steinbeck's 'do'.

"Well, Happy New Year then!" I said, and suitably emboldened kissed her on both cheeks.

She didn't seem to mind and even managed a smile.

"Let me get you a drink," I said trying to carry the moment. I went to the punch bowl and drank two glasses in quick succession before returning to Fenella. We sipped our drinks in silence.

"Shall we dance?" I suggested, before she had a chance to drift off.

"Why not?" she replied, consentingly.

It was not a particularly good record. It was 'Angry Bruvver Muzik' by Black Chaps on E, and as such involved a lot of shouting but was sadly lacking in rhythm.

The vodka had removed my inhibitions, but in the process it had also ransacked most of my co-ordination. I felt I was about to fall over with each move. I also had half a pint of air in my gut that I had to get rid of. There were a lot of people dancing. I reckoned if I let my flatulence out one bit at a time no one would notice.

I eased it out, slowly. So drunk. Just dance. Fart. Shimmy. Fart. Jive. Fart. Damn! A smeller... won't go away... move away from Fenella. Fuck! Bit pungent. Oh no! It's a freckler - watch your pees and poos! In my attempt to be subtle I had followed through. *How embarrassing*! I felt a warm sensation between my buttocks. *Bit of a skidmark,* Mr Wydmark? The smell was, to me, painfully apparent, although judging from Fenella's *sang-froid* it hadn't hit her yet. In retrospect I often wondered whether I was a victim of my own incontinence or if the incident marked the first instance of Christine's Curse.

I was most uncomfortable. The room started to spin with centrifugal abandon. I felt sick. That was all I needed; a huge wall-to-wall vom to complete the effect. *Cancel the audition for the Bond movie*! My mind went into drunken over-drive. I had a mental turbocharger that took over in such circumstances.

As I danced I increased the distance from Fenella with each twirl until, in the middle of a turn, I scuttled out of the room. I collected my coat and squelched into the street without looking back. I took a million tiny steps home to minimise the damage. The cold air sobered me up and I managed to get home without being accosted by any late night revellers. I went to the loo to clean up. I'd ox-tailed quite badly. I left my underpants to crust out on the radiator. My not so lucky underpants. It was 1:30. I had escaped undetected. A bit of a waste of Dutch courage on Fenella but at least I'd avoided social burial. I would live to fart another day.

At work I hadn't forgotten Rebecca, but I had neglected to see if anyone was interested in hiring her. So I was caught off-guard when she called up the following week to see whether I had made any progress with her case. In order to do some emergency groundwork I asked her for her number and said I'd call her back. I had a quick think about what I was going to say. Being new and a relative lightweight in the business, I didn't have many contacts. If anyone was hiring I wanted to see them first for *my* benefit. I grabbed a bank directory and flicked through it, trying to think of some plausible person I could call up, but I didn't know anyone well enough. I got back on the phone to Rebecca and bulldozed as much bullshit as I could muster.

"Rebecca I'm really sorry but I've been too tied up this week to give my undivided attention to your situation... also, it's not the best time of year with so many people still on holiday and the markets not in top gear. But what I can do is give you a list of my contacts to speak to and let you know who does what. Will that do for the time being before I get something more concrete...? Good, well why don't we meet sometime...? I'm not very good for lunch but how about after work? Shall we go somewhere slinky for a drinkie?"

She was working in Covent Garden the following week. We agreed on a date and a bar in the area. I knew the bar vaguely. It was a favourite after-work spot of Christine's. I put the phone down and smiled. Great! That gave me four days to get my body into shape, lose twenty pounds and grow three inches. The hook was in place and all that was needed was a few subtle twists of the reel and I'd be cooking fish for supper. Even if Rebecca wasn't.

I left work early on the appointed day and went through my customary pre-attack freshening up ritual at home. It was important to play from a position of maximum advantage. I operated better on a mouthwash and a clean shirt.

Rebecca was waiting for me by the time I got to our agreed venue. It was a blood-sucking joint; the sort where the barman handed back the change in a saucer to induce tip-guilt. Rebecca looked good, but not quite the goddess that I had in my memory, which was no bad thing as it lessened the chances of me turning into a jelly. I had some photocopies of the bank directory from work, which I hoped to fob her off with as genuinely useful. After the initial pleasantries, I told her who the best people were to contact adding, for professional reasons, that I'd rather she didn't use my name. It would have been embarrassing if she'd found that none of my so-called contacts had ever heard of me. I kept half an eye out in case Christine happened to drop by, but I didn't see her.

I gradually turned the conversation round to Rebecca and asked her about herself, steering the talk away from business on to a more personal level with each successive question. It emerged that she was another divorcee. She lived miles away, in some place in the Projects I'd never heard of, which was a bore - convenience is a natural aphrodisiac - but at that point it wasn't an issue.

We had several more drinks and by the time the bar closed our conversation was becoming distinctly personal. We had been talking solidly for three hours.

After a quick peck on respective cheeks we went our separate ways, but not before a mutually effusive summary of the evening, declaring that we must meet again sometime. Rebecca gave me her new temporary number. I was sorry that Christine Hale hadn't happened to make an appearance at the bar. Rebecca would have been a satisfactory snub, even though I knew deep down that Christine was beyond any real sense of jealousy.

I deliberated for a couple of days over the best method of keeping things alive with Rebecca. I had to move quickly. She would soon discover that all my contacts were duds and that the whole wretched display of caring about her career objectives was a sham.

When I called her at the end of the week she sounded pleased to hear from me. To my relief she hadn't tried to reach any of the names that I'd given her. I suggested supper and said I'd call her the following week to fix a date.

I contemplated pulling the same stunt that I had used on Yasmin by changing the venue at the last minute to my flat. I decided that in Rebecca's case it wouldn't wash, and when I called her I simply asked her to come straight to my flat. She was a big girl and by then, having spoken to her on the phone several times, it didn't seem such an outlandish suggestion. It had a slightly obvious ring to it but my delivery was pat. Rebecca didn't appear to have any objection.

As I put the phone down I wondered if women actually quite liked going out with me, and whether I should abandon my policy of trying to bamboozle them into a corner with every move. Perhaps the time had come to stop trying to fool them into thinking that I was an alpha male. I shrugged my shoulders. All seduction was trickery. It was the only way to get things done.

When the evening came I booked the most up-market restaurant within walking distance and waited for Rebecca to come to my flat. As she arrived I was interested to see that she had brought a chunky canvas bag with her that had a curious, overnight look about it. I fixed some drinks. We talked for a bit about work and London. Once again her *trompe I'oeil* looks didn't quite come up to my bombshell first impressions. She was pretty rather than beautiful. After another drink I suggested going to the restaurant. It was one that I hadn't been to before and I was anxious that it would set the right tone. It was supposed to be a favourite with various younger members of the House of Windsurfer, which was probably why I hadn't tried it.

It was a bit of an overkill with drapes everywhere. The waiters were from better backgrounds than most of the customers. The effect was slightly oppressive, as if dining in a salon rather than a restaurant. I tried to speed-drink myself into a jolly mood, but with little success. Rebecca was not particularly talkative and my reservoir of conversation began to dry up. I concentrated for a while on her ex-husband, who sounded a bit of a wally and an alcoholic, i.e. a good bloke, but it was heavy going.

We finished the meal and I asked for the bill. It wasn't late. Rebecca could have made a bolt for the last train if she had wanted to, but she didn't appear particularly worried about the time. The bill was reasonable and I almost forgave the decor for its vulgarity. The food had been quite good too, and if it wasn't for the fact that the restaurant was so obviously a converted drawing room, I would have made a note to go there again. We walked back to my flat. I decided not to try to put my arm around Rebecca, but when we got back I levelled with her and asked what she wanted to do about getting home. It transpired that she fully expected to stay the night, albeit not in the same bed as me. Things were looking up at last. She used the bathroom first and when I gave her the choice of the sofa or the bed, it was as if by rote that she opted for the latter. I found some sheets and blankets and made up the sofa once again.

We said goodnight and got between our respective sheets. After ten minutes of darkness and silence, in time I hoped to catch Rebecca before she nodded off, I called out gently:

"Rebecca?"

"Yes?"

"It's not very comfortable down here."

"Oh?"

"Would it be a real pain if I shared the bed with you?"

Pause.

"OK... as long as you promise to be good and leave me alone and go straight to sleep."

"Sure, no problem," I called back, perhaps a little too eagerly.

I yanked on my undies, shot up the stairs and dived into the bed with the grace of a marlin. I lay still for five minutes before casually turning over. I brushed her shoulder. There was no reaction or counteraction. I manoeuvred my arm around her and drew her close to me.

"Sleep!" Rebecca barked. "Or back to the dog basket!"

Another five minutes went past. My arm started to go fizzy and I was forced to remove it from under her. Rebecca stirred, gave a bad-tempered grunt and let out a long sigh. I turned over in the opposite direction and fell quickly into a sickly stupor.

The next morning I woke up early. My liver was kicking like a Thai boxer from all the alcohol I'd whacked back the night before. I had my customary bladder-filled erection and a dry mouth. I slipped quietly out of bed and went downstairs to relieve both conditions. I brushed my teeth and quickly dry-scraped my face to get rid of any infant prickles that might've appeared overnight. I went back to the bed and cast off the false modesty of my underpants. I nuzzled up to Rebecca's dormant carcass. She smelled rather sexily of sleep and the previous evening's *Eau de Lancome*. She was wearing a T-shirt as a surrogate negligee, but it was a poor substitute and provided scant refuge for her nudity.

I stroked her thigh gently, monitoring the expression on her face, with particular attention to the furrows of annoyance that could have appeared on her brow at any moment. I managed to slip my stroking hand between her legs without detection and gently touched her genitalia. I got to the entrance of her vagina with my index finger and explored the layout. It was a small but plump piece of work with an attractive pube-to-labia ratio, but despite its soft and fleshy promise it was dry as a bone. I carefully withdrew my hand and spat into my fingers, taking in her aroma as I did so. It had a pleasing bouquet of fresh limes that marked a pristine uterine canal. I slipped my fingers back and attempted to coax her plumbing into a state of arousal. My penis, which up to that point had been playing an ardent but non-proactive role, started to egg rather unattractively on her thigh. I was not a creamer by nature but in this instance my testes had jumped the gun in a Pavlovian anticipation of the morsel ahead.

I was beginning to feel a general change in the level of viscosity between Rebecca's legs and could just detect the beginnings of a rich vein of artesian flow, when she stirred. I froze. She lapsed back into unconsciousness. I brushed my mouth softly past her cheek and shifted my weight for better access. I went into my own world. Everything else ceased to exist. Time stood still. My mind and genitalia entered into a childish starship dialogue with one another.

"We are on target, sir."

"Proceed, Lieutenant Penis."

"We are about to enter the twilight zone, sir."

"Continue Lieutenant, and upgrade thrust to one millimetre a second."

"Aye aye, sir! ... (rising excitement)... we have entered the twilight zone sir... sir, we are now at The Gates of Moisture that lead to The Tunnel of Eternal Ecstasy."

"Proceed, Lieutenant."

"Sir, the gates are opening; they are showing very little resistance... sir... I think we are now two centimetres into The Tunnel of Eternal Ecstasy."

"Increase thrust Lieutenant, to three millimetres a second. Lieutenant, I do believe we are on course for a successful mission."

"Sir, sir... (hysteria)... I think we're losing control, something's wrong... or right... involuntary thrust action taken over sir... autopilot override negative, sir... (tears)... sir... sir... speed of entry in total free fall sir... I don't think I can hold this baby much longer."

Rebecca woke up with a start and screamed.

"What the fuck are you doing? Get it out! Get it out now."

"Mayday! Mayday! Reverse thrust, Lieutenant. Abandon all stations. Evacuate the bridge immediately!"

"You bastard!" Rebecca screamed. "You disgusting, dirty little boy. Oh yuk, what's this skank on my leg? I can't believe you. You're a filthy dirty little man. Get out of this bed at once!"

Things had been going so swimmingly that I was caught totally off balance. With no suitable riposte at hand I had little choice but to comply with her command.

I jumped out of bed like I was on rewind.

"Sorry, Rebecca... "I mumbled, "... I thought perhaps you wanted to... I thought you were awake, or pretending to be asleep... or just quietly lying back and enjoying it."

"You're disgusting. What time is it?" Rebecca demanded, looking crossly at her watch. "My God, it's only half past six! Now go away and don't come back. I'm going back to sleep. If you so much as lay a finger on me I'll scream and you'll never hear from me again."

I skulked off with bent shoulders, my penis sticking out like some obscene garden gnome's fishing rod. There was nothing worse than having a non-negotiable hard-on without a home to go to.

I had a bath and finished myself off by hand, reliving the episode but inserting a more satisfactory conclusion. I wondered if I'd ever be successful and do it for real with her one day, not that I particularly cared now that I had relieved my frustration. She was a sarky bitch and not worth more than a toss anyway. With that I got out of the bath, dressed and went to work leaving Rebecca fast asleep.

I didn't think any more of the incident and assumed that that was the end of it. I went back that evening to an unmade bed and the flat in a mess. Rebecca hadn't written so much as a 'thank you' note. Cow. Still, one meal and a near miss wasn't such a disastrous trade. I could live with the loss.

A few days later I'd all but forgotten Rebecca and did a double take when I heard someone call out:

"James! Rebecca Huxtable! Line five!"

I kicked into line five.

"Hi," I said as nonchalantly as I could, given that I had only one syllable to play with.

"Hello James. How are you?"

"OK, I suppose. What can I do for you?" I said brusquely, wanting to keep formalities to a minimum.

"I just wanted to thank you for such a lovely evening the other night."

That got me between the eyes. I was completely thrown. *Lovely evening*? It had been a disaster. What was she on about?

"Oh, it was entirely my pleasure," I croaked, lamely. "I'm sorry if I was a bit pissed and randy."

"That's all right! Boys will be boys. I'm sorry I got so uptight, but I'm always a bit bolshy when I'm about to start my period; it's just the way I'm made, but no - I had a really good time and I love your flat. I overslept and was late for work, otherwise I wouldn't have left it in such a state."

"Oh, for goodness' sake, there were only a couple of glasses to wash up. It was good to see you. We should do it again sometime," I said, wondering what quite I was saying, but blundered on blithely.

"To quote the Three Degrees: 'When will I see you again?' Soon, I hope."

"I'd like that very much. Maybe we could go to a movie."

I was still stunned and slightly at a loss as to how best to react.

"Yeah. Good idea. Why don't I ring you towards the end of the week and we'll see what we can squeeze in?" I proposed, slightly regretting my choice of words.

I called Rebecca on the Friday and she came round later the following week, this time clutching even more conspicuous overnight arrangements. We went to see 'Castaway' with Oily Reed and Amanda Donohoe at the local fleapit. The cinema smelt off-puttingly of popcorn and old fart. The film was quite pleasantly dull and gave us something to talk about on the way home on the 'Wouldn't it be nice to get away from it all?' theme. I put my arm around Rebecca as we discussed desert islands and whether either of us would have made a better job of it than Oily and Mandy had done. If I'd been Oily I would have clubbed Mandy to death at the merest hint of her not coming across with the goods. I didn't tell Rebecca that. We got home and kissed properly for the first time. When it was time for bed it seemed perfectly natural to go upstairs together.

We made love compatibly rather than spectacularly, but we were a good fit and I was pleased with the way things had turned out.

We started to see each other once or twice a week for a while, but it turned into a similarly socially stunted relationship to the one I'd had with Yasmin. Rebecca wasn't interested in going to pubs or meeting any of my friends and I wasn't bothered about meeting any of hers. Anyway from what I could gather she only had one – Judith - with whom she would go out on Saturday nights for a rave.

Rebecca's looks started to get on my nerves, which was odd as they'd been what had attracted me to her in the first place. She began to put on weight at an alarming rate and her elegance evaporated as her face and body went from the dainty to the bovine. Her bosoms seemed to shrink as her hips and arms vied with each other for flab. I started to notice a particular smell about her that hadn't been apparent when we'd first met. It was a smell that I associated with hangovers and over-indulgence; a blend of formaldehyde and cabbages that suggested she was a secret drinker. I felt strangely repelled being in contact with someone with the same disease as myself.

The final straw came one day when we were in bed together. I was taking Rebecca rather expertly from behind when she turned round and in almost wordless rapture whispered:

"It's exquisite."

"Exquisite?" Not "Fill me up, Big Boy!" or "Fuck me till I fart!"

'Exquisite' summed up Rebecca's little world. I decided there and then that this would be our last time together.

I never took Rebecca out after that although it wasn't the last time I saw her. As luck would have it, her employment agency sent her back to Parker Barrow for a six month secondment with Mr 'Bouncy' Castle, which meant I saw her every day. I would sometimes catch her looking at me with a slightly hurt, confused expression, not so much as if she was pining, as wondering how worship could turn to indifference so quickly. I said to her once or twice that we should go for a drink after work, but we never followed it up.

Girls came and went. Some were from the office but I started to look further afield. With each relationship I tried to purge myself of Christine Hale's memory, but with little success. I occasionally bumped into Christine, but I knew she was a lost cause. She enjoyed toying with me nonetheless. One moment she'd be pleasant and I'd raise my spirits in the vain hope that one day we could be friends again and maybe, with luck, even restore our relationship to its former glory. Then the next time I'd see her she'd revert to being supercilious, telling me how wonderful her life without me was, how stupendous her job was and how marvellous all her friends were. Blah. Blah. Blah. In reality her jobs would start promisingly enough and then fizzle out a couple of months later. I met most of her friends in the course of time. They weren't people that I felt comfortable with, but I couldn't say anything to Christine. I smiled impotently and tried to look interested, if not impressed by her narcissistic hallucinations. I still waited on her every word. I knew if I told her to shut up and drop the act she'd run away and I'd see even less of her. It was as if by putting up a facade she expected me to forget that we had once been intimate.

Then one day something happened that took my mind, temporarily at least, off Christine.

# Chapter 3: On the Road

I got fired. There had been plenty of rumours about possible redundancies going around the firm ever since it'd moved into its new, ridiculously over-priced aviary with its pathetic attempt to recreate a rainforest in the foyer. It was part of a new office complex that had aspired to combine imposition with environmental harmony. Something had gone badly wrong along the way. Hundreds of walk-ways busily led nowhere past cascading fountains, hanging gardens and silly fad shops. The *piece de résistance* was the ice rink, the size of a cake base that nestled in the centre of it all.

   Inside the office, next to the minimalist lavatories with their minimal privacy, was the state-of-the-art dealing room. It looked like a futuristic amusement arcade, which, in a sense, it was. On the floor above were the dining rooms for the fat cats. There were seventeen such executive pigsties. As my salary and net cost to the company were the same as a carpet tile, I assumed that I was too small a fish to be worth frying. And besides, I was starting to do a good job. I wasn't drinking in quite such massive quantities as before. I was functioning better than I had for a long time. I could almost stand my ground when the traders tried to take the piss out of my voice gave me lip about my technical naivety - both of which were becoming less apparent with each passing day. The Head of Sales, a gangly, insipid American with goatish eyes who looked about twelve, assured the sales force at one of the daily meetings that there weren't going to be any redundancies; our jobs were safe. With a London presence of a couple of thousand people and about a zillion others elsewhere around the globe, it was difficult to get a feel for which sectors were most vulnerable or how well the company's fortunes were faring on a day-to-day basis. But I saw no reason to disbelieve him.

Life up until then had been improving. I had sold my flat for four times what I had paid for it a few years before through no particular business brilliance or commercial acumen on my part. Anyone who'd bought property at the beginning of the decade could have done the same. I moved into larger premises a few doors down for only a fraction more. I'd just met a promising and presentable new woman whom I was successfully negotiating out of another relationship into one with me. London, at last, was working for me.

   The second hint of trouble came two weeks later at another morning meeting. The Head Trader made a reference to the new group of graduate trainees that was due to arrive in a week's time. They were, in his words, "lean and hungry... hungry for your job and hungry for mine."

   I muttered, out of his earshot, but loud enough for those near me to hear:

"Well, you were the cunt who hired them."

I got a chuckle. It missed him but he glanced in my direction. The Head Trader was not a bad sort. He was a small man with a big car and a big BO problem. Typical of the type, he took himself extremely seriously and I later wondered if the remark had got back to him.

A week later, the following Monday, there was a commotion on the trading floor. People were being called one by one into Mr 'Bouncy' Castle's office, having their notices handed to them in brown envelopes and being told that their services would no longer be required at the firm.

Halfway through the afternoon, I was joking with a colleague that now was not the time to ask for a pay rise, when the caprine Head of Sales came up to me with a big shit-eating grin and asked me to accompany him to Mr Castle's schloss. I love a Monday. My sphincter went into spasm. I walked, ashen-faced, to Mr Castle's office. Old man Castle was standing triumphantly behind a pile of redundancy envelopes. He told me to sit down.

"I'm sorry, James," he said. "This is a New York driven thing."

Like fuck it was.

"I don't like this any more than you do," he said qualmlessly, showing no obvious signs of remorse.

Oh, like, yeah.

"It's not my choice," he continued. "If I'd had my way you'd have been the last person I'd be doing this to, but that's not the story. Part of the re-structuring deal means that we've got to make cuts on the sales force. The Retail Desk has got to close. We can't reposition you on one of the other desks because they've had to cut back too. So, much as I regret it, you're one of the guys who's got to go. I'm very sorry but here's your package."

He handed me a brown envelope from the pile. Judas! Traitor to your class!

"Why don't you go home and think about it for a day or two," he went on. "Come back, tell us how you feel and I'll see whether there's anything we can do to help."

Quite what going home and thinking about it would do to get me my job back eluded me but I was too shocked to say anything. I could feel myself go an interesting shade of burgundy puce. I felt so ashamed. I tried to think where I had gone wrong. Maybe I'd nobbed one secretary too many.

Castle continued his monologue.

"There's a re-settlement course that's not to be sniffed at. Basically, if you want to work out your month's notice we can find you something to do in the settlements department or you can leave now and take three months' pay, tax-free, with no further questions."

Such choice!

"If you want to go to an industrial tribunal, we can't stop you. You'll have to forgo your three months' redundancy and I think, as you haven't been here two years, you won't have much of a case. Even if you did, it'd probably be too expensive for you to fight and it wouldn't guarantee you any more compensation at the end of the day."

I opened the envelope, glimpsed at the terms and conditions and realised that there was no point in fighting a foregone conclusion.

I said "Thanks," expressed my own regrets briefly and left the office.

Outside, the dealing floor was buzzing with the overload of gossip and speculation about whose turn it was next to go in. I felt a perverse sense of euphoria come over me. I wasn't exactly thrilled about losing my security, status and livelihood, but it would be a change, albeit not of my own making. A sharp jab in my ribs shook me out of my trance so unexpectedly that I farted rather loudly. I turned round and saw Yasmin, her large, brown eyes brimming with tears.

"I'm so sorry, James. It's such bad luck. You were the last person who deserved it. Why didn't they get rid of the real dweebs like Ramatool Upaboy or Mustafa Waz on the Middle East desk? They do fuck-all all day. I'm on the hot list too apparently, but they said they might have a secretarial number for me going in Commodities downstairs, which is bloody marvellous."

I couldn't help but be touched by the way she shared my plight with hers after I'd been such a shit to her. She went on.

"Everyone's meeting for a drink at 'The Egotist' if you want to compare notes. I'm going down at five if you want an ear, but I'll probably be out on my arse too, so I may be in need of a bit of moral support too."

I was impressed with Yasmin's sensitivity under the circumstances. Ever the sucker for a foul weather friend, I thanked her for her sympathy and said I'd call her at five.

I started to clear my desk and made a few phone calls to break the news. My parents couldn't quite grasp the situation. They kept asking me what I'd done wrong, as if I'd been de-prefected at school. After a while I gave up trying to explain and said I had to crack on. My more fortunate colleagues who'd escaped execution rushed around me, half out of curiosity and half in relief that nothing had happened to them. Dancing on graves. Some of the more senior members of staff came up and glibly expressed their outrage that I should have been picked to go. I was mildly embarrassed that most of the people who had been given the bullet were from other departments. There were very few casualties from my area. As the afternoon went on it became apparent that I was one of only two bond people who had been axed. Mr Castle and his sidekick had been more than economical with the truth. The other person who'd been fired in the bond section was a complete turkey. I was obviously cast in the same light.

I tried to think of possible culprits who might have wanted to get rid of me, but I could only come up with two candidates who might have had a hand on the knife. Unless of course it had been a straight forward case of Sod's law. Or Christine's Curse.

The two people in question were relatively junior but not, admittedly, as junior as I was. The first suspect belonged to one of the groups of American alpha males who, drunk on their own endorphins roamed the company like conquistadors across the pampas. This particular peach was special because he possessed an almost radioactive level of arrogance. We'd never been wild about each other. He frequently asked me to get him photocopies and generally tried to pull seniority stunts on me despite the fact he was nothing special. I always told him to fuck off.

The other suspect was the closet librarian-object whom I'd sat next to who'd helped me settle in when I first arrived. She'd later turned out to be a dragon. She took to eavesdropping on my conversations and contradicting everything I said. I counter-attacked by clicking my biro all day in an attempt to drive her mad. I thought that she might've been the other possible contender, as she'd just returned from a trip to the Head Office in New York. I wondered if she'd blown the gaff on me to get rid of my biro-clicking scam.

Who or whatever was responsible, I was a casualty and at a loss what to do next. The nature of my work had been to look after the Parker Barrow branches around the world rather than to establish my own client base. An unfortunate aberration, I was later to find. In the end I came to the conclusion that the new building had been my real executioner. The Parker Barrow management, in their haste to show off and buy everything in sight had been severely ripped off by the property developers and had signed a lease that they could ill afford on a rainy day.

I got shit-faced that night. I met up with the other firees, most of whom seemed better quality people than those who remained at Parker Barrow. Yasmin, normally so wet and devoid of inspiration, thrived on my dilemma as her budding maternal instincts came to the fore. Compassion, an emotion to which some women so easily submit, had sunk its jaws into her eager, young heart. She followed me from bar to bar and we eventually went back to my flat.

The next day I could hardly move. I was almost glad that I was out of a job and didn't have to go to work. The day after, however, I went in.

I was the only one of those who'd been made redundant to go back. I didn't know then that it was normal procedure for people who were given the push to clear their desks and not look back. The people who'd escaped dismissal themselves were civil to me, if slightly embarrassed by my presence. I was the walking dead. A few of them gave me names of contacts at other firms or came up with vague suggestions. One gave me the name of a firm of head-hunters who were looking for people to work at Consolidated Maxima - 'Conmax' for short - a futures broking boutique which had a small
bond department. I called and arranged a meeting with the headhunters. They seemed quite slick. I already knew that Conmax, on whose behalf they were acting, was not regarded as top drawer, but I wasn't in a position to be picky about who I worked for and readily agreed to be put forward for an interview. I had a few contacts at some of the more blue chip organisations but at that point I had nothing else lined up.

On my last afternoon at Parker Barrow I noticed the Head of Sales talking to a security guard. They both looked in my direction. I suspected they thought I might try to jam the computer or do some sicko trades to mess up the trading book. I didn't have the expertise to inflict any damage and was too decent, or frightened to do anything that wasn't legitimate. Instead, as a private gesture of defiance, I stole the Head Trader's stapler on the way out.

And that was the last of Parker Barrow. I was sorry to leave, mainly because I no longer had a job to go to but I had to concede to myself that I wouldn't be missing some of the people who worked there. I now had the boring prospect of hitting the phones and traipsing from interview to interview until I conned someone into hiring me. It seemed as though I'd only been in the job for five minutes.

I forsook my embryonic relationship with the new girl I had in tow to go back to the less time-consuming attentions of Yasmin who, in the event, had escaped extermination from the firm and had been duly transferred to the Commodities Department. At that point I didn't really want anyone around, but Yasmin was OK because she didn't care what my job status was or whether I brushed my teeth before we had sex. We resumed the walk down our emotional dead end, and for a while were a comfort to each other.

Parker Barrow, true to their word, sent me and all the other duds to an outplacement agency the following week. After the first day, everyone except me and two others dropped out. The half dozen or so counsellors who were presenting the course seemed to be living in a dream world where redundancy was a utopian condition that automatically led to a greater state of fulfilment and self-awareness. There were frequent references to 'objectives'. They cited a case of a banker who'd been ditched by his firm and turned to painting for a living. House painting. That was the only radical case they could come up with. Otherwise they kept repeating, like a stuck record, that ninety-five per cent of people who were made redundant eventually found jobs again. The fate of the missing five per cent was never discussed.

Both sides, the counsellors and the counselled, realised pretty early on that there was a plausibility gap that couldn't be bridged within the programme. Aside from cold comfort, the counsellors were of little use and the course was disbanded half-way through the week. They'd managed to screw some money out of Parker Barrow, which was good, but they were otherwise ill-equipped. They didn't even have the facilities to re-vamp our CVs. I had to chocolate-box a Parker Barrow secretary into doing mine.

After that I became a pinstriped vagrant. I wandered between companies and telephone boxes. I freshened up in various public conveniences around the capital. Mansion House became my central office. It had excellent facilities, a cheerful but not too inquisitive lavatory attendant and a payphone that accepted money.

I was pleasantly surprised at how many interviews I was able to get once I got down to it, and the sort of companies who were prepared to grant me an audience. Kleinworts; BZW; Hoare Govett. My Parker Barrow pedigree had fooled them into thinking that I was hot stuff rather than a potential window-gazer who would, in time, cease to care. I was led to believe at one or two interviews that there was a strong chance I might actually be taken on.

By the time my interview with Conmax was due I was in a cocky mood. I wouldn't be needing them. Or so I thought. My appointment was at 3:30 in the afternoon, but I got drunk by mistake with Yasmin in the City at lunch. I thought about phoning them and cancelling but I didn't want to appear as though I was wasting their time. I stuffed a couple of ice creams from a whippy kiosk into my face in an attempt to sober up, but it only made things worse. By the time I'd made it to their offices in Holborn I was almost incoherent.

I was punctual but felt decidedly nauseous. The company was smaller than any of the others I had recently visited. There was a pot plant and a semi-attractive secretary to lend a sense of credence to the reception area. I had reached the point of indifference by the time the person who was due to interview me called me into his office. I undid my tie, lit a cigarette to cover the wine fumes, and slurred my way through the meeting.

My interrogator turned out to be a relaxed, easy-going Scot who thankfully did most of the talking. He outlined the operation without fanfare. The remuneration, except for a small basic salary was commission-based. There were no perks, no cars, no sports and social club, no company magazine and, a big selling point for me, no Personnel Department. The coffee machine was a kettle. It was the sort of company I could understand. When asked how many dealing tickets I wrote on a good day at Parker Barrow I told my interlocutor I used to write up to a dozen or so, which impressed him. I was honest enough to add that I had been dealing with their retail network rather than my own accounts, and might therefore be as much use to anyone as a chocolate radiator. He liked that. He hadn't heard it before.

I saw four other people that session who, through my alcoholic haze, seemed personable and had none of the affectation that had been such an essential feature of the Parker Barrow corporate culture.

Halfway through the interviews I was overcome with a bursting desire to go to the loo. I didn't want to give the impression that I'd been whacking it back by the bucket before I got there, so I tried to hold on until they'd finished reviewing me. The last session ended just in time for me to be able to ask in a sufficiently dignified manner if I could borrow the' amenities'. The incumbent inquisitor looked at me blankly. For a moment I was gripped by a panic that this was such a low budget operation that I might have to take a slash in the street.

"Lavatories! Toilets! That sort of thing," I spluttered.

"Oh yes, sorry - out round the corner and on your left."

Close shave. I had hardly whipped it out when the most almighty Niagara splashed back at me. I nearly wept I was so relieved; it was like a religious experience. I zipped up, washed and left the building slightly regretting having been quite so pissed. They'd seemed unusually civilised for the industry.

Over the next few days I continued frantically to arrange more interviews. I was on my way to one with Merrill Lynch when I bumped into the Managing Director of the head-hunting firm who'd put me in touch with Conmax.

"Oh hello James," he said. "I gather it went well with Conmax. They thought you were right for the job and will probably want to see you again early next week, if that's OK with you."

And I was just about to apologise to him for blowing it! I was speechless. How could they possibly have thought I was "right for the job" in the condition they'd seen me?

The position at Merrill Lynch turned out to be a hoax. I would have had to start at the bottom again. They had far too many new boys just out of the

Army or university and there seemed little point offering my services just to be another low paid suit. I continued discussions with Conmax the following week and we eventually agreed on a commission structure and a start date. In case they had second thoughts, I decided to join them as soon as possible. Subject to references, we agreed to a date two weeks later. I thought there was no harm in getting a contract under my belt until a better job turned up. I envisaged working there for a month, or two at the most, until something came up from the big boys.

The whole process from redundancy to re-employment had taken less than four weeks. It had been surprisingly painless. I had hardly got used to the seriously weird world of late night television and not having to get up in the morning when, all of a sudden, I'd found a job. I was stunned by my own initiative and the fact that I had an actual market value. I wasn't quite sure how I was going to go about doing any business, but I'd confront that problem once I got there. There was always a honeymoon period that went with starting any new job and then after that, with luck, I'd be out of there and lost deep in the bosom of some fleshy monolith with my troubles far behind.

My first day at Conmax happened to be 'Black Monday'. I wondered what had hit me. Even on a busy day at Parker Barrow, things had never been as chaotic. Everyone was pulling everybody else's hair out. I looked round at my new colleagues in the cramped dealing room. Amongst the pandemonium they seemed an odd but friendly mixture. At lunch one of them explained that working for Conmax was like working in a cesspit. It was impossible to get any lower and there was a lot of shit to put up with. Most of the staff were misfits or rejects from other companies. The commission structure was generous but the company lacked a decent balance sheet and it was difficult, compared to other banks, to get any business done. Half the other professionals and institutions wouldn't deal with the firm because it was perceived to be a corporate parasite and most fund managers turned their noses at all but the well established houses.

To begin with I was given a list of insurance companies and pension funds to call; accounts that everyone else had already tried but had got nowhere with. Most of the time I got a 'fuck off' reaction before they hung up. Occasionally my patter would give me a few seconds' edge before they asked where I was calling from and then I would get a 'Thanks, but no thanks'. By the end of the first day I realised why it had been so easy to get the job; nobody remotely sane could have coped with the constant rejection and abuse all day without losing their nerve at some stage.

To my surprise, most of the other people at the company were doing OK. Some, especially those on the warrant side, were doing extremely well.

There was no limit to the commission that could be earned and six out of the eighteen people in the dealing room had made enough to bank a couple of million comfortably. I learned, however, that there was a high failure rate for people who arrived at the firm without a solid client base. They had to go through the same 'smile and dial' routine that I was experiencing.

I began to worry when I realised that I had only been hired as a cold-caller. By a miracle, on the third day, I traded with a company with whom I had a passing acquaintance from my time at The Pan Asian Bank. Two days later I managed to do an asset swap with a merchant bank that had been introduced to me on a buddy-buddy basis. By the end of the week I was considered, mistakenly, to be a bit of a legend.

I was artificially bolstered by the first week's success into thinking that I could actually make a good living out of the company. There was a chart on one side of the dealing room with everyone's monthly performance, which made me think of time-share salesmen. It was slightly tasteless, I thought, being openly encouraged to rip clients off for as much as could be got away with. After the almost saintly banking tutelage at The Pan Asian, it went against the grain to tear our customers' eyes out. It didn't take me long to put my scruples to one side and take anything I could get, but it made for an extraordinary client-broker relationship. We were fully expected to suck the breath out of our clients and, at the same time, pretend to be acting in their best interests. Some of the other people in the firm were extremely adept at this, having been doing it for years and knew no shame. If they were blown out of the water by the person at the other end of the phone, they'd just shrug and try someone else. Some were so good at it, it was almost a pleasure watching them in action.

Knut, a Swede who'd been one of the people who'd interviewed me before I joined the company, had once nearly bankrupted a Scandinavian pension group by smooth-talking them out of their high quality government holdings into, by degrees, more remunerative but slightly lower quality issues. Eventually, after a year of slowly turning their portfolio, he got them to sell all their holdings and buy into a medium-sized oil company that appeared to be good value. A month later the oil company was down-graded by the ratings agencies. It was no longer an investment class name and suddenly every institution in the business was trying to sell their holding. The price 'fell out of bed' and the bonds became illiquid. In the resulting panic the banks pulled in their credit lines. The oil company went belly up and had to file for bankruptcy protection. The stock became practically worthless, and the pension group were left without a cent in their account.

I bet there were a few cross Swedish pensioners waving their pension books excitedly at the Norrkoping Post Office that day, but that wasn't

Conmax's problem. Knut had a house to run and a wife to keep in furs so, apart from having to find another account to bleed, it was none of his business.

In another area of the company there was an ebullient Spaniard whose main account was an insurance company in Madrid that happened to be run by his brother-in-law. During the week the two of them would cackle away in Spanish buying and selling bonds to each other, both taking their respective sales credits on each deal, and then have a laugh about it together at the weekend. Too much like fun! Wally Barker on the other hand, who was later to become a close friend, would sell his clients immensely complex deals that at face value looked profitable but by the time Wally had taken his cut, the client either just broke even or carried, in some cases, a small but unnoticeable loss. The shortfall would only become apparent when the trade was matched a week later, by which point it was out of sight in another department less involved in the intricacies of making a profit.

The pirates of Conmax plundered the sinking and purchase funds. They double dealt, bobbed and wove in a way that I'd never seen at Parker Barrow. It was all perfectly legitimate. Just. The most celebrated dealing ticket within the folklore of Conmax legend had been done by one of the directors who'd interviewed me. He had bought a block of zero coupon bonds from the market and sold them back to the lead managers while taking a $250,000 turn in the process. The lead managers were withdrawn from the issue week later, and yet there had been nothing illegal or improper about the transaction.

I made a little headway, but it was difficult to get into the game with all the performing accounts already covered. The first few months were slightly hair-raising and I was worried that I wouldn't cut it. After my initial flash in the pan I did almost nothing for ten weeks. The smiles from my colleagues became weaker. I avoided direct eye contact in case anyone said something snide. I knew my days were numbered unless I pulled something out of the hat. I adopted a different approach and developed the off-the-run currencies that nobody else could be bothered with. For a while I had some success within the Swiss Franc market, then an underplayed niche in London. Swiss Francs were cheap to borrow. With Swiss interest rates lower than anywhere else in Europe, it was easy to finance positions and make money. I tried to keep the other hiring opportunities that I'd had before I joined Conmax alive, but they died soon after the market crash.

Outside the office, life in its impecunious way limped on. Yasmin and I decided to part company for the last time. She realised that I only saw her when there was nothing better to do and so I let her drift off once again.

Although Yasmin had never exactly been a drain on my resources, I was happier flying solo while I sorted things out at Conmax. I was lucky that despite my paltry salary I could get by, mainly because I'd managed to sock away some cash from my time at the Pan Asian and as a result had only a small mortgage. I became an instant slum landlord and let out my two spare bedrooms. It was a bore having to worry about money constantly. All my friends could afford big ticket items such as cars and holidays. I only went to the cheapest restaurants when I had to, and it became increasingly difficult to run with the pack. I became a sexual nonentity and retreated into the goblin world of folksy gatherings in Fulham basements and Clapham semis. The world of screw-top wine, cheese footballs and holiday snaps of Thailand.

Then one day things changed.

# Chapter 4: Crystal

Diana Faber, an American girl I knew vaguely who lived just round the corner from my flat had always been a little coolly disposed towards me. So I was surprised when she called one day to ask me to fill in for someone who'd dropped out of a dinner party she was having that evening. At such times I never knew whether to be flattered or insulted, but unless I was doing something else I usually accepted. On this occasion I made no pretence about my availability. The proximity of Diana's flat more than made up for my own reservations about *her*. I had an aversion to running the gauntlet of breathalysers or spending a fortune on taxis just to eat a meal on the other side of town. Going to Diana's meant I could get nicely swacked and waddle home in my own time without having to be beholden to others for a lift or held hostage to the vagaries of a local taxi rank.

There had been a time when I'd no such qualms about drinking myself silly before driving home, until the night I was stopped by a policeman. I was so drunk that I was practically sick over him. I was immediately thrown into a police car and bundled off to the Earl's Court nick. They loved it. They'd nabbed a nob. The intoxicator machine was dead when we got to the station and a doctor had to be summoned to take a blood test. I waited on a bench for an hour with half a dozen other drunken miscreants while hobnailed rozzers strutted about importantly under the harsh yellow light. The officer on my case was delighted with his catch. It was so much plumper and juicier than catching a thief. A doctor eventually arrived and took some blood from my arm. Afterwards he asked if I wanted a plaster. I said, rather wittily I thought at the time considering I was so drunk:

''Who said anything about being plastered?!"

It wasn't quite so funny when it was brought up in court a month later by the bluebottle who'd been present at the blood-letting. I was handed a print-out with my alcohol count on it. The magistrate looked at me expectantly and asked for my comments, but the print-out meant nothing. I said that I was sorry but that it was 'All Greek to me'.

"Greek!" he exclaimed incredulously. "It's positively Olympian!''

I got eighteen months off the road and a two hundred pound fine. I resolved to take the necessary precautions to avoid repeating the experience when I got my licence back.

I didn't know any of the other guests at Diana's that night. They were an assortment of yuppies and Thatcherite spawn and corporatiive party padding. I was handed a drink and introduced to a slim, dark-haired girl, whose name I missed. She was attractive in an intense, child-murdering sort of way. I noticed that she bore more than a passing likeness to

Christine Hale. Her face seemed to hide the same repressed cruelty of a thousand unfought wars, although I soon found that this was a front for her underlying humour. She was tall in her heels, which was a drag as I had to stand to attention to look her in the eye. Her features were unflawed, except that her nose was almost too straight, like a runway, She was wearing rather tarty, rude lipstick which I liked. The effect, despite its ghoulish undertone, was oddly elegant and she looked as though it would take more than a box of chocolates to gain her attention: just the sort of woman I couldn't be doing with. We fell into the regular Q and A routine about where we lived and what we did.

"So what do you do to keep yourself in narcotics?" I asked, trying to make the best of an unoriginal opener.

"I don't know really. I work in a building, I guess."

"A building? No kidding? That's great! I do too. Isn't that amazing? What colour's yours?"

It turned out she worked for a firm of art auctioneers. Neither of us was particularly taken with our employment and we started talking about what, in a perfect world, we'd both like to do. She wanted to rebuild old ruins.

"You'll do," she said. Very funny. I said I would like to be in journalism; a columnist perhaps.

"Well, you've certainly got the height for it," she noted, delicately.

I gave a double take. I was supposed to do the jokes. I tried to cap her comment with an appropriate rejoinder but to my annoyance she dismissed it with a look. I was intrigued. It was a pleasant surprise to find a comedienne amongst such humourless company.

Perhaps I mistook her ability to amuse for a willingness to please, but I was glad when we sat down to supper that she was opposite me. She had two solemn-looking men on either side of her. One seemed self-opinionated and self-aggrandising barrister, the other as I was later to learn, was Patrick 'Dumper' Ballingall, a brooding investment banker with a face like thunder. Things were no better on my side of the table. On my left was a horror-head with pubes growing out of her scalp and to my right was a small, beaky woman whose views were of no interest to me. Out of desperation, my fellow jester and I were thrown together in conversation again. We continued our banter, however her asides became increasingly more barbed as the evening wore on. I started to get heartburn. The food had been prepared by outside caterers and was rich to the point of being practically indigestible, although I noticed that my new accomplice had no such problems attacking her plate.

Much as I wanted to get drunk, I was anxious not to numb my reflexes to a standstill. I tried to hit the jocular cusp between humour and absurdity. I aimed, missed, and became horrendously intoxicated instead. I turned to the poodle-headed hydra on my left and lectured her on colonic irrigation for a while. I was exhausted by the time coffee was served and decided to leave while I could still walk. At an appropriate moment I got up and slurred my farewells. I lurched back to my flat, pleased with the evening, if not myself. At least there had been one girl, the tall dark one, who'd been out of the ordinary, even if I hadn't got her name. Whether she regarded me as anything within the food chain was for me to investigate.

The next day I phoned Diana to thank her for an enjoyable evening and such an 'exquisite' meal. I casually asked about the dark-haired girl. It transpired that her name was Crystal. Crystal Frost. The fact that her appearance and name were not dissimilar to Christine Hale's didn't strike me as ironic at the time. She was twenty-seven and just in the process of severing an emotional tie. Perfect! I asked Diana if it would be politic to call her.

"How the hell do I know?" Diana snapped impatiently. "Why don't you find out? Wanna number?" Of course I did.

I left it, smoothly, until the following day before I called Crystal. There was no point being coy so I just said, "Hi! It's James from the other night. Free for a date?" Unceremonious but quick. There didn't seem to be any problem and she agreed a day and a rendezvous without putting up any pretence of being booked up weeks ahead.

I signed off saying, "Oh, one more thing: can you do me a favour?"

I could hear trepidation in her reply.

"Well, yes. What?"

"Can you wear low heels?"

I got a Woody Allen laugh and then we signed off. *Brilliant*, Mr Trilliant!

We met a week later. I had devoted a fair amount of thought to the choice of restaurant. I decided that proximity to home was not a relevant factor at this juncture, and chose an upper-spend bistro off the King's Road which I hoped would strike the right note.

I waited at the bar and sipped a seven pound gin and tonic very slowly. I caught my reflection in the mirror behind the bar. My hair wasn't quite right. Whichever way I flicked it, I still looked a prat. I felt uncomfortable sitting alone in full view of the other diners. I glanced at my watch. I wanted to chug back my drink and order another but then I remembered, however lovely the restaurant *I* was on a budget. Ten minutes turned into twenty. I reluctantly ordered another drink. I began to assume that I'd been stood up. My mood was about to enter a terminally negative state when Crystal finally arrived.

"I'm sorry I'm so late," she said, breathlessly. "I got lost and couldn't find anywhere to park."

I was sufficiently relieved to see her that I forgot my solitary wrath. She had her hair tied back and looked unapproachably severe. The table that we were shown to had a wobble and put me back into a state of chronic agitation until I got the waiter to coasterise the offending leg.

We chatted agreeably enough at first but there wasn't any of the spontaneity that we'd had before, and the conversation never got properly kick-started. We ordered our food and some wine. I made the usual mistake of trying to drink myself into a good mood but I only became belligerent. Crystal's wit turned to derision. I felt a rift growing that was putting her further from my grasp. As Crystal had her car to consider, she sipped her wine sparingly, which left me with the lion's share of the bottle and the rest. The gin and tonics hadn't helped. I kept having to go to the loo, like an incontinent moron. The food was bearable but I was too out of sorts to eat it. I noticed Crystal had no such qualms and devoured her helping with almost canine voracity. By the time I'd picked at a quarter of the plate I felt like an overindulged cockroach. I was glad when it was time to ask for the bill.

Crystal tried to pay for her share, which was nice of her but implied that she was reluctant to accept anything from me that might compromise the distance that she'd managed to establish between us. She offered to drop me home. I was sufficiently relieved that the evening was drawing to a close that I readily accepted without trying to linger around a second more than was necessary.

The drive back turned out to be a more relaxed job. Crystal asked me about my new flat. I asked her about the art market and her work. She drew up outside my door and to my surprise accepted my invitation to come up for a cup of coffee.

I was proud of my new flat. It was not particularly stylish but it was spacious enough. The drawing room covered the top floor and had a roof terrace at either end. It was, however, up six flights of stairs which did nothing to enhance its chic. Crystal said there was an air of downtown Manila about it, which I wasn't sure whether to take as a compliment. I regarded it as possessing a certain tree house ambience. She had a look round and continued with her appraisal while I was making the coffee. We talked for a while, then she finished her coffee and left.

I took Crystal out a few times after that but it soon became obvious that she wasn't interested in having an affair. She became disenchanted with watching me get drunk and the inevitable descent into unsophisticated behaviour that followed. I got the impression that she thought I was OK, but a bit of a sad case. A happy sad case, but a fraction second drawer. She asked me to a few social functions which I misinterpreted as the stirrings of requited interest, but otherwise she kept herself at arm's length.

Things at Conmax were still not exactly peachy, but I managed to hang on. I had the odd lucky break that kept me from being fired. Away from the office, Crystal's indifference began to grate. I thought I could offer her a measure of compatibility but, as time progressed, I knew that I was not what she was looking for.

Albert Carr, one of my fellow drinking advocates, summed her up one day by saying, "I give your tart minus four out of ten. Unless you've got a house in Chelsea and drive a Porsche, the only way you'll get to nob her is to rape her."

It was difficult to disagree. I could see I was onto a no-hoper, but however unreciprocated my feelings were I had at least discovered a use for her. At last I had found an antidote to Christine Hale. By nurturing another obsession, one effectively cancelled out the other. It was a painful cure but at least with Crystal I was squandering emotions on a project that vaguely existed.

I had all but given up any thoughts of having a serious relationship with her and had more or less thrown in courtship's towel when, in a disturbed moment, Crystal demanded that I slept with her. Bingo! I had no objections but she insisted that we both had a bath before we did anything, which somewhat detracted from the immediacy of the occasion, but I knew better than to complain. It was only when we got into bed that I realised how drunk she was. She started to spit all over me. I asked her whether she thought it was such a good idea.

She replied, "Oh yes, I like this game!"

I didn't. It had only been a few months earlier that I'd thought of Crystal as a rather poised individual. Once she'd drained herself of spittle she calmed down and we went through the usual routine of touch, feel, insert and thrust. I wasn't particularly sober myself and slightly regretted baiting the master with such alacrity in the office lavatories that afternoon. To my surprise Crystal turned out to have a far more womanly figure than I had envisaged. Her model-thin exterior concealed, in its clothed state, a feast of anatomical excitements and my tumescence materialised without any further protocol.

The next morning was not such a happy affair. Crystal woke up with a start, went from shock to panic and fled the flat with the speed of a whippet out of a trap, leaving me looking mournfully at my six o'clock erection.

We spoke on the phone later that day and were able to joke about the incident easily enough. I felt however bizarre the circumstances, that this could be the start of something. I didn't want to appear greedy, so I left it till the next day before I called to arrange another date. When I did, however, Crystal said she was busy for the foreseeable future, "... but how about Tuesday the 25th?"

That was four weeks away.

"Quit hand-jiving, Crystal. You can do better than that. Don't you think you're being a little stingy with the 'buy' signals?" I said, and prattled on for a bit. My plaintive bleating had no effect.

She said simply, "Goodbye, James," and put the phone down.

I felt dejected and wondered what to do next. My thoughts went back in time to a sex dictionary that had been sent to my parents by their Book of the Month club in a burst of 'sixties permissiveness. I used to sneak a peek at it when I was a child. It would have made therapeutic reading for anyone with a sexual or emotional complication, but I was too young at that point to lay any serious claim to either. In its naivety there was an explanation for every hang-up and deviation imaginable. Everything was 'perfectly normal'. Under 'J' for 'Jilt' there was a story about a man who'd been happily living with a woman for three years. The woman had turned round one day and announced that she'd found a new love and was off. Despite his resentment, the man put his feelings of umbrage to one side and sent her a bunch of flowers with the message:

"Thanks for all the fun."

The woman relented. They got back together and six weeks later they were married.

I headed for a florist near work and chose a tasteful eighteen pounds' worth. After several attempts to get my writing to look less like a psychopath's I wrote:

"Bummer. Never mind, it was a laugh while it
lasted.

Thanks for everything. Love, James."

If she didn't respond, at least my suspicions about her being a cold-hearted bitch would be confirmed. If she did, then maybe I could coerce her into another meeting and get a reprieve. She called the following Monday.

"Thanks for the bunch, Trunch!"

'Trunch' was the nickname that the two girls with whom I shared my flat had given me in mock homage to my 'love truncheon'. So not such a bitch after all? Crystal tentatively agreed to meet me at an unspecified but not so distant future date and we ended the conversation on a relaxed note with my ego, if not reinstated, at least out of detention.

I heard nothing from her for over a month. I could have phoned and asked her what was happening but I knew that she would just hang up on me again. Then one day, out of the blue, she called.

"Hi, Trunch," she said breezily, as if we'd only spoken the day before.

"Hello, Crystal," I said icily. "To what do I owe the pleasure?"

"Nothing special. Just haven't seen you around and wondered how you were doing."

"Don't come on all innocent with me, Cosmic. *Fait tomber le masque*, for Christ's sake!" I said. "You've been doing your level best to avoid me ever since we fucked each other."

"I'm really sorry Trunch, but I've been so busy. I simply haven't had time to see you. Do you want to go to a film next week? A group of us are going out on Wednesday. Why don't you come?"

I would have preferred to have seen Crystal on her own but if this was the only way to make contact I decided I'd have to accept her invitation graciously. We arranged to meet near the cinema at 'The Artist', a pub which was, although I didn't know it at the time, to become instrumental in the course of my destiny.

Things gradually began to get better at work and I actually made a small bonus one quarter. It was not that I was doing particularly well so much as other people in the company were doing worse, which drew some of the fire away from me. I was able, briefly, to shed the bottom-of-the-class aura that had become increasingly ingrained in my persona. People came and went within the firm. It seemed more of a temp agency than a job with a serious career path. I looked elsewhere for employment but the other companies were now only hiring dead certs. Someone had warned me when I joined Conmax that there were few places to move to that were lower down the employment vortex. The larger companies, unimaginatively, turned their thumbs down at Conmax employees, which was silly as there were some clever people there. I shivered with the realisation that without Conmax I'd probably be on my own. The prospect of being locked in and obliged to work there for another twenty years was pretty bleak.

Cinema day arrived. I got myself ready to go to the pub where we were due to meet. The film that had been decided on was an American pre-teen rites of passage affair which might not have been *my* first choice. I got to the pub and saw Chrystal with Diana, the American girl who'd introduced us and two young men. One of the men was making a fuss of his new mobile. The conversation was expensive holiday destinations, night clubs and 'serious dosh'. Mobile worked for Goldbergs and earned more money than God. I'd never met anyone I particularly liked from Goldbergs and Mobile wasn't proving an exception. The other man, who looked a bit of a wimp, was just rich from what I could gather. I was glad when it was time to go to the cinema. Mobile produced his gold Amex with a flourish to pay for his ticket. I sat next to Crystal and contemplated holding her hand once the lights went down but thought better of it.

At the end of the film, which was shit, Crystal went into a fit because her bracelet had fallen off somewhere. We all looked under our seats and along the aisle, but to no avail. Crystal was practically in tears. It had been a twenty-first present from a favourite aunt. Aunt they all? I offered to stay behind and help her look while the others went back to the pub, but Rich Wimp beat me to it and insisted I go on and leave him to help Crystal.

They rejoined us in the pub ten minutes later, *sans* bracelet. I noticed that they were unusually deferential to each other, but didn't at that point think any more of it. The closing bell rang just in time for me to miss my round. I wanted to get away from Hand-phone's cant and have Crystal on her own.

I turned to her and said:

"That was a great evening! Thanks for including me. What about coming back for a quick drink? We haven't really had much of a chance for a chat."

"James, that's really sweet of you, but I need my beauty sleep," she replied, evasively.

"You're not wrong there honey, but go on... just a quick one."

"James, I really can't. I'm getting a lift home with Stuart."

Stuart must be Mobile's friend; the one who helped Crystal look for the bracelet.

"Don't worry. I can order you a taxi from my flat. I'll pay," I said trying not to appear imposing.

"I don't think Stuart would like that much!" she laughed.

"Why not?" I demanded.

"Well, he's my boyfriend... I thought you knew."

I felt as though I was about to be sick. Stuart? Rich Wimp? Even Mobile would have been less of an insult. At least I could have blamed it on his overbearing confidence. To be pipped at the post by such an obvious weed was a humiliating blow to my already shaken self-worth. I tried not to let the disappointment show, but Crystal later told me that I looked as though I'd swallowed a lemon.

"I'll call you in the morning, Trunch," she said, as if offering a consolation prize.

"Sure you will," I said dejectedly, and walked out of the pub.

I stumbled home feeling as though I'd been kicked in the crotch. Bitch! Talk about going to the highest bidder. Whore! Why were so many women like that? Was money *that* important? It seemed to be the universal narcotic and everyone was hooked. I wasn't exactly a pauper; I didn't have much, but I didn't have any debts either, which was a start.

I couldn't sleep that night. I switched on Radio Nerdo and listened to the other demented insomniacs airing their problems. I twiddled the knob and caught Phil Collins wailing some dirge about inner city deprivation. What the fuck did he know about it? I went back to reassessing how a drip like Stuart was able to access cargo to which I appeared to have no licence. I kept having visions of his unsmiling face as he mounted Crystal from behind. And Crystal had been *so* subservient with him! She was never like that with me. If only I could become rich overnight. I knew I was on course for being a millionaire because I saved almost every penny I earned, but I also knew I would have to live for six hundred years to get there.

There had been some benefit from the whole episode. Crystal had definitely usurped Christine Hale as my major irritant, but her methods hadn't been as deliberate or calculating as Christine's, which almost made me rue Crystal's loss all the more.

I was too exhausted to get worked up about it. Christine had used up most of my emotional reserves. Crystal was just another false lead. Or so I thought.

# Chapter 5: Things Look Up

One of the questions that Yasmin used to ask when we'd been together was, "James, why do you hate everyone?" I'd always dismissed it, but after a while I started to take notice of what she was saying and began to analyse two aspects of the question. One: was it true? Did I hate everyone? Two: if it was true, did it show? On the first score I came to the conclusion that it wasn't everyone whom I hated. Certainly not everyone hated me. I'd received over a dozen Christmas cards the year before. Perhaps, I wondered, I just resented those who conducted their lives in a more fruitful manner than I did.

"But that's almost everyone, James," Yasmin pointed out. On the second theme, I conceded that perhaps I did seem a bit sour. With this in mind, I tried to present a more cheerful and optimistic front after the Crystal incident. It worked for a while and I found life became more pleasant. The three main sectors of my existence, namely the working, social and emotional aspects began to crystallise, despite being Crystalless, into a happy threesome. They snowballed, slowly at first, and then gathered momentum until there came a moment when life almost seemed pleasant. For a while I even wondered if Christine's Curse was beginning to tire at last.

At work I'd established, more by accident than design, a tangible network of business contacts. The commission I was earning became less haphazard and started to evolve into a regular flow. I was no longer quite so worried about whether I would last the week out and allowed myself the luxury of upgrading my employment horizon on to a monthly basis. I finally got my driving licence back and bought car, an unimportant event by anybody's standards, but that was before I had explored all its uses. I chose a rusting, tarmac-coloured BMW in a half-hearted attempt to conform to what I then considered to be a high-end chattel.

"Bemused Middle-aged Wanker," Wally Barker commented unkindly when I took delivery of it. I didn't care. To me it was a Mercedes and yet it was sufficiently unobtrusive to attract either the attention of the law maker or law breaker.

I met and started taking out Michelle, a pretty graduate trainee from Dundee who worked at Bankers Trust. Initially I made a determined effort to play things straight and keep all tricks and chicanery to the bare minimum. She had a good job but she was naive to the point of being infantile: the cream of the university milk-round. She had a 'Parking Wardens are nice people too' sticker on her car bumper and wrote unfunny captions beside the pictures in her photograph albums. I took it upon myself to purge her of her unworldliness.

Getting into her pants proved to be like playing a game of Grandma's footsteps. Whenever I cornered her on the sofa for an entwining session, and happened to unhook her bra *en passant*, she would freeze and look at me accusingly. I would have to stop and pretend that her bra-hook had come undone by an act of God or of its own accord. For all Michelle's prudery her stocky, pony-like body and its generous Zeppelinesque breasts held me fascinated. There was an element of the page three look about her that seemed at odds with her low church primness. I decided that if patience was required, I would give it all I had.

Her innocence restricted me in what I could do with her. If we went to see a film it had to involve Denholm Elliot sipping tea with a whole lot of other Brits behaving like spastics in turn-of-the-century Italy. To me, a film wasn't a film without cops, crims and corruption. Furthermore, there was a limit to the number of people I could introduce her to. Most people I knew would be bound to give the game away if they saw me trying to act all holy. I occasionally took her to parties and left her by herself while I took off and talked to other people. Fortunately she was pretty enough to attract male attention. I'd join up with her when we ready to go home. If anyone wanted to ask her out they were welcome to: if the master couldn't crack the safe what chance had an amateur?

After two months of strained elastic and denial, I decided that it was time to rattle my sabre. I picked a suitably inebriated moment -the office Christmas party as it happened - in which to pounce. Normally office parties were not my idea of a good time, but the people at Conmax were a sufficiently bizarre and diverse bunch that I thought, if nothing else, it would be different. I had no misgivings about taking Michelle. It went well. What few speeches there were, were suitably heckled down. The raffle prizes were appropriately naff, the food awful enough to evoke comedy and the drink plentiful. The restaurant had a small discotheque and we danced like beasts into the small hours.

I had little difficulty steering Michelle back to my flat afterwards but making her stay the night proved more of a problem. We assumed our usual teenage clinch on the sofa. I then said, in what I hoped passed for sincerity, that I sensed a special feeling growing between us and that like all special things, it was fragile. I continued, whispering softly, that I didn't want to do anything to destroy it and quietly slipped my hands into her pants. She agreed willingly with what I had to say and seemed sufficiently distracted that she didn't appear to notice my attempts to coax her crotch into a state of froth until it was almost too late.

"Taxi!" she declared abruptly.

Damn! I thought to myself. So close yet so far. Next time. I moodily called a cab from the furthest taxi rank in the book and got back to business. It was maddening work, teetering on the precipice of intercoursal bliss with only a few millimetres of lycra and cotton separating us, but the evening bode well for the future. When the taxi eventually arrived, I wasn't totally dissatisfied with the way things had turned out, given how spankingly wet Michelle was and the fact that she wasn't going to go down as one of history's natural nymphomaniacs. Other Christmas social occasions provided a good opportunity to take Michelle out without actually having to spend a fortune escorting her around half the nightspots of London. One evening, as I dropped her home, she foolishly asked me in for a drink. Once in her flat I speed-drank two large gins and promptly declared myself unfit to drive. Much against my wishes, I said, I would have to stay the night. Michelle hesitated for a moment but then yielded without a struggle.

It had taken two months and fifteen days to achieve my objective. Which was no big deal as it turned out.

Just as with Yasmin and Rebecca, the relationship was not particularly exciting. It was good to have female company around again; someone to share the pizza with, watch television next to and generally fool around. But the association never left the ground. It was like taking a camera to a funeral: somehow it wasn't quite right. I didn't know what I was looking for, but Michelle wasn't it. Her child-like enthusiasm for office life and thirst for recognition and approval at work clashed with my indifference to such trifles. For me, work meant drudgery and toil; the office was just a place to recover from hangovers. My life began at five in the evening. For Michelle it started at eight in the morning. Her superiors and colleagues were her heroes and role models. They dominated her life. Her conversation mainly consisted of conclusionless workplace anecdotes. "A really funny thing happened at work today..." was the inevitable prelude to some predictable account about the stiffs that she worked with. To my mind talking about work outside office hours was not only blasphemous but *déclassé*. When she spoke I could feel my face going into a weak, rictal smile, like watching a West End musical.

For a while I was prepared to put up with it, as being bored to the point of helpless amazement seemed a reasonable price for being allowed access to her magnificent chest, the likes of which I had only ever seen before in specialist magazines. However a man cannot live by tits alone, and one day I flipped.

Michelle had given me a present of a bath sponge in the shape of a lion. She came round to my flat one evening while I was having a bath. I buzzed her in and got back into the water. She came into the bathroom and, seeing the sponge, grabbed it and made mock-snapping noises as she thrust it towards me threateningly.

"I'm a big hungry puddy cat, tee hee!" she giggled, splashing me.

"Ho ho," I said, "most amusing I'm sure." But I wasn't in the mood.

"You're a bit like a puddy cat, aren't you?" she continued with mounting hysteria.

"Yes, I suppose I am a bit like a puddy cat," I said testily, wondering where the joke was.

"Like a naughty little puddy cat!" she cooed.

"This will not do!" I muttered. Here was this cretin with career prospects that I would kill for, with the mind of a small child. I could see the affair approaching its conclusion with increasing certainty.

I didn't drop Michelle there and then as I had with some of the others, partly because physically she was my ideal and she certainly wasn't a bad person. But we were so utterly different that it was unfair of me to have picked on her in the first place, let alone carry on for any length of time with what was, after all, another pitiful charade of a relationship. Michelle had her uses, if only as a platform to greater things, but she sensed my laboured attention and although my sexual interest in her remained unaffected, it more often than not went unsatiated.

Even morons have instincts and Michelle became increasingly reluctant to deliver the carnal dividend I craved. She started to make polite excuses about having to get up early whenever I raised the question of staying overnight. I blamed myself for the state of the relationship and decided to give it one final chance. I couldn't expect everyone, let alone Michelle, to share my point of view.

In the meantime something strange was happening with Crystal, that took me by surprise. Patrick Farrel, a vague pub-frequenting acquaintance who happened to work in the same office as Crystal, accosted me one day in 'The Artist' and put me in the picture about Stuart, Crystal's boyfriend. It transpired that Crystal and Stuart had been at university together and had been going out with each other on and off for years.

Then Patrick delivered a verbal slap in my face by saying, "Of course Crystal's nuts about you, James."

"You what?" I said with a mixture of disbelief and bashfulness.

"No, I mean it. It's practically all she talks about. She's always saying that she is in love with –'Trunch' but you don't care."

"Bollocks," I griped. "She's the one who gave me the flick. I haven't spoken to her for months. I can't believe she'd say that. You're winding me up."

"No," Patrick insisted, "you should give her a call. I believe that things aren't going at all well between her and Stuart and they had a most God-awful holiday a couple of weeks ago, which practically nixed the relationship. I'd give her a call, if I were you."

I did, the next day.

"Hi, sweet cheeks! It's Trunch. How goes it?" I chirruped, with slightly nervous familiarity.

"Trunch! How are ya babes!"

We exchanged banalities until I tentatively came to the point and suggested meeting for a bite to eat. We agreed on the following Saturday. She seemed friendly enough, but I was wary of her motives from past experience. I knew that she enjoyed stringing me along and I was not about to get sucked in again.

To lighten the load I arranged to join a group I knew who were going out to a restaurant that Saturday night. Crystal arrived at my flat in a bumptious frame of mind that I was in no mood to counter.

"I'm starving," she announced, looking at me as if it was my fault. "What have you got to eat?"

"We are going to a restaurant, you know," I said defensively. "If you can hang on for half an hour you can eat an entire waiter if you want."

"You must have something in the fridge, surely?" Crystal demanded, grumpily.

"There's last year's cabbage and some mouldy bread, but that's about it, I'm afraid."

"You're useless," she said, not in jest and went off to check that I was telling the truth.

I suffered her stoically until we got to the restaurant. Once there, with the benefit of an audience, I let my temper go to work. After two glasses of wine I was ready to go into action. I found an opening. Crystal made a reference to my flat which she described as "poxy". God's little acre? My pride and joy? That did it. I felt a rage coming on.

"At least I don't start gobbing over people while I'm doing it," I snapped, adding as an afterthought, "stupid bulimic arsewipe."

"Don't call me an "arsewipe", you idiotic alcoholic gnome," Crystal hissed. I upgraded the step from trot to canter.

"I'll call you what I like. How about 'Third-rate gold-digging whore,' for starters?"

"Well you're just a career corpse in a fourth-rate job, with not a hope in hell of getting on in life. And you masturbate too much."

"How do you know?" I asked, a little disconcerted.

"It shows."

"Well, I'd rather have a pretty wank than an ugly fuck," I said, glaring at her fiercely.

The rest of the table became quiet. Someone tried to calm me down but I shot him a look and he too became silent. I continued with my barrage of infantile vitriol. I noticed Crystal's eyes slowly filling with tears. She made a feeble attempt to interrupt once or twice but I cut her down before she could say anything intelligible. The tears turned from a trickle to a torrent, but I was too far gone to turn back. I continued with salvo after salvo of scathing, crude and mainly groundless abuse.

"Please get me a taxi," she gasped to a passing waiter.

"Where do you think you're going?" I demanded loudly. "You're not going anywhere without paying your whack, matey! You can think again if you thought you were getting away scot-free for just letting me have the pleasure of watching you act the silly bitch! Twenty quid or I'll cause a scene."

As if in a trance she reached into her handbag and fished out a £20 note. Her face had become a crumpled latticework of misery and liquid mascara.

"Please hurry with my taxi," she croaked to the waiter.

"Why don't you wait outside for it? You're putting me off my supper, and that simply won't do," I declared, primly.

Crystal started to weep in earnest.

"I've never been so insulted. You're just a bully!" she sobbed.

"*Au contraire*, my little bowl of wobbling plums. I see myself as a beacon of decency amidst the seas of injustice. This is just a sample of the sort of medicine you've been dishing out in scoops all your life. But it's not so nice being on the receiving end, is it? Your behaviour is never short of being anything but ill-mannered; it's crass and you've been specialising in it every day of your fucking sordid existence. Now piss off!"

Crystal wobbled as she got up and had a last attempt at breaking my delivery.

"Talk about the pot calling the kettle black. You're not right in the head, James Mallet. I know what you are... you're a screwed up misogynous shit, that's all."

I returned her volley with a little topspin:

"*Moi?* What an outrageous suggestion! Let's just say I've always been suspicious of anything that can bleed for a week and still won't die."

Crystal retreated aghast to the door and fled into the night. The others went into shock. I felt no remorse. In fact I felt the opposite; the heady mixture of power and arousal that I got whenever I saw tears in a woman. Tears that represented the teasing dividing line between emotional sadism and compassion that was such fun to test. It was a flashback to childhood when it was so easy to make a little girl cry; like pulling a pigtail or not letting let her be part of the bicycle gang. As a small boy it was about the only thing that I'd had any manipulative control over. It took a few years to work out that tears, of course, were themselves manipulative tools, but I'd learnt to ignore them long before that evening.

"Sorry about that chaps," I said. "A little dirty washing that perhaps shouldn't have been done in public. My apologies. The cabaret is over but the night has just begun."

I settled down and sat back to bask in a caddish glow of one-upmanship. That would teach Patrick Farrel to play Cupid! I hadn't fancied my chances of getting back into Crystal's pants again anyway, so I thought I hadn't lost anything. It had been an unnecessarily brutal incident, but enjoyable nonetheless; a satisfactory conclusion to what had otherwise been an unsatisfactory affair.

I thought I'd seen the last of Crystal, so I was surprised when two days later at work I received an official-looking envelope bearing Crystal's company logo. In it was a joke questionnaire that Crystal had typed asking me to answer why I was so psychotic. It was quite amusing. She had obviously spent some time on it which was flattering. It gave me an inkling that I had - not that I wanted it now -the upper hand at last. I coolly threw it into the bin and decided not to take any action, but at the end of the day I had a rethink and rescued it from the wastepaper basket.

Nothing happened for another two days. But then on the Friday afternoon Crystal called.

"Well fuck a slut, if it isn't old Crystal Frost," I said, feigning surprise.

"Did you get my letter, Trunch?"

"Sure did, sugar lump. Thanks. Very funny. I was going to give you a bell but I've been a bit busy lately."

"I'm sorry that I made you so angry the other night. I didn't mean to. I don't know what went wrong," she said, dejectedly.

"I do. It was a bit of a humdinger wasn't it? I suppose I should really be the one who's apologising. I'm sorry. It was out of order but I wasn't in the mood to take any shit and I suppose I overreacted," I said in mild understatement.

"Can I see you again?" Crystal asked, almost timidly.

"Sure. What are you doing this evening?"

"I'm supposed to be going to my sister's but maybe we can get together next week."

"Nah. I'm only on for an impulse purchase. Bust the trade with your sister and let's go for an interview."

"I suppose she won't mind, but it's a bit late notice."

"Do what you want but I'm not in the mood for playing around and making arrangements for some date in the distant future. And we all know what a problem my moods are now, don't we? Either you do it now or forget it. It's up to you," I said, getting slightly carried away with my tough guy act.

"OK. I'll give her a call. Where do you want to meet?"

"My flat. We'll take it from there. About seven-thirty."

"OK. I'll see you there."

What had come over her? I wondered ruefully.

I wanted to go somewhere where we could be relaxed and decided it would be a diversion to play at being rich Arabs at Raider Nick's Polynesian Bar beneath the Poor Reasons Hotel on Park Lane. If nothing else it was an original choice. The cocktails cost the price of a meal but they delivered a punch.

We drove there in virtual silence. What little we said was cordial and free from animosity. Raider Nick's was not particularly busy and we had no problem finding a space between the escort girls and Lebanese gangsters. We looked at our cocktail menus reticently and after the waiter had taken our orders I opened with a flash of colloquial brilliance:

"Well, here we are then!"

"Yes," Crystal said uncooperatively. We looked at each other awkwardly. I fumbled about for another conversational entrance.

"I don't know what we've really come here to discuss, but I suppose the very fact that we're talking to each other is nothing short of a minor miracle."

"It was awful the other night," Crystal replied, in a strained voice. "I don't think I've ever been so unhappy. You know how I feel about you. Why did you do it?"

"That's just the point, Crystal. I've no idea how you feel about me... I mean who's zooming who? All you do is tease, tease, tease. You've roller-coastered me for God knows how long, to the point where I don't know whether I'm coming or going and quite frankly by Saturday night I'd had enough. I thought it was time you mucked someone else around and left me alone."

"Trunch, I didn't mean to muck you around. It's all been such a mess recently. Stuart and I thought we'd get together again at around the same time that I met you. I suppose in that respect you lost out. Stuart was a known quantity and you were so strange sometimes I didn't know what to make of you. I wasn't sure that we'd work out. I appreciate that I must have looked like a complete bitch sometimes, but I suppose I was just holding back."

It all sounded a bit teenish.

"So that was my dilemma, Trunch, and in the end I was the one who lost out. Stuart and I had a wretched time when we went on holiday together. All I could think of was you, and what fun we'd be having if *we* were together. I realised my mistake, basically."

"Well, it's nice to hear your side of things. I'm actually very sorry I jumped down your throat the other night. However, my situation has changed somewhat in the last few months. I decided, as I appeared to be barking up the wrong tree, there no point hanging around. So when opportunity knocked I started seeing someone else. It' OK and I'm not sure whether I'm up for sale any more. Shame, I suppose, but should give it a go."

"Oh," Crystal said quietly. "I wasn't aware of..."

"One of those things," I butted in, high-mindedly. "It's a bit rich ditching one thing just to go on a wild goose chase for another."

"It wouldn't be a wild goose chase," Crystal protested, defensively.

"How do I know? Your past behaviour has been erratic at best. On the-devil-you-know basis perhaps I'm better off with what I've got and..."

"It won't be like that," she interrupted. "I promise."

"Well, I'm not totally without feeling as far as your case goes but you've bitten me on the nose once too often. How am I to know it won't happen again?"

"It just won't be like that, I swear. I'll give you every ounce I've got. I want to be around you, James, can't you see? I had to put you off the scent at times for your own sake. In the end I'm the one who's been messed about, even if most of it has been self-inflicted."

I thought for a moment, then said, "I think the only thing we can do is to play it by ear. I don't know how my current liaison *sans danger* is going to work out. We might not be ideally suited, but I wanted to give it a shot. Now of course this happens. Never rains, does it? The only thing is to give me some time to think it over." I paused, and then added sagely, "Maybe you should do the same," creating what I hoped was a sufficiently annoying level of sanctimony.

"But if you don't feel strongly about this other girl, why do you bother seeing her?"

"She makes my willie go big," I answered, flatly and truthfully.

"Oh... I see," Crystal mumbled, slightly taken aback, "I'm glad you agreed to see me tonight to talk it over. Obviously things are a little more complicated down your end than I'd bargained for, but these things happen, I guess."

We ordered some more drinks and the conversation moved on to lighter matters. Crystal reverted to her droll alter ego and the cocktails did the rest.

We finished our drinks and the olives that had sat like rabbit droppings between us and drove back to my flat. It was still early and so I asked Crystal up for a cup of coffee.

My flatmates were very much in evidence and the flat seemed busier than a backpackers' hostel. The spell between Crystal and me started to disintegrate. After she'd finished her coffee, Crystal made her excuses and said that she'd better go home. I saw her to the door. We hung around talking for a bit downstairs, when I plucked up courage and said, "Hell, why are we doing this? If you're so in love with me then why don't you put your money where your mouth is for once and stay the night."

"You're always so slow to move. I always think I'll turn into a sexual fossil when I'm with you," Crystal said, tartly. We kissed and made our way to the bedroom.

For the next two weeks Crystal and I spoke frequently on the phone. I made enough references to Michelle to make sure Crystal was aware of her existence but not so many as to frighten her off. In reality there was no contest. I knew I would miss the occasional northern exposure of Michelle's twin peaks, but Crystal's mammary arrangements were by no means inconsequential. I certainly would not miss Michelle's inter-departmental office melodramas.

One evening I drove over to Michelle's flat and gave her one last shot. I had endured an usually long tirade of workplace drivel when, towards the end of the evening, I suggested staying the night. I thought it was a rightful reward for what had otherwise been a waste of time.

"James," Michelle said hesitatingly, "I don't know... I just don't know if it's the proper thing to do. It doesn't seem right."

*Not fair*! I had just endured three hours of undiluted office anecdote and had nothing to show for it. I felt a rage coming on.

"Michelle," I said, "that's pitiful. What are you? Sexually constipated or just an old-fashioned prick teaser? Is sex so sacrosanct that you daren't do it? Is that what you're frightened of? However you dress it up, it's about cowardice, isn't it?"

"Don't get angry with me James. You always get into such a huff when you don't get what you want."

"I don't think that's surprising in the circumstances," I said, feeling extremely huffy.

"What circumstances?" Michelle demanded accusingly.

"The fact that you've taken to breaking the unwritten rule."

"Oh really? And what's that?"

"That men like me do not take out girls like you just to talk about the weather."

"Well James, that's just the point... you only want me for my body."

"No. Just your cunt."

"James, I'm serious," Michelle complained, brushing aside my crudity. "Can't we just be friends?"

"I've got friends coming out of my arse... I don't need another. I'm sorry but you know the terms of engagement... I have absolutely no interest in being your platonic stooge."

"Well it's a two-way street, buster," Michelle declared, in an unexpected display of cool, "and I'm not sure if I'm particularly interested in having a relationship that revolves solely around your sexual appetite. We hardly see each other these days and yet you act as if you can come round when it suits you and climb into bed."

"So you think some sort of sexual embargo is going to help?" I demanded angrily. "You're not exactly the easiest person to go out with, y'know. I reckon as a boyfriend I'm pretty low on your list of priorities. I mean top comes your frigging stupid job, and when you're not there you're at your frigging stupid gym. Then come those frigging wet office patsies you surround yourself with that you call your friends and their prissy little jokes. Then comes your entire attitude problem to having a relationship, and then about a billion rungs down the ladder, comes me. I'm fed up with being used."

"That's not the case, James, for goodness' sake."

"Bollocks. You're just a waste of time. Like every other fucking woman I know in London," I added, resentfully.

"James you're not being reasonable. We're both so different... I know you think I'm a bit common." *A bit*!

"I think I understand," I said, in a vague attempt to appear magnanimous in response to Michelle's spirited rear-guard action.

I left with my head held high and zoomed into the night vowing never to see her again. If my JT wasn't good enough for her, her company certainly didn't stand by itself. Either put out or get out. Yup. Now that I had Crystal lined up, Michelle wouldn't be seeing me for blue smoke I mused, as I made my way through the night traffic.

And so began a relatively happy phase. Crystal and I behaved well towards each other to start with and I was proud of her. Like some relationships the beginning was the most fun, with the illusion of promise to come. We were a popular couple. Life at work was good too. My days of being at the bottom of the production league appeared to be over and the sectors that I covered were doing well. A new Dutch salesman joined the company and found an untapped market for the bonds I happened to trade which boosted my turnover, and thus my profitability, in no short order.

The full vulgarity of summer started conspicuously early that year, with one hot, cloudless day after another. People thought they were seeing evidence of global warming for the first time and muttered darkly about the ozone layer. I didn't care as long as it was sunny. As so often was the case, I was unaware of my good fortune and disposition until long after the moment had passed.

Sociable as we were, Crystal's drinking was a problem. Her wasp-sized constitution, despite her ability to devour plate after plate of food, seemed unable to process the minutest amount of alcohol. After one glass she'd start to twitch and after two she became like a steroid-crazed Amazon. On reflection, at that point I regarded myself as a perfectly safe drunk unless goaded, in which case I was apt to become belligerent. Unfortunately Crystal was good at goading. This led to a volatile combination as Crystal and I went for each other's metaphysical jugulars, both of us ending in a heap, emotionally pistol-whipped and bloodstained, swearing that we'd never see each other again. We always got together a little later, but the familiar signs of relationship meltdown began to set in.

I knew we were starting to irritate each other in earnest as the summer came to an end. My libido, despite our occasional forays into the foothills of deviation and half-hearted attempts at anal sex, became less impulsive, which I knew offended Crystal. At the same time Crystal's faults and quirks started to assume elephantine dimensions. Her hair, for instance, tended, quite harmlessly, to shed itself occasionally. Although this had no cosmetic ill-effects, it revolted me out of all proportion to its actual repulsiveness.

In other areas, there seemed to be more joy in the anticipation of events than in their subsequent realisation. Between us we had an unnerving ability to kill a good time or quash a perfect moment. Crystal was too amusing to be killjoy, but her neurosis destroyed both her own positive characteristics and those of people around her. More things got on my nerves as time went by; her disapproving sister from Hell who hung around in the background like a huge, black bat whom, to my annoyance, I secretly fancied; her poky flat with its early Jetsons furniture that they both shared in the land of the "C" registered Nissans. And Crystal's vulpine, no, lupine gastronomic appetite became increasingly irksome. The list seemed to grow every time we met.

My fortunes at work continued to improve dramatically. The new Dutch salesman thought up an excellent tax wheeze for his compatriots and once one took the hook, half of Amsterdam wanted to jump on board. For a while we were making thousands of pounds for ourselves every day. My profit and loss account started to skyrocket out of control, bursting through targets and bonus schedules, picking up incentive awards and flavour-of-the-month prizes and for a fleeting moment I almost felt like a fat cat.

Crystal, poor thing, wasn't having such a good time of it. The art market she specialised in started to shrivel up and her services at the auctioneers where she worked became surplus to requirements. It didn't matter at first as she managed to turn her hand to sewing and making clothes for friends, but it was galling for her to watch others with half her brain make a fortune every time they blinked.

We stumbled along for the rest of the year, putting off our inevitable cooling off. One of my flavour-of-the-month prizes, won as a result of the Dutch tax adventure, was a two thousand dollar travel voucher. I decided to leave Crystal out of it and spend the lot on myself and go as far away as possible. I bought a ticket to Australia and with the change bought a year's membership to a yuppie health club. Now that I was Mr Moneybags, I had to have the body to go with it.

In the heat of the moment I seemed to be leaving Crystal behind, which was strange as it had been the other way round a year before. I started to look for someone else, which Crystal got wise to. She put a moratorium on my seeing any but the plainest women. Her paranoia finally got the better of her and, unbeknownst to me, she started to call my answerphone when I wasn't in and, by using the secret code, would listen for any calls from strange females, thus wiping out all the other phone messages in the process. I wondered why I hadn't received any recorded calls those last few months we were together.

Although I was only going to Australia for three weeks it signalled the start of our breakup. Australia was a dump and confirmed for me its reputation for being the biggest NCOs' mess in the world. Melbourne was a fly-blown version of Croydon, full of horrid children on skateboards and nothing beyond the city limits but desert. Sydney was makeshift and hick. It should have been called "Kevin". The cultural scream of its opera house seemed to reiterate the underlying shame of the city's fundamental sleaze. There was nothing of interest to look at or anything to buy except stuffed made-in-Korea Koala bears and Ken Done pop art sponge bags. The Australians, to their credit, were delightfully devoid of the pretension and surliness that ordinarily went with Anglo-Saxon social retention. The weather wasn't fantastic, which was a swizz having travelled twelve thousand miles to get there. I spent the time mooching around under a grey sky, slithering from bar to bar with nothing much to see or do.

By the time I got back to London my liaison with Crystal was in its last throes. I secretly switched my attention to a hard-bitten divorcee I'd met before going to Australia. She was a menu-driven restaurant whore but she had a Penthouse body and what little sex we had was, to my mind, faultless. The feeling was so not mutual. She turned out to be unreliable and constantly stood me up or flaked on arrangements at the last moment. I finally had enough when we went away together to some house party in the country for what I assumed would be a 'dirty weekend'. She, for reasons then best known to herself, decided not to be 'dirty'. I was silently furious. There was nothing else to do but copulate, but she was having none of it. All tit and no action. A waste of gin and tonic. I was told later that she'd fucked one of the other house guests while I wasn't looking, so I gave her the bullet. Or she gave it to me.

Crystal and I got back together for an argumentative two months. An uninspired and silly move as it turned out. Since my return from Australia I'd become restless and bored with London. My Dutch cash cow at work was running dry and my commission earnings reverted to the sporadic style of old. I was becoming stale and devoid of inspiration again. I had been back in the UK for over four years since leaving the Pan Asian Bank and yet I was no more balanced or accomplished than when I had started.
   I could no longer tell one month from the last. There were no landmarks to distinguish time. Life had become one big Groundhog Day. The homogeneity of each Saturday, and Sunday's inevitable Sundayness defeated the object of going through the misery of the working week. Every Saturday I made the pilgrimage to St Peter Jones of Sloane Square on some spurious errand and watched the immaculately groomed wives and their chinless husbands who worked at Credit Suisse First Boston ponder over furnishing fabric. Shop assistants went lethargically about their duties wishing they were somewhere else, while fashion accessory infants named after brave Third World countries gurgled pointlessly to their parents' weary gratification. *How dare they*! What right had *they* to stain the planet with their genetic pollution? Then to 'The Artist' for a pint or two to take in some friendly but nonetheless uninspiring chat with the Wine-Bar-Wendys and Doubles-All-Round-Dereks and all the other Anoraks-With-Attitude who seemed to live there. Each Saturday evening I got ready for some supper party in the Projects while half watching Filla Crack on 'Blind Rape' looking more and more like Mrs Thatcher. Sundays seemed to consist of wading through five kilos of indifferent newsprint until it was time to settle down to the weekly treat of watching the kittenish pygmy on 'That's Strife!' fluff his lines before I fell asleep. Then back to work on Monday.
   This state of ennui did not last forever. Fate, I thought at the time, came to my rescue and jolted me out of my safe, complacent boredom.

# Chapter 6: Roxanne

When I was happy I drank too much, which made me maudlin. When I was maudlin I drank more. I was well into a five week binge when Emma Longmuir, the only friend of Christine Hale's whom I liked, called excitedly to ask me to a fancy dress ball. I groaned.

"Must I?" I pleaded. My charity ball days were behind me and the idea of fancy dress just killed it.

"Emma," I said, "I'd love to, but, without being rude I'm not sure that I can be bothered. It's not quite my scene any longer."

"Nonsense James!' she said chirpily, "You'll have a lovely time. There's a good bunch of people going and besides, it's all in a good cause."

"Oh sure it is," I sneered, peevishly .

"It's only thirty-five quid and that includes supper and booze. Anything that's left over goes to the elephants in Africa. Can't get much fairer than that, can you?"

"I suppose you want me to bring Crystal?"

"You don't have to, if you don't want to. There'll be lots of other girlies there for you."

"Is Christine going?" I snapped.

"No. Or if she is, she's not in our party."

"Well, I suppose it's got that going for it."

"Don't be such an old grump. I'm not twisting your arm, you know. It'll do you good. Meet some nice new people. It's on a Saturday so you can drink yourself silly and not have to worry about getting up the next day."

"Fancy dress? What's the theme?"

"Couldn't be easier: Safari; it's a cinch. You can dress up as anything; a big game hunter, a hippopotamus, a Hottentot... whatever you like."

"Hmm. When is it?" I asked, petulantly.

"Three weeks' time: the twenty-ninth."

"Where?"

"Battersea Park, so it's only a two bob taxi ride. You can do a runner back home if you get into a state."

"All right. Count me in," I said, grudgingly.

"Yippee! I'm sure you'll have, well, a ball, but you will behave yourself, won't you?" Emma enquired, cautiously.

"What do you mean?" I quizzed, slightly hurt by her assumption that I might do otherwise.

"Well, you know what you're like after a couple of drinks. I've got two South African girls from work coming. They're new in town so don't shock them. Just control yourself."

"South Africans? Great. They arrive in London with a pair of clean knickers and a fifty pound note and leave a year later without having changed either," I reposted, spitefully.

"Rubbish. They're lovely girls. They're not freeloaders. They're proper accountants. They're quite civilised, actually."

A few days before the ball, Emma called to tell me that her group was starting the evening with drinks at her house. When the day arrived I took it upon myself to embark on my own alcoholic safari and tried to support the entire British brewing industry on my own at lunchtime before stumbling home and falling into a coma.

I woke up at six in the evening feeling disorientated and drunk. I still hadn't decided what I was going to wear. I had a moth-eaten fuzzy wig which meant I really could go as a Hottentot, but I looked silly and didn't have a grass skirt to go with it.

I dug around in the toy cupboard and found an old army jacket. I took the pips off and put it on. I didn't really look like anything. I tucked an old pair of camouflage trousers into a pair of boots and hoped I would pass for a white hunter type. I should have made a bit more of an effort, but the greater the attempt to dress up the more awkward it was for the rest of the evening. It was all very well making an initial impression in a gorilla suit, but not if one was expected to dance in the smelly thing all night.

It was warm that evening and Emma had the drinks in her garden. I arrived in a shocking state. The last thing I needed was more alcohol so I limited myself to a modest half dozen glasses. I wasn't expecting to meet anyone particularly interesting. I looked around. They were a collection of people who used to be young. Peter's Friends types. Most had made more effort with their outfits than I had. As my line of vision followed a passing drinks tray, my eye fell on a girl whom I hadn't seen before. She was also wearing a safari outfit, but hers looked good on her, with her pith helmet set at a coquettish angle. She had copper-pink hair, little-girl freckles round her nose and startling green eyes. A redhead! The most spectacular of all the orchids in the garden! Her baggy empire-builder shorts appeared to sport a pair of well turned legs. I scooped another glass off the drinks tray before it disappeared and wondered who she belonged to. It didn't really matter. She was too pretty for me. Out of my league.

By the time we were ready to move on to the ball I was past my best. We got into various cars and taxis and made our way to Battersea. There was a distance between the parking area and the ball marquee. I was having difficulty walking in a straight line. I introduced myself to a great big gusset of a woman in a lion suit and said as a drunken *non sequitur*, "... so you won't mind if I lean on you for support?"

The marquee was festooned with palms and hanging vines. There must have been about two hundred people there. I regretted being too pissed to properly take in the occasion. Once we'd got to our table Emma bossily told us where to sit. I was beyond caring and had no particular preference who I sat next to as long as they were able to cope with my drunken ramblings.

"Peter? You're there," said Emma, "and Jock, you're next to Sarah. Roxanne, you're there next to James. James, you're on Roxanne's right".

I didn't know any Roxannes but when I looked up to see who the name belonged to I broke into a sweat. It was green eyes in the safari suit. *Holy wank stains*! Why now, why today, when I could hardly think, let alone talk? Fortunately the girl on the other side of me was the belter in the lion suit who'd been moderately tolerant earlier.

We sat down. I introduced myself to Roxanne as politely as I could but my efforts to appear sober were fooling no one. She accepted my hand coolly and in a surprisingly mellow Afrikaans accent returned the introduction. One of the South African girls whom Emma had mentioned. My interest perked up. If she was new in town there was a fair chance she was unattached. I studied her face
again briefly. She had cute upside down Susan Hampshire eyes and sharp little Bantu teeth. I reached into my shirt pocket for a cigarette.

"Lung food? 'Velvet Puffs'... the very latest in smoking technology, wouldn't you know," I said, pointing the packet at her.

"I don't mind if I do," she said, and smiled as she took one. She was a smoker. A good sign. It meant she didn't take herself seriously and accepted risk to gain pleasure. Smokers fuck.

"It's always a good idea to light up a fag while you're waiting for a meal because if you're hungry, the minute you do, someone will come scurrying up with your supper and you'll have to stub it out before you get a second drag," I joked weakly. Roxanne looked at me blankly.

"Mallet's Law," I added idiotically.

"Mallet's Law?"

"My name... James Mallet."

"Oh, right." Her eyes wandered off into the middle distance in a cloud of perplexed boredom. I ran through the usual gamut of questions, searching in vain for something we might have in common. There was a bad-

tempered looking man on the other side of her who was trying to catch her attention but I cock-blocked him from getting in. By including the heifer on the other side of me
I managed to form an impenetrable conversational triangle which effectively iced him out.

The talk turned to national comparisons. I said that I had recently come back from Australia and that I hadn't been particularly impressed by the clip-on culture in Melbourne or Sydney, implying that all post-colonial societies were the same, but Roxanne didn't seem riled.

"That's OK. I'm from Cape Town and where I come from it's beautiful, so I couldn't give a fuck what you've got to say about anywhere else."

I was a little taken aback by her directness. It was at odds with her appearance. Words and figure differed.

I sipped my wine carefully. I knew if I did any more speed-drinking I'd start to see double and want to lie down. I didn't want to leave Roxanne with old Moody Guts on the other side ready to pounce. The heifer became distracted and started talking to someone else. I had Roxanne to myself. She was easy enough to talk to, but my faculties weren't in top form and I kept going off at a tangent. We had gone through just about every topic possible when I launched into a long, rambling, semi-insulting anecdote concerning a South African girl I'd once taken out. I'd managed to get the poor girl back to my flat and into my bedroom but despite my charms, she didn't particularly want to sleep with me. I was about call it in when she said, "Would you mind masturbating into my mouth instead?" I couldn't believe my luck! Music to my ears! I noticed Roxanne didn't share my enthusiasm for the vignette.

"Boy! She could suck the chrome off a tow bar!" I rhapsodised, with nostalgic relish.

"Incredible," Roxanne remarked, distractedly.

"Sorry, I thought it was a rather good story," I opined, feeling slightly hurt.

"Oh dearie me. What are we going to do with you?" Roxanne asked, with a sigh. "I think underneath it all you're just a little bit bitter and twisted."

"But I haven't even put it in *your* mouth yet," I ventured, shyly.

Roxanne shot me a sideways glance, thought about it, and then dissolved into a fit of giggles. I let my face drop and joined in. I knew then that I'd found a friend.

"I'm sorry Roxanne," I said, as our laughter subsided, "you've caught me on a bit of an 'off' day. Emma told me to behave this evening which was like a red rag to a bull. Out of spite I went to the pub at lunchtime and got a bit boozed up as you can see, and I haven't climbed down since."

"Well, I have a bit of catching up to do then, haven't I?" she said, as she poured the contents of my wineglass into hers.

Food came and went. For a mass-produced supper it wasn't too bad and there was no shortage of drink for me to avoid. The evening slipped by as Roxanne and I continued talking.

Supper finished and people moved between tables. I knew several other revellers outside our group and proudly introduced Roxanne to them. The discotheque had accurately gauged the vintage of its brethren and was pumping out a string of 'seventies favourites.

"Come on you silly boy. Let's have a bop shall we? Might help sober you up or clear your head even," Roxanne proposed, enthusiastically.

"Must we?" I pleaded, feeling full of food.

"Yes we must!" Roxanne insisted, firmly.

The dance floor was heaving. Beyond doing an occasional spasmodic hopping motion, nothing much was expected of me. I hated dancing at the best of times, unless I was really pissed, so by rights I should have been in my element, but the record had no metre or beat. I gyrated like a robot. Roxanne danced in a swanky sort of way which I could see she thought was dead sexy. I complimented her.

"You dance... you dance... like a receptionist."

In fact she danced like a man. It wasn't her only masculine characteristic, I was later to find. The record came mercifully to an end and we returned to the relative safety of our table. Once we were back I made sure that Roxanne was talking to someone of no consequence and then declared that I was off to look for a loo.

I left the marquee. It had started to drizzle refreshingly outside. In the dark I couldn't see anything. After I'd walked a hundred yards and still hadn't found a lavatory I realised that I had the whole park to urinate in. The joys of being a man! I peed behind a tree and looked back at the tent full of colour, people and noise tinkling in the distance and silently thanked Emma for insisting that I came. Things weren't turning out so badly, in spite of my own devastated state. I shivered, shook my manhood dry and walked back to the marquee, wordlessly rebuking myself for not washing my hands.

I cruised round the marquee for a bit to see if there was anyone else I knew. I spoke to a few people incoherently before making it back to where I'd left Roxanne. She wasn't there. I glanced round anxiously but I couldn't see her anywhere. Ferry was belting out "Hey good-looking boys gather around". Not me, Bryan. I became apprehensive that Roxanne had given me the slip or had felt the need to do so. Then I spotted her on the dance floor with old Moody Guts. An overwhelming sense of jealousy enveloped me, which was ridiculous as I had only met the woman a few hours before.

There wasn't much I could do short of rugby tackling her new dance partner and declaring Roxanne mine which, in the state I was in, seemed a reasonable thing to do. I put my head down and charged. I grabbed a pair of legs and felt the satisfactory clump of a person falling to the floor.

"*What the fuck*...?!" Roxanne cried.

Shit! Wrong legs. *Snafu*! Roxanne lay sprawled out on the floor, staring at me in stark amazement. Another fine example of Christine's Curse. Fortunately no one except Roxanne and Mr Grumpy took any notice. Mr Very Grumpy.

"Sorry," I said, sheepishly. "Most uncool, but I wanted to get your attention."

"Well, you certainly succeeded," Roxanne acknowledged, as I gave her a helping hand off the floor. Grumpy was so cross that he stalked off speechless, seething like a sergeant. I took a silent bet that my welfare wasn't high on his list of prayers that night. I looked at Roxanne.

"Well, shall we dance?" I asked, foolishly.

"I suppose we'll have to," she replied, exasperatedly.

At that moment the music changed and a new record started. It was a slow one. The absurdity of the moment left me temporarily lost for words. We clasped one another stiffly and started to rotate slowly, like a kebab on a spit. We stopped shuffling and I held Roxanne still. I moved my face towards hers and kissed her lips.

Everything went into a Babycham haze and to my relief, with only a moment's hesitation, Roxanne's mouth met mine.

She pulled back after a minute and muttered, "Bizarre."

"Bizarre, but not unwelcome, I hope," I proposed, searchingly.

"Let's say that it was a sympathy kiss rather than a mad desire for any adventures round your dentures," Roxanne discerned, reprovingly.

"I don't care what you call it," I retaliated, bravely, "... let's have another one."

I kissed her with less hesitation and evaluated the implications. Her mouth was dry and tasted of cigarettes and old food. Mine probably tasted the same, if not worse. She had, on closer examination, a fair dusting of facial hair around her upper lip. Its fairness had had me fooled. It was a good thing that she wasn't dark-featured as she would have looked like a Mexican bandit.

It was getting late and people were starting to drift off. Grumpy had left, seeing that there was no point hanging around for Roxanne. At two the discotheque played "Goodnight, ladies" and called it a day. Roxanne found her flatmate, who turned out to be the other South African girl, and we walked through the park to Chelsea Bridge to find a taxi. The drizzle had promoted itself to a downpour.

We waited in the rain for a while before I declared, "I'm quite hungry after all that. Who's up for a greasy hamburger and some soggy chips?"

"Me! Me! Me!" the South Africans shouted in unison.

We made our way to a late night burger stand by the bridge which was surrounded by desperado bikers. Normally I would've thought twice about going into a trough of quasi-Hell's Angels with a safari suit on and a girl on either arm, but I had the contempt for danger of the very drunk. We stood in the wet, eating our burgers and gazing at the lights on the Embankment. The river went about its business, moving its primordial *hors d'oeuvre* of Mars Bar wrappers and spent condoms up and down its course. For a moment London looked almost Parisian. French letters. I spotted a taxi and we threw our leftovers into the water.

"Where do you two live by the way?" I asked, as we got in.

"Deepest, darkest Fulham," Roxanne answered, in what could have passed for regret.

"Too easy, I'll drop you off... unless of course you want to come back for a coffee. I've got two spare beds and loads of hot baths and towels..." I proposed, slipping desperately and inappropriately into the old routine.

"No, Fulham will do fine," Roxanne said, but then added contemplatively, "... perhaps another time."

I dropped the two girls off and took the taxi on home. I'd had the presence of mind to ask Roxanne for her number which she wrote down on a scrap of paper quite willingly. Once home I took off my sodden clothes and dried my hair before collapsing onto my bed in a happy drunken torpor and farted myself to sleep.

The next day I awoke feeling fragile. I had over-smoked and was now lunged-out. My limbs were stiff with alcohol and my joints ached where the nicotine had seeped in. As I climbed out of bed my legs went into spasm in an involuntary celebration of incipient thrombosis. I hobbled to the bathroom and ruminated on the lavatory.

I thought through the previous night, reliving and savouring the best bits. I reckoned I'd just got away with it. Not a bad evening's work, however crudely executed. Perhaps if I hadn't been quite so drunk things might have been better, but then again maybe Roxanne and I might have only made polite conversation and then gone our separate ways. I looked at the number she'd given me. It wasn't a local one. It was either her work number or a dud. She hadn't put down her surname. Dammit. Probably a dud. I spent the rest of the morning with my face in my hands, awaiting the inevitable onslaught of alcoholic remorse.

I tried Roxanne's number from work the following day. I chewed my lower lip and took a deep breath. An operator answered.

"Hello. Spawforth and Fisher."

"Oh hello. I wonder if you can help me. I'm trying to track down a South African accountant called Roxanne, but I don't know her last name."

"I think I know the one. Trying to connect you."

Amazing, I pondered, how all switchboard operators had the same intonation. Maybe they were all the same woman, like Italian waiters were all the same man. "Some more black pepper, sir?"

"Hello, Roxanne Sullivan speaking."

That voice! As an accent Cape Dutch was not my favourite, yet with Roxanne it had the illicit flavour of an improper suggestion.

"Hi, Roxanne. It's a very quiet and sober James, from the other night. Can you speak?"

"Yes, of course. How nice to hear from you. How are you feeling? Recovered a little I hope? Never mind. It was a great night... different, that's for sure."

"Yes, it was fun. I hope I didn't spoil it for everyone else... well, you, I mean."

"No, it was a lot of fun and you were great as space cadets go. I particularly enjoyed the rugby tackle. That's what I like about you Brits... none of you have ever really gone to Cool School."

"Oh, I'm really sorry about that. I've been living with a dirty conscience ever since. Listen: is there any chance of having the privilege of your fluffy little company again sometime?" I wheedled, trying to distance myself from my former barbarous persona.

"Why not? But not on a Saturday night!"

"What do you mean? I don't get like that every weekend, you know. You just happened to catch me on a bad day."

"I hate to think what you're like on a good one, James," she remonstrated, teasingly. Or testingly. Trick or treat?

"Well, why don't you find out?" I challenged. "What's your week looking like?"

"It's OK," she said slowly, as if she was looking through her diary.

"Yep, it's pretty free. Can't do Wednesday or Thursday, but Friday's all yours if it doesn't clash with your schedule."

"Shit," I lied, "every day's free but Friday."

Friday would have been fine except that it was five days away and I wanted to catch some of the magic of the ball event before it disappeared forever. I had to move quickly; I needed to cash in on the enchantment of being unknown. By Friday my tawdry history might have reached Roxanne on the grapevine. I could always see her then anyway if things panned out well in between. I broke off briefly for effect.

"Excuse me Roxanne; I've got a call on the other line," I said, keeping her within hearing distance.

"I'll take twenty million," I shouted to no-one in particular. My colleagues looked up in stunned confusion.

"Make that fifty. Done? Good... I've gotta blow. See ya later, masturbator!" I came back to Roxanne.

"Sorry about that Roxanne. The market's gone crazy today. Look... obviously Monday nights are sacred... chat shows... ironing shirts and all that... I don't want to seem as though I'm shoving myself down your throat... but how about tomorrow night?"

"Yup; don't think there's anything on. Let's go for it," Roxanne assented, with what appeared to be ambient acquiescence. *Excellent,* Mr Bexcellent!

"Good," I said feeling relieved, "but just one thing; I've got to go to some fartatious charity meeting that I'm on the committee of at the beginning of the evening. I should be out by eight. Is there any chance that you can meet me afterwards, say eight-thirty at my flat... next to the Bates Motel? I've got some great snuff movies we could watch." Even I was getting bored with the script. I'd have to change it one day.

"Charming," Roxanne responded, sardonically. "That sounds OK. Where do you live?"

"Not far from you. Do you know Devon Gardens? It's in vomiting distance from Alphabet Street tube. Number 43. It's a peach to find... so see you tomorrow... at 8.30. I'll be waiting. Silk pyjamas and smoking jacket. Sober of course! ''

She seemed to have got my measure, but what she didn't know being a newcomer, was that this was pretty standard scuzzball procedure: to be appalling on first viewing and as good as gold on the second, and thus appear doubly nice. It didn't matter if I was the most dreadful man in the world the first time round. The chances were that either some lost and confused strand of maternal instinct or a masochistic desire to be mucked about would take a woman over. If neither worked then at least a good time could be had with nothing lost in the process.

I actually did have a charity meeting to go to that evening, but not one where my absence would have been noticed. I'd never been asked to be on a committee before. It was only the social committee, and as such was full of bogus yahoos on the take for a free drink rather than out to do anything particularly worthwhile. In this respect I took my duties seriously, even if all it meant was turning up just to whack back the best part of a bottle of cheap wine. My added value amounted to little more than muttering "Well, this is it," every so often and generally hanging around, being pleasant but useless.

I got back to my flat in good time that evening. It smelt a bit strange where I'd gone mad with the 'shake 'n' vac' the day before in anticipation of Roxanne's visit. I switched on the television while I waited for her. A pretty girl implored me to buy a French car as a forest fire raged in the background, and then a comedy about some old people came on. Roxanne rang the bell on the dot of half past eight. I buzzed her in and stood by the door.

"Welcome to Castle Kleenex!" I fêted, before I had time to check myself.

Roxanne had come straight from work and had the tired look of a woman who'd reapplied her make-up rather than started afresh, which in itself was not without appeal. I wasn't particularly apprehensive about seeing her again, but I wondered how we'd shape up without our safari suits or the benefit of half a vat of alcohol apiece. She entered the kitchen as I was opening a bottle of wine. Under the strong strip lighting I could see that she had a slightly coarse complexion; probably the result of too much time spent in the sun as a youngster. I hadn't booked a restaurant as I was going through a parsimonious phase that month. We talked until ten when I looked at my watch and exclaimed:

"Heavens! Is that the time? Fuck! We're a bit late for a restaurant. What a clot I am! What would you like to do? We could stroll down Alphabet Street and get a pizza or there are some tasty morsels in a packet that I can nuke up."

"I don't mind... whatever," Roxanne said, as though food was not the main purpose of the evening.

"Have another drink and I'll see what's available."

I opened another bottle and looked in the fridge. There was nothing except a pat of butter with mould growing on it that looked like an aerial shot of the Maldives and a half-empty tonic bottle. I inspected the freezer compartment. There, behind the three year old fossilised Viennetta log, lay two packets of Mean Cuisine.

"Chicken Tikka-Masala and Pilau rice... or mild prawn and vegetable curry?" I shouted.

"Yummy. Not fussed," she called back.

I put both packets into the microwave and returned with the wine.

"I'm sorry I've made such a Horlicks of the catering arrangements, Roxanne, but I hope to have the opportunity to make amends another time... it's very good of you to take your life in your hands and come round tonight. You must think I'm a madman after my performance the other night. It can't have been a pretty sight."

"It was a bit of a shocker, I'll grant you," she concurred, "but I've seen worse. Remember, I'm from South Africa, as if you'd forget, and South African men make you, James, look small time. I've seen blokes at parties set fire to their pubes, moon their arses off, fall over drunk and piss in the punch bowl to get a girl's attention."

"How enchanting. The South African Cool School, no doubt?" I enquired, politely.

"Not that I'm in the market for a repeat of Saturday night's extravaganza," she continued, ignoring my referral.

The microwave pinged conveniently a few moments later. I went to prepare the pitiful portions onto the smallest dinner plates on the shelf in an attempt to make them look less frugal, knowing that eyes could be fooled, but stomachs not. Stomachs knew when they weren't getting the right stuff.

"Mmm... 138... my favourite "E" number!" Roxanne enthused, as I deposited her portion of steaming slop in front of her.

Her easy-going nature was a refreshing break after Crystal's neurosis and she appeared, by my meagre barometer, to be quite accomplished. We finished supper. I made some coffee and sat next to her on the sofa. After a decent interval, I moved closer and stole an easy snog. I was pleased to note that there was nothing bashful about my genitalia's response to Roxanne's proximity. It was the first erection I'd had without using my hands for weeks, but the night was no longer young and I'd had more than enough to drink. I reluctantly but deliberately extricated myself from our embrace and said:

"Well, little fella, I suppose I'd better get you into a taxi. I think it's getting way past our bed times."

I knew my token gallantry would, as it always did, earn me more than enough kudos to move in for the kill the next time, but for the moment I wanted to reverse Saturday's image. I had the feeling that Roxanne was surprised, if not put out by my neutrality and ludicrously formal sense of decorum. Not that I would necessarily have got a hole in one that evening, but I knew that she felt robbed of the option of protest.

I rang for a taxi - a near one this time; I was still exhausted from the weekend and genuinely ready for bed. I returned to the sofa and we reassumed our amorous half-Nelson. I kissed her mouth again with its downy perimeter and breathed her in. Under the scent of 6 o'clock Rive Gauche, I could smell a mixture of tobacco and office aromas. The doorbell rang with the taxi before I could let my olfactory CAT scan run its full course. We untangled and I followed Roxanne down to the front door.

"Normally I'd drive you home," I insinuated, "but I think my level of intoxication might not pass muster with the gentlemen in blue."

Bollocks. It was never safe for me to drive at night. Or any time of day for that matter. I pushed a twenty into her hand, ignoring her objection.

"It's the very least I can do after you've taken the trouble to come over. I'm sorry I made such a nonsense of supper."

"Nonsense? It was fine, James. Thank you for a lovely night. It's turned out to be very different from what I was expecting, which is no bad thing, I suppose."

I smiled. She got into the taxi and left.

I skipped up the stairs with the spring of a mountain goat and flashdanced around my bedroom as I stripped for bed. *Walking on sunshine*! It was Mardi Gras! It was time to rustle my bustle! I was like a junkie who'd just been given some high grade blow. That was me. I was a love addict and the bigger the hit the better. I calmed down and assessed the evening. It had gone well and according to plan. For an out-of-town girl she was streets ahead of most her London counterparts, who were either parochial or simply dim by comparison. She wasn't perfect but then again, nor was I. Sure, she was a rough diamond, but a diamond all the same. Intelligent, but as tough as old guts. I wondered whether she was *the one*. Was this the end of my quest for genetic compatibility? I chastised myself for entertaining such a ridiculous notion and went to bed.

Roxanne and I spoke a few times that week with a familiarity that implied that we would soon be lovers. For my own sake I didn't want to rush things. I didn't want to put a premonition I had of her easy virtue to the test. I wanted to keep the illusion of some sort of roughshod farm girl virginity about her alive; unkempt but pure; outback but not out-on-her-back.

We slept with each other on our second date. Roxanne had her period which was, in its way, convenient as it meant I didn't have to ask any dreary questions about contraception and left us free to take our chances at the roulette table of exotic disease.

"Got the painters in?!" I asked excitedly.

"'fraid so," Roxanne affirmed, matter-of-factly. "I'd better unplug."

"I suppose you'd better," I endorsed, eagerly.

I placed a ceremonial bath towel under where Roxanne was going to lie. She had, as I suspected, rather small, apologetic breasts and slightly vulgar poached egg nipples. Small tits were like renting a Fiat. What was the point? She had an opencast vagina that lay close to the surface of her pelvis, like a gaping wound. There was something undeveloped and tadpole-like about her physique. Her bottom was large in relation to the rest of her and sagged like a canvas tent on a wet day. Her beauty was from the neck up and hadn't trespassed with conviction onto other parts of her anatomy. She was a face fuck.

We had a brief embrace and then got down to business. As a teaser I did my Japanese love trick of seven quick thrusts and one long one before rolling over, apparently satisfied. Roxanne looked miffed.

"Just kidding!" I teased, and climbed back on top.

I noticed her armpits were a bit rank and that the insides of her ears were brown with wax. Personal hygiene obviously wasn't her top priority, but nor, at that moment, was cunnilingus mine. The intensity of Roxanne's first orgasm caught me by surprise. Fortunately she was a thrasher rather than a screamer, but I was taken aback by the effect that my love gun had on her so soon after penetration. Orgasms were a man's business and over-enthusiastic displays of female rapture were, to my mind, bad form. A warning bell went off somewhere in my subconscious and I paused to wonder how many other people had brought Roxanne to such a state of delirium; this was a woman who quite plainly liked her sex by the bucket.

Once I'd properly had my turn we lay in each other's arms in complementary post-coital exhaustion. I tentatively asked her if she was OK.

"Fine, honey... just fine."

"Well, you never know first time. I mean I don't know what turns you on. For instance, are your tits sensitive, or do you go wild having your neck licked?"

"Nah. I'm basically a cunt woman," she said, putting an end to my laboratory of human response.

After a while I got up and ran a bath. I went back to the bedroom. It smelt like a badger's set.

"Bathie-kins?" I proposed assertively, proudly displaying my lack of muscle tone.

Roxanne stretched and yawned like a cat.

"Oh yes, please! Yes please! Yes please! Mr Mallet!"

I learnt that this was to be one of Roxanne's wangles; she the wilful schoolgirl always getting one over me, the mild-mannered school teacher, too meek to complain.

I ran the bath and went upstairs to make two large gin and tonics. I nibbled some cheese from the fridge and let out the loudest fart in the world. I'd forgotten how coitus made me windy. I came down with the ice clinking nicely in the drinks.

"James, was that you farting upstairs?" Roxanne asked suspiciously.

"I beg your pardon? I don't know what you're talking about," I replied, as earnestly as possible.

"Then maybe somebody just stepped on a frog," she said, giving me a knowing look.

"Who cares?" I asked nonchalantly. "An empty house is better than a bad tenant."

I looked at Roxanne and took her in. It struck me as strange how two parents from the other side of the planet, who had no idea of my existence, had cultivated and nurtured this fruit from their loins, unaware that I, James Mallet, would be sampling the harvest of their endeavour at the supreme moment of its existence.

The bath was ready. I turned the taps off and got in. Roxanne came into the bathroom and joined me in the tub. As she got in I received my first close-up of her bottom. It was not a pretty sight. In fact it was a disaster. It was the ugliest bottom I'd ever seen. Not only was it in the grandmother class for sheer mottled sagginess and size, but it was also an atlas of broken veins and stretch marks. I'd never seen anything quite like it. It was a catastrophe! I'd never witnessed such a profusion and variety of cellulite before. I felt hypnotised, like a victim in a B-movie, transfixed by the enormity of its awfulness. I thought I was going to faint but fortunately I had my drink close at hand to steady me. Roxanne sat down. I breathed a sigh of relief. It was ironic that someone with such an inviting face could harbour such a monstrosity. It was a pity because I could tell this would seriously hamper our relationship. If it was a horror now, what would it be like in twenty years' time? Or forty? It didn't bear thinking about. All I knew was that I didn't want to be around to find out.

We soon fell into a routine and Roxanne all but moved into my flat that summer. Instant girlfriend: just add sex and stir. There were a few clouds of incompatibility on the horizon, but Roxanne didn't seem conscious of their existence, and for my part they were at a sufficient distance to be ignored.

Crystal was perplexed by the abruptness of the turnaround in my affections and peeved that I had found a new partner so soon after our own relationship had gone into receivership. I saw her at a party soon after Roxanne and I had met. Perversely, I followed Crystal into a lavatory towards the end of the evening. We kissed with a passion normally reserved for a pontiff's ring. Crystal offered to drive me home and we left discreetly together.

I asked her up to my flat, but she declined and we had to content ourselves with the facilities of her small car. After Roxanne's body, Crystal's felt like Aphrodite's. The bunion in my trousers stirred to complement the gear stick. We were parked under a street light, in full view of late night pedestrians. I suggested we drove to a quieter spot. It killed the moment but it had to be done. Crystal drove round the corner to the comparative anonymity of Emperor's Gate and we clambered into the back seat. Peugeot 205s were not specifically designed for copulation and the car almost bounced out of its parking space with the ruction inside. Crystal also had her period. It was my lucky month for periods. I was *Mr Tampax*! She pulled her tampon from her labia minora and stuffed it delicately into the dashboard ashtray. We resumed our bouncing. My spermatozoa made their short, efficient journey from my scrotum to my prepuce in record time. It was uncomfortable, brutish and short. The best. Afterwards Crystal drove me home and we said good night formally, as if the previous ten minutes - our one for the road - had never happened.

The incident left me in two minds as to what to do. Roxanne's facial hair and various body odours were getting on my nerves, and there was no comparison between the aerodynamics of the two girls' design features. If I could have put Roxanne's head on Crystal's body I would have had the perfect woman, but technology had a long way to go before such things were possible. In many ways Crystal had more to offer by the sheer convenience of being English, but Roxanne was less effort and cheaper to feed. In the end I flipped a mental coin and decided to stick with Roxanne and ignore her bottom.

Summer merged into autumn. Life settled in to an inspiration-sapping routine once again. I let Roxanne and half of the Cape Province-in-exile take over my life. Roxanne was more comfortable with her compatriots than my "dickhead friends" as she called my slightly moth-eaten circle of acquaintances. I regarded myself as bigoted, but Roxanne and her fellow denizens seemed unable to digest the smallest cultural differences. They complained about "whinging Brits", in itself a whinge, and were never really happy unless they were having a go at something or complaining about the weather and how everything was so much better in "S'thifrica". Every time Roxanne uttered a derogatory statement about Britain I felt any chance of a permanent union between us slip further away. I gradually became tired of her constant knocking of what was, after all, my home. Her battle cry whenever we were caught in a traffic jam or supermarket queue of, "This country is fucked, so fucked I can't believe it!" eventually started to grate.

  The concerns I'd nursed concerning Roxanne's libertine leanings turned out to be not entirely baseless. She openly admitted, or rather, brazenly boasted that she'd gone through most of the male members of the campus population at university, and had continued in a similar modus after she'd graduated. It seemed as though I'd exchanged Crystal's appetite for ingesta for Roxanne's craving for aphrodisia. For all Roxanne's sexual proclivity in the past, her emotional maturity was relatively undeveloped, and she was, I initially found, easy to manipulate. What I had to offer in return - beyond being as British as a VC 10 and a few laughs - remained a mystery. Whatever it was, it was enough for Roxanne to fall in love. This became a problem as time went by and the tenure on Roxanne's work permit started to run out. I was boxed in and had to consider, or pretend to consider, whether we were going to take the matter a stage further into uncharted and, for my part, decidedly unfathomed waters.

By the end of that autumn things had started to pick up again at work. Just as my Dutch tax scam had run its course, access to the Canadian dollar market came to my rescue in the shape of a huge, clumsy, Alaskan moose of a bond salesman called "Desmond the Dork." Desmond the Dork turned out to be a whiz at ripping off his clients round the world. His easy-going North American style complemented my ridiculously uncompetitive prices and we managed, between us, to get the presses of avarice rolling once more. We finally sprung a beaut in October by selling a couple of million dollars of junk to the Bank of Switzerland in Grand Cayman and took sixty thousand dollars out for ourselves on the way. Our end of the year bonuses started to look worth hanging around for. My thoughts turned to buying some phallic sports car with a cosy wombed cockpit in the hope that it might help me sleep with more women and make me feel good about myself.

Conmax as a company was, in the meantime, experiencing problems. A trader on the warrant desk had boobed and taken a large position in a stock that had 'headed South' and found himself radically 'long and wrong' without a buyer in the world interested in his position. To make matters worse he had attempted to support the price by actively bidding the stock up in the market. The situation mushroomed as he took more of the issue on board and finally collapsed when there was nothing left to buy. The price imploded and Conmax had to 'take a bath'.

The company had had plenty of good years behind it and I was not particularly concerned about its own safety *per se*. The management had taken a few steps to retrench and it looked as though the company was capable of limping through to the next upturn in the market.

Ever since joining Conmax I'd tried to find a less precarious existence elsewhere but with little success. In one instance, a former Parker Barrow colleague of mine had tried to get me on board at a Japanese bank. I had six interviews at Sumimayo Trust before my application was quashed by the Brit Personnel dweeb at the seventh. Personnel managers had been the bane of my life ever since my Pan Asian Bank days, but the one at Sumimayo was the cat's pyjamas.

I wondered about going back to school on the proceeds of my bonus payment to do an MBA and learn about what I had been doing all along. I even contemplated the prospect of running a pub. Anything to get out of the repetitive nightmare I'd bricked myself into that relied on other people's whims and economic uncertainties that I had no control over.

November came and the end of the year target figure that would put me in for a healthy bonus payment inched nearer. Roxanne went weird on me and seriously began to cramp my stylus. Her affection for me mutated into an obsession. To make matters worse she started to sport an unsightly rash on her face. The rash was caused, admittedly, by my early morning stubble, but it was none the prettier for it. I became mesmerised by it and started talking to the rash rather than to Roxanne whenever we met.

I mused over these things one lunchtime while sitting in the jacuzzi with a drink at my yuppie health club. I was bored. A holiday or a nuclear holocaust was what was needed to break the tedium. I opted for the former. Christmas was just round the corner and a holiday abroad would provide a perfect escape from the annual family circle jerk around the Christmas tree. I wondered about the States, but there was so much of it on TV that an actual visit seemed pointless. I thought about paying a call on some relatives in ever-interesting Canada but decided that it would be too cold at that time of year. Africa? Eating spaghetti in the Serengeti? Nah. Too much AIDS and tsetse fly, not to mention the notorious unpredictability of the locals. My daydream moved to India. Cheap and more or less English-speaking. I'd never been there before and Christmas was as good a time as any to redress the issue. Roxanne was due to go to South Africa to see her family at the same time, which left the coast clear for me to go legitimately on my own without rousing her ire.

I left the club feeling uplifted and made my way to a takeaway pizza joint before going back to the office. As I was waiting for the creation of my 'hot 'n' spicy', David Hobson, one of my Conmax colleagues came into view, interrupting my contemplations. I wasn't mad about him. He was the only other ex-public school boy in the company but we'd never felt any empathy towards each other. I suspected, rightly as it turned out, that beneath his smile there lurked a viper.

"Hi James," he said in a friendly enough fashion.

"Watcha Doiv," I said, plebbing-down his name, which I knew annoyed him. I enjoyed nurturing our animosity.

"Have you heard?" he said.

"Heard what?"

"The company's in deep shtoop".

"Yes, well we all know that but nothing that it can't dig itself out of, surely?"

"Well, apparently Larry's calling a meeting with all the staff at three o'clock in the dealing room and that could be the end of it."

Larry Glitch was our slightly wide chairman.

"Don't be ridiculous!" I rebuffed. "That's just idle rumour. They've ordered the company Christmas cards, for Gawd's sake, so presumably they intend to hang on till the New Year at least."

"I don't know James. It's just what I've heard."

Oh dear. That would really bugger up the weekend. This Christine's Curse thing was getting seriously out of control. Good excuse to give shit Christmas presents though, I mused to myself. I went back to the office. People in the dealing room were jumpy and making wet little jokes. I had no particular desire to do any work at the best of times but there was little point even thinking about it if the firm was about to close down. I spent the hour before Larry Glitch was due to do his twirl calling up travel agents about India. I suddenly craved the Third World. Job or no job, I was now more determined than ever to get away.

Five minutes before three the office went quiet. The dealing room adopted a surreal atmosphere of polite apprehension, like the passenger compartment of a plane that was about to land in thick fog. The general consensus was that Larry hadn't summoned us to discuss the Christmas decorations.

The clock flipped over to 1500 hours and seemed to signal a digital death knell. Larry walked into the hushed dealing room and in an apologetic, staccato voice explained his predicament, the difficulties of the prevailing economic environment and the unforeseen circumstances that the company now found itself in. No mention of Christmas decorations. He concluded by declaring the firm closed for business.

"Please collect your redundancy packages on the way out from Karen. Any questions?"

We were too stunned to ask about our unpaid bonuses and any other questions would have been trivial to the basic dilemma.

"I'm truly sorry," he said, "but you have to go now."

With that he exited, leaving us all in silence.

The Neo-Nazi from Neasden who ran the options desk let out an undignified yelp and burst into uncontrolled girlish sobs.

Rather odd, I thought. He'd always been as hard as precision engineered nails on everyone else, but now it was happening to him he didn't appear to like it. For my part there was a dull thud of disbelief. Slowly the dread prospect of worklessness and all that it entailed started to sink in; the need to schlep humiliatingly around 'Jobland' from one interview to another again, desperately trying to appear to be a good egg and the right sort. The last time this had happened I was out for less than a month, but that was then. This time I knew it would be very different. This time it would not be so easy. I shivered at the prospect that the war, for me, might be over and that I was about to enter the POW camp of eternal unemployment.

I called Roxanne from a payphone on the way home and told her all about it. I looked at the effete logo on the call box with its homosexual connotations and wondered what sort of management committee would have OK'd such a design. I pocketed a couple of sex-for-sale flyers that were wedged between the glass and the telephone apparatus as I left. They made such nice postcards.

# Chapter 7: On The Rock 'n' Roll

Roxanne was sympathetic. Everyone was sympathetic. But they all had their own lives to get on with and their blessings to count that it hadn't happened to them. It wasn't the best time of year to start looking for a job again but I rang all the contacts and agencies I knew and managed to set up a few interviews. In between I organised the India jaunt, reasoning to myself that a holiday would be a good thing and a means of getting away from my immediate problems. I knew two girls who were going to Goa at around the same time and we agreed to join forces. They were both called Camilla and acted accordingly.

As Roxanne's rash grew worse she became increasingly irritated by my senseless socialising which she regarded, correctly, as just a front for my drinking habit. Being on the road again, I didn't really want her around anyway. I needed to travel light. Things came to a head when the tenancy on her flat ran out and she wanted to move into mine. From past experience I knew I operated better on my own when the chips were down. I made my excuses as to why she couldn't move in. She said she thought that I was a heartless bastard. I decided to bring forward her trade-in schedule despite not having anyone in mind to swap her for.

As she left my flat one morning, complaining about having to sleep on some strange sofa the next night, she said that she'd had enough of being an appendage to my self-centred existence and 'wanted out'.

"Fine," I reasoned, "but remember you chucked me. Don't expect any sympathy in a month's time when you find you're empty-glanded with no one to play with."

I breathed a sigh of relief as she disappeared down the street and out of my life. She had reached her sell-by date and it was time to look for someone else. I had become like the owner of an over-eager dog with a ball in its mouth that needed to be flung endlessly across a field, gathering more and more saliva with each throw.

Like an idiot I spoilt it by sending her a Christmas card a week later which gave her an excuse to call and thank me. After an embarrassing pause I was provoked into suggesting meeting for a drink. We met, slept with each other and went back to square one.

Christmas closed in. I sat at home scouring the papers, listening to octogenarian DJs on the radio ordering me to 'Keep it Capital', while pop groups with no previous history of Judeo-Christian beliefs milked the season for all its worth with an assortment of puke about children and peace on earth.

I got together with Michelle during the short time that Roxanne and I were apart and dragged her along to a nicotine pigsty of a bring-a-bottle party. We both got pissed. We declared undying love for each other in a taxi on the way home and, as we flashed past my street, Michelle asked if I wanted to spend the night at her flat. Silly question. It had almost been two years since I'd last had access to Michelle's huge working class bosoms and the proposition didn't warrant a moment's hesitation. I slipped one hand into the back of her skirt and kissed her lightly. Her lips tasted of sweat.

The taxi drew up outside where Michelle lived and we disengaged. I straightened my tie and ran my fingers through my hair, noticing that my hand smelt disconcertingly of shit. Once we were in her flat Michelle went into the bathroom and unpeeled a new toothbrush for me. I looked around her flat while she took off her face. There was a day-glo poster in one corner with a peace sign and the legend:

"What if they had a war and nobody came?"

How original. I looked at the other marks of her individuality. Every book on every one of her shelves was about work. I'd forgotten that in her employee-of-the-month sort of way she was my direct antithesis.

After Michelle had finished with her face I did my teeth and then collapsed onto her well-sprung bed and snuggled up to her well-sprung bod. We lay oozing £3.75-a-bottle Liebfraumilch from every pore. I couldn't be bothered to negotiate Michelle's pants off. I contented myself with rolling her into a spoon position and fondling the enormity of her barrage balloon-sized flesh rockets. The alcohol she'd consumed sent her off to sleep in moments, but my weather-beaten liver had processed the worst of the evening's indulgence and the rest of me was ready, in a limp sort of way, to go. I slid my hand into her crotch in the secure knowledge that even if the entire board of directors of her company had been in bed with her she wouldn't have stirred. I encountered her usual vulval desert. It felt like an overstuffed beef sandwich. I spat into my hand, as if by rote, and drunkenly made a mental note to bring a grease gun next time. Her vagina gradually started to moisten as I gently fed her horse. I moved her onto her back and manoeuvred myself so that my head was between her thighs. My tongue flickered through the matted undergrowth of her pubic forest. Yum... hair pie... *mon favori*! My mouth met Michelle's *labia majora*. It was like kissing a baby seal. I plunged my tongue into her vagina. It tasted quite nice, but my erection was starting to fade. I continued to lick her out, like a greedy child with an ice cream, but my penis had had it. The distant, foetal association with its briny wetness was no match for the Liebfraumilch. I gave up on my fruitless necrophilia and eventually fell asleep, emission impossible.

I woke up the next morning busting for a piss. I got up, had a pee and replaced it with half a gallon of water from the tap. I checked my reflection in the bathroom mirror. My face was covered in blood. I looked like a boxer who had just gone ten rounds. The bitch! It was her period. Not again! Little bleeder. Why always me? To be cursed with periods seemed a cruel irony. I must have been too drunk to have noticed her tampon. I was damned lucky not to have choked on it. That would have been awkward for everyone down at the coroner's office!

I washed, went back to bed and nestled up to Michelle again. She stirred. I tried to arouse her but she was still half-asleep. I placed her hand over my half-erect penis. To my delight she started to move her fingers with the dexterity of a pro. *Wild Palms*! Maybe that was her function at work. She certainly seemed to have had plenty of practice. She finished me off quickly and efficiently and for a moment I almost forgave her for boring the crap out of me every time we met. It was a pity, I reflected as I contemplated Michelle's surprising manual dexterity, that there weren't more women like her who had the gift for this much underrated hobby. Most of the women I knew were apt to pull it up by the roots or yank it back with the fervour of an over-zealous Rabbi.

I left Michelle's flat, pleased that I had found some sex, albeit somewhat forced and autoerotic in nature so soon after Roxanne and I had finished with each other. It proved that there was life after Roxanne, even if I was an unemployed layabout. I got back to my flat to find two job-related messages on the answer machine. Things were looking up. Hah! Roxanne and Conmax: who needed them? I ran a bath and relaxed into a post-masturbatory stupor before psyching myself up to make some calls. The first person I spoke to was Pete Divis, who worked at a recruitment agency. I asked him how he was progressing with my situation. Pete owed me some money and I knew he was keen to help me in case I called in the loan. He had a reasonable network of clients, but he was stating the obvious when he said that my Conmax background might count against me. He said he had nothing on his books at that moment, but would keep trying.

I kept in touch with most of my ex-Conmax colleagues. We made arrangements to meet for lunch three weeks after the company had closed, in case anyone had any bright ideas. None of them were there and I was left talking to the shifty ex-company financial controller from another department. Six of them eventually arrived, led by David Hobson, having had lunch elsewhere. Nice. They were reserved and evasive when I asked them how they were progressing with their respective job searches. Two days later I heard that David had arranged to get them all into a newly-formed Conmax clone via a head-hunter, with David pocketing a cool £40,000 kickback in the process. *Quelle cunt*! Thanks for including me in on the party! Typical. Another classic example of ex-public school stabmanship. The old boy network was dead. The proles had stepped in with their own clubs for their own private use. Most of the public school boys I knew had been shoved to one side with duff jobs as estate agents or life insurance salesmen. I had to laugh all the same. It was ironic that the months I'd spent heckling David Hobson had finally backfired on me so spectacularly. His gritted patience, never rising to my needling, had paid off handsomely. Nobody owed me a living, I once again reflected, least of all David, but I still felt a klutz for being left out of the game.

I returned the other message on the machine, which was from Leonardo Personnel who were fixing me up with an interview at a small Japanese house with an unpronounceable name. Annoyingly the interview clashed with a boozy lunch in the City that I was looking forward to. I had to keep my priorities in perspective, even though I knew from past experience that the Japanese were a waste of time. However pleasant I tried to be, it was impossible for me to disguise my contempt; they could sense the bigotry behind my smile. To me, they were just a nation of unethical, patent-infringing dolphin slayers (for scientific porpoises - my foot!). And what kind of people would proudly have death by overwork as a national characteristic?

The timbre of this interview proved no exception, although there was a glimmer of hope. They kept me in for three hours, culminating in a folksy interview with the Brit Personnel manager, who had the false flush of rude health that is an alcoholic's lot, who I naturally warmed to.

I phoned the agency the next day to see if there was any feedback from the interview. The person at Leonardo said I'd drawn a blank. Another waste of a day. I might as well have gone to the pissy lunch, for all the good it did.

Roxanne and I got together for our drink and as it happened, our relationship. Some things were better left for dead, as I was to find out in an opaque fashion later, but it was good to have her intuitive reassurance massage my troubles away. Temporarily. I felt obliged to put Michelle's breasts on 'hold' for the time being.

# Chapter 8: India

Roxanne left for South Africa a week later and the following day, Christmas Eve, it was my turn to trudge out to the airport. I met the two Goa-bound Camillas at Gatwick and we whizzed round on the toytown railway to the North Terminal. The girls were in high spirits and I found their excitement contagious. We checked in and then spent half an hour plundering the incredibly naff Gatwick Village of its sunglasses, sunblocks, cassettes and diarrhoea pills before treating ourselves to some 10a.m. £10-a-throw Bloody Marys at the reassuringly fake "Travellers Fayre" in the departure lounge. There was something mollifyingly cheerful about large airports: the smartly dressed cabin crews walking in confident unison and the glitzy shops selling all the last minute travelling gadgets that one would feel such a fool without. The soothing announcements that Flight BA956 from Zagreb was about to land, or the last call for Flight PX204 to Karachi, all led to an aura of technological pulchritude.

Once on board we were plied with drink. The service was unexpectedly indulgent considering we were in economy where the ugly stewardesses lived. ("Freshette, sir?") The trolley dollies gave us some rather good plastic food and then we fell asleep in front of a film we'd seen before. I woke up halfway through the flight and twiddled through the stations on my armrest, alternating between 'easy pop' and 'mellow funk', trying to define the difference, before settling down with the dependably ancient comedy channel three times over for the rest of the journey.

We arrived in Bombay on Christmas morning and took a ramshackle taxi to the hotel. There were only ramshackle taxis. We'd decided to stay somewhere smart as a Christmas present to ourselves before slumming it in Goa. The forty minute drive in gave a glimpse of the city's dilapidated energy. The traffic had its own logic despite every driver's determination to conserve brake pads and fuel by driving in fourth, irrespective of the speed. Pitiful women and old men in rags came to the cars while they waited at traffic lights. The women with emaciated babies stuck to their withered dugs; the men wandering confused, like hermits caught in a department store sale. Sunglasses were an essential foil to hide acknowledgement or, worse, pity.

I spent most of Christmas Day walking around central Bombay feeling relieved that I didn't live there, and yet I was aware of a pleasant sense of isolation from Christine's Curse. The poverty of the town was not as alarming as my first impressions. Aside from the beggars and vagrants, most of the male population appeared to be involved in one jolly street corner tea break, while the women strolled about the markets looking at the rubbish on offer and the Samantha Fox calendars. The hotel was an oasis of reason amidst the Bedlam of crumbling tenement blocks and garbage heaps. It wasn't the poverty that I found depressing, so much as the ever-present, omnivorous hunger for cash. Everywhere I looked someone tried to catch my eye to sell me something. What on earth was I, as an obvious tourist, expected to do with a broken-down toaster or a bit of ancient plumbing equipment? Or a Hindi movie fanzine or some state lottery tickets?

Even as I watched the sun go down from the fifth floor of the hotel there were beggars in the street trying to attract my attention with cries of "Over here! Yes sir! Over here!" One little boy had a performing mongrel which, if he hit it with a stick, would stand on its hind legs on a paint tin. I threw down a ten pence coin for my own entertainment, ran a bath and played with the hotel freebies in the bathroom cabinet. I put on a complimentary shower cap to complete the effect and let the only potable water in Bombay wash the dirt of the city off me. I felt like Cleopatra.

Supper that evening was a mistake. We should have stuck to the hotel but the two girls wanted to experiment and find somewhere more representative of the area. Their error was in being fooled by appearances. We found a restaurant that looked clean and, from the curling travel posters on the wall, appeared to have made an attempt to be cosmopolitan. Once settled at our table we realised that that was where the sophistication ended. We were handed a large laminated menu the size of a petition, acutely aware that the dingy kitchen that we could see from our table would be unable to accommodate with any competence the variety of dishes on offer. We opted, imaginatively, for the speciality of the day, chicken curry. When it finally arrived, it was a green and nasty deposit. We retreated, wiser but still unfed, to the hotel and pizza-ed up some room service.

I was up with a jet-lagged lark the next morning and with some trepidation went down to settle our bill. I was amazed, considering we'd murdered the minibar and eaten every meal in, that the bill for our suite, with Government Tax and all the bollocks, came to £140. In other words, as the hotel we were staying in was the most expensive in Bombay, it was almost impossible at the time to spend more anywhere else. A few days later in Goa I found that I could just about buy an entire hotel for £140.

Goa was an hour's flight away. We boarded a surprisingly contemporary aeroplane at noon. The local apothegm had it that the aeroplanes in India were in the nineteen-eighties, the cars in the nineteen-fifties and the telephones in the nineteen-twenties. We touched down in Goa and taxied past the gallery of dead aircraft on either side of the runway. We cleared our stuff through the delightfully silly little customs shed and headed for a beach village that had been recommended to us.

A beach holiday is a beach holiday, except that this was the hippy trail, and as such was an eye-opener for me. I'd been on backpacking holidays plenty of times before, but I had a feeling that a lot of the other holiday funsters in Goa had been there somewhat longer than the regulation two weeks. In fact most looked as though they'd been there for years, strumming their guitars, gazing at the sun as it went down and as it came up again; their faces turning to cracked leather; their eyes as vacant as the windows of abandoned factories.

We found a place to stay which wasn't exactly luxurious, but it was all that we needed. A night's stop was less than the price of a packet of cigarettes. The beach we were on was thirty-five kilometres long and interspersed with cafe shacks boasting such exotic names as "Surfers' Paradise", "Moon Rocket" and "Rick's Spliff Palace", blasting out old Santana records and "Like a Virgin" at ninety watts. It took over an hour to scooter up and down it. The civil unrest in other parts of the country had frightened off most of the package tours and family holiday makers. There was the deserted atmosphere of a ghost town about the place. The hippies and other layabouts that remained were mainly a detached collection of Euro-dirt and Australians who kept to themselves.

By the fourth day one of the Camillas was starting to get on my nerves. Fortunately she was pink-skinned and totally unsuited to a seaside holiday. She left to go on a cultural whirl around Delhi after a few days. I managed to convince the remaining Camilla that nice though our patch was, there were other places that we should visit. I made a complete reconnaissance of Goa on the scooter the second day there. It was no bigger in area than the Isle of Wight, but it was a beautiful, mad little spot with perfect Magritte skies and a fishing village ambience. And it cost virtually nothing. Every so often I skipped down to the State Bank of India waving a ten pound Tommy Cook traveller's cheque and in return received a huge paper bag full of dirty rupee notes that seemed to last for days.

We moved up the coast to a town where there seemed to be more happening. The first evening there we met an Australian called Danny who'd been in Goa for about a month and knew where things were kept. Together the three of us settled into a routine of late breakfasts and paper-backed the rest of the morning away, while fighting off the trinket sellers. By mid-afternoon it was cool enough to potter around.

The shops and stalls had a myriad of nonsense clothes and jewellery that looked great in the sun but I knew would look cheap and gaudy the minute

I got them home. But it was impossible to leave a shop empty-handed. The shopkeepers wouldn't allow anyone to escape. They clutched at my arm whenever I was about to leave and demanded, "How much? How much you pay for that carpet?" or some bauble that had caught my eye which I'd made the mistake of asking the price of, more out of curiosity than a desire to purchase. Usually I'd say "Nothing," because I didn't really want it or wouldn't have had room in my suitcase even if I did. Occasionally I was caught out by bidding what I thought was an unreasonably low price, perhaps sixty rupees when the original quote had been six hundred. There would be the inevitable "You crazy!" rebuttal, but when I turned to leave I would get "OK, OK, sixty rupees," and then would find myself the proud owner of a pair of gas green harem pants or something equally useless.

Most of the local population had no concept of any financial worth beyond a few hundred rupees. Several times I was asked how much I wanted for my camera, or my Walkman, or my watch.

I'd say, "Well, it cost me seven thousand rupees but if you particularly want it I would be happy to sell it for five thousand". Brows would furrow and then: "I pay you two hundred!", to which I'd say, "Why would I want to sell something that's practically brand new that cost me two hundred pounds a few months ago for two hundred rupees now? Make no sense, la?"

But they never saw what I was getting at. It was almost touching to see even in such a grasping environment as India, that actual money itself had a limited circumference.

After my afternoon strollathons, I would return to the hotel. It had seen better days, perhaps fifty years before Camilla and I had booked in. To have a shower I had to call for a bucket of warm water from the kitchen, and pour it into a Heath Robinson watering can contraption suspended from the ceiling, and duly wash myself, M*A*S*H unit style, before dressing for whatever the evening held for us. Supper or drugs. Or both. Danny had found a shack-bar that was set away from the road where we could smoke the local combustibles without upsetting the local constabulary, who were having a bit of a crackdown that year. On most nights a motley collection of no-hopers, dopers and can't copers gathered to stare into nowhere. I found the vibes weren't always to my taste unless I'd toked up enough to get high. There was an American family who'd been coming to Goa for years who frequented the drug shack each evening, or at least Dad and his two sons did. Dad was an extremely ungroovy middle-aged ex-hippie who actively encouraged his fat pubescent offspring to toke away all night. The local weed was not particularly strong or, for that matter, pleasant to smoke. I raised the point with Danny one evening.

"Yeah," he said, "you want to get yourself some acid. That'll set you up!"

"You must be joking," I said. "I want to arrive home refreshed, not with my nut half fried, thank you very much."

"Oh man, you can't do India and not do the acid. That's why we come here, man! I mean, it's like going to Paris and not doing the Eiffel Tower! I've had half a tab already tonight and I'm not acting like a fruit loop, am I?"

"Well, what's the point if nothing happens?" I asked, naively.

"Ah, I didn't say nothing's happening... in fact, as we speak my hand is doing something pretty strange," Danny said, holding his hand up and gazing at it in wonder. "You'd be OK on half a tab, I reckon. A quarter if you want, but I don't think that'll do the trick."

Eventually curiosity got the better of me and I yielded to Danny's suggestion to include me when he next saw the tambourine man.

The following evening we met and Danny broke off a corner from what looked like a stamp-sized bit of balsa wood and very carefully, holding it between his thumb and forefinger as if he was handling a piece of microfilm, passed it over.

"You've got to take it immediately. If you touch it too much all the good stuff'll come off on your fingers and that'll be no use to anyone."

I popped it into my mouth and embarked on one of the most unusual evenings of my life.

Being an LSD virgin, I didn't know quite what to expect. Nothing happened for the first five hours. We had some supper and afterwards a group came back to my hotel room. We passed a joint round and listened to some tin on my Walkman and its miserable auxiliary speakers. One by one people went their own way and I was left trading war stories about women with Danny while the remaining Camilla passed out, comatose, on the bed.

At about three o'clock I had a mild panic attack as the acid began to leak into my sanity. My swimming trunks started to edge towards my trousers on the makeshift clothesline I'd erected in the bathroom.

I called over to Danny, "Hey! Is it my imagination or are my swimmers and chinos over there moving closer to each other? If they are, I reckon they're in for a scrap."

Danny looked at them thoughtfully, and after a while said, "Nah. They're not moving... much."

It was late and Danny decided that he'd better go home. He left me contemplating my pugilistic leisure attire on the clothesline. After he'd gone I switched off the lights and listened to Camilla's reassuring snores. Initially there was nothing I could see to freak me out. But once my eyes had become accustomed to the dark I noticed that the ceiling fan had turned itself into a pearly rabbit. It mutated slowly before settling gently into a fluorescent cow.

Fortunately my hallucinations didn't wander too much further into the obtuse.

I spent the next two hours asking myself questions about my work and career, or the lack of it, and was given a series soothing 'no worries' responses. I asked about The Curse, which I had all but forgotten about for the last two weeks, and whether it had anything to do with my relationships going wrong. In return I was treated to a series of Disneyesque explanations, including one of Christine Hale. It was a psychedelic Addams family montage of her death mask on a casket pillow with "NO" in big letters on either side. My mind flicked over to Roxanne. My concerns about her almost feral sexual appetite and potential propensity to be unfaithful were met with a flat "Who cares?" heliotype.

As I went through all the other women I knew, my brain-computer got bored and changed the subject and started asking me odd, childlike questions.

"Fuck all this falling in love with other people to solve your problems," it said. "Have you ever thought about falling in love with yourself?"

"Not really," I said to myself. "Although, don't get me wrong... I'm not against the concept of self-respect."

"Same difference," said Mr Brain.

"But how can a single unit fall in love with itself? I can't be the lover and the loved all at once. If there's nothing there to like, how can I love? Especially when I hold other people, and women in particular, in such awe."

"Have you ever considered that you might be a woman yourself, James?"

Shit, I didn't need this.

"You mean a fag?"

"No, I mean a woman."

"No, I'll admit that I'm not fantastically macho, but I've never thought of myself as a woman. An inadequate male perhaps, but effeminate - definitely not!"

"Well, James, you're both. We all are in differing degrees. There are two halves to the brain. You can see that in laboratory models and brain scans. There's a purpose. We, as a race, have two hands, two arms, two nostrils, two testicles or two fallopian tubes. Notice how there's two of everything?"

"Well, I've also got one tongue, one nose, one tummy button, one arsehole and that's the way I'd like to keep it," I replied, petulantly.

"Hardly vital organs, James. You can't pick up a cup of tea with a tummy button."

"OK, what about the ultimate organ? I have, dare I confess, only one penis. Pretty necessary for propagating the species, even if it can't pick up a tea cup."

"Propagating the species perhaps, but also eliminating the planet. Besides you only use yours for recreational purposes, so it doesn't count as a vital organ."

"Pity. I thought having given so much happiness to its owner it might actually be of some use in the greater scheme of things."

"Dream on. Chop it off. It will never be of any use. Most of them aren't. Anyway we haven't come all this way to discuss your penis and I'm sure the laboratory technicians in Amsterdam or whoever concocted this mixture, this metaphysical lubricant that has brought us so pleasantly together, didn't do so with the express intention that James Mallet's penis be cast in stone, much as you'd like it."

"Oh," I said, dejectedly.

"The point is, James, there is a positive and a negative that go to form the psyche; you've got to come to terms with that."

"You mean there are two sides to me?"

Psychedelic fireworks exploded into a profusive "YES".

"Oh God," I said desperately. "You mean that I'm bisexual? Is this a taste of things to come?"

"No, you're missing the point again. Even if you were, you really shouldn't be quite so phobic."

"So there really are two separate distinct sides to the psyche? A yin and a yang? A horse and a cart?"

"Precisely. You're getting there at last." I could sense the two halves of my head dancing and getting funky with each other like two cartoon characters. They jived like the Jungle Book with increasing rhythm upon each passing realisation.

I looked at my watch. It was five-thirty. The birds outside were beginning to sing. I felt a sense of calm and inner wisdom that I hadn't experienced before. The trip was coming to an end. I murmured a toast to the kind chemists in Amsterdam or wherever the stuff was made for giving me such a gentle ride, rolled over and went to sleep.

Two weeks became one and then the days started to run out. It was time to take my leave of this dusty utopia with its infrastructure that seemed to be held entirely together by bits of string. I tried to forget the fact that I had no job to go to or rather that I had a task ahead of me far harder than any actual occupation. Two days before I was due to leave I decided to have one last acid hit and asked Danny to make the necessary arrangements. At fifty rupees a trip, to travel first class by magic carpet for four hours, it had to be done. And besides I had an important mission: it was my last chance to try to unravel the mysteries of The Curse by psychedelic means.

That evening Danny and I swallowed our respective bits of balsa wood and went to join the other deadheads for supper. I looked round the table at the empty, unstimulated faces that had swapped one reality for another. I wondered how many dropouts there were drifting around the Third World for every accountant, solicitor and computer programmer in the First, and asked myself who were the fools?

At eleven I said goodnight to everyone and wandered back to the hotel. I read for a bit. By twelve my eyes were becoming tired and I started to worry about when the acid would take effect. I didn't want to be absent through it because it would have been a waste of a trip, so I set the alarm clock for one-thirty and went to sleep. One-thirty came. The alarm went off. I woke up, tripless. I re-set the alarm for three and went to sleep again. Three o'clock came and still no trip. I began to feel like a child waiting for Father Christmas to appear. I'd been stood up. As a last resort I set the alarm for five and tried to get to sleep again. Five came. *Nada. Rien.* It must have been a dud tab or the acid had evaporated before I got to it. The mysteries surrounding The Curse were to remain an enigma.

I couldn't get back to sleep after so many interruptions, so I dressed and went for a walk on the beach. I watched the sun come up as the fishermen came back to the shore, their catch brimming over the gunwales of their dangerously unseaworthy long-boats. The shallows became a frenzy of activity and noise as the women, baskets on heads, sarees flapping, shouted to each other through missing teeth while their children ran around excitedly in the water. Seagulls squawked and made audacious dives at the sprats in the nets and baskets. The whole village became enveloped in a pleasing fug as the sun's warmth started to take effect on the fish and the nets left out to dry. The dark blue of the early morning sky turned into a vivid azure, assuring the prospect of yet another perfect day; my last golden day before returning to the cold, wet, unpaid bill of a country that my existence had become.

The return journey was long and uneventful, but not unpleasant. I didn't have the benefit of the remaining Camilla for company because she'd decided, wisely to my mind, to extend her stay in Goa by another week. I had a ten hour wait for my connecting flight in Bombay. I took a taxi to the largest and most opulent airport hotel I could find and installed myself in a comfortable air-conditioned bar that overlooked the swimming pool. I drank slowly from frosted glasses of beer served by deferential waiters and nibbled salted almonds like a maharajah. I only had to fart and someone would come running with another drink.

I walked around the cavernous lobbies and vestibules and peered into the immaculate but empty restaurants on offer until plumping, out of meanness, for the coffee shop where I ordered an exotic-looking pizza that tasted of old socks. I spent the rest of the afternoon wandering around the landscaped gardens and manicured lawns, delighting in the irony of the poverty outside, returning every so often to one of the hotel bars to sample another lager.

At six it was time to make my way to the airport. The experience had cost me less than ten pounds and in many respects was the most civilised day of the holiday. I collected my bags from the reception and was presented with a plastic 'Privilege Card' that entitled me to enter the hotel's nightclub, gymnasium, swimming pool, conference facilities and torture chamber, but alas I had to go. I waltzed past the air-conditioned taxis awaiting custom on the forecourt and the turbaned door flunkies touting for tips. Tips that were rewarded with either a gentle clunk or a thunderous slam of the car door according to the donor's generosity or intimidation. Once out of the confines of the lotus-eating environment of the hotel, I headed for the main road and hailed a sixpenny trishaw.

# Chapter 9: Back to Life: Back to Reality

Getting back to England in mid-January was a bit of a comedown after the previous few weeks' excitement. Roxanne was still in South Africa and not due back for another week. I resumed the odious task of phoning around and scouring the newspapers for work. Most of the Eurojobs I saw now required three extra languages, an MBA and a bulletproof client base, none of which I had. Other jobs were for peons in their early twenties with excellent "interpersonal skills", whatever they were.

One recruitment specialist to whom I had been recommended lined me up with what looked like a promising interview. When I arrived I found that the interviewer was not only ex-Pan Asian Bank himself but we'd both been to the same school, albeit at different times. It was too cosy. I knew, in the tradition of old school back-stabbing, that I wouldn't get the job however close a fit I was. Afterwards I headed forlornly for the nearest Underground station. A busker played a noteless noise on a penny whistle, more to establish a presence than out of a genuine attempt to entertain. A supermodel in a Wonderbra pouted at me from the safety of her billboard. I stared at the other posters on the platform. Maradonna's 'Ultimate Virginal Immaculate Conception Greatest Hits Collection Album'; Diane Toss, 'Songs for Spastics'; Cindy Puerile, 'Shit Tunes from a Pretty Face'. Old whine in new bottles. I wondered what they wanted the extra money for. I'd have been happy with the royalties from a flip side of one of their singles. It would be more money than I would see in my lifetime.

I got on the train and flicked through a copy of the 'Scum' that someone had thoughtfully left behind. It fell open at the opinion page: 'Cutting through the bollocks with Dave Shit.' 'Read Your Stars with Mystic Smeg.' 'Wot the Scum says...' I put it down and felt depressed again. I made a mental note to make an appointment with the dole office and to contact Pete Divis at his recruitment agency when I got back again. I walked out of the tube station into the winter slush, and headed towards the pub opposite for a reflective pint and a go on the trivia machine. There was a homeless oaf by the door trying to sell copies of 'The Big Issue'. What 'Big Issue'? His homelessness wasn't a big issue to me. I had a flat; my big issue was not having a job.

I couldn't be bothered to do anything when I got home. There was a message from Mike Dexter, another pariah struck down with the paralysis of unemployment saying that he was going to be at 'The Artist' that lunchtime. I felt I needed company and so with no further hesitation I got in my car and drove round to meet him. I pretended not to notice a life insurance salesman I vaguely knew at the bar as I went in. He was looking shifty as usual. I could see his eyes darting from table to table, ever on the lookout for some unsuspecting fool to pitch his annuity schemes to. I spotted Mike sitting in a corner. He was in his slightly nervous 'Jack-the-lad' mood that usually led to repetitious pettifogging and inconclusive discussions.

"Well if it isn't old Jamie Mallet. What a sight for sore cunts! How was India?"

"It was great. Like a time warp without a lavatory," I said, wistfully and enquired, "And how have you been in my absence?"

"Absolutely under the moon, old cock," Mike replied, morosely.

"Well what have you been up to then?" I asked, not really giving a shit.

"Just sittin' on the dock of the bay, wastin' time. What have you been doing since you got back?"

"Same sort of thing; just wandering around, lonely as a fart... been quite busy watching telly, I suppose. Otherwise are you all right?" I asked, trying to be a bit more specific.

"Tossing like a teenager, thank you; fings couldn't be better," Mike intoned, sarcastically. "Fuck me, is it a nightmare out there or what mate? There's nothing happening, man. I mean no one's hiring. Sending off for jobs is just a waste of stamps."

"Some people are hiring, Mike; they just don't happen to be hiring *us*," I said, hoping to avert a rant.

"That's because pricks like to employ other pricks."

"God does seem to smile on wankers at the moment, granted, but it can't go on forever," I remarked, unconvincingly.

"But I don't understand why it's always the cruds who get the best jobs," Mike said, with mounting despair.

"Probably because cruds make for better robots," I said in a last-ditch attempt to steer Mike away from the oncoming diatribe. It was too late.

"The bank's halfway up my bum. Chicks don't want to know... I got laid more often when I was a virgin. If you put lipstick on an Alsatian I'd fuck it, I'm so desperate."

"Tell me about it!" I said, entering into my own rant. "Trying to get any schtoink to climb on board when you're unemployed is like trying to wank with both hands tied behind your back. In fact, trying to do anything when you're out of work is practically impossible. Even getting a CV typed up becomes a major performance. You can't win."

"I've gotta get out of here, James. South America; that's the place, man. Wanna come? It'll be a real groove. Tons of sun, loads of other people's dosh; pussy crawling all over you... I just want out. This place stinks. What happened to us, James? I mean we were hot stuff not so long ago: cash and gash, cars and bars... where did it all go? The country's run by shits for shits, leaving us poor sods in the shit. We're stuffed! And does anyone care? What have any of our friends and all the other job pigs done to help? Absolutely fuck all. Each day they get stronger and we get weaker. Never in the field of human conflict has so little been done by so few. The worrying thing is, you know, I think they love it. And the Government doesn't give a damn either. If anything, they derive positive pleasure from exacerbating the situation and slapping VAT on everything that moves."

"When they're not too busy shagging the living daylights out of any secretary with a pulse, that is," I interjected. Mike looked at me and nodded. He resumed his monologue.

"I've had to sell my flat for less than the mortgage. I've got nothing left. This country can be summed up in two words: John Major. It's dull, grey and wanked out. Naive git. All he's good for is poncing around, having a good time in his tuxedo at official functions and looking pleased with himself. What we need is that Mrs Thatcher back. God she made me laugh!"

"Democracy and poverty are unhappy bedfellows," I said, quoting something slightly out of context that I'd heard on TV the night before.

"Whatever it is, it's gone to pieces: it's a con. Lloyd's... the Government... the whole thing's rotten to the core. The City's been taken over by proles and foreigners. Not surprising, I suppose. Neither realises just how awful the other one is. Contacts aren't prepared to put themselves out. Headhunters are a complete wanking exercise. So what are you left with? The square root of fuck-all, that's what."

I sighed in agreement but made a vague attempt to brighten the conversation.

"We are in a bit of a messy-poos, I suppose, but things could be worse. At least we're still single. I mean money's like confetti; you only really need it when you're getting married."

"Don't be an arsehole James," Mike cut in crossly. "How are you going to get married, or laid for that matter, without it? Women are like game fowl; they're bred to be hunted. But you've got to have the dough to go on the shoot in the first place. Otherwise you might as well sit at home with a sticky magazine pulling your todger to bits for all the good your killer instincts are going to do you. There's nothing that cunt likes more than money. And money *loves* cunt."

I'd heard it all before. It was sad watching Mike going more and more bonkers every time I saw him. He'd been out of work for over a year. Given time, I'd start to go to pieces too. If I hadn't already.

There were a few other boozers and losers who came to the pub each lunchtime who we joined tables with. We took it in turns to have a moan, or tell a sob story about an interview that had gone wrong or how three zillion other people had applied for the same job to be a road sweeper. It wasn't madly therapeutic. It just made me more aware of how bleak the situation was. We were all public school dinosaurs who'd been caught in a 'seventies time warp, without degrees or professional qualifications and scant prospect for the future. Victims of a lack of guidance and sloth in years gone by. We thrashed around like elephants in a drought. We were about to be the twenty-first century's sharecroppers, without a crop to share.

Mike suggested going to lunch somewhere, but the chop in my fridge was on its last day and besides, I reasoned to myself, it would only be another tenner down the drain, just for the privilege of watching Mike's dementia froth over. I stayed a bit longer and smoked my way through another pint. I exchanged some piffle with another gentleman failure I saw hunched over the pink tablecloth of the Financial Times. I left the pub, annoyingly sober. It meant there wouldn't be anything for me to sleep off and yet my bladder would be too awash to allow a comfortable afternoon's wank.

"Jesus," I cried inwardly. "What has the world come to that a grown man should sit at home, like a gorilla in a cage, with nothing more stimulating to pass the time than to *frappe la viande* all day?"

I bought a copy of the FT for myself on the way home. Being a Wednesday there might, I thought, be something in the jobs column for me, but there was nothing except some accountancy positions in Sordid Arabia. The only advertisement which looked vaguely promising turned out to be for an 'equal opportunities employer', which ruled me out.

The second post had come and with it two bills that I didn't particularly want to open. I'd been trying to balance the books without any proper income for the last two months and was finding that I was fighting a losing battle. One of the bills was the mother of all credit card statements with most of the India jaunt on it. In the cold light of day it looked the size of the entire country's national debt. The other was the 'leccy bill which wasn't much better and made me realise that I wasn't fooling anyone by turning the central heating off and living on fan heaters. I went into the kitchen and peered into the fridge. I found a half full bottle of 'Blue Numb', speed-drank it as if it was lager and went straight to bed with all my clothes on.

The phone woke me at five, interrupting an interesting dream I was having about Paula Abdul's bottom. It was Pete Divis saying that he had a potential job interview lined up for me with United Discount Securities – 'United Disco' for short - at a date yet to be confirmed. I thanked him and told him to "keep 'em rolling". I tried to go back to sleep, but I was too nauseous to drift off.

Roxanne came back from South Africa the following weekend. We lay in bed all Sunday, huddled under the blankets, comparing holidays and professing how much we'd missed each other. I welcomed her shapeless, sagging posterior like an old friend. At the time I didn't realise that my renewed feelings for her came largely from my own insecurity and sense of worthlessness rather than a genuine glow of affection from within. She was a good ear and had the patience to listen to my endless tirades about failed interviews and rejection letters. She had a knack of being able to reduce them to more digestible proportions.

Roxanne had to go back to work that Monday and I was left to face my paranoia on my own. I contemplated the birth of a new week. It looked deformed.

I gazed out of the window. The horizon was bleak and lifeless. I wanted to go for a spend round the supermarket just to get out of the flat, but apart from being dangerously low on peppercorns there was nothing I really needed, and besides, I wanted to save any shopping for Wednesday evening when it was 'Singles' Night' at Insanesbury's.

I sent a salvo of CVs in response to some inappropriate jobs I'd seen advertised in a business magazine and then went along to the DSS to sign on. I'd missed a month's worth of dole but at least I'd made a start. It was only forty pounds a week but it would help pay for the gin and tonics. I wasn't deemed poor enough to collect any of the other benefits. The staff at the dole office were surprisingly helpful and I didn't feel any sense of humiliation. People had talked of the shame of signing on, but I had no such qualms. I felt perfectly at home standing in the queue with all the other crusties and misfits. A youth with out-of-work-actor good looks and an earring tried to queue-barge past me just as I'd reached the front of the line.

"What the fuck's going on?" I protested.

"I was here first," he said, in an unconvincing cockney accent.

"Don't be a cunt. I've been waiting here for half an hour," I rallied, trying to be firm but fair.

"You watch your manners, mate. You give me any more gyp and I'll break your fucking face," the youth screeched, definitely rising to the occasion.

"Really? I've never been hit by a man with an earring. What's it like?" I asked, genuinely interested.

"Listen you stuck up git: do you want me to take you outside and beat your 'ed in?" the youth continued, starting to get hysterical.

"Oh for crying out loud; what's the point?" I questioned, in despair, injecting for irritation's sake, "We're exactly the same size. There's nothing to suggest that either one of us would come off the better for it, thus rendering violence inefficient... so why don't you get a job, *loser*?! People like you take all that's civilised out of unemployment. Your hard-man act doesn't fool me. It's patently obvious that you went to a grammar school – look at you – you look so wet! So why don't you cool down and take your turn like everyone else?"

The youth looked as though he was about to explode. A girl behind us came to our rescue.

"For goodness sake you two! Just look at yourselves. Sad innit? Fighting over who's going to to dot on first. What's the hurry? Missing somefink good on telly?"

The absurdity of the spectacle made everyone else in the queue laugh. The laughter turned into a wild cackle. I felt ruffled by the prospect of physical confrontation and the ludicrousness of the situation. The youth I suspected felt the same, and out of embarrassment let me go ahead. The woman at the signing station handed me my UB40 in an ominously durable plastic sleeve. Someone had written "small tits" on the counter with an arrow pointing to her.

I phoned a few head-hunters when I got home. They were little more than estate agents who dealt in human flesh and I was not, in their eyes, particularly hot property.

Time slid by again. Weeks became months and I still couldn't find any work. I came close, but a miss was as good as a mile when it came to paying the bills. Any advertisements that seemed to fit usually turned out to be for selling water filters or dodgy make-up products or some such hokum. One job actually specified 'Eurobonds', but when I went for the interview, it turned out that the commission structure didn't include even the smallest basic salary. It seemed a bit desperate. The company's smart Mayfair address belied a Dickensian basement office with no dealing equipment.

"What about screens?" I asked, thinking that a dealing room without screens was like having a kitchen without a cooker.

"Oh, we're trying to keep costs down," came the reply.

I suggested that if they really wanted to keep their overheads to a minimum they should get rid of the telephones and do everything by post. "After you with the office biro!" The point seemed lost on them, but to me the stigma of unemployment seemed better than the ignominy of working under such ludicrous conditions. They didn't offer me the job anyway.

By late spring I'd entered such a state of ennui that even going to the pub seemed too much effort. My flat became my hermetic sanctum against the outside world. It was the only place that I had any control over. Each morning I struggled with my agoraphobic fear of the front door to check the post and file the increasing stack of rejection letters into my 'blow-out' box. They seemed, as if by some strange phenomena, to match exactly the number of applications I'd sent out.

Habits that I'd cast off years before started to creep back; the early morning cigarette in the bath, flicking the ash into the soap dish, and then lobbing the butt into the loo, missing and jumping like a scalded cat out of the bath to rescue it. Then settling down to a regular nine o'clock gin and slimline. Roxanne appeared oblivious to my reduced circumstances and didn't seem to mind my new role as house-sitter. I carried her gym bag to the station as she went off to work each morning and was ready with a hot meal in the evening when she returned. She occasionally came back in an abusive frame of mind, but normally because she'd had one too many with the lads after work.

The country descended from farce to shambles. Christine's Curse seemed ready to take on the whole nation. Company after company went bust as the banks foreclosed on anyone they'd ever lent money to. It didn't help my case. It meant that there were more people on the street looking for my sort of work. At least I had a recession to thank for providing a cover for my feeblemindedness. My thoughts started to go round in circles as I snatched desperately at any idea that might get me out of my predicament. I had another think about going back to school and doing an MBA. I had a look at some of the entrance papers and decided it all looked too much of a wank. I'd never been exactly Professor Calculus at school so it was difficult to envisage being the toast of the common room now.

People came to me with ideas. Set up a restaurant! Open a nightclub! But I didn't want to blow what precious cash I had on hare-brained schemes that I didn't understand. I put my flat on the market, more for something to do than because I couldn't afford the mortgage payments. The thought of a healthy bank balance in place of my draughty garret and going back to India for an endless sabbatical began to grow more attractive with each passing day, although in my case I knew 'sabbatical' was just another name for a skive. As I wasn't on track for the chair at Barclays, I thought I might as well enjoy life to the full, but hedonism and corporate survival seldom mix. In the interlude I lurched from one gin and tonic to another, clutching at whatever straws I could find to achieve some form of escape.

After six months of being out of work I'd become something of an authority on the subject. I received calls from people I'd never met asking me about their unemployment entitlements and who the best recruitment agents were. I was an acknowledged expert on the ignominy of being jobless. I was even contacted by Allegro Television who were filming a documentary about redundancy. They asked if I would discuss my experiences with them with a view to appearing on the programme. I agreed to meet the producer and her assistant at 'The Artist', together with Albert Carr, who'd also been called to the leper colony of the unemployed.

The producer went through what she wanted to do. She was pretty, in a nun-like way. She had a slightly fluffy bottom that I mused would probably appear a *soupçon* over-generous in a bikini. The result, perhaps, of too much pony-clubbing in adolescence or sitting around at the Allegro offices all day. I said that I didn't think that I was interesting enough as a subject. I'd never been a particularly heavy hitter for a start and now that I wasn't working, I only had a modest mortgage to think of and as such could cope adequately on a day-to-day basis. In some ways I was lucky that I was in a position to survive on ten pounds a day: two pints and a slice of pizza on the way home. I told her that being out of work was turgid; that was all, and that if she wanted to do a parable about yuppie comeuppance, I wasn't interested in participating. She promised that she was endeavouring to document something of social significance rather than trying to stitch up two out-of-work toffs. In the hope of becoming better acquainted with her bloodlessly perfect face, I reluctantly agreed to be interviewed on camera, with Albert, at a later date.

Pete Divis finally managed to get me an interview with Dick Langley, the Head Yank at United Disco. When I arrived there Dick said he wasn't in a hiring mood, but after half an hour of giving him reasons as to why he should be and why he should specifically hire me, he gave in and changed his mind.

"OK, let's give it a shot," he said at last. "Thirty-three thousand basic, thirty-three per cent commission and three months' probation."

All the threes! Too neat! At last I had found someone with the sense to employ me. We shook hands. He told me to call his secretary with two references and he'd get the contract drawn up. I called Pete Divis and told him the outcome. We met at 'The White Sock' to celebrate and got completely bladdered.

I never heard from Dick Langley again. I waited a few days to hear from him about a start date. When no call came, I tried to contact him at his office. His secretary was evasive, and he was always busy. He never returned my calls. Two weeks later Paul Harrison, a parvenu I knew at NatWest called to say that Dick had resigned from United Disco and had gone to Parker Barrow. Thanks Dick. That really helped. I called United Disco to try to keep the thing alive, but nobody had heard of me and they weren't interested in reviving the matter. My confidence took another tumble and what little faith I had left retired to the back seat. In his own diminutive, bearded American way Dick Langley had seemed a decent specimen, but I was learning that nice guys were not necessarily the ones to trust.

Roxanne was due to go back to Cape Town for a wedding that May. Her reasons for going quite so far for a wedding so soon after having returned from South Africa eluded me at the time. Normally I couldn't be bothered to go out of London for such trifles.

Just before Roxanne left I received a call from one of the companies I'd written to. The voice sounded strangely disembodied and I was confused to begin with.

"Mr Mallet?"

"Yes."

"It's Karen from Kowshat International."

"Oh," I said, wondering if I'd done something wrong.

"Kowshat International? The Korean securities firm? You wrote to us in response to our advertisement in last week's FT. I'm calling on behalf of Mr Kim who'd like to see you for an interview next week."

I'd sent out so many CVs that I'd lost track. I stalled her for a moment while I tried to remember which advertisement she was referring to. I had no recall, but readily agreed to meet "Mr Kim" the following Wednesday.

Roxanne left for South Africa the day before my appointment. I was relieved that she was going away again for a while. My lack of employment was beginning to wear a bit thin with her. However proficient I was at housekeeping, I knew my credibility was definitely on an ebb.

My first meeting with the slab-faced Mr Kim was strange to say the least. After the initial questions about what clients I had and my product knowledge, he asked me about my salary expectations. I told him what I had earned on a good day at Conmax. He told me the salary range that he had in mind. It wasn't fantastic but as I hadn't been offered any other job I kept quiet. It wasn't the sort of salary that meant much would be expected of me. Mr Kim appeared to be looking for a reaction. I said that as I was single and without any dependants, I could survive, if not thrive, on the amount mentioned.

Quick as a flash he said, "How long you stay single?"

I shifted uncomfortably, wondering where his next question would lead.

"I have no immediate plans to change my marital status," I replied, after a moment's hesitation.

"I think you stay single because you a beautiful man," he declared fiercely, without the slightest suggestion of a smile. Before I could think of an appropriate response he went on in his halting English:

"I think you too beautiful, and you have too much good time to get married. I married to same woman for eleven years. I no like."

I didn't really want to know. In the interests of getting the job I kept my composure.

"We have an expression Mr Kim here in the England, that the grass is always greener on the other side. It's sometimes a lonely existence being single. I'm just waiting for the right woman to turn up. If she does, that is..." I hurriedly steered the conversation back to the question of my employment.

A few days later I had the magnetronic voice of Karen from Kowshat on the phone again calling me in to meet Mr Park, the imaginatively named Managing Director.

On my arrival Mr Park and I exchanged similar inanities to those I'd traded on my first meeting with Mr Kim. Eventually we came round to discussing the company's objectives. I attempted to put forward a convincing case about how I'd be a perfect fit within the firm and what added value I could bring. Mr Kim, who was also present, came out with another lavishly tooled *fallacia consequentis* and asked:

"Mr Mallet... you like alcohol?"

Jesus! Was it that obvious? I replied that I enjoyed the odd drink at Christmas and other religious festivals. Communion wine. That sort of thing. Mr Kim then turned to me and in a slow, tremulous voice that erupted with mounting ferocity, declared: "I like whisky!" as if challenging me to a duel.

"How interesting," I remarked. "Any particular sort?"

"Malt whisky – 'Royal Salute' - you know it?"

"Oh yes. That's very famous. The connoisseur's choice, or so I'm told."

"You drink it?"

"I'm sure I've had a glass or two at some point, but I can't recall actually purchasing a bottle as such... too expensive for my wallet... it's a rich man's game, Mr Kim," I said, smiling obsequiously and feeling myself squirm. How things had changed since my Pan Asian days when the boot had been on the other foot and I'd been perfectly horrid to the Orientals.

We waffled on for a bit about the joys and virtues of malts, single malts and non-malts. We went through every known label before returning to the question of my destiny within the Kowshat organization.

Mr Park asked if I would have any problems coping with a Korean work environment.

"Absolutely not!" I said, quickly and emphatically. "It would be an honour and a privilege to be associated with such a prestigious organisation," laying it on almost too thick, even for Mr Kim.

I left the interview feeling that I was as close as I'd ever be to clinching a deal. Mr Kim said that he would contact me in the next few days once he'd discussed the matter with the Head Office in Seoul. The firm was really a one man and his dog outfit, but being out of work was beginning to lose its charm. Once again, I was in no position to pick and choose.

Thus I continued to comb the newspapers for other jobs, but with little success, as I turned a blind eye to the inevitable "Wanted: Graduate with a first in brain surgery and comprehensive computer knowledge including Orifice 123 plus advanced spreadsheet proficiency," and wrote in regardless. It only cost the price of a stamp and gave me a certain amusement dividend. Like submitting a pools coupon. I knew most of the time that I didn't have a chance. There was the satisfaction of knowing that some creep in Human Resources would have to process the application and send back a rejection letter to add to my collection. Human. Resources. I think not.

I particularly enjoyed wasting the time of banks that advertised along the lines: "We are a first class organisation and only employ first class people. We are looking for tiptop, enthusiastic, hardworking individuals (i.e. morons) with proven track records, to embark on the privilege of working as a slave in our whiz-whiz equity portfolio management team. Preferred age: mid-to-late-teens."

The complacency of any particular company seemed to be in direct proportion to its size. Where were the jobs for the nice guys? Why were there no job advertisements that said, "Lazy, unqualified person needed to assist in making personal phone calls in congenial atmosphere. No cunts or MBAs (same thing) need apply. Age: over 35 and burnt out." If all these banks had been so "first class" and clever, how come they'd lent grillions to Maxwell, Polly Peck (silly name for a company), O & Y and every tinpot dictatorship in South America?

One ad caught my eye and looked quite promising in that it didn't have the usual squeaky-clean-mustard-keen job specs. It turned out to be for a Japanese house, which didn't bode well. Ian Pickering, the man at the search agency who'd advertised the position was so enthusiastic about my prospects that I felt the least I could do was to give it a shot, although I knew the exercise would have all the hilarity content of a Bundesbank meeting. The company in question was Taiayobo Securities. As my past experiences with the Japanese had all been abortive, I was slightly reluctant to waste any more time; I'd never been enamoured anyway with the concept of working for a race that had cheated and buggered its way through the twentieth century without showing an ounce of remorse to show for it.

It was the first seriously sunny day of the year the morning that I was due to go for the interview. I still felt drunk from a binge I'd been on the night before. I contemplated calling up and cancelling. I wanted nothing more than to have a stroll in the park, but I didn't want to let Ian Pickering down. My disposition was hardly improved by the queue for the newspaper bitch at the station. I must have missed more than a thousand trains over the years, suffering her cheerful geriatric squawking while she fiddled about making a balls of everyone's change.

I arrived on time at eleven and was kept waiting by the wanker from Personnel for half an hour. To add further to my displeasure I was made to wear a visitor's pass practically the size of a dustbin lid on my lapel. I looked like a game show contestant. I filled in the time looking at the people going about their business as they passed the reception area. Busy. Busy. Busy. A cute Japanese girl gave me a funny look as she passed by. I checked my flies when she was out of sight.

Eventually a youth with a feeble excuse for a moustache and the most peculiar voice procedure came into the reception area and introduced himself. It was the Personnel Manager: Essex man on a mission. My hopes rose. If a company was sufficiently inept to entrust its staffing matters to such an obvious oik, there was a chance that I might slip through the net unnoticed. He gave me a moist but confident handshake. Assurance was not a problem for people with jobs, especially when they were about to interview one without.

The youth directed me to a conference room where two Japanese salarymen, both with faces as smooth and featureless as Nakamichi tape decks, were waiting. Another Brit yob in a reflecting suit came in and introduced himself as the Head Trader. God help us, I thought to myself.

We sat down. The interview didn't get off to a good start. I wasn't feeling quite myself and longed to be somewhere else. On top of it all I had a thirst that water could not quench. My thoughts kept wandering to the prospect of having a beer on my balcony with a good book and getting my tits nicely sauteed in the sun, shirt off, answerphone on.

There was a pregnant pause for about a minute before embarrassment got the better of me. To get the ball rolling I started to ask a question.

Personnel amoeba jumped into action immediately and twanged:

"If you don't mind, Mr Mallet, we'll ask the questions. If you have any queries perhaps you can save them for the end of the interview."

I felt a rage coming on. Alright Cuddles, have it your way. My hangover swung into action. I would happily have got up at that point and slapped Personnel-git across the chops, spat in the Nips' faces and thumped the trader-wallah with my briefcase on the way out. For Ian Pickering's sake I restrained myself.

Finally the trader-thingie came out with, "How come you've been out of work for so long?"

I could see that things were not going to go smoothly. I didn't have the energy to go into a long and grovelling justification of why, despite being such an obvious prize, I'd been unsuccessful in finding an employer with the necessary vision to hire me. I answered simply, as if addressing a child:

"Well, you see, there has been a recession. This has led to a downturn in market activity, which has led to a job shrinkage within the securities industry."

"Oh, I see. Yes, Mr Mallet, I think I get your point."

After that he seemed flummoxed and at a loss what to say next. He started a question for the sake of it, but hadn't thought out what he was going to ask and became stuck.

I wanted to say, "You're stuck, aren't you?" But all the time I kept thinking of the saintly Ian Pickering and my duty to not let him down. I sat patiently attempting, I think successfully, a pleasant but annoying expression that I slowly mutated into a look of daft incredulity. Trader-thingie staggered on, trying desperately to clutch at a straw of authority, when finally the Personnel dweeb had the sense to step in and rescue him.

"What I think my colleague is trying to say is... is..." and then he got stuck too. I upgraded my expression to a crazy Jack Nicholson for a few moments, and then snapped back to normal,"...why haven't you had any luck with any of the other securities houses so far?"

"Oh, is that what he was trying to say?" I said agreeably. "I did wonder. Pity, I thought I'd already answered that one, but here goes: you see there has been a recession. This has led to a downturn in market activity, which has led to a job shrinkage within the securities industry."

Ian Pickering really couldn't have asked for more but I seemed to have caused some degree of agitation. The Nips, as expected, said nothing.

The Personnel 'nana tried to change tack and battled on saying, "I see from your CV that you didn't go to university. Why not?"

"Because I didn't want my creativity to be institutionalised. Also there's nothing quite like a boarding school to put a boy off any further education. Is there a problem? I'm just slightly at a loss with what this has to do with selling bonds. I passed my 'A' levels a year early, if my intellect is in doubt. I decided, for my sins, to go rather excitingly straight into banking after school. I didn't want to become a one trick pony and I couldn't see how a degree in, say Geology, could be of any possible financial advantage to anyone. Besides, as I wasn't going to get into Oxford or Cambridge, I didn't want to be pigeon-holed as a dunce for the rest of my life by going to somewhere second-rate like Durham or Bristol. Did you go to university? You strike me as a polytechnic man."

"I went to Durham," he said stiffly.

"Durham Polytechnic?"

"No, Durham University. I read Social Sciences."

"Oh, that's where you get it from. I can tell you're very social. I'm quite social myself, although I haven't studied it as a science. I felt it just came sort of naturally to me..."

At that point I Sloaned up my voice into a Prince Charles turbowhine and marked my sentences with "Yah", "Really?", "Oh, topping!" and "Splendid!" I was pleased to see that I was able to maintain a consistent level of agitation until I began to tire of the game. I kept wrestling with the problem of which lager I would go for when I got home. I was in a quandary. Should I chug back double-quick one of the tins of Carlsberg that I was trying to work through to get some useless promotional gift they had on offer, or should I quaff at leisure the last remaining can of Kronenbourg? I decided I'd re-stock on Kronenbourgs on the way home when I went past Weirdbins.

My eyes drifted towards the window and I stared longingly at the sunny world outside wishing I was there with a bucket of cold beer at my side, instead of having to endure the artificial intelligence in front of me. Personnel-thingie went on about the wonders of Taiayobo. To keep myself from looking bored I tried to imagine them all with no clothes on, then in nurses' uniforms, then in flowing Laura Ashley numbers ,with gathered sleeves and sensible necklines.

"... and where do you see yourself in five years' time, Mr Mallet?"

That old chestnut. Why five? Why stop there? Why not ten? Or twenty? It was all very well for him to ask. He at least had a job. He knew exactly where he would be in five years' time. Probably interviewing some other tired old schlep like me. It had to be most idiotic question devised by the human resources industry. I kept my reply brief.

"Fuck knows." At least I was honest.

He raised an eyebrow and moved on. "I notice from your CV that you haven't put down your interests."

"I don't have any," I snapped back.

"None?"

"Oh all right. Network paedophilia and heckling at weddings. Will that do?"

"Very good, Mr Mallet. Very droll. Very modern. Do you speak any foreign languages?"

"No but I know all the words to "American Pie" and speak English better than most foreigners," I said fixing him with a steady stare before adding accusingly, "and better than most of my own countrymen for that matter."

Personnel problem cranked to a halt and said after a pause, "Do you have any questions now, Mr Mallet?"

"Oh goody goods!" I answered suavely. "My turn: except I've forgotten what questions I was going to ask. No. I don't think I have any. There is nothing to question is there? Obviously this is *the* firm to work for. I've always known it, although I never thought for a moment that I'd pass muster to be considered worthy of an interview. And what a delight it's been; in amongst the City's finest; keen minds that never rest; lives given over to the call of commerce for the enrichment of mankind. Magnificent! The fusion of Eastern ingenuity and Western creativity, perfectly matched in this powerhouse of financial productivity: client and broker enlaced in peerless harmony."

I went on a bit longer until I ran out of drivel.

One of the Nips sparked to life like a dormant lizard that had just had a rock thrown at it, and machine-gunned me a short burst.

"How much money you make for Conmax?"

Oh rock on Tojo! Taking no prisoners here!

"About seven fifty U.S.," I lied, "but I could do a lot more from a prestige house such as this." Not even the Nips would buy that one.

"You could make a million dorrar if you worked here?"

Oh sure Tojo! Go find your own rain maker. I decided to keep my cool.

"I would feel comfortable with that sort of figure, all things being equal. Given a fair wind behind me, maybe more."

Fair wind just about summed it up. The imbecilic trader regained his composure and said something at last.

"You're positive about that?"

"Absolutely HIV," I replied, earnestly.

The Nips and the trader left in thinly veiled disgust, leaving me alone with Personnel-insect-thing.   He shuffled some papers and said:

"Mr Mallet. You've had your say but maybe you'd like to know a few things about Taiayobo Securities?"

"I'd rather be whipped, but I don't suppose that will stop you," I replied with a straight face. I was right. I left him to babble soothingly in the background as I retreated into a daydream.

"... Taiayobo was established in 1953 and has risen to be number seven in the league table of Japanese securities houses. We have six thousand employees and offices outside Japan in Hong Kong, London, New York, Paris, Milan and other major international financial centres. Our market capitalisation is..." It had a familiar ring to it. "... and we are leaders in the Japanese equity warrant market."

I knew they had no intention of hiring me and I could see little point in continuing the charade any further. I wasn't too upset. As far as I was concerned, the lot of them should've been nuked good and proper back in '45.

"So, Mr Mallet, you would be happy with the idea of working with Taiayobo?"

"Indeedy doody, Deputy Dawg! I can't think of anything more lovely," I said deliriously. Except sickle-cell trait.

"Well, we'll be getting in contact with you via, what's his name... Ian Pickering over the next couple of days and perhaps we can discuss salary and terms then."

And I was Frank Sinatra.

"Sure you will," I muttered to myself. "Call in the porcine air division!"

"Well, it's been nice meeting you Mr Mallet. Most interesting indeed."

I bet. I was happy with the deferential "Mr Mallet" peasant-to-squire address that he accorded me. I on the other hand addressed him by his first name, although I wasn't completely sure that it was the right one as I'd missed it when he'd introduced himself.

With that we concluded the meeting. Personnel person looked worse for wear. He saw me to the lift and extended his hand. I took it and raised it to my lips for a courtly kiss and minced off into the lift.

I swaggered out into the sunshine, feeling very much the man as I lit up a Marlboro Light. I spotted the cute piece of Japanese schtoink who'd given me a funny look when I'd been in the reception area. She was walking in my direction. I put on my sunglasses to look cool before she saw me. Easy peasy Japanesey, let me slip it up you, nice and sleazy. We smiled as we passed each other. I turned back.

"Excuse me," I said. "Do I know you?"

"Yes. I think so. Didn't you used to work for De Jenerette in New York?" She had a slick American accent.

"Nah. Wrong hunk. Nearest I've been to Wall Street is a four hour wait at JFK."

I took off my sunglasses and looked at her. I hoped my slight tan would have the effect of making my eyes, my only good feature, a mysterious shade of aquamarine. Her smile disconcertingly turned into a giggle. I asked if anything was wrong as her giggle mutated into hysterical laughter.

"You've still got your visitor's pass on!"

I looked down. Shit! How uncool! I blushed and hurriedly took it off.

"Your face rings a bell too," I fibbed, trying to regain my composure. "Maybe we met at a road show or some corporate bash."

"No. I thought it was New York. I'd know if it was here."

"Well, why don't we exchange business cards? If either of us remembers where we met, we can call the other one up," I said and then remembered that I didn't have a job. She looked in her handbag while I pretended to go through my pockets. She found a card and handed it to me.

"Damn!" I said. "I must have left mine back at the office."

I looked at hers. 'Teresa Batomata, Associate Director.'

Teresa? Not particularly Japanese.

"Japanese father, American mother," she said, perhaps to alleviate any confusion.

"Oh, I see," I said feeling relieved. I looked at her again. Apart from some spots that I could see through her make-up in the sunlight, she really was very cute. Not beautiful. Just very cute. In an ape-faced sort of way.

"Well Teresa, I'll pop my card in the post and if either of us thinks of anything, let's talk. Perhaps we can have lunch sometime, anyway."

She raised a quizzical eyebrow and then gave me a saucy wink. "Sure. I'll see you around."

Invitation or prophecy? She turned and wiggled her way back to the Taiayobo building.

Result! What a shag I'd so utterly buggered up the interview. I prayed she wouldn't make any enquiries about me with the Personnel dork. I was cheered that the morning hadn't been a complete write-off.

I suddenly felt tired. My Odor Eaters were slipping in my shoes. I needed to get away from the people and office blocks. I looked at the office lab rats scuttling back to their desks with their little bags of pastrami on rye. Busy. Busy. Busy. I turned and headed for the nearest sewer to take home. I got out at Alphabet Street Station, picked up a dozen Kronenbourgs from Weirdbins and some deep fried animal matter from Colonel Skidmark's and made my way to the flat.

My disposition was once again shattered when I got back by the stench of Mr Buenechea's rotting rubbish on the staircase. Mr Buenechea was the little Bolivian prick who rented the flat below. The Spaz from La Paz. He had a habit of leaving his garbage outside his front door to putrefy for days on end. Judging from the mail he got, he'd attended every business school in America, yet he still didn't have the gumption to take his trash down to the communal dustbins. He netted ten thousand a month at Credit Mayonnaise. I knew because I'd opened one of his pay slips when it came through the post one day. He was twenty-eight. What did he do with the money? I had left the occasional cryptic message on his door concerning the garbage to the effect that this was Kensington and not some downtown squat in Santa Cruz, but I could see that a stronger approach was necessary.

I spent a constructive afternoon composing a maniacal letter, carefully worded on Pan Asian Bank notepaper to look as though I was writing from on high. At the end of the afternoon and several Kronenbourgs later, I'd reached what I thought was the right pitch:

*Mr Buenechea,*

*Why are you being such a spastic about your rubbish? Is it that you think its aroma is so wonderful that you should share it with the other occupants of this building? I suspect not. I suspect it is because you are an ill-mannered individual who is too lazy and inconsiderate to carry it the short distance from your door to the dustbins by the basement. If this unacceptable behaviour continues you leave me with no alternative but to inform your employers of your total disregard for hygiene, your lack of consideration for others and request that you be repatriated to where you belong and where such unkempt and thoughtless behaviour is obviously the norm and deemed acceptable.*

I didn't sign it. With any luck, I thought, he wouldn't know who'd sent it. Unfortunately there was only one other tenant in the block, a quiet middle-aged doctor, so it was pretty obvious who it was from. I went down and sellotaped the note to his front door and resumed my position on the balcony. Ian Pickering woke me from my contemplations with a call at about five o'clock. I cursed myself for forgetting to put the answerphone on. He asked me how my interview with Taiayobo had gone.

"It was multiple," I replied. "They were a great bunch." Ian was relieved. He was about to give Taiayobo a call to hear their side of the story. I gulped and put down the phone. Ian was back in two minutes.

"No deal, James, I'm afraid. They thought there was no doubt that you could do the job, but for some reason they were a little worried that you wouldn't fit in." Too right I wouldn't.

"I'm sorry, Ian. I did my best. Pity, because they seemed such a cool team. I can't understand why they didn't ask me in for another look. Their loss, my toss I guess."

"Well, don't take it too badly; I've got you in next week with Redshields. You don't have any objections to them I assume?"

"Absolutely not. But who will I be seeing?"

"Initially the Head of Sales and then hopefully the Head of Trading and then, if they want to take it a stage further, the Managing Director."

"Groovy. Just as long as I don't have to see anyone from Personnel. Personnel officers, along with graduate trainees, have got to be the lowest forms of office life. What day?"

"Any day. When would suit you?"

"How about early Tuesday?"

"Should be OK - I'll confirm with you later the exact time and I'll brief you on what to say."

As I put the phone down I heard a fierce rap on the front door. I froze. *Holy sense of humour failures*! Oh no, it must be *The Spaz*! Frighty! I tried to get Petra, my rather shy lodger who was hiding in her bedroom to answer the door and say I was out, but she was having none of it. I timidly opened the door. The Spaz was holding my note.

"Hello," I said brightly, as if it was an old friend just dropping by.

"Did you do this?" he spat.

"Do what? Oh that. Yes, let me think... yes I think I might have done. Yes... actually yes... I definitely perhaps did it," I stammered.

"I can't believe how xenophobic and hateful you've been to me since I moved here. I never leave my rubbish out..."

I was taken aback by his cry of innocence in the wake of such overwhelming evidence to the contrary.

"...my maid leaves it out. She's Albanian and doesn't understand that the trash cans are kept down in the basement; that's all."

I didn't see how this had anything to do with the price of vaseline but in order to defuse the situation I went along with his logic. The things they must teach at Harvard.

When he finished I said, "OK. Well, whoever leaves it out, I wish they'd take it away. I'm trying to sell my flat and rotting rubbish cluttering up the common parts doesn't help. I'm sorry about my note - treat it with the contempt it deserves - but please try to co-ordinate something with your maid so that the refuse makes its way to the dustbins."

He grunted, turned and left. Such manners! A perfect Credit Mayonnaise specimen!


Roxanne arrived back from South Africa the following morning. She had been due back a few days earlier but there had been some complications with her ticket. I had thought about meeting her at Gatwick but decided I didn't love her enough. Nonetheless, it was good to have her back.

"It's your kissin' that I've been missin'," she said, as we took our clothes off and got into bed.

It wasn't the best session that we'd ever had and I noticed that we weren't able to co-ordinate our gyrations with our usual level of syncopation. I thought nothing of it. When we went back for fecund helpings an hour later, everything was fine. Roxanne didn't have much news considering she'd been halfway round the world and back.

I yammered on about my interviews and all the bastards who'd turned me away. I noticed her attention wandering and so I went out to get the papers. I couldn't put my finger on anything, but I had a sneaking suspicion that Roxanne was beginning to tire of my redundancy, however adamant she was that this wasn't the case. She said she didn't give a shit what I did or didn't do for a living. As far as she was concerned, she used to say, I was perfect and it was them -the world at large - who'd got it wrong.

I had a wedding to go to myself the following weekend. I only knew the nuptial couple vaguely and was surprised to have been invited. Both were rich, unattractive and ideally suited. I took a bus that had been laid on for the occasion from London and sat next to Albert Carr on the way down. He'd been drinking for most of the morning and was already doing aeroplanes before we set off. He'd taken the precaution of bringing a bottle of whisky to complete the effect. The bus driver thoughtfully stopped at a pub en route to add to Albert's alcoholic carnage.

We arrived at our destination and were dropped outside the church. There were a good six hundred or so people inside. The church had been built for a village parish and was too small for such a large gathering. There was nowhere to sit, so Albert and I stood at the back. Albert gazed in wonderment at the overstuffed pews and their unhappy occupants and said, a little too loudly to be funny:

"We can't *all* have slept with her."

The service started. The bride swept down the aisle like a lace hovercraft. A flotilla of frilly Daleks followed self-importantly in delta formation. The hymns were the usual motley selection of nineteenth century mantras, more in homage to Empire than Christian value. I looked around but all I could see was hats.

Halfway through St Paul's address to the Corinthians I began to regret the stop at the pub on the way down. The bride and groom exchanged their vows and disappeared to sign the register. The choir stood up and treated the assembled throng to a descant of pious birdsong. The signing took forever. I was entertaining the theory that the nuptial couple were illiterate when they reappeared, beaming as if they'd just been to lavatory. My bladder tweaked in envy.

The choir shut up and sat down abruptly. In their stead a sanctimonious-looking woman in a twinset and pearls stood up and in a quavering warble delivered a menopausal aria before the Wedding March mercifully took over, signalling the end of the ceremony.

A rickety procession of genial old walnuts, smiling idiotically, shuffled past at a funereal pace. I started to shake. I saw a side door by the vestry and made my exit unnoticed. Morning dew was not the only refreshment on the grave of Arthur Muswould, dearly beloved husband of Alice, that day.

The reception was a marquee affair at the bride's parents' gopping great mansion nearby. There was a mutton-chopped Master of Ceremonies in a huntsman uniform at the entrance to the marquee who bellowed the name of each guest in elaborate baritone. I noticed he had a Gorbachev-style port stain on his forehead. Albert rather childishly gave his name as 'Mr Iggy Pop' . Everyone looked round when he was called. Albert turned and glared accusingly at the announcer who, realising his mistake shot back a look that bristled with the class hatred of a millennium.

Albert and I became separated. I couldn't see anyone I knew at first. I took a glass of champagne and spotted Fenella Fellon, the society beauty, in the crowd. She looked immaculate, her couture capturing the essence of her freshness and untouchability. Audrey Hepburn with tits. She moved, a swan among the ducks. I caught snatches of matronly conversation as I wandered about looking for someone to talk to.

"... of course we were going to put Henry down for Ratminster but with this wretched AIDS epidemic they've got there we've had to think again..."

A waiter re-charged my glass. I turned and nearly knocked over Fenella Fellon.

"I'm sorry Fenella," I said, with genuine concern and added quickly, "... you look absolutely... absolutely..." but I couldn't think of a word that could do her justice, "... blemishless."

Her face broke into a smile that nearly made me faint.

"Oh thank you! You are sweet! Sorry. I don't know your name. I know we've met somewhere."

We had by then met several times, but there was no reason for her to commit my existence to memory. What possible use could I be to her?

"I think we've crossed once or twice at Annabel Dribble's," I said.

"Oh, that's right," she said. "How clever of you to remember."

As if I could have forgotten.

We spoke for a moment before an off-duty polo-playing god caught her attention and she moved on. It didn't matter. The closest I would ever get to seeing her undergarments would be if I followed her maid to the dry cleaners.

I picked up an unattended glass of champagne and drank it quickly before going in search of a waiter to fill my own. I nodded to one or two people I knew and finally joined a group of balding bachelors who'd commandeered a case of champagne and were heartily toasting their grossly exaggerated sex lives. Albert Carr had appointed himself in charge of braying.

"Apart from Fenella Fellon, the designer vagina - who as usual isn't taking any deposits this weekend - the standard of schtoink here is appalling. Anything half decent has got to be as rare as rocking horse shit."

"I don't know, Albert," one of the other men said, "I'm sure you could get one of the bridesmaids to oblige."

"I've already blown that one," Albert said with a satisfied smile. "I had a word in the ear of the littlest one on the way into church and told her the only reason why we were all there was because her mummy had gone up to Heaven to meet Baby Jesus. *Silly mite*! Her mother was standing right behind her, but that didn't stop the little brat from bawling her eyes out for the rest of the service!"

I had a few glasses with them before I went people-spotting again. The drink and effort of standing up was making me tired. I suddenly felt peculiarly drunk and then I remembered that I hadn't eaten anything all day. I went in search of some profiteroles to give me ballast and noticed Katie Cutress standing alone and made straight for her. I had an old score to settle. I knew Katie had colluded with Christine Hale on proceedings that had led to my eviction from Christine's life. I also knew that she was recovering from a particularly unpleasant miscarriage that she'd had a few weeks before.

"Well *hello,* Katie," I effused, with as much artificial warmth as I could muster.

"Hello James," Katie responded, looking uncomfortable.

I held my smile and tried to look pleasant.

"Had any more dead babies recently?" I enquired, affably.

At that moment her husband made an untimely appearance and I was obliged to make myself scarce before I had time to savour her reaction. I went into the main house in search of a lavatory. There were lots of paintings everywhere with posey little lights above them, as if the pictures were *that* good. I eventually found a loo and took a piss.

When I got back there was a loud tapping sound. The toastmaster prayed silence and announced the first of the speakers.

A crone got up and told some unamusing anecdotes about the bride and her family. I looked around at the other guests. I felt a bit common. Everyone seemed to be called 'Rupert' or 'Imogen'. There must have been five per cent of the country's GNP under the marquee that afternoon. Centuries of inter-breeding and fleecing the proletariat had left them with an air of constipated detachment.

Once the crone had finished, the bride's father got up to have a spout. Deferential 'hear-hears' followed the end of each sentence. Eventually he stood down and let the drip of a best man have a go. The groom looked indulgently at his gormless new acquisition. A dog is for life. The best man banged on unconvincingly about what lads he and the groom had been in the past. Twenty minutes later the guests were ordered to raise their empty glasses and toast the bridesmaids. The cake was cut, symbolising the bride's imminent defilement, and then it was all over bar the shrieking.

It had been a loveless event, devoid of any depth; a contract of convenience between two cosseted individuals to perpetuate their mutual opulence and ease of existence.

The bride and groom changed and then came down to fight their way through the storm of confetti and inebriated well-wishing. Albert tried to climb into the boot of their limousine and had to be restrained by the bride's father. Albert mistook him for the chauffeur and called him a cunt.

It was time to go home before Albert had a social fatwah placed on him for ever. We hung around a bit longer, making astringent comments about the remaining guests before hurrying to catch the bus as it was pulling out of the drive. I looked back at the house and wondered how it was, that the more elaborate the wedding, the more naff it was likely to be.

Halfway back to London we stopped at a burger joint for sustenance and urinary relief. Albert by this point was doing his 'Toxic Avenger' impression and tried to start a fight with a group of Hell's Angels, but they appeared bored, if not saddened by his drunken hectoring. Eventually one of the wedding party took Albert by the arm and escorted him back to the bus.

We arrived in London and went our separate ways, I had been witness to another milestone in two other people's lives. A snapshot of bunting and fantasy, frozen, unlike its subjects, in time forever. A big day for two minuscule components of the universe and a litany of false hope for the charlatans in attendance.

The weather reverted to being grey and became as cold as charity. During the day I was reduced to masturbating every two minutes just to keep warm. I was now beating the bishop with such white-knuckled ferocity that it had started to go septic. Roxanne and I went into our customary social hibernation of suppers in front of the television and weekends surrounded by newspapers. I became more despondent and short-tempered as each morning brought another batch of rejection letters. I had one quite promising reply from Bank of Chicago who wrote to say that I was on their shortlist of possible candidates and that they would get back to me in due course to arrange an interview. I never heard from them again.

Crystal Frost later told me that Patrick "Dumper" Ballingall, who happened to be Head of Sales there, and of course had been an erstwhile admirer of hers, had binned my application as it crossed his desk. Thanks Patrick. Another public school knife job. He'd always loathed me since I had pipped him at the post with Crystal, although at the time I wasn't aware of his animosity . Crystal told me he had never had a chance with her after he blocked her loo with an enormous ferret. It had lurked there for a week before she'd summoned the courage to chop it up with a bent coat hanger and flush it away. Enough to put anyone off, I suppose. Fat tit. I'd tried to placate Patrick's envy some time after Crystal had originally told me about his jealousy, and even asked him to supper with Crystal's bat-like sister. We went to a nightclub afterwards but he'd forgotten his wallet and I got clobbered with the bill. For every ten pounds I'd been earning, he'd been earning a hundred. The financially astute can be amazingly forgetful at times.

The interview with Redshields went well and they asked me back to meet the Managing Director the following week. I duly presented myself at the appointed time. The Managing Director sported a grey bouffant and was standing with his chest puffed out as I went into his office. He resembled a regency dandy, but for his cheesy Rolex and Armani spectacles. I looked at the photograph of his trophy wife or daughter on his desk and watched him talk for a bit. My attention became more focused when he started dropping names, on the assumption that if he was out to impress me, then I must be worth impressing. He told me that the company had been formed under his stewardship on the directive of Lord Redshield, who owned half of France and a couple of ski resorts and was, he added, "a most delightful man." I remarked, perhaps unwisely, that with his sort of money even I could be "a most delightful man".

The Koreans, whom I'd almost forgotten, kept me on hold, but just when I was about to write them off, I got a call Mr Kim to say he'd received the green light from the Head Office in Seoul to hire me. *Eureka*! At last I'd found someone with the requisite lack of common sense to take me on. Great! Once I had some money coming in again I could go back to drinking in earnest.

I went to see Redshields a few more times. They got to the 'ho-hum' stage when the Managing Director with the over-washed hair decided to flake at the last moment. I wasn't unduly put out. They didn't have much to offer and weren't quite the gentlemen's club they thought they were. Like everywhere else. That left me with the Koreans, which was better than nothing. Just.

# Chapter 10: The Chipmunks

I signed the contract with the Koreans and started work the following week. I was given a staff handbook in Korean hieroglyphics and told to keep it close at hand along with my copy of the company song. It was good, after nine months, to have a desk to put my feet on as I contemplated how best to achieve an acceptable level of mediocrity within my new workplace.

I wasn't allowed to take any dealing positions and so doing any dealing was virtually impossible. Furthermore, it wasn't in the Korean character to communicate to foreigners. No one spoke to me for days or told me what was going on. It suited me fine. The vital matters that were discussed with such brio by my Korean colleagues in the conference room each day remained a mystery. Mr Park, the Managing Director, insisted that I gave him a review on the state of the markets each morning and an activity report of what I'd been doing prior to leaving the office in the evening. The morning review was no trouble as I just taped 'Dawn Raiders' on Radio Nerdo as I got into the bath each morning and wrote it out in long-hand before I left for work. After a while I stopped doing even that when I realised no one read it. I rotated half a dozen different reports and changed the date at the top each day. No one seemed to notice.

The daily activity report presented a bit more of a problem. As I did nothing but make personal phone calls all day, I had to make it up as I went along. I spun out frightfully important events that never happened. The Koreans spoke in "chopstick" the whole time, generating enormous mounds of paper but no actual business, while I was left to my own devices. I fabricated fictitious deals that I always seemed to miss by a hair's breadth and mandates I was just about to clinch, which somehow never actually materialised. Always at the cutting edge but never quite drawing blood. Occasionally Mr Park called me in to his office and asked me to explain some point that had caught his eye. I would reply in some long-winded financial Esperanto that he couldn't possibly understand, and then would ask to be excused on the pretext of closing some big deal, leaving Mr Park looking dazed and confused. I knew from my Pan Asian days that it would be contrary to Oriental habit for him to chance his "face" enough to question me in any more detail. After a month he gave up.

It didn't take me long to come to the conclusion that I was only there to pad out a labour law requirement. There was no point trying to be a one man broker, so I concentrated on mastering a computer game on the PC. I occasionally endeavoured to dream up ways of playing on the company's strengths, but there weren't any beyond being Korean and having a silly name. Once or twice I tried to whip up interest in European products in Korea and Korean products in Europe. I got no response out of the Head Office in Seoul and as far as the European investing public was concerned, Korea might as well have been a moon of Saturn for all the business enthusiasm I generated.

Being back at work gave me the confidence to call Teresa Batamato, the Japanese-American doll at Taiayobo and ask her out to lunch. We agreed to meet at some nouvelle cuisine nightmare on Fenchurch Street. I felt a bit unhinged on the day and hoped that she wouldn't notice that my shoes didn't match.

I waited at the bar until she turned up. I saw Uri Rimlicher, who I knew from my Parker Barrow days talking to a small group of Scandinavian types. He saw me and waved.

"Hi, James! How's it going?"

"OK Uri. How about you?"

"Ask me next week when my bonus comes through, ha!"

He always was *so* interesting. 'Eighties scum. Teresa arrived, looking the epitome of chic: Chanel suit and Hermes handbag, makeup perfect and eyes twinkling with self-assurance. We were shown to our table. I nodded to Pete Divis, my pet head-hunter, who happened to be sitting nearby. He gave me a collusive wink in deference to my lunch companion. Teresa and I sat down and we started to chat.

Teresa turned out to be an easy conversationalist but I soon felt out of my depth. Not only was she a pleasure to look at but she was also indecently witty and articulate. In four languages. Suddenly my two hundred metres breast stroke certificate seemed rather unimportant. She smoked, knocked back her drinks and laughed. There was nothing to dislike about her, except the gradual realisation that having lunch with me was, as far as she was concerned, a minor inconvenience to be endured; a charity run. We worshipped different gods. Hers came from job satisfaction and the rewards that came with it. Mine came from a bottle. She was go-ahead and thrusting. I'd put my thrusting days behind me. With her intellect and work ethic she was able to make her employers five million dollars a year. I was lucky if I had ever made a tenth of that. She was, not surprisingly, very corporate and talked about her 'crients' as if they were intimate friends which, I subsequently heard on the grapevine, was not far from the truth. I asked her out a couple of times after that, but she was always busy with her 'crients'.

It was during our last conversation that I realised I was barking up the wrong Bonsai and handling goods that I couldn't afford. I asked Teresa to a Billy Joel concert in a last ditch attempt to appear cool.

"Billy Jowl? That spiv? Jesus Christ! You must be joking! He's about as hip as rheumatoid arthritis," she laughed. She was about to take a week's vacation in Honolulu before going on to New York to see some of her infernal 'crients'.

"You live in a different world," I said obsequiously. "It's all so jet-set and glamorous."

"That's what you get from working hard, James," she said, reprovingly.

"Yes," I concurred. "*And* I don't have a vagina to fall back on."

I never heard from her again. I thought she missed the point. Perhaps I should have said "pretty face" instead of "vagina". The incident was not important in itself, but it proved what I had already suspected. I'd lost the edge. What had worked well a decade previously was now tired and obsolete. A brilliant start was turning into a disastrous end of term. It was all part of the package of The Curse. What had once been so full of promise was no longer perceived as a going concern. It had happened so quickly. I contemplated ways of reversing the trend, but I couldn't think of anything. It was too late. I was too set in my ways. Bachelordom and dissipation had set in for good. The dog, knowing its limitations, couldn't be bothered with any new tricks. It was no longer a question of decline. Only the rate of descent was now at stake.

Soon after I'd joined the Koreans, Justin Game, an old Conmax colleague who'd been part of David Hobson's job putsch, called me to ask for a bid for some Korean bonds he had to sell. I spoke to Mr Loon, my esteemed Head of Trading, and asked him if he would show the bonds to our counterparts in our Seoul office. He replied with a simple, if slightly chilling, "No" and resumed reading his newspaper with the same air of quiet logic as a dog lapping water from a lavatory bowl. Not "What price?" Just "No". Even if the bonds were free, the Head Office wouldn't have been able to place them. I wondered why they bothered being in the market. If the Koreans weren't prepared to invest in their own companies, it was difficult to see how anyone else could be expected to. I questioned what Kowshat or any of the other Korean security houses were doing in London. It was, after all, a professional and competitive market that was already hopelessly over-broked.

The Korean authorities had, just at that point, been magnanimous enough to open their stock market to foreigners. It had promptly hit the floor. Nobody in his right mind would touch it. The process of investing in Korea was complicated and bound in red tape. A dozen separate transactions were necessary to execute a single order. To add to the mayhem, corruption there was rampant and the stock exchange was rigged. The authorities were somewhat taken aback when nobody wanted to invest in Korea, as investors looked to the more remunerative markets available elsewhere in the East.

I'd been in the company for a couple of months when I awoke at home one morning knowing that something was going to go wrong that day. I'd been unwell the previous evening and had spent half the night curled around the lavatory. I got up in a daze and made a pot of coffee without thinking what I was doing. I made it far too strong and was twitching like a severed limb by the second cup. I was practically entering an epileptic fit on the third, when it was time to leave for work.

As I left the flat I saw a middle-aged bag in a puffa jacket taking her dog for a dawn crap. The pooch was sniffing at my doorstep as I closed the front door. It started barking at me for no reason, as all dogs did when I was around. I loathed dogs in London. To me they were just four-legged jobbie machines and I hated their owners even more. As I stepped onto the pavement I could see that the mutt was about to assume the familiar strained squatting position associated with canine defecation. I felt a rage coming on.

"If that fucking thing shits anywhere near my doorstep I'll kick it to death," I said, as viciously as possible to its owner.

The woman looked at me in disgust and replied in a haughty voice, "It's been trained not to."

"Well, it must be you that's doing it," I said spitefully, turning on my heel.

"You've no right to talk to me like that," she said, her voice cutting through the peace of the early morning, but cutting no ice with me.

"So what are you going to do about it, you old witch?" I shouted over my shoulder.

I felt a bit guilty as I walked away, and mildly rebuked myself for being such a bully. I'd never have had the audacity to be so rude to a man. If the dog's owner had been younger or prettier I would probably have stopped, patted the brute on the head and offered to let it take a dump on the hallway carpet. I never saw the woman or her dog again. Occasionally, there was some method in my madness. Half the world brought their dogs for a dump in my street. The road sweeper must have wept whenever it was Devon Gardens day.

I got out at Moorgate tube and passed some students loafing outside the City Business School. My taxes were going towards their education. Education that would ultimately render what few qualifications I had obsolete. With any luck, I mused bitterly, there wouldn't be any businesses left for them to go to by the time they matriculated.

As soon as I arrived at the office the phone went.

"Bonds 'r' Us. How can I help?" I enquired, perkily.

It was First California Securities. A voice asked me if I had access to any bonds for Dickwoo Corporation, a Korean conglomerate and indicated the sort of size and price he was looking for. I couldn't believe my luck! Out of the blue someone was at last buying some Korean paper! I got on the phone immediately and spoke to the Head Trader in the Seoul office. I said that I had a potential buyer in London and gave him the details of the issue. I gave no indication of the price and size at that point. I thought it would only confuse the matter. He called me back and said that he'd found a seller of a million of the same issue in Hong Kong at 98½. I told him my buyer was looking to purchase a similar size at around 97½. I said that I'd work on trying to up the bid if the Seoul office could endeavour to talk down the offering price from their end.

I reported back to First California Securities and said their price was on the low side. I suggested that 98 would be a more workable level. They said they'd think about it and get back to me. Five minutes later the trader in Seoul called me up and proudly informed me that he'd bought the million at 98½ and now it was up to me to sell them.

"What?" I shrieked. "I said I had a potential buyer. That was all. At no point did I issue any instructions to buy the bonds, and if I had it certainly would not have been at that ridiculous level, you lemonhead!"

"You tell me to buy the bonds," he said defensively. "Now you sell them."

"Listen, Fartsworth," I said, "I did not have a firm order and I certainly have no intention or capacity to sell those bonds at the price you bought them. You sell them back to whoever ripped you off in the first place. There's no trade as far as I'm concerned. Who's the seller anyway?"

"First California, Hong Kong."

"That's just wonderful. My buyer is First California, London. So we've just managed to screw ourselves up the arse and lose ten thousand bucks in the process. You turd biscuit. Are you off your meds? This is not my mistake, do you hear? I had no fucking intention of buying those bonds at that level. I can't understand how you could've misread me when I gave no price, amount or settlement details along with all the other stuff that passes off as established procedure. You're nuts!"

I called Wally Barker, who was now working at Korean Banking Corporation, and explained my predicament. He thought for a bit and then said he was sorry but he had no use for a million at that point, especially at that level. He said he could pay 97 for a fiver, i.e. five million and swap it out, but that was about it.

I called back Seoul and told the Head Trader that we definitely had a problem. I got an indignant response:

"But you say you could sell them."

"No I didn't, you prick. Not at your price. What planet are you apes on? For goodness' sake get a grip. We're going to hold on to those bonds till either the market picks up or we find a buyer at the right price. We can hedge them for the time being or repo them out or, failing that, just fund them for a couple of months, ride the coupon and still make money. It's not the end of the world."

"We can't take position," he said triumphantly. "We have to sell today."

"Oh rah, rah, Rasputin! If we sell today, it'll be at a loss and the company will be ten thousand bucks down. If we can hold on for a few more days we may be able to dig ourselves out of this mess with a bit of dignity. I assume our company is happy with the name of the stock? Dickwoo's just about the largest company in Korea and it's only for a million bucks for fuck's sake. That's not exactly a mammoth position."

I rang off in despair and called Wally Barker again. Wally was pretty astute. I knew he'd give me an honest view on what to do and perhaps even warehouse the bonds until I found a buyer. He'd done some homework since we'd last spoken.

"James," he said, "I hate to tell you, but Mani Hani have got a block of the issue - five million I think - going at 97½. I might buy yours at that level, but obviously there's no way that I can pay eight and a half. I'd buy up all Mani Hani's but I can't take the size at their price but, if it helps, I'll buy your position."

Mr Loon opposite me had, in the meantime, been having a heated diatribe in chopstick with the trader in Seoul. When he put down the phone I explained the latest development. I told him that we had the option to sell our one million at a loss or we could buy Mani Hani's five million at 97½ and with a little luck, I could sell both lots on to First California London at 98, without raising their suspicion that most of the bonds were coming out of London rather than the Far East. I could then cover the loss on the million and still come out with twenty thousand dollars profit in the bank.

I went downstairs to Café Grebo to get a Coke and cool down but I got stuck behind some zombie from outer space ordering sandwiches for half the universe and had to give up. I came back into the dealing room a few minutes later to overhear Mr Loon talking in his anachronistically polite but broken English.

"Hello? Mr Harcourt? It's Loon here from Kowshat. How are you? Yes? Good. Good. I understand you have interest in US dorrar bonds for Dickwoo Corporation. Yes. I have one million to sell at 98 ½... I see... I see... you no want? I see... I see. OK, Mr Harcourt. Solly to trouble you Mr Harcourt. Thank you velly much, thank you. Goodbye Mr Harcourt." I felt another rage coming on.

"I can't believe what I've just heard Mr Loon," I said, as coolly as possible. I continued, "Mr Harcourt? Is that Mr Harcourt from Mani Hani?"

"Yes," said Mr Loon, matter-of-factly, his face a picture of unblinking stupidity.

"You spermhead! Why are you showing our one million at 98½ to Harcourt when you know perfectly well he's got five to go at 97½. It makes no sense, for crying out loud!"

"It is important to improve our relationship with Manufacturers Hanover," he replied, resolutely.

"Mr Loon. You are such a dicksplash. Mr Barker at Korean Banking Corporation told me Mani Hani's position in strictest confidence and you go and blow the whole thing by offering bonds back to the seller a point higher than where he's selling them. Just what drugs are you on?"

"Mr Harcourt my friend," said Mr Loon, his voice beginning to adopt the wavering pitch of confrontation peculiar to smaller rodents.

"Like fuck he is. Mr Harcourt's everyone's friend. He's even my friend and I haven't got many these days. He's still a fat tub of guts and doing such an arsehole thing with price sensitive information is not going to help our case, Mr Loon," I said, trying to retain my cool. "If he sees a Korean house showing bonds at 98½ he's going to think he's doing something wrong showing bonds at 97½. It's just going to ramp the price up and my friend Mr Barker is never going to speak to you, me or any of the other vaginal rejects in this company ever again. Do you think that's really good for business, Mr Loon?"

"If the price go up we make money."

"Oh Mr Loon, you're such a big swinging Richard!"

"We make money mean Head Office will be velly happy."

"No, you silly cunt, it means Mani Hani will raise their price and still no one will buy their bonds and Mr Barker, First California and I will be out of trade as a result of your fat, stupid mouth. Bugger our million. That's history. Dead. Gone. No more. Kaput. What I want is to get the other five million working and repair some of the damage you little fucks have done to the company's profit and loss account."

"Mr Mallet, please calm down."

"No, Mr Loon, I won't calm down. What you did was unprofessional, unethical and downright stupid. Even by Korean standards you've managed to excel yourself with this almost Napoleonic act of wankerdom. You've made us and the company look complete idiots. You should consider yourself lucky that I'm such a nice, reasonable person because if there was anyone else standing here you'd have this telephone rammed halfway up your bottom by now."

"I have good friend at Korean Banking Corporation who say he will pay at 98."

"OK fist-fuck," I said. "Go ahead and sell them at 98 if you can, although why he would want to buy them at 98 when he knows he can get as many as he wants from Mani Hani at 97½ beats me."

Like most Koreans, Mr Loon had a simple approach to business. He assumed that by taking people to lunch they would automatically deal with him. The Japanese had done much the same twenty years before when they first opened their London offices and showered everybody with hideous corporate gifts at every conceivable opportunity.

Mr Loon called one of his compatriots at Korean Banking Corporation and launched into a semi-automatic torrent of foreign nonsense. I called up Wally and came clean about Mr Loon's market meanderings. Wally laughed. I told him Mr Loon was talking to his Korean counterpart as we spoke and trying to get him to pay 98.

"He won't," Wally said, "because I won't let him!"

"Good boy," I said, "and in the meantime, could you send me a fax reprimanding the firm for our breathtaking stupidity and abuse of trust in using information that you told to me in confidence. Really spank our little bottoms - get my drift?"

"Sure," Wally said. "I'll get down to it right away."

With that we hung up and I tried to think who I could show our position to, now that the matter had become so public. There were precious few people interested in Korean bonds. I had until the end of the day to get rid of them. I phoned up a trader at Merrills who knew a little about the Korean market, but he said he couldn't pay more than 97½, and that was on a favour basis. By then, my original buyer, First California London, had got wind of Mani Hani's bonds and had dealt directly with them, icing me out of the deal.

Mr Loon finished his conversation and put down his phone.

"Well?" I said.

"He pay only 97½."

"Of course he pay only 97½, you dopey arsehole. It's time you guys got into the real world."

Although Mr Loon was technically my superior, I knew he was a coward and afraid of me. Half my insults were lost on him anyway, but he must have got the gist of what I was getting at. Poor little turd. He was only trying to help.

We sold our bonds at the end of the day to Korean Banking Corporation at 97½ and took our ten thousand hit manfully. It was no big deal but it wiped out any of the gains that I had made previously. It was just annoying in that it was all so unnecessary. Mr Park, the Managing Director, called me into his office at the end of the day and told me to "write three page report" on the incident. All reports had to be three pages. I was lucky that the little jerks hadn't asked me for a graph, which was their other trick. I went home wondering whether it was worth continuing with them. It was only a matter of time before they sacked me. It was a depressing existence with nothing better to do than endure the white noise of their incessant chatter all day. Working for a bank was bad enough, but working for a Korean bank was the pits. It was like living in a psychiatric ward.

When I got home matters were not enhanced by a message on my answering machine from the local council. As a courtesy, they said, they were calling to inform me that the space where my car was parked was being dug up and my car had been taken away. I looked out of the window. *Holy parking bay suspensions*! One side of the road was completely carless. I took a deep breath and decided against punching the wall.

I walked round to the car pound and paid my ninety pounds and the VAT they'd thoughtfully tacked on. The day would come, I could see, when I'd have to pay VAT on Christine's Curse. I saw a lot of summonses with Devon Gardens on them. I spoke to the old black dude behind the counter. He must have had to deal with more lost tempers in one day than anyone in the world.

"How many cars did they scoop on that road job in Devon Gardens?"

"I'm afraid I'm not allowed to say, sir."

"You're having a laugh, aren't you? Go on, give us a clue... thirty... forty?"

"Something like that, I would guess sir."

Oh rock on! Three cheers for the Royal Borough! Four thousand pounds for a morning's work. Not bad. Let's go out and dig up some more roads, boys! We can all be millionaires by lunchtime! I debated whether to write a deranged letter to the local MP and complain about such obvious extortion, but then thought better of it. There was no point. I'd never get my money back, although writing outraged letters to people in authority was fast becoming a major pastime of mine. I thought of all the instances when I had scrimped and saved; ten pence here, twenty pence there. Taking a bus instead of a taxi. Going for the two-for-the-price-of-one specials. Then the council, bless them, the very people I paid to protect my interests, go and shaft me. Like I really needed it.

I called Roxanne when I got back home from the car pound. She wasn't in. I didn't want to see her in my current mood anyway, so I sat alone with a bottle of wine in front of the television and watched some working class people getting stroppy with each other till I fell asleep.

I was woken up some time after ten by the phone. I picked it up.

"Party switchboard, operator James speaking," I said despondently.

It was Chris Seymour, a scruffy pigeon I knew who ran a small public relations company. He came straight to the point. He was looking for someone to help him raise money and general interest for a charity event his company was involved with. He asked whether I'd be interested in helping him with the project and some other ideas that he had in the pipeline. High finance indeed! I explained that I was tied up with the chipmunks but that I was coming to the end of my tether. He said that there was no hurry but, if I was interested in joining him, to let him know. There were a number of ex-public school dinosaurs involved in fund-raising and charity sponsorship at around that time. Why not me?

The next morning I was called into Mr Park's office to hand in my report on the previous day's fuck-up. I had written it in the style of a Shakespearean tragedy. I inadvertently handed it to him upside down. Mr Park looked through it thoughtfully without turning it round. I explained in simple language that there had been a breakdown in communication which had been compounded by the company's gutlessness in not taking a contingency position till we sorted things out.

"Head Office no like to speculate, Mr Mallet; Head Office velly conservative."

"Head Office also velly stupid, Mr Park. If they could hold a position for more than five minutes without running around like headless dicks they might, heaven forbid, actually make some money one day."

It wasn't surprising that their grammar never improved the way I spoke to them. For the sake of appearances I apologised for the incident. No more was said about the matter although I knew that all my Korean colleagues secretly held me responsible for the episode.

I went back to the playpen-sized dealing room. Mr Kim did his ten o'clock fart without fanfare. I sometimes wondered whether Mr Kim was personally responsible for the state of the ozone layer. Mr Lee coughed, hawked and then gobbed gracefully into his wastepaper basket. My thoughts cast themselves back wistfully thirty years to my James Bond Dinky car with its ejectable Korean. I phoned Pete Divis at his recruitment agency and told him to get back on my case as quickly as possible. He told me to fabricate a new 'Charlie Victor' for him immediately and we agreed to meet at 'The White Sock' for a nerve-steadying drink at lunch time. It was the worst pub in the world but I rather liked it.

I got there at one and saw Pete at the bar. I elbowed my way through the swamp of foreign exchange dealers with their pints of lager top and grabbed Pete by the arm. We got our drinks and made our way to a semi-quiet corner. I told Pete about my predicament and together we assessed the situation. I could have gone on for another two months before I either went mad or the chipmunks expelled me from their den, or I could resign now and feel quite good about it. Pete responded with the usual head-hunters' spiel about it being easier to find another job while in work. I didn't totally agree with him. All the time I'd been at Conmax I'd looked for other jobs and nothing had come up. As far as I was concerned, I was unemployable whether I was in work or out. I told him I'd been toying with the idea of chucking it all in, selling the flat and going back to Goa for as long as it took. Getting cute in Calangute.

"Oh, that's a really smart career move, James," Pete slammed in, crossly. "It's daft, or whatever comes after daft. You'd be better off organising a whoring expedition round the ports of East Africa if you want to do something really sensible. Come on, James. This is life. This ain't no dress rehearsal. It's all about staying on the heap and being part of the game. There's no time to wallow in the mire. If you're not happy with working for the dog-gobblers, you've got to try somewhere else. Nobody ever got rich by watching TV, James. What are you trying to be? The Patron Saint of Unemployment? The whole world's a circus... don't you be the clown. Have you tried Lemmings? Apparently they're on a hiring drive."

"No. They make you do a handwriting test. I doubt if my DTs would pass muster. I couldn't work for a company that believed in such balderdash. Besides, I only have to look at a picture of their fat slob of a chairman and I start to feel quite violent. Silly git refuses to do a handwriting test himself, of course. And they say that he's tipped to be the next Lord Mayor. It's no wonder the town's in a mess."

"What about the Americans? Organ Manly are looking for..."

"Pete, don't make me puke," I cut in, abruptly. "I think I'd almost rather work for the Japs than the Yanks. Parker Barrow was bad enough with all the deranged Harvard Business School jerks calling meetings just as you're about to put your coat on and go home. Or holding pointless weekend seminars just to bugger up what's left of your social life. All so that the little pricks can have someone to spew their silly half-baked ideas to. Organ Manly's worse, with their closed-circuit TVs trained on you all day and their stupid fucking microphones under your desk. It's all so sneaky-beaky and unnecessary. I wish they'd all grow up one day. As far as I'm concerned Americans are living proof that Mexicans used to fuck buffalos."

"Old joke - but good. So where would you like to work, James? You don't like the Yanks or the Brits. You can't stand the Japs and, as far as I can see, you're making a complete dog's breakfast, literally, of the Koreans."

"I must admit I'm at a bit of a loss as to who to turn to," I said dispiritedly. "I don't suppose you know any Australian banks? I've always had a soft spot for the Ockers and..."

Pete suddenly smacked his head in the middle of my flow.

"James, while we're on the subject did you know Billy Mytton while you were at Conmax?"

"Sure I did. Old bugger. Worked at BorDom before. He'd only been at Conmax for a couple of months before the bloody thing folded, poor sod."

"Yeah? Well not that I'm one to gossip, but have I a trunk load of shit for you: he topped himself last Sunday."

"He what?"

"Did a hosepipe job in his car."

"Stupid fuck; he'd have only been out of work for less than a year. That's nothing these days... happens to everyone."

"Well, that's just the point you see, James. You said "old bugger". That was the problem. No one said he couldn't do his job properly, but employers in their wisdom want to hire adolescents. They want a clean slate... something that hasn't been scribbled on so they can apply their own graffiti. They claim that youth is naturally more energetic, creative and flexible, and they want next year's model now. Of course it's all claptrap dreamt up by Human Resources departments to provide a respectable cover for the truth - that employers prefer youngsters because they come cheap and they're less likely to complain. They want earnest graduate trainees or mini-skirted schtoink, but above all what they really want is conformity. Only the naive need apply.

"Billy Mytton didn't have any of those qualities. It was the system that got him. He had a big mortgage, a wife and two veg... there was no way he was going to get a job at his age in this economic climate, or any other climate for that matter. He'd become, to re-coin a phrase, Mytton dressed as lamb. I guess it all finally proved too much for him. So before you start poncing around with your esoteric ideas about selling your flat, dropping out and going for another jolly around India smoking funny cigarettes, remember you may not be an 'old bugger' yet but we all have to take our turn at the table sometime. And for some of us, that's not so far away. If you don't want to end up middle-aged and washed up with only a box of Kleenex for company, I'd start pulling a finger out double quick before it's too late."

"Yeah. You know you're growing old when the rent boys start to look so young," I said, in an attempt to lighten the conversation.

"Can't you be serious for a moment, James? Could we have a little reality here perhaps?"

"OK," I said dejectedly. "But you know it's not my strong point."

"Have you tried calling Errol Slush at Grabon? He gave Charlie Neville a job."

"No," I replied. "He may have given Charlie a job but to me he's hardly the embodiment of human kindness. He wouldn't look at me. He's another method wanker. I might get in the way of his complacency..."

"Well don't let your complacency get in the way of your objectives, James," Pete remonstrated, sharply. "Don't alienate The Alien! It's a sad fact but anyone born the wrong side of 1965 has a fart's chance in a thunderstorm of getting back into the job market."

I thanked Pete for his cheering advice and we moved on, mercifully, to another subject.

"What's happened with that piece of sushi I saw you with at the restaurant the other day?" Pete asked, referring to Teresa Batomata.

"Mellow Yellow? Nothing. No sale. She's a job snob and only puts out for clients or directors, according to Jim Party at Paine-in-the-Webber, who seems to know about these things."

"So? All women are like that. It's in their nature. Just as men prefer women with higher reproductive values, the sort of women we know look for men with larger resources. It's the only thing they really understand and the only way you'll get a bit of wobbly on your nobbly. I can't see why this one's so different."

"I'm not a client or a director: I'm a job slob. Never mind. It serves me right for being a hypocrite and taking her out in the first place. I've never exactly hit it off with the Japanoose."

"Can happen. The fairer sex of other racial groups often appear more acceptable than their male counterparts."

"That's true," I concurred, without really analysing the statement.

"How old?" Pete asked.

"Quite old. I mean younger than me, but quite old in girl-years. I'd say maybe thirty-two."

"So she's got another fifteen years before her looks head South and her plumbing starts to fall apart. Wait till she realises she's carrying nothing more than a teaspoonful of dead eggs... that'll wipe the smile off her face. It always does."

"Yeah, but by then she'll be someone else's problem. For the time being the dice are loaded in her favour. At the moment she'd rather have sex with an amputee than give me a second glance."

"One of those, eh? When they're at their most desirable they can afford to be snotty... they're treated like Royalty. As they get older and lose 'the power', they have to pipe down a bit... which they never do, of course. In the meantime if they're grateful, give them a plateful. If they don't thank, wank."

"Quite," I said, starting to get a little bored of Pete's homespun aphorisms. "The trouble is, as you said with reference to poor old Billy Mytton, time waits for no-one. Not even for us sleazeballs... eventually we all end up looking like shit."

We talked about girls a bit more. Pete asked how things were with Roxanne.

"Still motoring along. But her work permit's running out which is making things a bit heavy," I explained, morosely.

"You could always marry her," Pete counselled, well meaningly, unaware of the *faux pas* he was committing.

"Are you out to lunch?!" I challenged, choking on a cocktail peanut. "Who are the happiest people on the planet? Single men and married women. Doesn't compute, does it?"

"So Roxanne's nothing special?" Pete questioned, slightly taken aback.

"Not to me she isn't. That's the problem; she'd make someone a dam good wife... but I ain't looking for a wife. Just something to fuck until something better turns up," I surmised, with slightly forced arrogance.

"What's she like in bed?" Pete enquired, on the assumption that I wouldn't be bashful in my response.

"Very moist. Bangs like the back end of a 1930 Volvo, and so she should: she's seen more pricks than a pincushion. But I need a change. You can't feel what you don't feel."

"Bowling alley genitalia?"

"Pete! Hush your mouth! That's not exactly what I meant and since when have you ever known me to speak ill of womankind?!"

"Have you seen anything of Christine Hale?" Pete asked, ignoring my riposte. I'd forgotten that he and Christine had once had a brief affair. He had a sour look on his face. I wondered whether he too had been on the receiving end of her evil eye.

"Not recently. Why? How is Her Imperial Smugness? Have you spoken to her?"

"I talk to her from time to time," Pete replied, "but she's so up her own arse it's difficult getting any sense out of her."

"That's what happens with these girls who spent all day at the office pretending to be blokes. Where's she working at the moment?"

"Afro Devo, I think."

"What in heck's name is that?" I asked, i

"Some misguided Third World bank."

"That girl is one hundred per cent dishonest! She has no right to work in a bank," I declared, crossly.

"James! Are you kidding?! Banks are the biggest crooks in the world. Look at the people they employ. You should know; you've worked for enough of them."

"I suppose they're not in it for love. But tell me more about Christine," I said, wanting to get back to the subject.

"There's not much to tell. She's still going around as if she's got a secret that she's not about to share with anyone."

"They say you should never trust a girl with a hooker's butt, although she's actually not as pretty as she looks," I remarked, with convoluted logic, but slightly wide of the point.

"It's not that, although she's definitely chunked out a bit; her appearances are no longer quite the unique selling point they once were. No, there's definitely something very rum with Christine. I pity the poor sod who ends up with her. He who wishes to own beauty must be prepared for its loss. And then what's left?" Pete asked, pensively.

"Not much. Whatever the female equivalent of a wanker is; not a particularly savoury specimen, that's for sure," I replied, suddenly aware that I'd hit on something quite important.

"Exactly. She's completely lost the plot. And she's slept with everything that's walked God's Earth in trousers. She's like a sixteen year old who's just woken up to the fact that she's got a vagina... she really thinks it's quite the cleverest piece of instrumentology this side of the Trent. She was born with the flippin' thing for Christ's sake!" Pete cried in exasperation.

I sniffed disdainfully.

"I must say I've always been impressed by her lack of moral compass. She's unable to distinguish between what's right and wrong and what's in her own interests," I declared, feeling the warm, sickly lungs of hypocrisy breathing down my neck. "I wouldn't pay any attention, if I were you."

"I suppose you're right," Pete said tersely. "My God, Old Johnny Female's a damned tricky customer, y'know. Bloody women! There's a war going on out there."

I was glad that I wasn't the only one to have been subjected to Christine's obtuse behaviour, but Pete didn't have time to elaborate further. We finished our drinks and went back to our offices.

I was shaken by the news of Billy Mytton. He was only fifty, but fifty was too old in a young man's world. He'd sat opposite me for the brief time he'd been at Conmax. I hadn't particularly liked him but he'd been a tough bastard and had worked like a dog to get things done. He must calmly have taken a view one day and decided that he'd had enough. He must have asked himself: "What is the point?"

I had to admit the question was beginning to cross my mind.

There was the Pavarotti extravaganza in Hyde Park that evening. It was raining. I mooched around in my raincoat taking pictures of people getting soaked, some of the sillier ones in their long dresses and dinner jackets in deferential salute to the great Neapolitan pasta mountain. I wasn't tall enough to see the stage through the sea of umbrellas and I could only make out one of the huge television screens in the distance if I jumped up and down. Hardly in the spirit of grand opera. I watched in wonder as some of the dumber animals solemnly got their picnic hampers out. They were surprised when their smoked salmon-gorged paper plates were trampled into the mud by the crush. It was all very cheering. It restored my faith in British wallydom that set us apart from other nations. No wonder we'd been so resilient at the Somme. It had been a picnic.

I got up early the next day to go for a run and headed for Hyde Park to check the aftermath of the concert for any rich pickings amongst the debris and abandoned flotsam. The clearing-up dudes had beaten me to it and everything was neatly packed in black plastic bags by the time I got there. I cursed myself for being so slothful and not getting up earlier and ran home without so much as a discarded sweet wrapper to show for my endeavour.

The chipmunks were reaching new levels of poison. A new arrival, Mr Dong, had been specially parachuted in from the Head Office, supposedly to beef up the London operation and was starting to be a serious threat to my privacy. He spotted me immediately as a phoney and began to apply some very unwelcome pressure on me to do some work and make a few business calls. He, too, was terrified of me and was apt to break into uncontrollable hiccups every time he asked me to do anything.

I was fed up with the demeaning process of cold-calling people who weren't remotely interested in anything to do with Korea. Instead I tapped the keys on the Reuters board with renewed intensity each day, pretending to be James 'The Street' Mallet, bond trader *extraordinaire*, in touch, on the phone, always there, lightning reflexes, bobbin' 'n' weavin', duckin' 'n' divin', in and out, no market safe from my killer instincts. Fast decisions, Worldwide. But all I was doing was looking at the sports pages and the funnies while making personal calls, thinly disguised as business. I would call Albert Carr and say in a loud, hearty voice, "How's your market looking today?" and then proceed to compare, *sotto voce*, the previous evening's state of inebriation.

Albert was by then working in a shoe shop and had nothing to do with my line of business. I hoped this was lost on Mr Dong. It didn't stop him from wafting garlic all over me and asking what I was doing every time he passed my desk. As with my other colleagues, I pretended that I was doing something immensely important and was just a millimetre away from pulling off 'the big one'. I'd look Mr Dong squarely in the face, knowing perfectly well that he knew that I knew that he knew that I was a complete fraud. I also knew that this charade couldn't go on forever. It would continue with increasing intensity until one of us snapped or, perish the thought, I did some business. The other option was to resign, but since my meeting with Pete Divis I'd resolved not to leave without a fight.

One of the benefits of this extraordinary working environment was the group of Brits who worked at the other Korean houses. A lunch club existed of ten or so lowlifers who met every week to exchange tales of Korean woe and wrong-doing. We all had exactly the same cultural and procedural problems with our employers. On the first occasion that I attended, one of the group proposed what I later found out was referred to as 'The Toast'.

"Death to all Koreans!" To which Wally Barker would respond darkly: "Slow death!"

Peregrine Blücher, who worked with Wally at Korean Banking Corporation was an old Etonian who'd been at the game for nearly three years and knew all there was to know about the peculiarities of Korean behaviour. I congratulated him on being able to succeed with them for so long.

"Succeed is the wrong word," he said. "No one succeeds with the Koreans. At best one survives. In that respect I suppose I am a success."

I asked him what he did all day.

He replied, "Not a lot. It's vital that you develop a hobby or an interest to pass the time. For my part I manage to fill these vast tracts of tedium by studying genealogy. My genealogy in particular. It's a rather specialised subject of limited interest to others, but it's kept me sane."

I looked at him sceptically.

Ian Smiley from First Exchange Bank of Korea told us that he had spotted one of his Korean colleagues drying his hands under the hot air dryer in the lavatory.

"Is that a crime?" one of the others asked.

"Well," said Ian, "he hadn't actually washed his hands but he was definitely drying them, if you see what I'm getting at."

Wally Barker groaned and pushed his plate to one side. I mentioned that there was a new Korean geezer in my office who was making my life a misery and asked what I should do. Peregrine Blücher gave his verdict in his slightly over-clipped tone.

"Never do anything he tells you unless you are absolutely sure you want to do it. Should the situation arise that this is not the case, you should look him straight in the eye and say, "Yes sir!" and promptly do nothing. If he asks you later why you haven't done anything, all you have to say is that you weren't aware of being given the order. When he tells you again what to do, ignore it and repeat the process until he gives up."

That was more or less what I'd been doing all along at Kowshat anyway but I drew comfort from the fact that it was established procedure. I put forward a theory that I had been formulating since joining the company.

"Gentlemen," I said, "I believe that I may have an answer to some of the mysteries surrounding our lords and masters of the dog-eating persuasion. I believe their London subsidiaries are being used, at least in part, for covert operations. In short, I think we are being used as a cover towards ends far more sinister than the humble pursuit of mere profit."

The table went quite and all eyes turned to me.

"I believe, comrades, the principal objective for setting up these London subsidiaries is espionage."

No one contradicted me although Ian Smiley asked plaintively:

"But what is there to spy on, for goodness sake?"

I answered his question as thoroughly as I could.

"Exactly. What is there to spy on? The answer is certainly not of a military nature. The Koreans have a war machine infinitely better than our motley selection of girl guides. It can't be industrial espionage because as a country we don't make anything except chocolate biscuits. It could be for commercial espionage purposes but even that's a bit of a joke, unless they want a textbook study of mismanagement and executive overpay. I believe they have come here, sirs, to spy on a lifestyle, report on it and perhaps eventually take it back home with them."

Everyone looked relieved and some started laughing.

"Quiet everyone!" Peregrine Blücher demanded, authoritatively. "I think James has a point, if indeed he isn't stating the obvious."

As Peregrine had been working with the Koreans the longest, his views on the subject were taken seriously. He took the floor.

"Having first-hand knowledge of one culture enables another to exploit it all the more effectively. In reviewing tastes and trends here and in Europe, the Koreans are able to report back to their Head Offices with the necessary information, which in turn is passed on to their government, the industrial conglomerates, the commercial enterprises and so on. The next thing we know, the whole country here is awash with Kylie dolls, nasty petrol station nick-nacks, squash rackets that break on impact and horrid, cheap little cars. All mysteriously made in Korea in the safe knowledge that this is what Joe Public wants. Makes the invasion that much easier."

Wally Barker, who'd been listening quietly for most of the lunch, came to life and started to speak.

"It's all beginning to make sense," he said. Wally had only been in the game for a few months longer than I, and was thus a relative newcomer. "If you notice, everything's spoken in Korean, written in Korean, faxed in Korean. God is Korean. I mean we're never included in any internal meetings, thankfully, and not one of them ever tells us what's going on or what's being discussed. Yet they're perfectly happy to watch us twiddle our thumbs and do nothing all day. And do you notice something about the British support staff? They're stupid."

"All support staff are stupid," Ian Smiley interjected, gruffly.

"Yes," Wally persevered, "but ours are particularly stupid. Notice when the Koreans come to recruiting they always advertise directly in the press? They daren't use an agency in case they might get someone intelligent. Yet the Koreans themselves, although you'd never guess it, are all supposedly top-notch. They have first class degrees from the best universities... all ex-military. Yet all they do all day is write report after report, never generating one red cent's worth of business and remaining totally ignorant of how any of the financial markets actually work. "

"I agree: James may have a point," Ian Smiley interjected, at last coming round to my idea. "They're like alien observers... cultural and commercial cartographers... spies by any other name. We should report them to the Securities Association for masquerading as legitimate trading houses. They just waste everyone else's time. If they want to operate cultural missions, then they should go through the appropriate channels."

"Well done Ian, but then we'd all be out of a job," Peregrine Blücher chipped in adding, not without levity, "I think the important thing is not to make it too obvious that we know what they're up to and continue with business, or the lack, as usual. If they ever get an inkling for one moment that we're onto their game, anyone of us could end up somewhere face down in a lake."

We concluded the discussion and got the bill. I went back to the office relieved there were other kindred spirits suffering similar dilemmas to my own.

At home Roxanne was beginning to be a nightmare again. She'd stepped up her complaints about my 'dickhead friends' and the 'shithouse weather'. Then one day she suddenly announced that she'd had enough and was going to go back to South Africa. I felt nonplussed and remarked that I didn't blame her. I said that I would do exactly the same in her shoes. She was taken aback by my indifference but I wasn't in the mood to beg her to stay. Our relationship had gone as far as it was ever going to go and now we were just marking time. I was as fond of Roxanne as she was of me, but I couldn't marry that bottom or live with those deformed little breasts for the rest of my life. If I ever got married I was going to treat myself to the biggest pair of tits in the world. An ironic prophecy as it turned out. And her early morning breath, her 'poo sandwiches' as she called it, was just too much to handle on a permanent basis.

So Roxanne gave her three months' notice at work and our relationship started, by necessity, to wind down. We celebrated our first anniversary of being together quietly at a restaurant. On the way home Roxanne seemed reticent. I asked her if she was OK. She remained silent. I put my arm around her and kissed the side of her head gently. I assumed she was being reflective or even a bit remorseful now that time was running out for both of us. I was way off target.

"James. There's something I've got to tell you."

That I was the most fantastic person she'd ever met? That leaving me was going to break her heart? That she'd cancelled her plans to go back to South Africa?

"What is it, muffin?" I asked softly.

"Well, the last time I was in Cape Town I met a guy who took a bit of a shine to me. ''

That was not unusual. Lots of guys took a shine to Roxanne.

"So?" I said.

"Well, he wants to go on a trip round Europe."

"Can't see the problem."

"But he wants to come to London before he goes around the Continent."

"I can't stop him."

"You see, he doesn't know anyone in London so he'll probably have to stay with me."

"Shouldn't be a hassle."

"The thing is, he wants me to go round Europe with him before I go back to S'thifrica."

"And are you?"

"You know that there's a whole lot from Cape Town who are going round Italy and France in a couple of months' time?"

"I didn't, but I do now," I said.

"Well, me and this bloke might hook up with them."

"You suit yourself, lollipop, as long as you're happy. I can't start getting jealous of a person who lives eight thousand miles away, although I think you've picked one hell of a funny time to tell me about it. In fact, it sucks. How long is he coming over to England for?"

"For about a week and then we intend to zip round Europe for a month before heading back for S'thifrica."

"Fine. Let's go to bed," I said without further ado.

The implications of what Roxanne had said didn't register with me immediately. It wasn't until I asked for further details a few days later that I had any grasp of what was really going on.

"So this guy who's coming over to the UK and going round Europe with you, when did you meet him? Have you known him long?" I asked, convivially.

"I met him briefly when I went back home at Christmas and then saw him again when I went back for the wedding last time."

"Roxanne, are you trying to tell me something?"

"Well, sort of, I guess."

"So you got pissed and had tongue banjoes?"

"Something like that."

"Something like what?"

"Something a little more than that."

"Fish fingers?"

"Little bit more."

"Cape rape?" She nodded. *Et tu*, Roxanne?

"Oh great," I said. "That's really wonderful. Thanks for letting me know. Just on health grounds it would be nice if you'd inform me of who and how many people you've slept with every time you go on holiday, or leave the house, so I at least can have some say as to whether I want to chance stuffing my dick up your diseased pipes."

I was bluffing. I was playing the role of outraged boyfriend. I wanted to see how far they'd gone. I was still convinced that Roxanne, in spite of her sexual dipsomania, would never deliberately be unfaithful to me. I was her stud and soulmate, after all.

"We used condoms," she said hesitantly.

*Condom-s?* I felt an instant bolt of cuckold's nausea hit me somewhere in my lower abdomen.

"I do believe I'm going to be sick," I said, and quickly went into the bathroom. I gagged without vomiting. I brushed my teeth, composed myself and had a think. Was this natural causes or Christine's Curse at work? I was stunned at Roxanne's duplicity, although at the back of my mind I couldn't help but feel a sense of relief that I'd been let off the moral hook. At least I had the ethical advantage of being the offended party. Roxanne was going away and her revelation now brought the finality of the affair into perspective. I weighed things up. I couldn't pretend that I was in love with her. This interruption meant that I could leave the affair with a clear conscience and quietly close the door behind me. It was important not to repeat the mistakes that I'd made with Christine. The last thing I needed was another curse to contend with. Knickers were not to be twisted this time. After all, it was only companionship. It wasn't as if money or anything tangible was at stake. I had been wronged, questionably, but that was not to become the all-consuming issue. Or so I told myself.

Roxanne had been pretty free with her favours before she met me, so what was I to expect? Her love had been almost masculine in its intensity; its high octane had flared spectacularly, but briefly. What I needed was some slow-burning diesel. Anyway, what was so wonderful about my penis that it should command instant monogamy wherever it laid its salacious head? It was just as well that I'd seen Roxanne in her true colours now rather than ten years down the line. I now had no doubts about her impending departure. I was apt to be vindictive but, in this instance, I decided to spare Roxanne my ire. I'd always known that she was susceptible to flattery and I'd ceased flattering her for a while now; it was natural that she would look elsewhere for affection.

Her South African liaison was not due in town for another two months. Till then I wasn't going to let a little infidelity get in the way of my fun, although I thought it was a bit rich of Roxanne to expect me to melt into the background the minute her other romantic ligature stepped into the country. England was my patch. He would have to wait his turn. One week and then he could have her for ever, with my blessing.

Roxanne came into the bathroom. "I'm sorry, darling," she said commiseratively.

I turned round and looked at her sadly. To my annoyance when I spoke, my voice had gone hoarse.

"I had no idea it was quite so serious when you said you had an admirer. I didn't realise you admired the admirer in return."

"It wasn't meant to be a big deal. The first time I went back it was just a holiday fling and no one would have been any the wiser."

"What do you mean *the first time* you went back? This cunt with teeth was slipping you warm bananas back in December? Do you mean I've been having sloppy seconds all this time?" I said starting to get cross.

"Or he has... depends which way you look at it."

"Don't fuck with my head, Roxanne... you can't be serious."

"Serious as cancer, baby blue."

"Jesus Christ, Roxanne! You manhole! You really know how to debase the coinage. Is this your idea of revenge for me not loving you enough? When are you going to upgrade your life from some sort of sleazy striptease to a class act? You've got about as much style as a backstreet abortion. At this rate you're going to make someone a wonderful slut one day."

"Oh shut up. Take a chill pill. Work it out; nobody owns me. Till I take those vows at the altar, I can do what I like."

"Oh yeah. As if vows will make any difference. You only open your mouth to change cocks."

"Listen, fuckwit; do you want me to talk this through or do you want to call it quits, in which case I'll leave now?"

"You don't leave me much choice. You might as well get on with the story."

Roxanne paused for a rest before delivering her next emotional Exocet. I'd taken so many hits that there was nothing much left to destroy.

"Well, after my first trip back to S'thifrica, I heard that this guy had gone sweet on me. He called me up and offered to pay the air fare if I came out to see him for a couple of weeks."

"So you screwed each other the first time you went back over Christmas?" I said, more for dramatic effect than as a rhetorical question.

She nodded again.

"And the wedding you were going to?" I asked falteringly, bordering on dumbstruck.

"There was no wedding," she said quietly. "I know I sound like a complete two-timing bitch, but I had to try him out. He was my escape from something that was, for me, turning into a nightmare. I'm afraid truth has to be the first casualty in these things. I would've kept quiet about the whole thing, except he wants to come to Europe via England. I wasn't going to tell you because the last thing I meant to do was to hurt you. You know you're special to me."

"They all say that," I said petulantly. "Like they all say I'm so cool in bed... like I'm *Mister* Orgasms... while all the time they're probably being quietly shagged senseless every lunchtime by Greg from filing."

"So what? It's only sex."

"That coming from you..."

"I don't know if I even particularly like him," she said, ignoring my sarcasm. "Of course I found him attractive but I don't know him really, and now you mention it, he's not exactly Luke Skywalker in bed. In fact he's a bit of a dud fuck in that department, but I'll soon change that. Otherwise he's just an ordinary South African boy. I'm going back home and I guess someone like him represented the future for me. You weren't going to marry me and there was nothing else here for me to hang around for. I was stuck like a dope with a thing called hope, but eventually, what with my work permit running out, I had to protect my own interests. I'm not going to be twenty-six forever and we all know how men go cold as women grow old... there are some things you can't cover up with lipstick and powder. I guess he was my ticket out. I was just trying to look after myself. I didn't want to get stung. You know what a grip you've got on me. You're like an addictive drug that's devastatingly bad for me but makes me feel so good. The only way to wean myself off you was to go cold turkey. You, you're OK... you can look after yourself. I can't. I didn't deliberately go looking for an emergency exit but I guess Bernard was my only hope of making the break in one piece."

"*Bernard*? You shittin' me? What a name! I wouldn't follow someone on to a bus with a name like that, let alone sleep with him. How could you?" I bleated, pathetically. "Oh, and by the way, thanks for thinking of me, mate. Just as long as your emotions are OK, that's the main thing," I added, affecting wounded pride.

Roxanne sighed despondently and then said:

"I know. It's not the way I wanted things to turn out either, but I couldn't throw all my eggs into one ovarian basket with you. I adored you with all my heart and all that I could give, but I knew you weren't able to return the compliment, and never would; you couldn't say the words I wanted to hear. So when I found someone who loved me with the intensity that I'd loved you, it was difficult to ignore it and ultimately turn it away.

"I've been drained in every sense by my emotions for you, but I know that there's nothing I can do to make you feel the same. Not that you should feel obliged to anyway. It just wasn't coming naturally from you. You're always looking over your shoulder at someone else. You're tough... you know the game... all the rules and tricks. I couldn't keep up with such a seasoned campaigner, you understand? You'll move onto the next one or whatever it is you want, and I'll just be another photograph in your album: "Oh yeah, the cute little South African girl I used to go out with. I wonder what she's up to now?"' she said, doing a reasonable impersonation of my voice and a not inaccurate assumption of what I might have been saying in a year's time. Or so I thought. I let her continue without interrupting. I was quite enjoying myself.

"With Bernard, on the other hand, he's on my level. He's my background... my age... from my country. We're both at the same stage of development and can help each other along at the same pace. With you I was tossed, turned around, dumped and left for dead as you went about your frantic little life with me barely hanging on by my fingernails. I was just a fashion accessory to you - just a minor subsidiary of James Mallet Inc. Someone you could say "Hey, guys! Look at the little redhead I've got this week and, guess what? She's no bimbo; she's an accountant. Wow! I must be good with girls." It was lovely while it lasted and I even wanted it to go on forever but I knew it wasn't to be. Don't pretend, James, that it was going to be forever for you either."

The more she talked, the more I could see that she had a point. She had an accountant's knack of aligning the figures to match the bottom line. She was also making me out to be a bit of a legend, which I liked. It took the wind out of my indignation, but it was flattery that I didn't deserve. Beyond being a drunkard, there was nothing special about me.

At work the next day Mr Dong rudely interrupted me just as I'd turned my fountain pen into a cargo jetliner. It was about to taxi down the runway towards the hole puncher when he summoned me into Mr Park's office. Mr Loon and Mr Park were already there. Cool and the gang. From their expressions, not that they really ever had any, I sensed that I was not being called in to discuss my bonus. I put on my best Captain Sensible facade and tried to look serious.

"Ah, Mr Mallet, Head Office ask me why there no movement on profit and loss account for last four weeks," Mr Park said, assuredly.

"I hope you told them that, without their approval to apply some funds to the trading account, things are not going to move at any great pace," I dictated, earnestly.

"They will give us credit line when we start to make money, Mr Mallet," Mr Park parried back, bravely.

"But we cannot make money out of thin air, Mr Park. Without money, no credit line... no credit line, no money," I whined, achingly. "We cannot do spread plays, arbitrage, new issue syndications or have anything of any value to offer our clients while we have nothing in the account in the first place. I know that Head Office is scared about giving us any credit, but this is the price they have to pay for not properly committing themselves to the market: zero business. If you can't pay, don't play; you have to speculate to accumulate and all that. I try to do my best, I promise you Mr Park, and there's nothing that I'd like to do more than earn this company lots of money and keep Head Office happy but, without the necessary tools to do the business with, it's very difficult to get anything done."

A look of complete incomprehension crossed Mr Park's prehominid features. I yabbered on before he could come up with a rejoinder.

"I think we've been extremely successful in raising the company's profile in London. I mean, everyone's heard about Kowshat International *now*," I fibbed, unconvincingly.

"And I'm sure, given time, there'll be lots of business coming our way. At the moment, what with the Korean Stock Market as it is and no money to go into a bond play, I am unable, along with a lot of other people in my position, to make money out of nothing. You cannot till a field without a plough. I'm trying to generate business in other areas but I don't think I can be blamed for the fact that nobody in Europe is particularly enamoured with the whole Korean funky groove thang at the moment," I spluttered, desperately groping for words.

I paused briefly for breath and then went on:

"As far as bonds are concerned it's already an overcrowded, overbroked market with far too many intermediaries chasing far too few genuine clients. Coming in at this late stage as a diminutive player with bugger all to offer is suicide. If you want to try someone else in my job, just tell me and I'll go, but he or she won't be able to do any better."

"Mr Mallet," Mr Dong pleaded, "we know your job not so easy, but we pushed by Head Office to show results. We show no result, they get angly."

"I appreciate that Mr Dong, and I will do my best to cultivate business as best I can. Next week I have lunch with Mr Forrest at Kleinworts and then Mr Shunmore at Scan Asset. I will bring you feedback as to what view they have for Korea."

Mr Park and Mr Dong looked at each other uneasily, as if they'd heard it all somewhere before. I tried a different tack.

"Hey fellas... fellas... look at it this way; we're making more money than Euro Disney, and they've got thousands of people working for them. There's only ten of us here."

I concluded the meeting by asking if they had anything more to say and then piously asked to be excused as I had 'some important work to do'. Like organise next week's social life.

Fuck! It was getting hot in there! I gave myself a maximum of another month of this bullshit before they gave me the push. It was only because they were too polite or lacked the guts to sack me that I was still in business. They didn't know what to do. I reckoned it would probably be Head Office who would pull the plug. I had ceased to be an entity in the dealing room. The Koreans no longer spoke to me at all. I was left in silence for weeks at a time. They'd long ceased to take any of my phone messages.

I phoned Wally Barker to report my recent close shave.

"I'm glad you called James. It's nearly tea time and I can hear the kettle boiling."

"What do you mean?" I asked, puzzled.

"I just wondered if you would like a cup of 'tea', as it were. Perhaps we can meet somewhere halfway, like 'The Plough' in its adorably nonagenarian setting of the Barbican for something a bit stronger?"

"No, I mustn't," I answered, feebly. "I'm in deep enough shit already, much as I'd love a drink. I'll go downstairs and get a Coke."

"But it's not quite the same though, is it? Go on... just a quick one."

I slipped out to the 'The Plough' unnoticed. Not that my presence registered any more with my colleagues.

Wally was already waiting with Peregrine Blücher by the time I got there. They had a pint of 'Neverhards' lined up for me. The pub was empty, except for some grungy late shift LIFFE traders discussing their Ford Tiaras.

Peregrine passed me my drink saying, "Wally was just telling me about your brush with your reptiles."

"Yes. It's all gone a bit Amstrad in there."

"Oh dear. It sounds as though you've rather had it, old boy," Peregrine said stiffly. "It can only be a matter of time. It always was a case of "when" rather than "if". I mean I don't wish to appear condemnatory, but you are the Grand Wizard of the personal telephone call. Things aren't helped by the fact that all the other Korean houses have started to sack their white men. You know how if one does it, they all do it. The Koreans march in phalanx. It will be Wally's and my turn next."

Ian Smiley had been sacked from First Exchange Bank of Korea the week before, for no apparent reason after two and a half years blameless service. As an inspired parting gesture he anonymously booked a stripper for a customer presentation his bank was conducting a few days before he was due to leave the company. The confusion, so Ian subsequently informed us, justified every penny of the eighty pounds it had cost him. Peregrine continued:

"I suggest, James, that you keep your head down and hang on for as long as possible. Treat each day as an added plus, if you can call it that. Think of it as being another £75 that you've deprived the Korean economy of. Your father would be proud."

"You're absolutely right, Peregrine," said Wally, "but, that being said, I do feel a 'conference' coming on."

'Conference' was our euphemism for going to the cinema in the middle of the day under the guise of business. Peregrine took him up on the point.

"Actually, there is a real conference on next week on futures and options at the Chiswell brewery, admission free. It's not going to be very exciting, but it would get us out of the office. Obviously the key words here are 'free' and 'brewery'.

We chucked down another pint and returned to our offices. I was tired and full of beer when I got back. I picked up a copy of the 'Standard' and made my way to the third floor lavatory. There were no tenants on the third floor. The conveniences were unused and spotlessly clean. I put the newspaper on the floor as a mat and lay on it. It was important to use only the 'Standard' in such circumstances because it was smudge-free. After that I covered my eyes, using my tie as an eye mask just as Peregrine Blücher had taught me, and fell asleep.

I woke up an hour later. It was time to go home. I went back to the dealing room to get my jacket and briefcase and, without saying goodnight, made my way to the tube station wondering whether £75 a day was worth it for such a pointless existence.

That was another worry. Mr Park might try to chop my salary. The money they were paying was enough to cover the bills, but my evenings were still divided into two categories; CNIs and CNOs. Cheap Nights In and Cheap Nights Out. On the other hand, if push came to shove, it was important to make sure I wasn't categorised as having been made redundant by my own choice in case it disqualified me from getting my unemployment benefit.

I was fired a week later. I suppose it had nothing to do with The Curse this time. The television profile on Albert Carr and me from when we'd been unemployed had been screened the previous evening. We both came over as a couple of brain dead chinless prats on some weird ego trip. Albert looked a complete berk and I looked as if I'd just come off heroin. The documentary turned out to be nothing to do with redundancy. It was a record of how two rather idle hoorays passed the time of day while down on their luck. The producerette was a product of Allegro Television's in-house graduate training scheme and had done everything to a set formula, including soppy shots of me feeding the ducks in the park. In her view that was what redundant people were supposed to do. It looked ridiculous. Imaginatively handled the piece could have been a record of genuine national comment, but instead it merely lampooned two ex-public school buffoons. Albert and I were stitched up, but then we knew we would be. And to cap it all, the producer-bitch wouldn't let me have her phone number.

The day before Wally, Peregrine and I had, at lunch time, ventured out of the confines of the City to the 'Needle and Spoon' revue bar in Shoreditch which had an all day strip show. We stood gawping along with the solemn-looking fund managers and other low grade scum as each girl in turn mechanically removed her clothes to the thud of some arbitrary background music. Once naked, they manoeuvred themselves into a variety of contortions so as to afford the audience optimum command of their urogenital display. We all chipped in a pound when the hat came round. At two o'clock the pub started to empty. I wanted to get back to the office. If I was going to be useless at work, the least I could do was to be occasionally punctual about it, but Wally and Peregrine, both being married, hadn't had their full ration of smut. I left them hypnotised in front of a gyrating, perfectly plucked pudendum and got some more drinks.

By three o'clock, we were the only customers left and the girls had given up any pretence of dancing. They sat in a state of semi-undress, talking and smoking to one side while the duty stripper lay motionless on the stage with her legs wide apart. Wally and Peregrine eventually became bored and agreed to walk back with me to the City. On the way we discussed with Epicurean relish each of the girls' finer points and which were our favourites, before re-entering the real but grey world of Officeland.

I had hoped that none of the chipmunks would see my appearance on television. If any of them had, I'd intended to come over all innocent and say that I had done it years before. I never got the chance.

I was Thunderbirding my felt pens around my desk the morning after the programme ("Green hi-lighter to red biro. Come in red biro! Come in red biro!"), when my line rang. It was Parksybaby.

"Babycakes!" I trilled, rapturously.

"Please come into my office, Mr Mallet," Mr Park said grimly, brushing aside my brotherly good humour.

I assumed I was being summoned to explain my late return from lunch the previous afternoon. I had an appropriately earnest-sounding seminar and a three page report at the ready for an excuse. As I entered Mr Park's office I noticed that he had a naughty little smile on his face. I stood to attention in front of his desk.

"You on television last night, Mr Mallet. That against company rules," he said, sternly.

"Ah, you noticed. Yes indeed. It was something I did before I knew I was joining the company.”

"Company rules: no publicity without Director's approval."

"But I wasn't working for the company at the time it was being filmed, Mr Park. It was a documentary about a social dilemma. It had nothing to do with Dogshit, sorry I mean Kowshat Securities, and even if it had, it should have been very good publicity for the company."

"I inform Head Office and they say you must go."

His face became a study of joy. He handed me the standard brown envelope with my P45 and all the bits in it. I wasn't surprised. I would have sacked myself months ago. It was the only smart thing the company had done since coming to London.

"Two months' salary. You may keep your season ticket."

He was delighted that he'd found a bulletproof excuse to get rid of me and seemed better disposed than I had ever seen him before. For a minute I thought he was going to burst into tears of euphoria. Bloody Head Office! I knew they'd be my downfall. It was now my turn to lay on the insincerity with a trowel.

"OK Mr Park. I'm sorry I didn't work out for you here. You've been a marvellous employer and I hope that my replacement is more compatible with your requirements. I still say that Head Office is being silly not committing any money to the dealing room but I won't go into all that again."

"I hope you not hold this against us, Mr Mallet," Mr Park said in reconciliation.

"I can't hate little children," I said, confident that any sarcasm would be lost on him. "Especially retarded ones, Mr Park."

We both got up and shook hands. I clicked my heels, saluted rather camply, turned and gave him one of my finest flounces as I catapulted myself out of his office for the last time.

I strutted proudly into the dealing room, shoulders back, chin out and emptied the contents of my desk drawer into a carrier bag I happened to have kept handy for the occasion. The chipmunks had their heads down, pretending to be reading studiously through their miserable reports, occasionally underlining a word they understood, such as 'the' or 'it' or 'and'. No one looked up. Cowards. They were fraudulent as I was. They hadn't made a bean between them in all the time I'd been there. At least I'd supposedly lost some money. Mr Dong was contentedly eating a banana. He looked just like a monkey.

Mr Loon started speaking into his phone in petrified English. "Ah Mr Dirrion... er... er... this is Loon from Kowshat Securities... er... how you today? Yes... yes... very good... yes Mr Dirrion... I was wondering if your company... er... was interested in investing in the Korean Stock Market". Stock phrases.

"Don't do it to yourself, Mr Loon," I said, pityingly. "In the unlikely event that BP Pensions actually wanted to do something in Korea they'd go to the Club... Schroders, Boring Brothers, Lemmings... not some bucket shop like ours or, more accurately, yours."

"Maybe... well... maybe... er... maybe... I send some information on Korean stock market to you..." Mr Loon continued, ignoring me, "and maybe I can meet with your company for a presentation... or maybe we take lunch together... or maybe you take beer with me at the pub yes? Maybe tomorrow? I see. You have no interest in the Korean Stock Market? I see... OK Mr Dirrion... very solly... er... yes... goodbye... yes... thank you... goodbye Mr Dirrion."

I curled at the thought of some sabre-toothed fund manager having to fight off armies of Samsonite-wielding Koreans with their tasteless corporate gifts and piles of useless research.

I finished emptying my desk and went up to Mr Dong to say goodbye. He was coy and shifty about his new quisling role and burst, predictably, into a fit of hiccups.

"Mr Dong, I've come to say '*au revoir*'. I can't tell you what an honour it's been working with you these past few months. Your acumen and dedication are second to none. Your knowledge of matters Korean is formidable. And so dishy with it," I added, knowing it was all wasted on him. I shook his hand and said to the others with a wave:

"Bye lads, I'll miss you."

Mr Loon looked up.

"Especially you, Mr Loon. I would say your support has been nothing short of incredible. In fact, I think perhaps I should take it a step further and say it was nothing short of *uncredible*. Your arrogance is, as an art form, only marginally surpassed by your ignorance."

"Perhaps we take beer together sometime," Mr Loon suggested, oblivious of what I had just said.

Not if I see you first, I thought, but out of courtesy or cowardice replied:

"What a lovely thought, Mr Loon." Like needle stick injury at an AIDS hospice.

I left Mr Loon to his futile grovelling. And so ended my Korean adventure. So much for my cultural espionage theory. I opened my redundancy package on the tube. I was glad to see that the cheque had been correctly made out gross of tax and with holidays in lieu by the bearded accountant-thingie. I felt demob happy and pleased with myself. I'd managed to net over eleven grand in the four months I'd been there which, considering I'd done bugger all, wasn't bad. More money than I'd made for them, that was for sure. Silly fucks.

I stopped off at Micky D's to order an 'Egg McToilet' before their breakfast menu was withdrawn. I had to stand behind four busloads of astonishingly plain Japanese language students. I read some leaflets saying that Micky D's were not ecological rapists and that eating twenty hamburgers at one sitting was actually rather good for you. By the time I'd got to the front of the queue the breakfast menu had been withdrawn. I didn't feel like a hamburger so I turned round and walked home.

I had the rest of the day to myself again, and Ian Smiley round the corner to go roller-skating in the park with any time I wanted. I had, before Kowshat, become quite at home with my role as a dosser and tripping down to the Post Office with my Giro every fortnight. I knew I'd slip back into the routine quite quickly. Back to watching morning television with its politically correct children's programmes and cartoons about outwitting environmental baddies. And the seductive advertisements for impossibly expensive toys just to make life hell for parents. 'My Little Pony' cost more than my little dole cheque and 'Sonic the Hedgehog' was out of the question. And 'Tiny Tears'. She cries. She wets. Give it time and she'd start menstruating.

I realised I had, at last, found my metier as a government statistic. It would be nice to see all the familiar faces at the dole office again, although

I knew I'd miss my City lunches. Was it called the dole office because everyone had such doleful expressions?

It was a sunny morning and I decided to take my folding bicycle out for a spin. The trees smelt agreeably of sperm as I whistled round the garden squares. I cycled between the pretty girls in their ditsy open top Mazdas on the King's Road, forlornly aware that I could afford neither as I made my way to 'The Artist' for some refreshment.

It had been quite a week: girlfriend confessed to having an affair; got fired from work and, judging from the reviews on Albert's and my TV appearance, our idiocy and insolence had taken the world by storm. It was universally panned and the fame that Albert and I had fleetingly thrust upon us came with the full force of half a million outraged viewers' letters behind it.

The producer-bitch from Allegro said they'd never received so much hate mail before from the public for a documentary. Albert and I seemed to have that effect on people. I was delighted. If a job was worth doing at all, it was worth doing badly.

My mother called the following day. I told her the news. She'd become immune to the blight of my vocational ineptitude. Her disappointment had turned to indifference. Thank God.

"Then you'll have more time to see your Mummy, won't you?" she said, only half in jest.

"Yes I suppose so," I said weakly, and before I had time to come up with a diversion was summoned to lunch the following day.

The next morning I emptied the car ashtrays and drove with the windows open through the suburbs in an attempt to purge the vehicle of any tobacco pongs. My parents suspected, but had no proof, that I smoked. Out of respect, or spinelessness, I'd decided a long time before not to confront them on the issue. Anything for a quiet life.

I knew the route so well I could glide from lane to lane to achieve optimum short-cutting without having to think. I turned off the main road into the gin 'n' Jag tranquillity of my parents' neighbourhood. I parked in their modest driveway and looked at the house. It spoke neither of money or the lack of it, nor of conspicuous comfort or any particular austerity. It was a mute abode that narrowly defied the ordinary and yet achieved the same sense of sterile homogeneity as its neighbours. Each house had been built to order from a catalogue. At a guess I would have thought my parents' design would have been called 'The Westlake' and the next house along, 'The Tudorberry'.

Just about everyone in the area was retired.

"Welcome to Jurassic Park," I muttered to myself.

I crunched up the gravel drive past the geraniums and Habitat stone urns to the front porch affair. There was a wrought iron boot jack on one side and a Peter Jones carriage lamp on the other, as if denoting a baronial existence of equestrian pursuits and rustic attainment. The closest anyone would come to any rustic attainment in that house was to shoot the ducks off the wall.

I punched the doorbell. It ding-donged with Taiwanese glee. I peered through the frosted glass of the front door and could just discern the reproduction Annigoni portrait of the Queen against the purple hessian wallpaper in the hallway. In recent years I'd started to have serious doubts about my parents' taste. It had entered an inverted time tunnel of aesthetic principle, either through peer group assimilation or of its own hapless volition. It combined the reliquiae of yesteryear with the artefacts of modern mass production. Imperia vied with Lladro; Victoriana with Ikea. The art deco looking glass screamed across the drawing room at the portrait of some ancestral lunatic from the past. The watery outline of my mother appeared through the mottled glass of the front door. I straightened my tie.

"Hello Blossom!" my mother said dotingly, as she opened the door.

She had, once upon a time, been a district nurse. The experience had left her with a tendency to fuss when given the opportunity.

"Hi Mum," I said limply. I noted with dismay that she was wearing a housecoat.

My father appeared and hovered obligingly in the background as my mother and I embraced. She'd obviously just had her hair done as it smelt of napalm and looked as though I could bounce a tennis ball off it. I shook hands firmly with my father. Anyone married to my mother deserved a medal in my book.

We went into the drawing room. My father poured me as decent a gin and tonic as he could into a silly cut-glass egg cup. I shivered as I took in the twiddly porcelain figurines and china dogs on the mantelpiece and inspected the 'At Home' cards behind them. Farnham, socially, had a permanent high season.

"Well, chaps," I started, "you certainly are *the* popular couple. No party complete without the Mallets, eh?"

"Indeed not, James, I'm sure," my father replied in the Pathé newsreel vernacular that was the *lingua franca* of the locale. My mother scuttled off to look at the potatoes. My father and I continued our small talk. He was a quiet sort of man; a gent, if not, by limitation of background, a gentleman. He had been a middle-ranking civil servant before he retired and now spent most of the day avoiding my mother's shadow. I'd never really got to know him and felt uncomfortable whenever we were left alone. I looked down at the go-mad spiral carpet pattern and then peered through the French windows into the garden. It looked immaculate but lifeless. Inside, the imitation hearth fire blazed, heat-free with its sanitised decoration logs beside it. I began to feel claustrophobic. Another gin and tonic came to my rescue.

"So, James," my father intoned, "have you ever thought about working for a proper organisation, like a merchant bank, perhaps?"

"I certainly have, Daddy-O," I replied, dully, "but there doesn't seem to be a mad rush to make use of my services. They're a cartel, you see, and as such never employ outsiders such as me. I regret to say that my doughnuts have been well and truly dunked in that department. God knows, I've tried, but I'm just not quite the right sort of sapling for that particular thicket, I'm afraid."

"I see," he said, taken aback. "What about industry?"

"I wasn't aware there was such a beast. At least not in this country," I dismissed, dismissively.

"But there must be *something*," my father insisted, his eyes bulging with Churchillian intensity.

"Oh I'm sure there's a Japanese car manufacturer somewhere in Northumberland or an oil refinery or something in Wales, but that's about it, isn't it?" I replied sourly, wanting to get off the subject.

"I only wish there was something we could do to help," he said, unhelpfully. "We just don't have the connections in your sort of field."

"Dad, even if you did, it doesn't work like that anymore."

At that moment my mother returned from the kitchen and announced that lunch was ready. We went into the dining room. There was the usual assortment of life-shortening morsels riding aboard the Tricity Hostessette. A pound of butter had been crucial to their creation. We helped ourselves and sat down.

It was my mother's turn to apply the interrogatory treacle.

"So darling, what are your plans?"

"I don't know, Ma. Early days at the moment. I've been thinking about learning another language. Most of the jobs I go for now require at least one other European language. They never specify which one. I think they just like having another language for the sake of it. I was thinking about Spanish and spending three months or so going round South America. I've been trying to get into the Latin American debt market and it might give me the edge at an interview. Even if there's no job at the end of it at least I'll be able to impress the waiters at the local tapas bar."

My mother paid no attention to my frippery.

"You know that South American Spanish is not considered to be correct?" she said, authoritatively.

"Ma," I said, feeling my temperature rise, "must you always be quite so judgemental? I can't win, can I? I know you mean well but there's always a snipe or a niggle. Why the fight? It's quite extraordinary how so few people over sixty have any manners these days. If I ever do get to the level of Spanish where anyone can tell the difference, it'll be a miracle so I wouldn't worry about the social niceties of the accent for the time being."

I noticed that the passage of time had started to make my mother look like the stupid one from 'The Golden Girls'. All of a sudden she fixed me with a stare and, as if she'd just hit on an idea of Newtonian inspiration, declared triumphantly:

"I've got it! Why don't you work for a merchant bank?"

Oh God! I reached across to the bottle of wine and refilled my glass. Their conversation was stuck in a loop. It always was.

"Because, Ma, merchant banks are held together by bullshit and other people's gullibility. They shouldn't be allowed to exist. And they wouldn't employ someone like me anyway, as I was telling Dad."

Bad language, so long as it wasn't blasphemous was tolerated, if not encouraged within the family dynasty.

"Patsy Mordant's son, Christopher, is a director of Lizards," my mother said defensively. Her capacity to finesse the annoying comment had never ceased to impress me. I felt a rage coming on.

"You say that every time I come down, Ma, and every time we end up having the same absurd discussion and arriving at the same acrimonious conclusion that Chris Mordant is a fat nose-pick," I said, slightly overstepping even my family's liberal sense of decorum as my father's gins finally got the better of me.

"Besides I'm not director material... my attitude, unfortunately, doesn't quite match the curtains. I've been thinking about doing a computer course... or learn to type or something."

"But surely you'll have a secretary to do that," my mother interjected, indignantly.

"Ma, it's not like that anymore. Everyone is now expected to be computer friendly, and that means knowing how to type. I'm the only one at any of these places that I go to who can't work a computer. It's no wonder I keep getting fired wherever I go."

"You've never been fired," my mother observed, archly. "You've just been made redundant, that's all."

"Don't spoil a good story Mum; it's the same difference. Employers want class acts, not snobs," I said, beginning to sulk, and yet feeling a little sorry for my parents at the same time. They'd wanted little Lord Fauntleroy. They'd got little Lord Fart. Their vision of City life was of a gentleman's club, where courtiers bowed to one another in studied deference as flunkeys ran to and fro with bits of paper to be initialled by various company glitterati. My mother resumed her monologue.

"Apparently Shell's a very good company to work for."

"You *are* knowledgeable today, Mama," I said, in exasperation. "I had no idea that you had such an eye for the obvious. I didn't think your business acumen stretched that far. "

I put my knife and fork together, leaving half my lunch. It was too much. I had no more room.

"Darling, you've hardly touched your food. You must eat something," my mother wailed, perturbed.

"I can't, Ma. I'm as full as an egg."

My mother looked at me doubtfully for a moment, before resuming her appraisal of my career objectives.

"What about business school?" she suggested, trying a different tack.

"Look," I said, beginning to feel brutal, "I inherited yours and Daddy's DNA which makes for a pretty limited gene pool, *n'est ce pas?* It's no wonder you bred a dud. I mean, why don't you go to business school if you think it's such a good idea?"

My father winced. My mother became quiet at last and concentrated on her food. I took the momentary break to assess their point of view. They were locked into another era and were unable to comprehend or adapt to the second half of the century. Theirs was a time, war or no war, when men were chaps and women simpered.

Lunch was over. We went back into the drawing room for coffee. I noticed for the first time that the house was beginning to smell ominously of pee and dried flowers. *Eau de Nursing Home.* My mother started talking about her latest misguided charity project. It involved giving hundreds of pounds away to African babies who'd never see it. Nor would I. The conversation drifted onto the Queen, as it tended to with my parents. I retreated into a daydream. It wasn't my subject.

I finished my coffee. It was time to go. My mother protested, but I made some excuse about avoiding the traffic that seemed to satisfy her. When it came to road safety I knew I was on firm ground. My mother's doubts about me included my driving ability. She insisted on putting the lunch leftovers in some tin foil for me to take home.

They saw me to my car. I could see my mother's beady eye checking the inside for cigarette ash. We said our farewells and I left them to their strange little world. I saw them waving to me in my rear-view mirror until they were out of sight. I wound down the window, reached for a cigarette and hurled my mother's cosmic doggy-bag into the stratosphere.

I sighed, partly in relief and partly in sadness: I was a heavy cross for them to bear. I would get heavier.

# Chapter 11: Losing It

As I got back to the flat later that afternoon I noticed three small boxes, each the size of a photocube on my doorstep. I picked one up and looked at it. It was a free starter pack of Radon Ultra Micro Washing Powder with a plastic bobble object.

"Yes," I thought, "I'll have that," and picked up the other two boxes. I took another four boxes from next door, and then realised I hadn't got enough hands and arms to carry them all upstairs. I looked at the other front doors around the square and saw that they all had at least one box still on their step and some had as many as half a dozen. They were like little extra-terrestrials waiting to be let in. Of course! They couldn't fit through the letter boxes! My heart started to race. I rushed upstairs and got two holdalls and a large suitcase out of the cupboard. This was a military-style operation and military-style planning was required. I decided to designate my car as Mobile Headquarters. I toyed with the idea of changing into combat gear but then had second thoughts about looking too conspicuous. I decided on The Man from U.N.C.L.E. look and put on a suit.

I dumped the case in my car and went to work with the holdalls, keeping an eye out for tetchy curtain twitchers and the long arm of the law. When I'd made sure the coast was clear, I started to scoop up the boxes. I knew it wasn't exactly larceny on a grand scale but I thought I'd look pretty ridiculous if anyone spotted me and tried to stop me. I was thirty-five after all. Alexander the Great had conquered the world and been dead for two years by then. So who was the loser? I pressed on with my mission. In no time I'd filled the holdalls. I went back to the car (MHQ) and lobbed them into the boot. Booty!

I drove to a nearby no-through road, decanted the boxes into the suitcase and drove back to the flat. I hauled my catch up the stairs and poured the boxes onto my bed. I was panting with exhilaration. What fun! I hadn't had so much excitement since I used to swipe off Mercedes stars as a kid. There were some messages on the answering machine but I left them alone. I had more important things to do.

After grabbing a second suitcase I headed downstairs again. At ground level I looked around. There was no one about; the streets were completely deserted except for the fine old cannibal down the road with his supermarket trolley full of rather smart matching Euripoff bags. The joys of mid-afternoon petty thievery while everyone was cooped up in their offices! I continued harvesting the little spacemen in the next door garden square. I had a bit of a scare when a bluebottle rounded a corner just as I was leaving someone's porch. I looked pretty shifty and felt like a mafia stooge with a stash of forged readies in my bag, but P.C. Plod didn't even give me a second glance. Dozy fuck. I probably looked like a yuppie on the way to the gym.

I continued working until I'd filled both suitcases. I'd have been quite happy to have continued going all afternoon, but as I'd cleared most of the quieter streets nearby, I thought three suitcases and two holdalls' worth was enough. Leave a bit for the others. I got back to the flat and counted my takings: three hundred and seventeen boxes, and another two hundred-odd in the boot of the car. The ones in the car would have to stay there; I hadn't got enough room in the flat for them.

I felt as happy as a prospector finding a vein of gold as I gloated over my swag. I ran a bath and lay in soak, savouring the adventure. When I got out I listened to the messages on the answering machine while I dried myself. There was one from Roxanne. I hadn't told her about the Korean debacle. She sounded bored. She'd called me at the office only to be told, "He no work here anymore," and had the phone slammed down on her. Thanks boys.

The other messages were all from excited friends of mine who'd also tried me at the office.

Everyone loves somebody who's just been fired. For a day. I returned Roxanne's call.

"So, what happened?" she asked, listlessly. I told her.

"Well, you knew you were chancing it when you made that fucking programme. Not every employer or prospective boss wants to be on record for hiring a loser," she snapped, not exactly bursting with sympathy.

"Oh don't you start. It probably would've happened anyway. They were a load of wanks... they were getting me down," I retaliated, lamely.

"James, they were the only people who were stupid enough to employ you and you did dick all to try and keep the job. You blew it. You just don't get it, do you? You think you can piss your way through life without lifting a finger of responsibility. Really James, when are you going to get into the real world and grow up? Life's not all about going to parties and having a laugh with jerks like Albert Carr. It doesn't stack up. You're about three minutes away from middle age and what have you got to show for it? Nothing. No career structure... no career, in fact. It's time to act your age, not your shoe size.

"You're a worry, James Mallet," she resumed. "You can't spend the rest of your life sitting in your flat - Tissue Towers or whatever you call it - getting trashed out of your gourd on cooking sherry and masturbating like a marmoset all day. You get smashed on the pretext of being unhappy, when in fact it's just an excuse to do nothing and grab a one-way ticket to Muscatel heaven or wherever the Hell you seem to spend half your stupid, methylated existence. What is wrong with your life that you must get drunk every night? You're a lovely guy, James... you've got so much going for you, but you're your own worst enemy. You've got to realise it's tough out there. No one's acting the fool any more. Except you. You can't afford to do that in a competitive environment. It's funny at twenty-five: it's downright sad at thirty-five. "

"What's it to you, rough-stuff?" I asked, feeling slightly hurt. "It's only a job, for fuck's sake. It's my life. I don't have to watch 'Dynasty' to have an attitude. You know I'm different from the others and have different values. All we have is time. Empires come and empires go. You know that material things, expensive holidays and all that guff don't turn me on. I reckon nothing really matters as long as you speak properly."

"That's crap. People who speak 'properly' as you put it are invariably bogus and perched on the verge of bankruptcy. Career advancement and financial security are the principal driving forces of twentieth century society. You're living in a material world, wild child. As environmental resources run out there's a rush to grab what's left. You simply don't have the smarts, or the cash to bury your head in the sand and pretend that you don't need to be part of the action. And you know it. It's in your conversation... I'm sick of listening to you being jealous of everybody the whole time and complaining about not having the same toys as the other kids on the block."

"OK, so I admit I have my limitations," I conceded, "but not as many as some people give me credit for. All I want is enough to get by - which I do very nicely - and have a good time, and then die. And stop being such an old bag. You're off with Bernie Brownpants in six weeks' time, so why do you give a shit?"

"I still care, James. You know that."

"Well, don't waste your tits worrying over me, honey pants, because I did something far more constructive with myself today than I ever did with the Koreans."

I told Roxanne about the Soap Powdergate scam.

"You dink! You're mad," she said, giggling at last.

"What do you mean, mad? At the rate of one wash a week they'll last me ten years. Now who's calling who dumb? Hey! Stick around with a winner like me and you'll never have to buy any washing powder ever again."

"Oh fuck off," she said, amiably.

We finished our conversation on a relaxed note. I told her not to worry about me and we agreed to meet up in the next day or two. We no longer saw each other every night. It was all part of our defamiliarisation programme instituted in the run-up to Bernard's arrival.

I had a drinks party to go to that evening which cheered me up. Since Roxanne had dropped the news that she'd decided to go back to South Africa, and then the Bernard thing, I had been casting around for someone else, but with little success.

That evening was no exception. Christine was at the party which set me on edge. There was something mushroom-like about her posture that I hadn't noticed before. It was as if her spine had mysteriously concertinaed itself into her pelvis since we'd last met. 'The telltale seedlings of infant osteoporosis?' I asked myself, hopefully. She was wearing a white bodice with some black satin hot-pants and a pair of cheap 'take-me-home-and-fuck-me' platform boots. As a finishing touch she had a chiffon scarf round her neck. *Très porno*. Although she wasn't quite the vessel of temptation she'd once been, it did little to quash my infatuation.

I looked around at the other guests. There were a few café minimalists in polo-necks, as if attending a Spock convention and some tired-looking London girls on the make. I spoke to a blonde girl with a spot on her chin who'd imaginatively painted her mouth to look like a vagina. She struck me as the sort who'd have heavy periods. I asked a few questions. She didn't ask any back. She looked utterly disinterested in the conversation and did little to hide the fact that she wasn't in the mood to be chatted up by an old poop such as me. After a while she excused herself and went to talk to someone else. That was standard procedure since I'd lost my bottle and developed 'redface'. The market was never wrong. Women can smell desperation.

Christine came up to me to say 'hello'. She was unusually friendly which made me feel even more shifty.

"How's it going with the chonks?" she asked, breezily.

I told her what had happened to my job and braced myself for the inevitable trip to Snubsville. She said she was sorry about my job and then proceeded to tell me how marvellous her work situation was, the salary she was on and how nice everyone was to her. Blah. Blah. Blah. She could fart butterflies. It didn't matter to me how much she earned. I'd never get back the money she owed me. She told me about a skiing holiday she'd recently returned from with a great bunch of people. Jesus! All she did was treat herself to holidays. A junket junkie. I asked, as politely as possible, if she had a man in her life. She started to tell me about a millionaire who sent a Rolls-Royce round to pick her up whenever they went to the ballet. Ballet? I never got it. Just a load of perverts watching pubescent girls doing the splits,

I listened patiently to her social fantasia and thought back to when we had been in love. Then, as now, nobody had particularly liked her, which had somehow added to her appeal, but I was tired of her trying it on whenever we met. What was it about her little po face and translucent body that I missed so desperately? I still went down on my knees at the altar I kept to her memory in my bedroom - actually a cabinet retained under extremely tight lock and key – for whenever I was feeling morose and there was no one around to witness my madness. It had become a ritual. I would kiss every one of the letters she'd ever sent me before gouging her eyes out in one of the old photographs I had of her from the time we'd been together. I'd almost run out of photographs by then, but I had the negatives and could've ordered plenty more to keep me going.

Once Christine had finished her pastiche of the good life, she waved excitedly to a confused-looking man at the other end of the room who didn't appear to know her. She ran off and pointedly kissed him on the lips. She gripped his arm and started talking to him animatedly.

I turned and saw Lorraine Grabbings, the super-charged, go-getting bitch from Zanybucks, the new up-and-coming PR agency. All the money in the world couldn't save her from looking common. I did a body swerve and had a pleasant conversation with a fat woman with legs like upside down Perrier bottles.

"Why can't thin girls be nice?" I cried to myself.

"Because they don't have to be," Mr Brain replied.

Hippo hips had to waddle off to a dinner party. I said we must get together sometime and then forgot about her. I didn't feel drunk enough to go home so I stayed for a few more glasses and talked to an Army barmy who was over from Germany . At about eleven, our hostess called out with slightly neurotic over-enthusiasm:

"Come on everyone! I'm a member of 'Dangles'... let's go dancing!"

I didn't feel up to it. Nightclubs, I had decided, were not the right backdrop for short, round-shouldered thirty-five year olds. I could only enjoy them if I was coked out of my pretty little nostrils or off my face on disco biscuits. The confident angular women, their arms flailing like windmills, and the young men in their expensive leather jackets (gentlemen should only wear textiles) who frequented such places intimidated me. I still hadn't recovered from my last visit to 'Dangles'. The gorilla on the door had looked at me as if I needed to be carbon-dated. Once in, it took me about two hours to scrape up the courage to ask some hippy chick for a dance. I might as well have tried selling her a disease.

"Hi, cunt! Fancy a dance?" I asked, in an erroneous attempt to be massively cool.

She sprayed out her drink in shock and spluttered:

"Fuck off, corpse!" before turning her back on me. All we are saying is give sleaze a chance! What she had to be so snotty about escaped me. She wasn't a patch on my magazine collection.

Christine was still at the party. She had to get up early for her whiz-bang job in the morning and wasn't interested in going to the club. She offered me a lift home. I went to get my coat and fetched her poncho. As we were leaving she tackily slipped, I suspected for my benefit, her business card into the pocket of the man she had been talking to. He looked utterly bewildered. After we left Christine asked if I wanted to see her new flat on the way back. I thanked her but declined, saying that I'd already masturbated that evening.

She dropped me off at my flat. My patience for enduring her drivel without riposte did not go unrewarded. As I said goodbye she invited me to come down sometime to a cottage she rented in the country. She said she'd call me the following day.

I woke early the next morning, feeling bilious and worried. I had arrived at my destiny. I was going to be a single male buck forever, expelled from the pack, left to roll in the dirt, mateless and functionless with my fellow failures, doomed to a life of self-abuse until it was time to expire. At least I didn't have a big mortgage and could live off my flatmates' rent for the time being. I thought about the current incumbents for a moment. Arthur, the tall, sardonic food and beverage analyst from Kidder Peebreath, who was apt to pass judgement where comment would've sufficed. And Petra, the quiet Irish physiotherapist with the model's figure, whose bones I wouldn't have minded jumping but for her grebo Bosnian doctor boyfriend who was the one and only interest in her life. She'd gone a bit weird on me lately, added to which she had taken to leaving unsightly poo stains in the loo bowl. I had mentally demoted her from 'flatmate' to 'flatcunt'. I was contemplating giving her a go, subtly, once Roxanne had left. It would save on porn mags. Arthur had always warned me about shitting on my own doorstep whenever we had discussed Petra's gravity-defying physique, but my doorstep, I had decided, was the only place to shit these days.

I snapped out of my wet dream. I had a busy day ahead of me. I had to re-register at the dole office. At least they would be pleased to see me again. A familiar face. They might even recognise me from the telly programme. There were now more hoorays on 'the rock 'n' roll' than proles. I made a note to change into my top hat and tails and take the latest copy of *The Tatler* with me to flick through in the queue. Now, more than ever, appearances were essential.

I had to bank my redundancy cheque and buy some stamps and envelopes for the CVs I would have to re-write. After that I had to phone around the headhunters and tell them that, once again, my services were available.

I'd managed to paint myself into yet another corner. It wasn't an earth-shattering scenario. It was just boring. The thin dividing line between employment and unemployment made all the difference to other people's perception of an individual and the quality of life that went with it. Without employment I was dodgy; a tramp. Yet with it, although I was exactly the same person, I fitted in: I was a contributor, I could be categorised and thus was acceptable. I didn't need to be successful, although I was sure that wouldn't have hurt, just as long as there was a pigeonhole to fit me in. Unemployment was something that those with real jobs could only imagine. To them it represented a quaint form of shiftlessness where eccentricity went unchecked.

Once I had done my other chores, I called Chris Seymour at his PR agency and asked if he was still looking for someone to help him raise money for his various charity projects. He was pleased to hear from me. He hadn't found anyone else for the job and said he'd be delighted to have me on board. He was no longer in a position to pay me even the hundred pounds a week he had previously suggested, but he said he'd pay me a good percentage on any money that I managed to raise. I said that was fine and we agreed to meet the next day.

I parked outside Chris's office in Belgravia the next morning and fed an hour's worth of coins into the meter. Chris's office was a converted dump on the top floor of what had been, once upon a time, a smart Edwardian house. We chatted for a bit and then went out to a nearby pub for a drink. I was impressed by the way Chris kept asking the barman for 'a gentleman's' whenever it was time for another round. It was a polite metaphor for a treble measure. We talked about money. It didn't matter that he was unable to give me a weekly wage. All I needed was a phone, a photocopier and a kettle. People in work had no idea how expensive it was not to have access to office facilities. It cost me at least £20 a day to be out of work, just on calls and distractions to counteract the boredom.

After another drink, I briefly excused myself to look at my meter. I was two minutes late by the time I got to my car. There was a ticket on my windscreen. A bloody parky had beaten me to it. Bang went another forty quid I wouldn't have had to shell out if I'd been working. How petty of The Curse to have stooped so low. I made a resolution to send one of my 'Buffy Frobisher' loony letters to the Westminster Parking Office. I came back to the pub feeling slightly miserable.

"Welcome to Belgravia!" the camp black barman declared jubilantly when he saw me with my ticket. "That's the way they do things round here, darling!"

At least Chris and I had agreed that there was plenty for me to work on. He said I could join him any time I wanted; the sooner the better as far as he was concerned.

I drove home and concocted a letter protesting my innocence to the Westminster parking authorities. Afterwards I went to Insanesbury's and bought as much as I could for fifteen pounds, sticking to the special offers. *Toujours broke*! I had been eating the same food from the same shop for the last six years, and was now in a virtual state of constant constipation. It was time to give my colon a holiday. I could sense it was getting fed up with having to push through the same old crap every day.

I bought a magnum of plastic wine and half a dozen rolls of shit tickets that had been reduced. I added up the contents of my trolley and found I still had three pounds left to spend. I bought a box of man-sized (i.e. wanker-sized) tissues and a pork chop, a packet of powdered potatoes and some frozen peas because they were cheap. I pushed my rogue shopping trolley, crabwise, past the other unemployed fucks and all the horrible French people blocking my path. Numerous old bastards shuffled around inspecting toothbrushes as if they owned the place. Finally I went to the checkout and had a fight with an unspeakably fat Arab woman who was trying to jump the queue.

I got back, took the phone off the hook and went to bed for the rest of the afternoon, wondering how Chris could do any work with half a dozen 'gentleman's' sluicing around inside him.

I awoke in the evening with such industrial-strength breath that I practically had to gargle in Harpic to get rid of it. I got dressed, had a beer to wash away the alcohol and went down to 'The Happy Masturbator', a.k.a. Mr Patel's girlie mag shop on the corner of Alphabet Street to get a copy of the 'Standard' to see what was on the telly. While I was there I reached past the felch'n'squelch, rim'n'grin gay mags and flicked through the latest issue of 'Jiz'. I'd seen all the girls before in other training manuals. I put it down and picked up a copy of 'Spurting Life'. I looked at the contents page. There was a picture of Jack Rutter, the magazine's frazzled billionaire founder, looking slightly cross-eyed. Years of onanism had done him no favours; too much jerk had made Jack a dull boy. He'd been running a regular pictorial feature on 'Chelsea' - they're always called 'Chelsea' - a girl so perfect that it almost seemed an act of charity for her to share herself with the great masturbatory public. The profile of a nymph rapt in ecstasy , as her immaculately manicured fingernails parted her buttocks to reveal the glistening intimacy of her anus. The innocence of her smile somehow seemed at malevolent cross-purposes with the graphic cruelty of the snarl between her legs. I wanted to live in Chelsea. All this and half a dozen other lovelies (why do they always wear their shoes in bed?), staring at me in a perfect mixture of contempt and coquettish supplication while proudly flaunting their entrails, for just two pounds. A couple of quid for a harem of conspiratorial submission. Despite my reduced circumstances it was too good to resist. I bought it sheepishly along with my newspaper and rather wished that the Pakistani woman behind the till was quicker about giving me back my change.

She shot me a disapproving look and muttered, "Wanks a lot."

That was too much. I felt a rage coming on.

"What *did* you say, Madam?" I spluttered.

"I said 'Thanks a lot,' sir."

I was definitely starting to lose it. I turned and staggered out of the shop.

I was pleased there was nobody around in the flat that evening, but not just because of the magazine. I felt like being a slob, doing one of my five minute lonely bachelor meals that I was becoming proficient at and getting elegantly wasted in front of the box with a friendly bottle of Rio Tinto. Man, bottle and television locked in perfect harmony.

My five minute solo meal turned out to be a disaster. I had difficulty doing justice to the texture of the reconstituted potatoes. It was like mixing cement. I kept adding more powder, then more hot water, trying to get it right, until I'd used up all the potato lint and was left with ten helpings of sludge that I didn't know what to do with. While I'd been trying to sort out the potato fiasco, the pork chop had burnt itself to a cinder. I'd got the peas right, but I was damned if I was going to eat them on their own. I threw the whole lot away and radioed out for a pizza.

I was fed up with the kitchen. It had turned itself into my own private hellhole. The washing machine had recently decided to blow itself up and all the other white goods had gone on the fritz in sympathy. Everything was in a state of chaos. It was no wonder I couldn't find a job. What I really needed - fat chance - was a good woman; something nice and warm to rub my genitals against who could organise my life. Catch-22. My mind went back to a crude inscription I'd seen tattooed on some yob's arm which read: 'No money: no honey'. How true. I seemed to have had it tattooed on my forehead.

Once I'd wolfed down the pizza I settled down to inspect my new magazine in detail. It was a bit of a swizz as the corker on the cover wasn't featured inside, however the stormer in the centre pages more than made up for it with a stunning close-up of her bunghole. It was big enough to let the cat out. I unzipped and pulled out my tool. I manoeuvred the page and pressed my cock against her half open mouth. I pretended it was the Chairman of the Pan Asian Bank's. His head bobbed up and down obligingly in time with my lowly frottage. I was beginning to get a conscience about my colossal masturbation habit, added to which there was the worry that I might develop repetitive strain injury.

"What the heck," I reasoned to myself, "cuts out the middle man," and resumed my activity.

I was just getting stuck into the delights of Chelsea's innards when the phone rang. It was Christine Hale calling to invite me to her cottage the following weekend. I continued playing with myself as she talked. There was another couple going down with us. Another couple? Did that mean that she regarded us as 'a couple'? Surely not? Just a slip of the tongue. And even if she did it was all part of her stop-go policy of blowing hot and cold, being nice one minute and a bitch the next. Silly girl. Silly me for having anything to do with her, but at least it provided a diversion from Roxanne. By then there were only five weeks until Bernie Brownpants turned up from South Africa. Roxanne still expected me to wait on her. She whipped herself into a frenzy if I so much as mentioned another woman. I was actually quite looking forward to Bernard taking her off my hands. Poor sod. He didn't know what he was letting himself in for.

I kept Christine on the line for as long as I could and asked her lots of stupid questions to keep her talking. I managed to hold her just long enough to allow me to ejaculate over my shirt as she was crapping on about her latest boyfriend, and then I let her go.

I picked Christine up the next Saturday. She insisted that I inspected her new flat before we left. It was OK, but the decor was decidedly early American trailer home. We set off together for her cottage near Gloucester and talked equably for most of the journey, pausing occasionally when a good record came on. She knew if she tried to get too clever I'd make her walk. I took the opportunity, as we were alone and I was feeling brave to broach her on the subject of The Curse for the first time.

"Christine," I said, "I don't want to appear spiritualistic so early on in the weekend, but ever since we parted company as a love match, I've been dogged by some kind of bad luck. It's as though a cloud of misfortune is following me wherever I go, and if I stand still for more than two minutes it catches up with me and then proceeds to piss down on me with the wrath of Zeus."

"I know," Christine said with a little smile.

"Is there anything you can do about it, like call off the hounds or something?" I asked, slightly alarmed that she seemed to know exactly what I was talking about.

Christine shrugged, which I recognised from our time together as her body signal that she wasn't interested in discussing the matter further, and so I dropped the subject.

We stopped at some concrete colostomy outside Swindon (good parking facilities) to stock up on provisions. When we arrived at the cottage, we put clean sheets on the beds and did the necessary chores to make the place comfortable. The other couple turned up as we were preparing lunch. I hadn't met them before but they appeared pleasant, if a little smooth for my taste. I was flattered that Christine had risked introducing me to them.

Lunch, windswept walks and all the boring things that the country has to offer filled the afternoon. In the evening the girls watched 'Blind Rape' on television while the other man and I peeled potatoes and chopped beans. It was reassuring, being stuck in the middle of nowhere that the same homogenous Saturday evening tomfoolery was being beamed out all over the country. The silly *der-dup, der-dup, der-dup, der-dup-dup-dup-dup* music that accompanied Filla Crack's hysterical shrieking seemed a cheerful reminder that there was some corner of a foreign field that was forever weekend television. What a laugh!

"Funny how Filla Crack looks more like Mrs Thatcher every week," my co-peeler remarked, thoughtfully.

"Yes, I'd noticed that... I think all women eventually end up looking like Mrs Thatcher," I said, pleased with the idiocy of my assertion.

"Indeed," my co-peeler concurred. "But it's when they start to act like Mrs T that I get worried."

We swapped over when the Bond film came on and the girls set about the more technical culinary tasks. Supper was ready, predictably, halfway through the film. I knew Christine wouldn't let us have our meal in front of the television. It didn't matter. I'd seen the film a dozen times before, and besides, they were all the same.

It was folksy in the kitchen with the candles on the table. Very rustic. I fleetingly felt the benefits of getting away from London. The conversation was witty and interesting until I became drunk and banal. The other man asked how Christine and I knew each other. I turned the question over to Christine.

"I prefer not to admit to knowing James," Christine answered, mockingly.

"Christine's never mentioned you," the man stated, in earnest.

"No, that's Christine for you," I started to explain. "In, out and wipe it and then on to the next one!"

"That's not true, James," Christine refuted, calmly. "We had a good couple of years, although you did make the most extraordinary faces whenever you were about to come," she added, for embarrassment's sake.

"Thank you for sharing that one with us, Christine. At least I *could* come," I said, eager to get off the subject.

"So what happened then?" the man asked, becoming more curious.

"Well, it wasn't the most pleasant of separations," I said, deciding that letting Christine give her version of events was not a good idea. "Christine lost her heart to a starship trooper while I was abroad and our love became a funeral pyre. It's all bollocks about absence making the heart grow fonder. It makes it indifferent, that's all."

"He was a solicitor," Christine protested, as if she wouldn't have been seen dead with a starship trooper.

"It was a bitter pill to swallow," I batted on, ignoring her with mounting recklessness, "but it was a blessing in disguise. I'm thankful things turned out as they did."

"In what respect?" the man asked.

"I was at a low ebb when it all went wrong. I would have given anything to get Christine back - even married her."

"What's wrong with that?" he persisted.

"Well it would have meant that Christine would have married an alcoholic and I'd have married a useless sack of shit," I said jokingly, but feeling my courage about to spin dangerously out of control.

"That's a bit hard, James, don't you think?" the man retorted, in a vague effort to contain the verbal pyrotechnics.

"And I'm not useless," Christine objected indignantly, but otherwise apparently satisfied with the assessment.

"We wouldn't be married now of course," I persevered. "We'd be divorced and I'd be down several hundred grand in the process."

"Several hundred!" the other girl exclaimed, venturing at last into the conversation.

"Half my worldly goods. My flat's got to be worth *something*, even in this market. Christine would've screwed me for every penny. No, it was an emotionally expensive experience but, apart from a few bounced cheques, it was good value compared to what *might* have happened."

We moved on to other matters and talked quietly until it was time to go to bed. I contemplated slipping into Christine's room once all the lights were off, but had second thoughts. I didn't think I'd be welcome. It would have been embarrassing if I had been turned away. Besides, I would probably have been too terrified to get an erection in the unlikely event of her welcoming me in. Of course there was always The Curse to consider, and oddly enough I was more frightened of the spell itself than its sorceress. But the idea of entering into sexual congress with Christine at this stage didn't seem sufficiently imaginable to warrant making a pass. The next day she was back in bitch mode and we resumed our Mexican standoff and, with hindsight I was relieved I hadn't tried it on. It was high time I accepted that there could be no triumph in this war of lost love.

A week later I joined Chris Seymour's organisation and entered the exciting world of charity fund-raising. Not being paid anything, I could come and go as I pleased. I liked going to work in jeans and having a beer at my desk when the mood took me. There was just Chris, his wife Caroline and a part-time student there. We spent most of the day talking about nothing. I knew a lot of people, so selling ball tickets was easy, but trying to raise sponsorship from companies was like pulling teeth. I didn't bother de-registering with the dole office as I had no money coming in until I got my first commission cheque from Chris. I managed to sell a hundred tickets at short notice for a funfair event that Chris had arranged at Chiswick House. After that, in Chris's eyes, I could do no wrong. I asked Roxanne along to it, but she declined. She said it wasn't her scene. I knew the thought of a thousand screaming yahoo Brits let loose in a fairground would make her feel ill.

The event was deemed a success and enjoyed by all who went. Unfortunately it failed to break even. Poor Chris. If only the weather hadn't been quite so dire earlier in the week perhaps more people might have come. It was beautifully organised with bumper cars and carousels, flame throwers and jugglers, discotheques and blackjack tables; all against the floodlit backdrop of Chiswick House. The evening turned from a sepia twilight to a clear blue-black night. All that was needed was another three hundred people and everything would have been OK.

I had no problem getting people to come to the next charity event that Chris was putting on and the cheques started to pour in. Perhaps I really had found my forte at last.

Time was running out for Roxanne and me. Not surprisingly, we continued to grow apart. I no longer cooked supper for her on a regular basis and when I did, it was only because she wanted to save money for her holiday with Bernard. Nothing like subsidising other people's peccadilloes, I thought to myself.

I had all but given up any hope of ever getting a job back in the City. I played the last card in the pack that I'd been holding in reserve and called up the Head Prole at Stear Burns. He'd hired one or two Conmax people in the past, but he wasn't interested in me. The company had moved to Docklands, so I didn't think it was any great loss. I preferred to work for nothing in Belgravia than be a slave in some morgue out in the Canaries with its Fisher Price railway that took two hours to get to and hadn't so much as a fad shop to show for itself once there.

At work I was getting worried about Chris. He'd developed a twitch. A constant flow of 'gentlemans' crossed his desk from noon till dusk. Then Caroline took me aside one day and put me in the picture. Their accountant had made a nonsense of their tax return and they owed the VAT man twenty-two thousand pounds. With the further three thousand pound loss on the Chiswick House event, it was touch and go if they could struggle along for another month on the off-chance that a miracle might save them.

Not long afterwards I came to the office and found no-one there. I stooged around for a bit and made a few calls before Caroline phoned in to say that they had decided chuck it in.

They were losing a couple of thousand pounds a month and had come to the conclusion that they'd have to call it quits now rather than later. The receivers were brought in. For the next two days Chris and Caroline were tied up with banks and accountants. They asked me to hang around the office to field any calls and messages. It was fine by me. It was all I did anyway and the least I could do to help.

Roxanne and I had another two weeks before Bernard was due to turn up. The following weekend was the last that we were going to have together. I wanted to end on a good note and had thought up one or two things to do. Nothing too frilly like going to see a play or a concert or any such foolishness, but there was an 'I'm-gonna-dust-off-a-few-cops-with-my-Uzi' film on in the Fulham Road that I'd convinced Roxanne we should see. I thought I would combine that with taking her out to a decent restaurant, for a change, on the Saturday night. Another film. Another restaurant. Blah. Blah. Blah.

I had to call up the people who'd given me money for Chris's last charity event that now wasn't going to happen. It was OK for the people who had sent cheques in. I hadn't banked them and so I simply ripped them up. I said to the cash dudes that I could either send them their money back or hand it to them at 'The Artist' that Friday after work. Most people opted for the latter as a good excuse to go for a drink. Everyone was happy. Except Roxanne. She hated 'The Artist' and the people who went there. And she couldn't believe that I was out of work again.

"Yeah," I said, "I guess someone up there doesn't like me. I'd hardly had time to learn the new phone number... everything I touch goes bust or turns to dust."

"It was a dickhead job anyway," Roxanne remarked, unkindly.

"Thank you," I responded, meekly. "I don't suppose its demise will alter my life plan drastically."

"James, don't kid yourself. You don't have a life plan beyond the next pub opening time. And talking of pubs, do we have to start the weekend at 'The Artist'? You know how much I loathe that fucking place."

"Angel, you don't have to be there. You can do your usual after office things with your work friends and come and collect me from the pub afterwards. I'm just going there to give everyone their money back from Chris's ditched do," I said, unconvincingly.

Roxanne rang off in a grump. She was getting worse. There had been a time when I'd had total control of her. She'd started to get out of hand ever since the Bernard thing had flared up. I didn't care. Anything for a quiet life. I'd take all the shit she had to throw at me. It was all going to be over in a fortnight.

I fiddled around in the office, helping myself to whatever stationery I needed. I was now the proud owner of seven staplers from all the various firms I had worked for. I made use of the photocopier with the latest version of my 'Curriculum Vitae' or rather 'Tissue of Lies' as it was rapidly becoming, as fact turned to fantasy and dates faded into fiction.

There was nothing for me to do, so I left the office early that afternoon. When I got back home I noticed two letters for me. One was a rejection from Allied Bank. I'd never wanted to work for the cunts anyway. The other was a standard letter back from the Westminster Parking Department in reply to my parking whinge:

*Dear Sir/Madam:*

*Road Traffic Acts - Parking Places.*

*Thank you for your letter received in this office. I would explain that all meters are regularly inspected. There is no record of the particular meter you used failing to function correctly on the day in question, or of it being the subject of complaint by any other motorist who made use of it at that time. On the information before me I regret I am unable to cancel the Excess Charge Notice and accordingly shall be pleased to receive a remittance in settlement of the charge.*

*Yours faithfully,*

*for Director of Planning and Transportation S.M. Fuller (Miss)*

I went to my desk and sat down. I thought for a moment and wrote:

*Dear Miss Fuller,*

*Road Traffic Acts - Parking Places*

*Thank you for your mimeographed letter of 15th July. It made me feel very special, even if it did imply that I was a liar.*
*Despite having two witnesses who will confirm that I was parked on the meter in question for less than one hour, I have decided to pay the fine in question with no further ado, as a gesture of faith and goodwill to the City of Westminster*

*I do not wish to appear as though I enjoy wasting your time any more, I am sure, than you enjoy wasting mine, but one little thing worries me: you did not return my parking ticket and I am terrified that if I pay my remittance without the ticket there will be no record of it and you will send bailiffs around in the dead of night to frighten me. I only want to do the right thing and, as a bureaucrat, you know that it is the right thing to do the right thing because the right thing is the right thing to do.*
*Please therefore give me exact remittance instructions with appropriate reference details or re-issue me with a ticket, allowing sufficient time to enable me to pay it.*

*Yours sincerely,*

*James Mallet (Mr)*

I popped down to the Post Office and sent it recorded delivery. I didn't want such a work of art inadvertently getting lost after so much endeavour. I wanted my forty pounds' worth of agro.

Chris and Caroline came back to the office towards the end of the week to relieve me of my lonely watch. They both looked exhausted but at least Chris had stopped twitching. It was as though he'd had a lump removed. I gave them the usual tea and sympathy that I accorded people when they found themselves occupationally challenged. I told them, perhaps unconvincingly, that life still went on and that there was still air to breath and television to watch. I gave them details of the DSS handouts. They were going to have to get rid of their hyperactive child's nanny. As they hadn't been able to keep up their mortgage payments the building society had helpfully decided to foreclose on them and repossess their flat. They had to move to Chris's mother's house in Reading until things sorted themselves out. Chris was in the process of filing for bankruptcy. Caroline was going to try to find some secretarial work while Chris looked after the child at home. Another Sloane sub-species was about to go the way of the dodo. Although I drew no pleasure from it, I thanked what little luck I had that I wasn't in their predicament. My mind went back to a translation of a hieroglyph I'd seen in a temple in Goa: "I complained I had no shoes until I met a man with no feet."

As the phones in Chris's office were about to be disconnected I saw no point in hanging around. I said my goodbyes and wished Chris and Caroline well. A futile gesture in the circumstances. Chris was apologetic about having used my services without reward, but I told him not to worry about it. I'd cranked up their phone bill more than enough to compensate.

I left wondering what I was going to do next. I'd only been there a month. It was back to daytime TV and the canned chuckles of 'The Flintstones'. Back to trying to make a five pound note behave like a fifty.

"Why," I asked myself, "won't anyone let me back into real 'Jobland'?" Was it too much to ask? All I wanted was one teensy-weensy job, but I was getting nowhere. I'd missed the gravy train. There was only standing room left and I hadn't so much as a platform ticket to wave at my departing companions as the 7:15 for Prosperity pulled out of the station.

My thoughts turned to Goa again where I could live like a king on sixpence and the weather was free; somewhere where I didn't have to explain to everyone why I wasn't working. I could almost taste the Ambre Solaire on my face and feel the sand between my toes. I was more than happy to throw the whole thing in, drop out and go round the world but, thanks to the property market going into a nosedive, I couldn't sell my flat. I was beginning to tire of the endless job rejections and having to account for myself the whole time. The prospect of another jaunt around India, with nothing more demanding to do all day than to skim pebbles across the water and take recreational drugs was an enticing alternative. Or Thailand. Pick up a cutie in Bangkok and go up country. Travels with my slant.

I got home and scrabbled through the doormat litter of pizza dump flyers and promises of travelling alarm clocks from the Sun Alliance. I eventually found something that was for me. It was a brown envelope from the Department of Employment. My dole cheque at last? I opened it. No, it was a letter:

*Dear Mr Mallet,*

*I am sorry to tell you that your claim for Unemployment
Benefit has been disallowed because it appears that you
have not been paid, or been credited with, enough National
Insurance contributions in one or both of the two past tax years.
This disallowance, while its grounds remain, will also apply to
any future claim for unemployment benefit.*

Great! That was all I needed to add to my smorgasbord of problems. And just as I was beginning to enjoy the recession and every day being Saturday. Not only could I not find a job, but I was considered to be so useless that I wasn't deemed enough of an entity to be eligible for unemployment benefit. I'd ceased to exist. Curse or no Curse, I was an utter failure. I was even a failure at being a failure.

I went to the loo for a crap. It was a breach birth and I practically had to pick it out. My shit smelt of kerosene from all the accumulated alcohol in my system. I picked up a copy of *Contempt* magazine that was lying by the lavatory and leafed through it. There was an article on Timothy Crawley-More whom I'd been friends with at school. He'd been a strange child. He once sent the Queen a false moustache for Christmas. He now ran a successful chain of hair salons. He'd dropped me when his business started to take off at around the same time that I'd given my life over to alcohol. I nearly gasped when I read how much he was making. And he looked *so* well in the accompanying photograph. Renaissance man in a Ralph Lauren suit. His confident smile seemed to taunt. There he was, rich and successful, looking good; while here was I, unemployed and sitting on a lavatory.

I threw the magazine down and finished my business. I pulled the chain. Nothing happened. I pulled it harder a couple of times but its throat was dry. My shit sat there like a clutch of Belgian chocolates, looking back at me resentfully. I peered into the cistern. The ball cock had snapped off its pivot. Roxanne was right. It was a tough world. It was too tough for me.

I went into my bedroom and started to cry.

# Chapter 12: Bombing Badly

I felt a strange sense of foreboding that fateful evening, even before I'd really thought about what I was meant to be doing. The bath water wasn't hot enough to have its usual restorative effect and my bones felt chilled as I got out. I debated whether I should take my car to 'The Artist' as I knew I'd be in for at least a four-pinter. I hadn't had much to eat that day, but I wanted to be mobile for when Roxanne turned up. I knew that she wouldn't want to hang around the pub for a second more than was necessary. She was fed up with my cronies and for some reason no longer derived any pleasure from watching me guzzle pint after pint. Some girls were funny like that.

I decided in the end to take the car because I thought it might act as a psychological restraint on my drinking, which was foolish as it had never stopped me in the past. I arrived at the pub at half past six. There was the usual Friday evening camaraderie of office people which I found difficult to share. I whacked back two pints to get in the mood and finished the business of handing back the cash for the aborted charity event to the ticket holders. My unease continued. There were too many people I knew and the rounds were getting out of hand.

Graham Ruddock passed by me looking bellicose and satisfied with his pathetically beautiful Stepford-wife-type girlfriend clinging to him like a dog on a leg. Beauty and the Beast. They'd obviously come up with some sort of cash-for-looks deal. Graham disliked me intensely. I found him too ridiculous to hate, but I admired him for mastering the unusual combination of obsequiousness with a total lack of charm. He was massively successful or, more probably, lucky in his work. He was a lawyer on seriously big bickies in the Corporate Finance department at Goldbergs; definitely, to my mind, one for the 'God Smiles on Wankers' drawer. He seldom bought his fair share of drinks, but for his own account he was Mister Conspicuous Consumption. He drove a car that looked like the Battlestar Galactica, although Graham himself was hardly the epitome of astral greatness. I was pleased to note the denuded state of his hairline. The joys of male pattern baldness! His once thick yellow thatch was now a Tintinesque wisp.

I checked my reflection in the looking glass behind the bar for comparison. I had to concede that time, with the able assistance of alcohol and tobacco, was doing a first class job in destroying what little was left of my farty TV presenter looks. I still had my hair but my wino's nose had assumed a clown-like imbecility. I made a mental note to try to lose some weight and have one last attempt at getting some definition back to my face. I'd started to avoid mirrors recently. Even when I leant down for a line of coke, I had to close my eyes. I looked back at Graham. He caught my gaze.

"Had any good jobs recently, Mallet?" he enquired, with sly bonhomie.

"Bought any good drinks recently?" was all I could think of as a riposte.

He'd never been wild about me since I'd screwed his sister and promptly told everyone about it.

"Who's the schtoink?" I said looking at the girl he was with. "And more to the point how much was it?"

They both looked at me incredulously.

"Well, it must've gone for your wallet," I went on, enjoying his agitation. "It couldn't have been your personality. You don't have one."

"Oh fuck off Mallet. She happens to be my fiancée. Come on Simone, let's get out of here," he said, turning to go.

"You've always had such a thing about me ever since I porked your sister, though God knows why. I was only doing her a favour. She was a dud fuck anyway," I said, trying to get one more insult in before he left and borrowing, not for the first time, Roxanne's patois, adding, "but I expect you already knew that."

He let the girl go on ahead and swung round as if he was about to hit me, but thought better of it and instead said:

"Listen, butt-fuck: wind your neck in. If you want to vent your frustrations or display your obvious inadequacies to me that's fine, but don't take it out on some poor girl you've never even met before."

"Oh come off it Ruddock. Are you blind? It isn't your smouldering good looks that makes a girl say "yes". You've had such a massive charisma bypass all your life that anyone who goes out with you must, *ergo*, be a whore."

"Is that what you think, Mallet? Well maybe that's the way of the world. Wad is God. Cash is King. And I've got plenty of it and you ain't. A simple case of winner takes all, wouldn't you say?"

"Perhaps. But that's only because you keep your fist so far up your clients' bums they can't move, and anyway it doesn't alter the fact that you're an arsehole. And you know it."

"OK, you ridiculous piece of fanny snot, get this: either you shut up or I'll be landing a bunch of fives across your kisser."

He turned once again and stalked off towards the exit.

"Mind how you go now... don't be a stranger!" I called out pleasantly, mildly relieved that my face hadn't been split open, adding, when he was safely out of reach, "But remember: you might not count when the new order comes; however important your employers may make you feel, you're just another digit."

By that point I realised I was a bit pissed. It was nine o'clock and there was still no sign of Roxanne. I was on my fourth pint of "Nasty" and had yet to get my round in. I too had a reputation for being a moth wallet, which was unfair; I just wasn't flash with my cash. I always had to make up for it and normally bought more than my quota of drinks. I now felt obliged somehow, in my reduced circumstances, to keep the flag flying and show that although I was down, I wasn't out. Yet.

After I'd finished my fifth pint I managed, despite the crush at the bar and slow motion service of the staff, to buy a round of drinks. The order came, miraculously, to under twenty quid, probably because people had started to drift home or go out to supper.

By nine-thirty Roxanne still hadn't appeared and I felt like making a move. I wanted to drive home although I knew I was over the limit.

I was prepared to run the gauntlet to my flat with the bumper-to-bumper Friday night traffic and, with luck, go unnoticed. The police had enough on their hands just coping with the burgeoning pedestrian population that was out enjoying the pseudo-Mediterranean ambience of the evening.

When I got back I found a message on the machine from Roxanne. I played it over a couple of times to gauge her mood. What a little madam she was turning out to be, although on this occasion she apologised for not coming to the pub. She said if I wanted to call her when I got back she'd be glad to hear from me.

I turned on the telly. There wasn't much on. There was a 'yoof' programme hosted by two patronizing poshos. I pressed the squeezy and channel-surfed through the other programmes. 'Mega-Morons' were bashing each other about with their huge, giant cotton buds on ITV and there was a quiz show with five thesps trying to out-clever each other over on Allegro. I was bored, and yet it was too early to go to bed. I went into the kitchen and had a look in the fridge. There was a half full bottle of Sauterne on the bottom shelf. I reached for it, pulled the cork and glugged back the contents in two mouthfuls. I wiped my lips and shoved the dead bottle into the swing bin. It had been too sweet to justify the reward of the extra alcohol and I felt nauseous. I went to the bathroom to brush my teeth. The toothpaste gave me a momentary hit of sobriety. I went into my bedroom and sat bolt upright on my bed. I composed myself, picked up the phone and dialled Roxanne's number. I suddenly needed her.

When Roxanne answered she sounded pleased it was me.

"I ache to see you," I said. "Can you come round?"

She caught me by surprise when she said she "couldn't be arsed", but added that if I wanted to go over to her house, she'd be happy to see me.

"You wanna put some of your pus into my guts, eh big boy? Why don't you get your horny little ass round to the love shack and we'll see what happens."

"As you put it so charmingly, it's difficult to resist," I said, encouraged by her suggestion.

I wasn't ecstatic about tooling around in my car half crocked and yet it seemed sacrilegious to pass up the opportunity to indulge in some leisurely Saturday morning sex the following day for what would probably be our last time together. In the end I capitulated and said I'd drive over. A taxi would have sufficed but I only had ten quid left over from the pub which I wanted to spend on a Lisa Stansfield album I hankered for. There was a quick route to Roxanne's but it was via a main drag out of London which was normally crawling with Feds. I hated the Fulham eggbox where she now lived. It backed onto a railway line, but her bed was comfortable enough.

I went apprehensively down to the street and got into the car once again. I adjusted the rear-view mirror to optimum scan, and started the engine. The steering wheel was covered in nose oysters. I hit the Cromwell Road and drove the slow lane. The traffic had died down. It was a clear night with a full moon. I could feel I was starting to trip a little as all the drink I'd consumed settled in my stomach and the alcohol made its merry way into my bloodstream.

By the time I got to Roxanne's house my head was spinning. I gulped as much air as possible in an attempt to hyperventilate my way back to sobriety. Roxanne greeted me at the door. I was pleased to note that none of her flatmates was around. She was watching some programme with a lot of American lawyers and judges yelling "Objection!" and "Objection sustained!" at each other. She liked that series. It glamorised an otherwise mundane profession. Afterwards we talked for a bit. I apologised for being a tad drunk and said that it was only because I'd been waiting for her to turn up that I'd gone beyond my regulation three pints.

"Bullshit," she said crossly, but I knew she no longer cared what I did with my liver. Or my life.

I could tell I was beginning to babble as I talked excitedly about what I'd done that day, which was basically nothing. I didn't want to appear a total waster. Roxanne half listened distractedly as the television continued to spew its junk. An adolescent weather girl came on and told some half-truths in a regional accent.

"And how many pints did you have at lunch time?'' Roxanne snapped, out of the blue.

"A couple," I fibbed. "You know I have to get out of that flat from time to time or I'd die of loneliness. You don't know how lucky you are having something to go to each day. Even commuting to and from work, a thing we normally all deride, is a form of belonging; a sort of herd movement which gives, however false, a sense of security and by the very nature of getting from "A" to "B", an illusion of purpose to everybody's everyday existence. Believe it or not, work is sexy. It's a club... a great big sex *club.*

"When I'm alone I have to put language tapes on in the background just to give myself the illusion of company. It's no wonder housewives hit the bottle: there's nothing else to do. Do you know the other day I listened to the news thirty-seven times? And sometimes the phone doesn't ring for days at a go. I have to interrelate with someone at some point during the day. That's what pubs are about... they're for lonely people."

"That's pathetic," Roxanne said, in a low growl. "I'm getting pretty fed up with your self-pity, you know. It's long past time you got a grip, James Mallet."

I went quiet. Roxanne had little more to say and languidly suggested going to bed. She led the way upstairs. I brushed my teeth again and got into bed while Roxanne went through the womanly ritual of removing her make-up and slapping some sperm-coloured moisturiser on her face. She climbed into bed next to me and we talked for a bit. I felt more comfortable in bed as I thought my drunken slur might pass for fatigue. I put my arm round her and with my free hand stroked her genitals.

"Don't!" she objected.

"Why not?" I asked. It was unlike Roxanne to decline sexual stimulation.

"Because it turns me on and I know you won't be able to do it."

"Well you could try fiddling with mine," I suggested, in the hope that if I concentrated, my flaccid, near-dead penis might hoist itself gloriously to attention. 'The grub', as Roxanne called it. In vein! I removed my hand from Roxanne's groin and turned over to go to sleep, promising Roxanne that I'd rectify the situation in the morning.

I must have been in a coma for an hour or two when either a night train or my bladder woke me with the full force of three quarters of a gallon of "Nasty" pressing against my abdomen. I had no idea where I was. I got out of bed to go to the loo and felt my way round the bedroom, stumbling over a chair and crashing into the dressing table in the process. I eventually found what I thought was the door but was, in fact, a cupboard.

Roxanne woke with a start.

"James! For fuck's sake, what do you think you're doing?" she screeched.

"I'm trying to go for a pee but I can't find the door," I replied, apologetically.

Roxanne switched on the bedside light and caught me pitifully climbing the wallpaper.

"For crying out loud!" she shouted, not pleased. "Get a life! Look at you, you fucking drunk."

I sneaked out of the bedroom to the loo and had the longest piss in the world, occasionally missing the bowl, miscalculating the power of my jet as I leant, pixilated, against the lavatory wall.

I finished off and gave it a good shake. I looked at the mess I'd made and wiped it up as best as I could with some loo paper before I pulled the chain. I washed my hands, glanced at myself in the cabinet mirror and saw a sorry sight. My hair was banked up all on one side where I'd slept on it, and my eyes were barely visible through my puffy lids.

I turned out the bathroom light and once again found myself in total darkness. I groped my way back to the bedroom and opened the door. Wrong bedroom. Fortunately it was empty. I fumbled around trying to find the right one. I found it eventually but as I climbed back into bed, I knocked something that fell to the floor with a thud.

Roxanne sat bolt upright and said in a slow, measured voice between clenched teeth:

"You stupid bastard. You've woken me up for the last fucking time."

Another prophetic statement, as it happened. She continued.

"You're nothing but a drunk... a stupid miserable drunk. You'll never get another job and you'll probably never get another girlfriend."

Fighting talk. I began to wake up. I felt a rage coming on. The ungrateful bitch! After all I'd done for her; stuck by her; practically given her a second home; cooked for her; tolerated her meanness and body odours; even tried to play the good sport when her infidelities finally came to light.

She went on as I sat up and prepared to launch a return volley. Somehow everything she said sounded all the more scathing through her accent.

"You're a loser, a waster, a drunk and about as much bloody use to anyone as pockets on underpants and I can't fucking wait to get rid of you. You should get help, James Mallet. You're a case: a hopeless, silly, fucking case and I'm glad I'm getting the fuck out of here and away from your pathetic little world."

That was it. I'd had enough. My mind went berserk as what was left of my reason collided head-on with my anger. Attack seemed the only means of defence. I opened fire with all guns blazing.

"And I can't wait for you to go back to your stupid Nintendo game of a country and your... umph... glmph... blmph... mmmph..."

Unfortunately everything started to come out as an incoherent slur as I tried to articulate my good points and her bad ones all at once.

"You see what I mean? You pathetic little creep," she hissed. "You couldn't fart your way out of a paper bag. There's nothing there. You're just a stupid, unemployable, undesirable, drunken wimp."

The frustration became too much to bear. I grabbed Roxanne's hair with one hand and smacked her face in a half punch, half slap with the other. She tried to resist but I had the uncontrollable strength that alcohol and anger can produce to such devastating effect.

My hand went up and down and from side to side across her face as I gathered momentum. I shifted my weight to get into a better position. No more Mr Nice Guy. I got on top of her and changed my hand from a slap into a tight fist and rained blow after blow down on to her face, scoring one unopposed hit after another. I could hear the satisfactory sound of jarred teeth with each punch. Down. Whack. Back. Reload. Down. Whack. Back. Reload.

"You cunt!" she screamed in muffled panic. How original. And then I remembered that I wasn't at school, hitting some snotty-nosed kid in the back yard, but hitting someone I supposedly loved. Loved to death. I held my fire momentarily and then, as an afterthought, gave her one last blow for luck, into the centre of her face, like a Minuteman missile locking onto a target. Well she'd asked for it and had got it back good and proper. There were several ways to win an argument and this was one of them, I supposed. I didn't know. I'd never really won an argument.

It had gone quiet after all the shouting. I took stock of the situation. I put on the bedside light, still straddled across Roxanne. I looked down at her.

"Oh my God," I whispered to myself. "What a mess! Just look at the state of it!"

I sobered up with a jolt and thought of Roxanne going to work with her face all mushed up on Monday. I wondered if she put some sunglasses on and said she'd tripped and fallen on her face, whether anyone would believe her. I doubted it somehow. Her face looked like a child cruelty advertisement. It was just a swollen piece of meat.

I jumped off and went downstairs to the kitchen to get some ice. I was beginning to feel a little remorseful as the adrenaline wore off and my head started to fill up with alcohol again. That last swig of Sauterne had been a really inspired move. I felt uncomfortable and flushed after my performance. My tongue started to stick in the dryness of my mouth. I went back into the bedroom. It was not a pretty sight. I wrapped the ice in a towel to make an arctic poultice and gently put it on her face, careful not to shock her. I felt a mild sense of catastrophe, like dropping a bottle of wine on the pavement and not knowing quite what to do.

"I'm sorry pet," I said. "I didn't mean it to be this way. I only came over in the first place because I wanted to be with you."

I shook my head and reiterated my apology.

"God, I'm sorry, but you should know better by now than to provoke me when I'm pissed. I didn't mean to be your sledgehammer. "

She must have passed out cold as she made no comment.

"Silly cow," I mumbled. "Look what you've gone and made me do."

There was nothing more I could think of for the time being. I figured we'd have to review the situation in the morning and perhaps go to a hospital to see if her nose or anything else had been broken.

I felt groggy again and couldn't think of anything nicer than laying my head on the pillow and putting everything off until the morning. With luck, in the clear light of day, somehow her injuries might not look quite so horrific. I put the ice pack down, leaving it seeping on the floor and re-arranged Roxanne so she would be comfortable. As I pulled her down the bed I noticed her head flop disconcertingly to one side.

"Fuck, that doesn't look good..." I muttered to myself.

A brief spasm of nausea gripped my stomach. Just temporarily. I tried to keep my calm and reminded myself that this was only a lovers' tiff. Happened all the time. I tried feeling her pulse but I wasn't sure where it was. I hurriedly got on all fours and put my ear to her heart. Nothing... no... something... maybe something. But it was my own heart thumping like an engine room. I held my face over her mouth to check her breathing. Her night breath was always foul. I normally had to turn away if she ever rolled over in her sleep and breathed on me, but I couldn't hear or smell anything.

"Shit, that's torn it," I said, aloud. "We're in for a real telling off this time, James Mallet. Not many people are going to get the joke. How are you going to explain this one to Mum?"

What was I to do? Say: "Sorry everybody, I was trying to impress Jodie Foster"?

Slowly the gravity of my actions and their consequences dawned on my stupid, half-pissed mind. I tried to think quickly and idiotically wondered what Clint would have done in such a situation. I clumsily clamped my lips on to Roxanne's mouth and tried to breathe some life into her. My breath just came out of her nose. I tried breathing down her nose, holding her lips together as I imagined I'd seen on the First Aid notices at the swimming baths. However hard I blew and sucked I couldn't get anything into her. I started to freak. I jumped on top of her, thumping and massaging her chest as they did in television hospital dramas when things went wrong. I rolled her over and whacked her back as if she had swallowed something. No response.

I rolled her back again and started to punch her chest, as hard as I had previously punched her face. It was like hitting a rag doll.

"The Curse!" I cried. "This just doesn't happen... it must be a dream. I've had nightmares about this sort of thing before. This doesn't happen to normal, middle class English boys."

With a jolt I felt I had hit on the root of the problem. Of course! I might be middle class and English but I certainly wasn't normal. All my life I had stood apart from the crowd and been different. But now was not the time to get philosophical. It was simply a mistake. What a soft machine the human body was. Very soft. Very fragile. Very human. But it *would* be me who'd go the whole hog and totally flatline another person. For all I knew I was insane anyway and it was a bit of luck that it hadn't happened before. Mr Hyde always was bigger than Dr Jekyll.

Roxanne's silence spoke volumes. I felt small and at a loss as to what to do. There had recently been a spate of sordid *crimes passionels* which had ended in tears when the perpetrators tried to cover them up. I didn't fancy putting Roxanne under the floorboards and coolly joining the police in the search, like the New Zealand dude who'd accidentally corpsed his girlfriend had done a couple of months before. I wanted to call an ambulance just in case something could be done to save her, but by the time I'd come up with the ice I'd been away five minutes. It felt like a million o'clock. I looked at my watch. It was a good ten minutes since I had swung the last blow. Bloody stupid idea that final punch. That was the straw that had broken the camel's back. Good shot though. Must have snapped her neck or spinal cord or pushed her snout into her brain. It would be another ten minutes before they could get the ambulance round despite the fact that the hospital was only a block away. By that time she would have started to go cold.

So I sat on the bed next to my late ex-girlfriend, trembling, and lit a cigarette. Viewed from a normal perspective what I had done was unacceptable. Yet from an esoteric standpoint I had done nothing particularly exceptional. Similar instances had happened up and down the ages, across the planet. Murder was nothing new and in my case it had been a natural mistake. I decided the only mental state in which I could cope was to treat the situation on a surreal basis. I thought of the limited options available to me. I could have done a Lord Lucan and lain 'doggo' somewhere, stuffing Roxanne into the back of the car, planting her in the middle of a field and gone into hiding. On the other hand, I couldn't bear the prospect of all the publicity and then being hunted down like an animal.

It was the small hours of Saturday morning. I would have perhaps three days before anyone raised the alarm, giving me until Monday evening. Roxanne's nosey flatmate disapproved of me and knew all about the Bernard situation. She'd probably be the one who'd blow the whistle. Poor little Bernie Brownpants: he wouldn't have anyone to play with when he arrived in London next week. All that way for nothing! It was unlikely that I would evade capture for more than two weeks, even if I was able to make a bolt for the Continent. I was just one of those people who, even if I wore an oatmeal cardigan and a pair of grey cords would look suspicious. If I tried to catch a plane to South America on Saturday or Sunday, it wouldn't help as I wouldn't be able to draw out all my money from the building society. Anything to keep me going after that would be traced. My accounts would be frozen. There might have been an element of fun being on the run for a couple of weeks, but being caught would not be so amusing.

The logic of it all suddenly became plain. There really was only one sensible course of action open to me. On an eye for an eye and a tooth for a tooth basis, I could get rid of myself once and for all. That way, in a rough sort of manner, justice would be done for Roxanne and I could avoid the shame and ballyhoo surrounding the whole sorry affair. In the back of my mind I'd recently been thinking about running things down anyway and then doing 'the decent thing'. Roxanne was right, for the very reason I'd hit her; I was unemployable, unlikely to find another girlfriend, certainly not of her calibre, and was, as near as damn it, a terminal alcoholic. I wasn't even fit for unemployment benefit; I wasn't fit to be a failure. I was a poor man's Mayor of Casterbridge. If I did 'the decent thing' and took myself out, no one would really miss me. My parents and friends might for a while, but they'd get over it. The planet itself wouldn't mourn my passing. It would be as if I had never existed. In the big scheme of things, no one would be any the worse for it.

I wondered what would be the best way to go about it. I'd never really seriously thought of how to go about suicide before, except the week before my 'A' levels. I had no idea what was the most effective method of despatch. I couldn't shoot myself because I didn't have a weapon as such and to borrow a friend's shotgun at that hour might have looked a bit odd. I didn't have access to any pills to overdose myself with and the thought of quietly slitting my wrists and getting into a bath seemed a little primitive. If I'd tried to hang myself I'd probably make a nonsense of it and just end up looking foolish at the end of a rope screaming for help. Besides, there were no rooms with high enough ceilings in my flat to hang from, yet alone a handy bracket or beam to slip a rope over. It wasn't exactly the sort of thing I could ask a person to help me with. I might be able to hang myself from a tree, but then I couldn't imagine climbing up and throwing myself off with a rope around my neck.

And then it hit me: Billy Mytton of course! The Conmax man who couldn't find another job who'd gassed himself in his car. That was it! If it was good enough for Billy Mytton, it was good enough for me. I would get a length of garden hose, attach it to my car exhaust and thread it through the back window and 'bingo', everyone would be happy. By then I wouldn't know, or care for that matter. The clichéd fume-filled BMW. *Too simple*, Mr Dalrmyple!

I stubbed out my cigarette and got to work. After I had put my clothes on I looked out a nice dress for Roxanne. She was coming too! We were going to be united in the fourth dimension forever! I thought her favourite black number was the most appropriate for the occasion. I picked out a new pair of dark tights, some clean knickers, a bra and her smartest shoes and started to dress her.

It was a difficult task at first as she was all floppy and uncooperative. As I leant to put on her bra, over what Roxanne used to refer to as her "breasticles", I slightly insanely thought about giving her 'one for the road', just to see what it was like. Who'd know? But on second thoughts I didn't think I was really up to it. Maybe I was just old-fashioned or a romantic fool, but having just murdered her I thought it was really going beyond the bounds of good taste. Besides, when I turned her over to put her pants and tights on I noticed that she'd rather prettily shat herself. Bummer. That bottom of hers had given me nothing but grief from day one. I supposed her sphincter must've seized and gone "ping" when I killed her. Never happened like that in the movies. Maybe she wanted to go for a dump before all the action started. I skilfully wiped it off with some tissues and flushed them down the loo. I wondered about putting some make-up on her, but her face was such a rainbow of colours it would have made her look ridiculous. I had second thoughts about her shoes and decided they'd just get in the way or drop off the whole time.

Eventually I managed to get her arms through the sleeves of her jacket. I inspected my work. Something was missing. Jewellery of course! I got a pair of pearl earrings, a gold choker and a bracelet I'd given her and put them on her. I took a step back. She looked much better. As a finishing touch, to make her seem more alive, I dabbed a little cologne behind her ears.

I looked at my watch. It was two-thirty. Roxanne had been dead for nearly half an hour. Now that I'd made up my mind about what I was going to do I moved quickly and efficiently. My mouth had gone even drier after the cigarette. I went downstairs to get a Coke from the fridge. As I was going back up the stairs, I heard the main door open. *The fear of God*! It was one of the flatmates back from a night on the town. I hoped whoever it was hadn't seen the kitchen light on. I disappeared into Roxanne's room and closed the door behind me, almost sick with fright and covered Roxanne with the duvet. It was definitely a man, and not a very sober one from the footsteps I heard coming up the stairs. He stopped at the lavatory and I heard a gushing sound that went on for nearly as long as mine had some thirty minutes earlier. I wouldn't have minded having another slash myself. He pulled the chain and left without washing his hands. Mucky pup!

I heard him go into his bedroom and close the door, indifferent or oblivious to the light in Roxanne's room. I waited for him to come out again to clean his teeth, but after five minutes I heard nothing. I tiptoed out onto the landing and saw that his door was shut and the light off. He was obviously beyond caring about such minor details as dental hygiene and had passed out immediately. I wondered what time the other flatmate would come back; the girl, the nosey one, and then I remembered that she spent most of her weekends at her boyfriend's place.

I went downstairs again and opened the front door to see if anyone was about. The dormant flatmate's curtains were drawn. The coast was clear. I did a quick tidy of Roxanne's room, wiping a faecal graze off the sheets with an odd sock which I then threw out of the window. *That's obscene, Mr Green!* I noticed the full moon again and wondered if there really was a connection between lunation and lunacy. Perhaps there had been a tidal upset in my constitution that evening. If the moon could affect entire oceans, why not me? After all, I was seventy per cent water. I shook my head. The real problem was that I was seventy per cent beer. I pulled the duvet to the top of the bed and plumped up the pillows.

I had several attempts at hoofing Roxanne onto my back in a fireman's lift but she kept slipping off. I eventually carried her in my arms, like a child. I turned off the light and staggered downstairs, glad that I'd decided against putting her shoes on her. Once outside, I closed the front door and stumbled with her towards my car. I wanted to put her in the boot, Aldo Moro style, as I didn't like the idea of her flopping all over the place and distracting me on the journey home. I needed all the faculties I could muster to negotiate the car safely back, but the boot still had a zillion Radon boxes in it. In the event I lobbed her onto the back seat and we vamoosed into the night in an orderly fashion.

My psyche had changed as my guilt and remorse were replaced by the practical considerations of evading capture. I'd stopped sweating and my palpitations were now under control. I made it back to Devon Gardens in ten minutes. I parked the car as close to my flat as possible and pondered about what to do with Roxanne. I didn't want to leave her in the boot as I thought it was an undignified, claustrophobic tomb and it would have involved shifting the two hundred-odd Radon boxes to make room. And the weather had been unseasonably warm lately. I didn't want Roxanne turning putrid on me and making things even more unpleasant. I could have left her in the basement dustbin area but there was the risk that Mr Buenechea's maid or some busybody would find her, even if I did a good job of covering her up. I didn't particularly want her in the flat as it was a long climb with a body. My flatmates quite often used the downstairs phone in my bedroom and there was nowhere else I could hide her effectively. Even if I put her in my bathroom, the prospect of having a dead Roxanne watching me go about my ablutions spooked me out a bit.

I scratched my head and wondered what to do. Perhaps I could eat her? I finally hit on the idea of using the cupboard halfway up the stairs. It was in the demilitarized zone between the second and third floor and contained old paint pots and bits of carpet underlay left over from when the common parts had last been decorated. It would be cool during the day and there was plenty of room for a body; in fact there was room for several if I ever felt like going on a murder spree, now I'd got the hang of it.

I fumbled with Roxanne's corpse and manhandled her up the stairs to the halfway cupboard. I left her face down on the stairs. I wanted to wrap her up in a sheet or a blanket, partly out of respect for the dead and partly because it seemed to be what people did when they'd murdered someone. Although Roxanne looked perfectly respectable in her, and for that matter, my favourite outfit, I felt some sort of shroud was necessary to complement her newly acquired deceased status.

I quickly popped up to the flat. It was late and unlikely that anyone would be around. If anyone happened to stumble across her, I could always say that Roxanne was drunk, although I noticed that her limbs were beginning to exhibit the unnatural stiffness of rigor mortis as her blood turned cold and the last vestiges of human warmth left her carcass forever. I was glad I hadn't hung around her flat for much longer as it would have been a problem moving her about if she'd been stiffed out like a starfish. As it was I had to close her eyes. Her corneas had clouded over into a milky white glaze and had begun to look most peculiar.

I rolled her up in an old blanket that smelt of dirty hair and sat her down amongst the paint pots, at rest and looking composed at last. Two hours earlier she had been alive and kicking - literally. All her brains and beauty hadn't done her much good in the end. In fact if she'd had less of either she'd probably have lived to have told a different tale. I shut the cupboard door and went back upstairs to my flat. It was just after three o'clock. What a night! From social drinker to homicidal maniac in under five hours! I was exhausted. I poured a large Scotch to knock me out and turned myself in for the night.

But not to the police.

# Chapter 13: Things Look Down

I slept the sleep of Mengele, but then awoke early with a start. My head was in a fug and my body smelt like an oily rag. Outside a solitary bird sang where there had once been thirty. I sat up and blearily tried to piece together the previous evening's events. I had a feeling that the night had not been a qualified success. *A bit of a hammering*, Mr Mainwaring? Predictably, I wondered if events as I recalled them were for real, but I knew it was a false hope to assume that any dream could have been quite so vivid. I decided I would put the matter to the test by checking on Roxanne when I went downstairs to collect the post.

I wasn't quite as euphoric as I had been the night before about arrangements concerning my own destiny, however I concluded that there really was no alternative but to go through with it. It was like a wank; I'd started, so I had to finish.

I had a bath and then listened to the radio as I made some coffee. Steve Winwood was singing something that didn't make any sense. I thought again about the previous night's outcome. If only Roxanne had met me at the pub I'd now be making a pot of coffee large enough for two. But it was time to stop thinking along 'what if' lines and just get on with the job.

The tasks for the daylight hours were quite simple: to get a length of garden hose that would accommodate the exhaust pipe; to contact the two friends who were best qualified to assist me in the technical details of what had to be done and, finally, to fill the car with Mr Esso's finest.

The most difficult thing would be not arousing suspicion from the two friends whose professional advice I sought. I fixed myself an aspirin omelette and popped open a Bud from the fridge; quite the best breakfast beer in the world.

At nine I went downstairs to check the post and poked my head into the halfway cupboard to check that Roxanne hadn't decided to come back to life and run off. No such luck. I didn't linger long as the brooding spectre of Roxanne's corpse gave me the creeps. I continued downstairs and checked the mail. There was a rejection letter for me, which was a treat. Most companies had stopped bothering with such courtesies long ago. I wasn't surprised; my niche had become a tomb. Good news came by phone; bad news came by mail. It was from PNB Capital:

*We have studied your details with interest but due to
the very high standard of applicants we feel that your
qualifications and experience do not quite match our
present needs.*

Talk about rubbing it in! Tactless cunts.

However we will keep your curriculum vitae on file
and contact you should any suitable opportunities arise.

  Like, sure you will. They would be glad on Monday when all was
revealed, that they hadn't picked *me* for an interview!
  I went out into the sunshine to buy a newspaper and stopped off for a
croissant at the patisserie. I wasn't going to let the fact that I had a little
blood on my hands stand in the way of my Saturday morning
gratifications. When I returned to the flat I rang Angelica, a doctor with
whom I was friendly, and one of the two people I wanted to contact for
advice on my morbid predicament. Fortunately she wasn't on call that
weekend and was able to meet me for a drink at lunchtime.
I then called Freddie, a solicitor and my second would-be advisor, whom
I'd been friends with since school. I enquired what he was up to that
evening. He said he was going to a party, but when I asked him if he could
pop round to my flat beforehand, he said that it wouldn't be a problem.

I spent the rest of the morning tidying the flat and doing the usual weekend
domestica. I walked down to the ironmonger on Alphabet Street, bought
four metres of one inch gauge hose and went to fill the car up, giving it one
last wash 'n' wax at the petrol station. The swami at the garage slyly tried
to forget handing over my Tiger tokens. He must have been a Tiger token
tycoon! For my part, it was a pity I had to go so soon. I was nearly two-
thirds of the way to amassing the necessary tokens to qualify for a pair of
secateurs for the solitary rose that stood guard on my balcony.
  I picked Angelica up at one and we went off to 'The Artist'. I knew at
least four other doctors I could have contacted, but Angelica was the one I
knew best. Apart from some locum work, she was having great difficulty
finding a job within the NHS. She was becoming increasingly disillusioned
with the whole Hippocratic Oath thing and, in such circumstances, I
thought she'd be the best for advice on my objective. She smoked like a
chimney and did all the things that doctors weren't supposed to do. Best of
all, she had a soft spot for me. I never knew whether she actually fancied

me. I suspected not, but I think she regarded us as two of a kind and we'd always enjoyed a bolshy rapport. I got her a spritzer and a pint of lager for myself rather than the usual pint of 'Nasty', which had rather nasty connotations at that point. It had got me into quite enough trouble for one weekend. We found a quiet corner and I got to work. We chatted about mutual friends for a bit. I asked Angelica about her sister, Alex, who had a pop group called 'Alex and the Nosebleeds'. Angelica exhaled a puff of smoke angrily.

"The Nosebleeds walked out on her about a month ago. Pity. They were just about to go skyrocket in Malta. The band's now just called 'Alex'. There's no one else in it. The whole thing's pretty hopeless."

I saw the glorious stained-glass window of opportunity that I was looking for.

"Yeah. The whole world's gone mad. A friend of mine committed suicide the other day. He'd had enough. Hose-piped himself in the back of his car."

Angelica took the bait without hesitation. She launched into a medical tirade on various ways and means of committing suicide. After she'd exhausted her repertoire on the subject, she concluded that carbon monoxide poisoning was the preferred form of self-obliteration and had the seal of approval of one in three suicide cases. She went on to say that it was not a particularly pleasant way to take the final bow. In fact, she said, it was no more enjoyable than being shoved into a gas chamber. I coaxed her gently to go on. Angelica paused for a moment and then started to describe the intense nausea that accompanied car fume absorption which frequently led people to bottle out halfway, leaving them alive but looking foolish. She said it was easier for people to go through with it if they were heavily sedated, i.e. drunk. I had no intention of doing otherwise. She answered my questions matter-of-factly, unaware, I thought at the time, of my mental tape recorder.

"How long does it take to have the desired effect?" I asked.

"Depends on the make and age of the car, whether it's properly tuned and so on."

"OK, but normally?"

"Carbon monoxide poisoning used to cause loss of consciousness within a few minutes and death within half an hour, but catalytic converters have cut emissions by ninety percent."

Shit! I could have been there for weeks! I thanked God I'd never been a victim of environmental sentimentality and converted my car to catalyticism.

Once I'd satisfied myself that there was no point in going any further with the subject, I suggested that we made tracks and offered her a lift home.

I had things to do in the flat for the rest of the afternoon. I gave 'Mr Loon' and 'Mr Park', the two dope plants that I had growing on the balcony, a haircut and made a salad out of the trimmings. I put some photographs into an album and generally fussed about doing a series of fiddly jobs to keep myself occupied. The sun started to set. I switched on the TV. Women in tight white trousers leapt like springboks across the screen while proclaiming the virtues of a brand of sanitary towels. I settled down to watch 'Doogie Howser MD' for the last time. I was going to miss the magic box in the corner that took me to distant lands and introduced me to people I would never meet.

The doorbell went. It was Freddie - a bit early. I pulled out a couple of beers from the fridge and went through the same procedure as I had with Angelica, although in Freddie's case, a trap was hardly necessary. Criminal acts and the administration of justice were all part of Freddie's nine-to-five. I only had to ask him if he'd had any juicy cases recently and we were practically on subject. He'd recently acted on behalf of a vague acquaintance who'd been involved in a drink-drive rap.

I asked casually, "Obviously drink is not considered a mitigating circumstance in this instance, but are there occasions where it might be taken into consideration?"

"Like what?" Freddie asked. "Stealing pub window boxes after closing time?"

"Well, something a bit more serious. Let's think. I know... how about murder? Or accidental murder, for instance."

"Difficult. I don't think it would affect the apportionment of guilt. It might alter the charge from murder to manslaughter, but someone who's capable of murdering another person would normally be perceived as possessing a reasonable degree of co-ordination. It would all depend what grounds there were to consider, such as provocation or self-defence."

"So what's the difference between a manslaughter and a murder verdict?" I asked as nonchalantly as my nerves would allow.

"With murder, it's a mandatory life sentence, which is normally twenty-five years but can be commuted down quite a bit with good behaviour and stuff, whereas with manslaughter a person might get away with five years, or less if he's lucky."

We switched over briefly to girls. Freddie had met Roxanne a couple of times. He asked how we were getting on.

"It's over, I'm afraid," I replied, calmly. "For me, she no longer exists."

"That's too bad," Freddie commented, commiseratively. Freddie had always taken a healthy interest in my love life, although he tended to be reticent about his own. He went on.

"You seemed to be having a laugh together. Have you lined up any replacement nob fodder?"

"Not really," I answered reflectively. "Not since my pheromones went weird on me."

"Money is the only pheromone at our age, pal," Freddie remarked drily.

"Quite," I concurred. "In which instance I rest my case."

Freddie had to leave for his party. We said our farewells, promising to meet again in the near future.

After he'd left I went into my bedroom and settled down with a glass of wine to relax the man's way with my porno collection; my 'friends' as I liked to call them. I opened the pages at my favourite bits and had them scattered around me on the bed like attendant disciples. Play wristy for me. After I'd finished I put the entire library into a couple of black bin liners and took them down to next-door's dustbins. I didn't want as an epitaph on my gravestone:

**James Mallet**
**1956-1992**
**Wanker**

Of course, like everything else I'd done recently, I managed to fuck it up. I suppose I should have been grateful that my own ineptitude or The Curse occasionally backfired on itself, and let humble misfortune come to my rescue.

It was properly dark by the time I emptied my ersatz boudoir buddies into Number 44's dustbins. I decided to have a practice run with my mobile gas chamber. To get the hose from the exhaust pipe into the car I had to leave a gap between the window and the sill. The gap would have to be sealed with a wet towel. I thought of driving out of London and doing the dreaded deed in some pretty neck of the woods, but in the end I elected to get it over and done within the same locality as where I lived. There was the no-through road that I'd used in the soap powder heist nearby where I could park in privacy. Like everywhere else in the area, it went to sleep at weekends. I reckoned after the success of the previous evening's manoeuvres, any time after half past two in the morning and I'd have the streets to myself.

I went back to the flat and got out a bottle of my favourite tipple, 'Old Fraud' malt and chugged back two large glasses in quick succession. "Well, why not have a drink or five?" I asked myself. After all, it wasn't as though I had to worry about a hangover the next day.

My flatmates were away that weekend, which was convenient and meant I could go about my business without any distractions. I felt a slow bowel-moving sense of apprehension and went through the now familiar routine of asking myself whether I was doing the right thing. I got up and fixed myself another whisky.

I hadn't got round to writing a will, so I just wrote down who should get what on a piece of paper. I had, once upon a time, entertained the idea of setting up a covenant with a view to leaving all my wordly goods to my old school on the condition that I was buried in the headmaster's drawing room. I dismissed the idea now as being too absurd, even by my standards and tried to think of more sensible means of distributing my assets. I decided to split the proceeds of the flat, which I assumed would be sold, between my parents and my sister and decreed that they could have their choice of the contents. The cash in my deposit account, most of it, £15,000 odd, was to go to Roxanne's parents to do with it whatever they wanted; perhaps start a 'Roxanne Sullivan Memorial Foundation' if they so wished. I split the remaining £6,000 into lots of £1,000 between Freddie, Angelica, Crystal, Michelle and, just to show that there were no hard feelings, Rebecca and Yasmin from my Parker Barrow days. I left nothing to Christine Hale. If my madness had had any justice, it should have been her, not Roxanne, who was sitting in the halfway cupboard.

The legacy wouldn't go very far, but I thought it would be unfair to my family to dilute my contribution to the dynasty's fortunes any further. I would have loved to have given something to everyone whom I'd ever shared a bed with, but I didn't want to look as if I was posthumously boasting. It was terribly sad, really, having to say goodbye to all my possessions and memories, not to mention all tomorrow's parties.

I realised, just as I was finishing the instructions concerning the disposal of my car-cum-gas chamber, that without witnesses the will wouldn't be worth the paper it was written on. There was no one I could call at that stage of the evening without arousing suspicion. Then I had a brainwave. I ran quickly out of the flat and got Ali at the all night Deli on Alphabet Street to act as one witness, and Brian, the Australian at Weirdbins down the road, as the other. Neither appeared surprised by my request and I went back to my flat, happy that I'd done the job properly. After I got home I put the entire works of Felching Ron on the CD player, and sat back, relishing every note and word, which made me feel doubly remorseful. But it was for the best. There I was, getting all sorry for myself, when really it was penance for Roxanne that was at stake.

After my fourth Scotch I decided that I must make a tape recording explaining all and saying how sorry I was. I wanted my motives to be clear and to remove any doubts about my sanity. I had a few attempts with the tape recorder, but I wasn't very coherent. In fact I sounded as crazy as a fox when I played it back, so I abandoned the idea and chucked the tape in the bin and wrote a short note of self-condolence instead.

At about midnight I went to get ready and make myself look lovely. I ran a bath for the last time and relaxed in the bubbles with my fifth Scotch. I contemplated the plastic razor in the soap dish. I picked it up and fiddled with it. I started to shave my arms. My skin felt so soft. I continued with my legs and chest until I had no more body hair left, concluding my eclectic topiary, as an afterthought, by pruning my pubes into the shape of a heart. That would give them something to talk about down at the morgue! I rinsed myself off and stepped out of the bath. I dried my new svelte body, put on a fresh shirt, a clean pair of jeans and my best gay boy Marks and Spunks mountain boots. I didn't want people to think I was a slob. I did everything slowly and deliberately, as if not to rush the occasion; to delay the moment of truth. I combed and blow-dried my hair. It was at its best length, encasing and enhancing my face without being too scruffy at the back. I looked at my reflection and, through the whisky, thought that for an unexciting looking man, I'd never looked better. I didn't appear mad. Who gave a fuck what I thought? I was wondering what else I should do when the phone went. Two minutes later it went again. Like an idiot I answered both calls.

As fate would have it, unbeknown to either of my unwitting accomplices, or myself for that matter, Freddie and Angelica were destined to go to the same party that evening. The Venn diagram of coincidence was not so extraordinary. They knew each other and were part of the same crowd. It was I who'd introduced them in the first place, and they'd even had a brief, but now undiscussed affair.

They gravitated towards each other as the evening wore on until, almost when it was time to go, as they subsequently told me with such relish, they turned to each other and spoke. They had little in common now that their brief fling was over and I was the only point of conversation where they had any mutual ground. They established that I had contacted both of them unexpectedly that day to meet for no apparent reason. Angelica remarked that I had taken an unusual interest in the technical advantages and disadvantages surrounding various means of suicide. Freddie said that he'd also been subjected to some rather strange questions by me. Especially the ones concerning the different criminal implications of manslaughter and murder. They spent some time comparing notes on the oddities of my behaviour, to the point where embellishment got the better of them. Both of them
agreed that if I wasn't stark raving mad, I was somewhere close.

"I hope he's all right," Angelica said, casting aside her physician's mantle in a rare display of maternalism.

"I know this lack of a job thing's getting him down," Freddie remarked, with a solicitous grasp of the obvious.

"Do you know how it's going with Roxanne?" Angelica enquired.

"I asked him that this evening. I think they're finished. James didn't elaborate. He just said: 'For me, she no longer exists.'"

Freddie shifted uncomfortably and thought for a moment.

"There's something not quite right here," he said, halfway through his ruminations.

"Are you thinking what I'm thinking?" Angelica asked, more out of hope that their mutual telepathy might rekindle a momentary spark of attention than out of any serious concern for my welfare.

"Perhaps. I'll give him a call when I get home," Freddie replied, subconsciously distancing himself from Angelica's metaphysical bonding, but added wistfully, for excitement's sake, "I must admit, I'm getting decidedly whiffy vibes about the whole thing."

They tired of the subject and briefly went on to other things before they went their separate ways. They rang me independently when they got back to their respective houses.

Freddie's was the first call. He came straight to the point.

"James, I saw Angelica this evening. You didn't say that you'd seen her at lunch time."

It was nearly midnight and my fifth scotch had transformed itself into my sixth.

"I didn't think it was important, old boy."

"Oh fuck off James. Someone with your social antennae and propensity for gossip would jump at the chance to dissect a mutual friend you'd just seen a few hours before. Are you hiding something... some sort of skeleton in your cupboard, James?"

*A bit close!*

"I don't know what you're talking about," I said desperately, which led him to his next question.

"What's happened to Roxanne?"

"What do you mean?"

"It's only a question James, not an accusation."

"I don't know. I don't see her these days."

"Because *she no longer exists?*"

"Oh come off it Freddie. Don't get heavy."

"James, I don't like what I'm hearing. You need help. I'm coming over."

"For fuck's sake, leave me alone," I said, panicked by the prospect of my cover being blown. But the phone was dead. Two minutes later it was Angelica.

"James, whatever you're thinking of doing, for God's sake don't do it!"

"Oh yeah, like God's been a real sport to me, besides, I'm doing nothing."

"There's something dreadfully wrong. I don't know what it is, but I want to help in any way I can. I am a doctor, after all. Whatever hole you're in, the main thing is you've got to do something about your drink problem before it's too late. I mean even now you sound completely off your face..."

"Correct. And frankly my dear, I don't give a dram," I said, and with that yanked the phone jack out of the wall. If anybody wanted to talk to me they'd have to contact me in the next world.

I had to get moving. Although neither Angelica or Freddie lived particularly close by, there was no time to be wasted. I wasn't too worried. I'd be out of the flat, and probably this life, by the time either of them arrived. They'd never find where I'd parked the car, even if they had guessed what I was up to.

I brought the schedule forward two hours. I placed my makeshift will and farewell note in my back pocket, grabbed a bathroom towel and soaked it under the tap. I turned off the CD player and left my dear flat forever. I tiptoed down the staircase to the halfway cupboard. I had a peek at Roxanne and saw, not surprisingly, that she hadn't moved since I had last checked her. She looked an eerie but rather pathetic bundle in the semi-darkness, sitting forlornly among the paint pots, like a badly drawn Modigliani in confession. I pulled back the blanket and looked at her face. Some black mucous or toxins had unattractively started to ooze out of the corner of her mouth. I tried to feel love but the bruises on her bottle-blue face and her flattened nose made her look slightly porcine. Her expression was not one of my favourites. It was the cross, disapproving scowl that I used to call her 'shut up' look that she put on whenever she wasn't getting her way. *Don't frown*, Mrs Brown!

I looked at her for a few moments longer and thought how different life would have been if we'd never met. It was too late now for regrets. I tried to feel a sense of pity but with my own fate in the balance that didn't work either. I even tried to feel hatred and blame the whole thing on Roxanne, but she wasn't the one who'd got so pissed in the first place. I relived her last few outbursts and still thought she'd been stupid, in the circumstances for provoking me in such a way. A bright girl like her should have known better, especially when she was aware of the extremes I could go to when I was drunk.

I waited for the time switch light to go out and went further down the stairs. I stopped and listened at Mr Buenechea's door. I couldn't hear anything. I hoped to God he was in bed. It would've been extremely awkward to have bumped into him with Roxanne on my back. I would have had to pretend that I was taking the rubbish out! I went to the bottom of the stairs and had a look outside. I moved quickly towards the car. I took the tube out of the boot and placed it on the back seat with the wet towel. I switched off the inside light so that it wouldn't go on when I next opened the door. I left the door unlocked and quietly scuttled back to my block of flats, keeping to the shadows, checking to make sure that no one was dawdling by a window. My heart started to race again. The adrenaline came as a welcome chaser after all the whisky I'd hoovered. The events of the last twenty-four hours were beginning to make me feel exhausted.

I went back to the halfway cupboard and waited for my eyes to adjust to the darkness. Now was not the moment to use the time switch. I opened the cupboard door. I could just make out Roxanne's grey silhouette from the outside light by the stairwell. I bent my knees and put one arm under her legs and the other around her waist. It was a delicate manoeuvre. I didn't want to make a clatter with the paint pots and, at the same time, I had to be careful not to put my back out. I would have looked an idiot doubled up on the stairs with a slipped disc when Freddie and Angelica came haring round!

I eased Roxanne out and sat her on the stairs, propping her against the wall. Her rigor mortis had obligingly made her easier to manipulate. She no longer flopped all over the place. I noticed that her head was stuck at an appropriately crestfallen angle. I closed the cupboard door and was able, this time, to yank her onto my back in a fireman's lift. I attempted to walk as quietly as possible down the stairs. Now that I had Roxanne on my back she didn't feel particularly heavy. Her blanket smelled faintly of an unbecoming mixture of paint, turpentine and death. Once I was down at the bottom of the stairs, I opened the front door slightly and peered out with Roxanne still on my back.

"God, this is exciting!" I muttered to myself.

And then I remembered that it wasn't a game and that I was about, albeit rather sheepishly, to meet my Maker.

I dashed, like Quasimodo, into the darkness once more and made my way stealthily towards the car. I opened the passenger side and put Roxanne on the seat. I took the blanket off and swivelled her slightly to give her the appearance of being curled up asleep. I looked around to make sure no one was spying on me. It had all gone so well! I wished I'd been a commando on a daring night raid rather than a common murderer, but the exhilaration was about the same.

I drove the short distance to the cul-de-sac I had chosen and parked discreetly away from a streetlight between two cars. I got the hose out and wedged it into the exhaust pipe. I was pleased with the fit. I passed the pipe under the car and through to the back window. I got into the car, closed the door behind me and fed the pipe properly through the window, jamming the towel between the sill and the glass as I rolled the window up as far as it would reasonably go to make it airtight. I clambered into the driver's seat, unceremoniously dislodging Roxanne from her position. After I had re-aligned her, I sat behind the steering wheel and adjusted the rear-view mirror to have a look at myself. I didn't look as composed as I had before. My face had become distorted by the alcohol and my hair was all over the place. I briefly thought about going back to the flat to redo my mop but dismissed the idea as being too ridiculously vain at this late stage, and besides, I was running out of time.

I pushed down the central locking tit and turned the key slowly in the ignition. The radio sprang to life. The Gerbil Twins were taking the piss again with a clone of their previous hit. I regretted not bringing down a Felching Ron tape with me. I found a channel that was doing some midnight mellow madness thing and an in-depth musical profile of Simply Ill-Bred. I turned the ignition another centimetre. The engine coughed to life and then settled to an agreeably quiet purr. I took the will and farewell note out of my pocket and placed them on my lap where they wouldn't be missed.

Just as Angelica had said, the car started to fill with fumes almost immediately. Initially it didn't smell particularly deadly; it just smelled of fumes. I had no problems breathing and wondered whether I was doing it properly. Looking at Roxanne sitting faithfully beside me, I couldn't resist stroking her hair. I should have combed it before I turned the engine on, but I couldn't think of everything, could I? I reached over and tried to hold her hand as I thought it would make a touching sight for whoever found us, but it wasn't a natural pose, so I left her alone.

After about ten minutes the fumes began to have their effect and I started feeling decidedly queasy. My head started to roll and I thought how strange that Roxanne and I would probably be found in the same dejected pose by the time it was all over. I tried to see my whole life pass before my eyes, like they say you do, but I couldn't concentrate with all the fumes and whisky, so I just listened to the radio. The music was becoming increasingly faint and distorted. What a life! Way to go! A fitting end to such a shambolic and erratic existence. *Finita la commedia!*

I wondered what it would be like on the other side. I had two visions of Heaven. One was of a celestial version of the Harrods make-up foyer, with marble fittings and perfectly powdered worker-drones in attendance everywhere. The other was of a huge Elysian drive-in, playing endless repeats of my various acts of abasement in front of an audience of the trillion souls that had been created since the dawn of time. I reflected that although I hadn't been long on earth, I'd had two years longer than Jesus had at his first attempt, so really that made me two years older at chucking out time than Him, although He was, really, nearly two thousand years older than me. My head started to spin. I became light-headed and giggly - not so much out of euphoria as a sense of not understanding what was going on with the flashing lights and stamping sounds.

As the music began fading, I was just thinking how much I preferred Take Smack to Non-U 2, and asking myself whatever happened to 'The Dukes of Hazzard' and why Citroen made such ugly cars and why French bicycles were crap and whether Beatrix and Dennis Potter were related, when there was an almighty crash.

Everything went blank.

# Chapter 14: Slime and Punishment

Perhaps subconsciously I'd wanted things to turn out the way they did, but *prima face* my intention had been to finish it off once and for all and at least have the final say in my own destiny. I'd sealed Roxanne's fate, so it seemed appropriate that I should secure proper retribution on her behalf. Unfortunately, it wasn't quite so straightforward.

Freddie immediately called the police after he'd spoken to me and the fuzz were on the case by ten past twelve. Once they'd phoned my number and found that the line was dead, they were out of the station by twelve fifteen. It took them ten minutes to reach my flat. They had a description of my car, "a grey BMW", but, alas, *dans la nuit tous les BMWs sont gris.* They spread out and had a foot rozzer for each street. It should have been easy to hear my car idling but for the fact that I was parked away from the Gardens. The distant thunder of late night juggernauts on the Cromwell Road muffled my modest contribution to the nocturnal noise pollution. My greatest ally on the noise front though, was the constant scream of police cars arriving at the scene, their sirens wailing like banshees, which more than covered up the gentle throb of my Teutonic neutrality. I had been unaware of the rumpus until I was teetering on the edge of consciousness and about to black out.

Eventually a policeman noticed the towel covering the gap in the back window and saw Roxanne and me slumped in our seats. He had the presence of mind to pull the hose off the exhaust pipe as he called his other colleagues to the scene. Not being car thieves, it took them a while to smash open a window, unlock the doors and switch off the engine. Angelica and Freddie were at the scene by the time I was discovered and told me later that an ambulance was there within minutes. Apparently the medics were super-quick about putting oxygen masks on us, although obviously it was a little late in the night to be of much use to Roxanne.

The other residents who'd been woken up by the excitement either rubbernecked the blue activity from their windows or came down to get a closer look. The area was quickly cordoned off and Roxanne and I were shoved into the back of the ice cream van and whisked off at great speed into the night. It must have been fairly obvious that Roxanne was a goner because she looked so stiff and lifeless, but Freddie said later that he sensed I'd be OK. After a brief discussion, Angelica and Freddie came forward and identified themselves as the tip-off merchants.

A pick-up truck came to remove the car, as evidence I suppose. The chief bluebottle asked Angelica and Freddie to come back to my flat with him. The flat had been set up as a command station after the police had requisitioned the keys from my car. There were four policemen there, so Freddie later told me, two of whom were in plain clothes, taking pictures and painting fingerprint dust all over the place, the purpose of which escaped him. They'd seen one movie too many. The other two were dressed to look like policemen and took their statements accordingly. Angelica's and Freddie's respective professions had given them ample training for handling the pedantic ritual of police enquiry and they were allowed to leave once they'd given their details.

For my part, I had my last night's sleep as an unconfirmed murderer, oblivious to the fact that I was still alive. I came to slowly and leadenly, not knowing where I was, and then lapsed back into unconsciousness. I awoke properly when I was disturbed by a conversation at the end of my bed. I had no idea who the conversationalists were or what they were doing. When I looked up and saw that one of them was a policeman, I wondered whether I'd been involved in a train crash or been run over by a bus. I could feel no pain and, as I was able to wiggle my toes, I assumed that no particular harm had come to me. My face felt odd and then I realised it was the mask of a respirator sinking into my skin. My awakening had a dramatic effect on the policeman at the end of my bed.

"Good aftable consternoon," I said gaily.

The policeman immediately darted out of the room to get the 'super' without saying so much as a cursory "hello!"

The minutiae of questioning were held back for the rest of the day while I recovered. After the initial earnest "What you say may be taken in evidence" malarkey it became pretty obvious that I was in big trouble. After that I was taken into police custody. I got a lot of 'Section 23', whatever that was, waved at me whenever I gave my version of events. They'd found the abortive tape that I'd tried to make on my last evening when they were going through my rubbish bin and had played it through a million times. For some reason they overlooked or spared me the embarrassment of making reference to the denuded state of my body hair, nor was there any mention of the dope plants on my balcony. My handwriting was analysed by experts who pored over the will I'd made that night. When I started to recount the preceding forty-eight hours, I realised that I'd been right in trying to settle the issue myself. I could see it would take endless man-hours, mainly mine, answering the same repetitive questions and satisfying the authorities' ghoulish desire to go through and reconstruct events over and over again. An endless stream of quacks and shrinks, 'tecs and dicks - not to mention lawyers - filed past me in the 'Counselling Room'. It gave an entirely new perspective to the phrase 'helping police with their enquiries'.

I was detained for questioning for three days before I was officially charged and then everything went quiet for a while. I didn't bother with an application for bail. I knew I wouldn't get it. Besides I wanted to delay the embarrassment of showing my face to the outside world. I was bundled off to a magistrate's court where I was remanded in custody pending trial, and then left to contemplate my fate.

I felt almost more sorry for my parents than Roxanne's. It was bad enough for any parent to have a ne'er-do-well son. But having a murderer in the family was almost as shaming as having a homosexual, in the eyes of the Farnham bridge set and the other licensed hypocrites at the golf club. The Surrey Neanderthals would be very nice to begin with but, little by little, they'd be sure to exclude my parents from the geriatric social whirl that was so much part of all their existence.

Roxanne's parents came over from South Africa to collect her body and sign various bits of paper. They met my parents and, in the circumstances, got on very well with them, so much so that my mother suggested that they stay with them until it was time for them to go back home. The Sullivans excused themselves and said they wanted to be in London to be near their daughter, or something. Roxanne, posthumously, could do no wrong in everyone's eyes and went past martyrdom, through celestial canonization and on to sainthood in the space of a week.

Although I was now technically the ward of the prison service while I awaited trial, due to a bureaucratic hiccup or prison overcrowding, I was handed back into police custody. For some reason it seemed safer and psychologically less oppressive than being in an actual prison. I was taken to a remand-cum-don't- know-what-to-do-with-you centre where there was no one around to talk to about the outside world, although there was something oddly cathartic about being surrounded by authority. It took matters well and truly out of my hands. It was like closure. But it wasn't.

I was pretty much kept in the dark about what was happening except for what I heard from Freddie when he came to visit. I wasn't allowed a TV in my cell but I was permitted access to a black and white number in the 'Recreation Room' at certain hours. It had an indoor aerial that only worked if I stood behind the set and held it over my head, like a fool. The only newspapers I saw were lent to me strictly according to the whim of the policeman on duty, so I spent most of the time listening to the radio that Freddie had brought in for me.

More about Freddie. Naturally I was a bit peeved by what Freddie had done to foil my exit, but as a friend it was a comfort to have a smile among all the stern faces. Furthermore, out of guilt for upsetting my plans, he boldly offered me his services in a professional capacity at mates' rates. I readily accepted. It was good to have someone to forgive after having done something so utterly unforgivable myself. I knew he would see me through the bullshit in this new, confusing world of reprimanding grown-ups that I'd been thrust into. Despite his role in saving my life, Freddie seemed genuinely remorseful about my current predicament. The least he could do, he said, was to try to help me get out of it. The publicity surrounding the case was bigger than anything he'd ever handled before. He told me that I would be up against the toughest bastards in town. He retracted his original opinion that there wouldn't be any point in pleading manslaughter, as he reasoned that in my case, with all the psychoanalysis I was getting, I could have a claim for acting with diminished responsibility. The shrinks reckoned my entire life had been one act of diminished responsibility, which was nice of them. I didn't really care. As I'd been quite happy to kill myself, imprisonment came as an unexpected plus, but Freddie said there was no point in hanging around in jail for any longer than was necessary.

I realised then that however hellish things were at that moment, they'd get worse once I went on trial and the whole cross-examination process was repeated. As it was, each day was a long, bureaucratic nightmare of endless questions, tests, interviews and counselling sessions. At least there were no beatings or any physical nonsense. I had admitted my crime and co-operated immediately, agreeing to more wrongdoings than an entire Catholic mass in confession. I went along with whatever they wanted me to say or do. Some of the police interrogators were a bit chippy, so I kept any wisecracks or displays of impatience to myself, but in reality I'd lost my appetite for life and was beyond caring one way or the other what really happened.

My existence reverted to being boring and pointless. As for the court case, it didn't take an incredible amount of legal insight to know that the cards were stacked against me. I was guilty. The only thing in dispute was the severity of the punishment. Five strokes or six? Cane or slipper? I just wanted to get the bloody thing over with and then face whatever firing squad they had lined up for me.

A few days after I was charged I was allowed my first visitors. A lot of people wanted to see me now that I was a quasi-celebrity, but I was only allowed an hour's worth of visits each day, so initially I only saw my family and close friends.

The first people to visit me were my parents. I'd had a brief and unsatisfactory conversation with them on the phone a few days before, but I wasn't prepared for the shock I got when I saw them. They'd aged ten years. They looked small and worried as they did everything they could to keep a stiff upper lip. I wanted to weep for their pitiful attempts to appear normal and correct. My mother, the coiffed crusader, was smartly dressed, as if she were going to a prep school sports day. The first thing she asked was whether they were looking after me and if the food was OK.

My parents were funny like that. In their eyes I hadn't changed since I was six. It was as if they would have my little red bicycle with its stabilisers waiting for me at home when I had done my sentence and expect me to go tearing around the garden waving my Johnny-Seven-One-Man-Army screaming "*Quis? Vains! Ego 'D'*! I'm going to play conkers with Scruffy... make way for mad-cap Mallet, terror of the lower fourth!" I wondered if they'd insist on me wearing my corduroy shorts with their snake buckle 'laccy belt and if I'd be allowed to cross the A30 by myself. Then, with a jolt, I realised that they might not be there when I got out or they'd be all old or loony and locked up somewhere themselves.

We talked, a little awkwardly, about home and various relatives. For once Her Maj didn't get a look in. The conversation came round to Freddie and that led to the whole shebang. I cut the crap and with tears in my eyes looked up and sobbed, "I'm sorry."

It was a cop-out, but we needed an escape valve. I was more upset that my parents had to concern themselves with such a fuck-up at their late stage in life than with my own predicament. Especially when all their friends' children were so normal and doing so well. Bastards. I'd managed, with six pints of 'Nasty', to crown the summit of my parents' lives with such misery that it all but cancelled out the things they'd striven and fought for. There was nothing left for them to rebuild. It was too late. For the moment they were acting true to type; the darker the hour, the stronger their resolve and support. But only time would prove whether their Dunkirk spirit would be enough to see them through.

"We know it was all a mistake," my mother said, consolingly. "We love you more than ever and pray for you all the time." I gulped as she continued. "We know you were under enormous pressure and didn't mean it. You're a good man at heart... we know that and we couldn't ask for a better son." I thought the last bit was slightly over-the-top but I appreciated the sentiment nonetheless.

I also realised that their life, as they knew it, was technically over. They were too old to move to another town. The stigma, courtesy of the golf club fascists of the region, wouldn't be allowed to die. It would live with them until it was their turn to sink the final putt.

They left, bowed and sad, both of them trying to be as pleasant as possible to the staff on the way out, as if canvassing for my innocence. It only seemed a week ago that they'd been, in their own way, a groovy 'sixties mixed-martini type of couple. Now they were old. I watched them go and had to wipe away another tear at the sight of the sheer misplaced decency that I had fought so long to resist.

The following day was more tricky, as it was the turn of Elspeth, my elder sister and erstwhile competitor for our mother's nipple. She had her weird husband with her. Elspeth was a jokey, gentle person but I knew in her own no-nonsense way that I wouldn't get off quite so lightly with regards any sympathy. Elspeth felt partly responsible for my actions as she had been given the task of looking after me whenever my parents weren't around when I was younger. She more or less let me do what I liked and I was happily smoking my first cigarettes by the time I was nine and constantly being sick on cheap sherry all over her cheap little flat.

They didn't have much to say. I knew their lives wouldn't be particularly affected. They were from a more contemporary generation that had a comprehension of the video nasty mentality and scuzzy side of life. Bursting into tears and saying sorry would be no good as an emotional decongestant under these circumstances.

Elspeth took the lead and made as light of the matter as was possible. She had to get back to her kids before long. The incident simply represented another chapter in the disastrous events surrounding her problem little brother. She was practical and asked how long I thought I'd have to go down for. She said when or if I ever came out, I'd always be welcome to stay and rehabilitate with her and her husband until I found my feet.

It was a pleasant and optimistic vision of the future with them in their sixties introducing me to the local divorcees and widows. They'd love to meet a real murderer, I bet. The thought of helping my brother-in-law with healthy outdoor activities such as chopping wood and generally badger-baiting around the garden was a comforting prospect. They left jauntily, with my sister asking me if I would now make some attempt to acknowledge the devilish charms of alcohol and accept the seriousness of its abuse. It was as if she had transferred the responsibility of my actions onto commercially available beverages. After they'd gone, I felt more cheerful about my predicament than I had for quite a while.

Visitors came and went, asked questions and gave me advice. On the whole I got the kind of sympathy that I'd received when I was unemployed, namely that if this sort of thing was going to happen to anyone, I was the best person to cope with it. Easy for them to say. I even received a visit from Mr Loon of Kowshat, which was very Korean of him.

I wasn't put into prison pyjamas at that point. I was given a whole jumble of clothes that had belonged, at some time, to other passers-by. I resembled a 'seventies fashion victim, complete with shirts with jumbo collars and patterns of vintage cars racing off in opposite directions and a pair of gorblimey trousers that made my arse itch whenever I sat down. Eventually my parents were allowed to come to my rescue with a suitcase of my stuff and I began to feel normal again. It became like doing an extra long spot of detention at school. It was just another institution really. The police gradually accepted me as an ordinary bloke who wasn't going to pull any stunts. I started, in my own way, to turn their hatred into indifference and eventually into a grudging form of friendship. I was doing what I was best at, namely achieving social osmosis, only this time I was being downwardly mobile.

After another week I almost started to feel good again. I was sleeping better. The absence of booze meant that I had to make my own euphoria, but on the plus side it meant whatever my remorse, at least the situation wasn't being amplified by alcohol-induced moral hangovers. I missed my smokes and noticed that I hadn't masturbated or felt the need to since I had tried to commit suicide. It was as if I had gone into sexual mourning out of respect for Roxanne. Actually, it was well nigh on impossible to get an erection with the closed-circuit television cameras and peepholes all over the place. I had been exposed to enough humiliation being labelled a murderer, let alone a wanker. I wondered what they would have done if I just unzipped and calmly got on with it. Would alarm bells have gone off and a dozen burly men in hats burst through the door and grabbed my arms to restrain me? I decided not to put it to the test. It wasn't as if they had placed a box of perfumed tissues by the bed.

About three weeks after I'd killed Roxanne the psychiatrists and lawyers gave up squeezing any more information out of me. It was as if they'd become exhausted by my repertoire. Then I was told I'd be moved to a more permanent address pending my trial. I was going to be upgraded to the status of proper fully-fledged prison inmate. That was not, however, before the last and most nerve-racking set of visitors came to see me. Roxanne's parents were just about to leave for South Africa with their forlorn frozen cargo when they decided they'd pay me a visit.

Roxanne had shown me a picture she'd taken of her family when they'd last visited Britain. They were on a river boat near Greenwich. They looked like any other badly dressed tourists; her parents seeming slightly shell-shocked in their shell suits, while her bolshy little brother looked back in anger at the camera, obviously out of sorts about having his machismo associated with a family outing.

My armpits went into hydro-drive the hour before they arrived. For the first time since I had been carting their daughter's corpse up and down stairs, I started to shake. The *delirium tremens* of guilt.

When they eventually turned up I found it difficult to look at them on a level, as anyone would, I supposed if they'd just murdered the apple of their eye. They hadn't come to reprimand me, which made me feel worse. They wanted to know the details. Had she died quickly? Had she been happy for the last few months of her short life? I warmed to them gradually and could see where Roxanne had got her personality and guts from. They were no-bullshit South Africans who wanted answers rather than blood. Dad Sullivan offered me an Old Port cigar which I remembered Roxanne saying was his favourite toke. I used to smoke them when I was a kid. It tasted like nectar after a month without tobacco and made me feel slightly trippy.

I started to relax and stopped being obsequious. I described how Roxanne had fitted in, and yet had not totally immersed herself into London life and how, on a one-to-one basis, we'd clicked so well, perhaps better than either of us had ever experienced before. I admitted that we'd had our fair share of arguments. I tried to stick to the facts but felt obliged to give her character the benefit of the doubt and present a reasonably rosy assessment of her behaviour. I concluded by saying that we brought out the best and the worst in each other, and that had ultimately been our undoing. I still wanted to give them the fifteen thousand in my deposit account in her memory, but thought better of it. Freddie could handle the matter.

They left looking drained. Ma Sullivan said she hoped everything would work out OK for me, but I suspected her mind read 'Burn in Hell'. They weren't going to the trial. They said they couldn't see the point: it wouldn't bring their daughter back. They wished me luck.

Freddie became my lifeline. He visited me almost every day and briefed me on the progress of the trial. He kept me informed of the gossip, what people were saying about me and the various 'Jack the Ripper' jokes that were doing the rounds of the dealing rooms and the dinner party circuits around the capital. I was a star. It was like being the first to have measles at school.

It was on one of these visits that I heard about Christine's crash. She'd been cycling down a hill when she lost control of her bicycle and gone at about thirty miles an hour, headfirst into the back of a parked van. Her face was a mess, though not beyond repair thanks to the wonders of modern plastic surgery, but she'd lost the sight of one eye and severely damaged the other. She would have to wear glasses for the rest of her life. The sort with one lens frosted over and the other pebble thick.

My heart missed a beat. The photographs! *Holy schadenfreude!* Who said voodoo dolls didn't work? Had I the power to cast my own spells? It was too late to do anything about it now. Nobody could prove anything and even if I came clean, my confession would be dismissed as the ramblings of a madman.

"Well I never!" I said aloud. "They actually worked!" Freddie looked at me oddly. I didn't bother trying to explain. That should shut up Christine's twitterings about the good life. Tee hee!

On another occasion, Freddie brought an official-looking letter for me. I opened it. To my surprise it read:

*Dear Sir/Madam:*

*Road Traffic Acts - Parking Places*

*Thank you for your further letter received on 18th July. The matter has been re-considered and, whilst there is no evidence that the meter you used failed to function correctly, in view of your assurances I have decided to take no further action with regard to the Notice which may now be considered cancelled.*

*Yours faithfully,*

*R.C. Bum*
*Director of Planning and Transportation.*

"Yippee!" I exclaimed. "Isn't that marvellous?" I'd struck a blow for 'confuse-a-cat' silly letters.

One of the stranger things that happened at this very strange stage of my life was that I received a letter from Fenella Fellon asking if it was OK to visit me. I asked Freddie to pass on my flustered assent and a few days later Fenella came to see me. I was suspicious at first that she was on some weird Lord Longford do-good trip, but her motives appeared selfless.

When she arrived even the warders went quiet. I sat across the wide visitor's table lost for words. Her simple beauty and elegance made a mockery of the surroundings. I felt idiotic and humble in my everyday clothes. I thanked her for coming and then let my silence ask the questions.

"James," she said looking at me pityingly, "I was so worried about you."

"That's most odd, Fenella," I said. "You hardly know me."

"Yes, but I've always felt a certain empathy with you whenever we've met that I've never found with another man. I don't know why. All men want to worship or abuse me because of my looks, but with you there was something different. It was as thought you could read beyond my appearance and see the real me inside."

"Don't kid yourself sugar puff, but go on," I said in cynical self-defence. Fenella continued.

"The few times I've met you I have come away with an odd feeling of warmth and closeness."

What was she on?

"You see, James, I don't really like men. Morally. Spiritually. Or physically. I have my girlfriends, but you're the first man I felt I could have relied upon to make me happy and maybe provide what I've always been looking for. It's a pity we never got to know each other properly."

"Now you tell me," I said, rolling my eyes to the heavens.

"I know. It's silly, isn't it? Fate's such a useless bastard sometimes."

"No, there's nothing particularly exceptional about the matter," I said quietly. "People frequently spurn compatibility, although in this instance it's a shame we missed each other."

Then I thought for a moment. Suddenly I realised what Fenella was saying.

"Fenella, when you said you have your girlfriends, do you mean that you're a les..."

"Don't say that word, James," she interrupted, before I could finish. "Shall we say that my tastes and tendencies tend to exclude men from the equation? That's why you're such an interesting case."

Fenella smiled and got up from her chair. I stood up. Her eyes were glistening.

"Goodbye, James," she said, "I'll see you soon."

With that she departed, leaving me and one of the warders who'd been within earshot looking lost for words. All that remained was the scent of her cologne.

The trial was immensely embarrassing. In fact it was an exercise in total mortification. In and out of police cars with blankets over my head; people I'd never met screaming "Bastard!" at me whenever I appeared in the open and all the poncey gits in court with their wigs on. Even though I admitted being guilty as charged, they still insisted on confusing me and making me look even more ridiculous. The barrister who Freddie had instructed turned out to be particularly useless and out of his depth. At times I seriously wondered whether he was batting on my side.

Fenella appeared almost every day in the public gallery, a rose amongst the nettles. I was sure that the jury's verdict was biased by the fact that she'd come to see me rather than them. In his summing up the judge described me as "a thoroughly rotten egg and a deviant to boot," although I subsequently heard from Freddie that His Lordship was reputed to be unable to 'do it' without the assistance of a vibrator on full throttle up his bot.

My manslaughter plea was thrown out and I got life. Sheer penis envy. With Christine's Curse operating at maximum overdrive anything less would have been a disappointment. Reasons to be cheerful.

The Press was the worst thing that I had to contend with. The reporters had a field day. They had all the necessary ingredients for the perfect scandal. I came out, as was to be expected, as black as soot. Pictures of my pathetic old school, St Dweebs ('Top People's School') that I'd left over half a lifetime before and had absolutely no allegiance to beyond being an 'Old Dweebian', appeared in every tabloid newspaper. It was as if the school itself had committed the crime. There were long articles about my scandalous lifestyle - cocaine hoovering, glue sniffing and ecstasy swilling debauchery. It was a pity they'd missed the real bacchanalian culprit. They referred to me as "Unemployed Mallet" or "Mallet, unemployed" as if all was explained by the entire unemployed population's natural propensity for murder. The artist's impressions of me in court made me look like an arrogant but rather unintelligent shit. Quite a good likeness, actually.

With Roxanne, predictably, it was the other way round. Each day she moved to new pinnacles of celestial perfection. Pictures of her in the newspapers were captioned 'Much Liked', 'Gentle Disposition', 'Honour Student', 'Promising Accountant' and 'Budding Executive', all of it cut down as the full bloom of womanhood was about to begin. There was no mention of 'Sluttish Tendencies', 'Promiscuous Disposition, 'Putrescent Body Odour, 'Selfish Temperament' or 'Horrendous Bottom'. There were the usual photographs of her as a child on the beach with her loving family and every conceivable device to make her seem cute and vulnerable. Among the more recent photographs of her they'd found a particularly flattering one that made her radiate a certain vitality and intelligence. It became the trademark for most of the articles concerning the incident, rather like the one of the pretty blonde girl with the baggy eyes holding a monkey, who'd been eaten by game wardens in Kenya the year before. I wondered whether the media would have been quite so interested if either girl had not been quite so photogenic.

I was led away from court and frogmarched into another life. To start with it was tough adjusting to the new regime. It was my first real prison, although having been to a boarding school, I knew roughly what to expect.

I had the piss taken out of me, partly because of my accent and partly because being a murderer, especially of a woman was pretty low in the prison society pecking order, being only slightly above that of the child molesters and sex offenders.

My social skills came in handy again and I learned the new rules fast. I kept myself out of trouble. Although I was thirty-six by the time I was put away, I still had a neat, inoffensive body and a full head of hair above my plump schoolboy face. I was the object of considerable unsolicited and unwanted attention. Like every new boy I was a novelty and, as a result of my supposedly privileged background, or for some other reason, I was sought out by one or two of the other inmates as if I was a bitch in season.

Prison routine was, of course, different from the outside world. There were certain laws and codes of behaviour that weren't in the rule book but had, nonetheless, to be adhered to. These were not the rules as laid down by the prison governors, but the lore of everyday prison life. Rules made by the inmates for the inmates. For instance, if a bigger and more important inmate came to me and asked to have my radio, my shoes or anything of mine that he desired, this was a reasonable request. I either parted with whatever he wanted and nothing more was said or I didn't, in which case something not very nice would happen to me a few days later. I might be fortunate and just find a turd under my pillow at night or be the luckless object of fun in the showers and end up being flicked to near death with wet towels by a dozen party funsters until I was black and blue all over. Just like school. Obviously worse things could happen. I might have wound up with a couple of broken fingers or be the object of a casual gang rape; "bum fun" as it was graciously called.

There was, however, one way to protect myself against this sort of occurrence. I could become part of the prison insurance network. Instead of giving my radio to my would-be assailant, I could give it to a 'protector'. The 'protector' would in return ensure my safety and guarantee that no harm came my way. The same principle applied to parts of the body. By appointing an appropriate chaperon, I could insure my general safety in return for granting access to those particular parts of my anatomy that he desired. I had a number of requests to become various people's 'bitch' or 'jessie'. For about two months I held out. I complained to the deputy governor about it. He was sympathetic but said that there was very little he could do; it was just one of the many perplexing aspects of prison life.

Then I met Tufty Olmes. Tufty was a big, powerful man of about fifty, in the ex-boxer mould, who was also in for murder. He was a quiet but respected member of the prison hierarchy and nobody asked for *his* radio or messed him around. He had a Gorbachev-style port stain on his forehead that rang a bell. He spent most of his time reading crime novels. With his bald pate and glasses he affected a donnish air. The most important thing about him was that he had the collective ear of the prison officers and thus, although he wasn't 'King Rat', he had considerable sway in the behind-the-scenes politics of the prison.

I'd just about given up the concept of maintaining my anal virginity much longer and was calculating the most profitable and painless way of disposing of it. There was a disease out there and I was not in the market to be one of its customers. The solution, with luck, lay in Tufty.

Tufty was a little more subtle than the others in his approach. He joined me in the canteen at lunch one day. At first he didn't say anything. The strong, silent type. Then he spoke.

"I hear one or two of the lads are giving you a bit of trouble."

"The bum's rush I'd say," I replied.

Tufty told me that he could put an end to it if I wanted. I asked him what he expected in return, and was not totally taken unawares when he looked at me squarely and said, "You."

I thanked him for his flattering offer, but asked him what the difference was between being buggered by him as opposed to anyone else.

"A lot," he said knowingly.

It transpired that he desired companionship and 'a good woman' rather than nonstop erotic cabaret. He wanted someone to discuss his books with. Someone cultured and educated-like; a sort of valet; a gentleman's gentleman. Of course he expected his conjugal rights as any man would, but he said he wasn't a "tart or a poof, if you understand what I mean." Another plus that he pointed out was that I would be on practically full privileges in no time, which meant quite something if you were doing a long stretch. I would never get hassled by another prisoner or warder ever again. We would be "the dream ticket", he said. With my contacts on the outside and his on the inside, the years would just slip by. In no time I'd be out, none the worse for wear and safely back at home again. He even said I could keep some of the presents and food parcels that my family sent me.

Like me, Tufty had years to go before he was eligible for parole. If I was going to get out of the joint alive with all my T-cells intact, I could do worse than throw in my lot with Tufty up my bum. At least he was older and probably wouldn't do it so often, but as I hadn't had any previous experience of botty banditry, I didn't know what to expect.

I asked Tufty what he'd done before he'd been sent down. He told me that he'd been a builder for most of his life, but he'd also done some part-time work as an announcer at some of the bingo clubs in his area and as a Master of Ceremonies at various social functions.

"But it all got too much for me," he said. "One day a punter was getting to me, so I let him have it." The rest, he said, was history. I made no comment. The Venn diagram of coincidence had struck again.

I told Tufty I was very touched, even honoured by his kind suggestion, but added I would be grateful if I could be given time to consider his proposal first. Then bashfully, like a shy Southern belle leaving her handsome beau, I got up from the table to go to the gym. The prison food was indigestible to the point that there was little purpose in allowing it time to settle.

I thought about it, as any person would, and resigned myself to the inevitable. I was literally going to have to lay my arse on the line with Tufty, or someone else would get there first. T Olmes = No Resistance.

It was funny how on the outside I had been so indifferent to my fate, but now that I was back in an institution I wanted to survive and come out of it in one piece. Half the cons in the prison were jacking up on horse or anything they could lay their hands on. They all shared their works together. There wasn't a clean needle in the joint. Goodness knew how many people were carrying the dreaded 'American' disease. To add to it all, the social niceties of safe sex had not, at that point, reached voguish proportions within the prison community. There had already been half a dozen AIDS-related deaths and there was Terence - they're always called Terence - a suspiciously gaunt-looking character with the telltale blotches of Kaposi's sarcoma on his face, who hung lugubriously round the sanatorium in a dressing gown all day. Tufty was sufficiently old and ugly to be away from the mainstream of prison buggery and he didn't look the drug abusing type. In many respects his timely intervention was a blessing in disguise. He did say he wasn't a "tart".

The next day I dropped a note in Tufty's cell saying that I accepted his proposal and asked him to let me know what he wanted next. At lunch a delighted Tufty joined me amidst a few jeers from some of the other inmates at a nearby table. Tufty was positively beaming and said he'd arrange to get me transferred to his cell in a week or two. I was not to worry about a thing. All would be fine and dandy.

Tufty was true to his word and within a fortnight I was transferred with my meagre belongings to his cell a few corridors away. Tufty greeted me like an Edwardian grandee, a blazer over his prison overalls, freshly shaven but smelling rather revoltingly of Old Spice. He offered me some 'Stingray' fortified wine in a coffee mug and we toasted our new acquaintance. How civilised! Whatever next? Guacamole and tortilla chips? A log fire? A little Richard Clayderman in the background, perhaps? Tufty was convivial to the point of being avuncular in showing me where I was to put my belongings and which drawers were mine. He was at pains to point out that I didn't have to do anything I didn't want to do as long as he could do what he wanted to do first.

I hadn't had any alcohol for nearly four months and I found that the 'Stingray' was hitting my emaciated stomach at the right spot. I felt a devil-may-care, do-your-worst-big-boy attitude envelop me. I think Tufty was expecting me to be a little more coquettish about his advances, but as it happened he didn't need to make any.

I just said to him, "Tufty, I don't know the score; you do. I'm in your dear little building-site hardened hands, so go for it."

Tufty was a bit taken aback, as if I were an under-aged but slightly over-direct virgin. It struck me as funny that however much bravado a man or a woman could muster in public, so often in private - on a one-to-one basis - their bluster turned to a childlike coyness.

He helped himself to another mug of 'Stingray' and, as an afterthought, refilled mine. He sat next to me on my bed and started talking about his books, his life and his aspirations. All of a sudden I realised why I'd been getting it wrong with women so much of the time. Every man regards himself as the most important thing in the universe and is perplexed or occasionally outraged when all his dreams come to nothing and his achievements are of no consequence. It makes for very boring copy. I was beginning to enjoy the subtle manipulation that is a good listener's art. Especially, I imagined, a woman's.

I crossed my legs as if I was wearing Dior tights and held my rolled-up cigarette as if it were a Virginia Slim. I wished at that point that my hair was longer and that I could shake it and feel it on my back and neck. I felt that if I had that, I might be able to achieve an air of mischievous vulnerability, like Natalie Wood, but with my fierce prison haircut I had to adopt second best and go for a come- hither Mia Farrow look. There was no way that I could go through this charade as a man. Manliness, which I'd had in scoops before, belonged to another life. I wasn't going to desecrate my masculinity by confusing the issue with buggery. For that I would have to turn myself into a woman.

Halfway through my third cup of 'Stingray' I began to feel a bit sick. The chat-up was over and the business part was about to begin. I had a sense of *déjà vu*. I now knew how a woman must feel sometimes when an evening turns serious. Tufty moved closer to me and I tried to retreat into a gap that wasn't there. I tried to think about tomorrow, next week and the week after. Tufty put his arm round me. I hoped that no one whom I'd ever taken home had experienced the sense of dread that I felt that evening. He made a move to kiss me but I avoided his mouth as best as I could without wishing to appear frigid. I wasn't exactly exuding 'buy' signals. Tufty gave up on my lips and nuzzled into my neck. The smell of aftershave and 'Stingray' made me want to vomit. He cupped his hand rather pathetically on my chest. I recoiled foetally and feigned sleep. I supposed Tufty interpreted this as submission or bliss. He took his trousers off. I was relieved to see he had an agreeably small, pencil-thin penis. He waved it in front of me and asked me to kiss it or touch it but I shook my head and squeaked:

"Surely not on our first date?"

I went into a state of shock but had the presence of mind to ask him earnestly if he could be gentle. He got a tub of prison margarine from the cupboard, pulled down my tracksuit trousers and slapped the marge across my bum, like the well-practised brick-layer he was.

## A few years on.

I won't go into the technical details for those who haven't been buggered, but for my part it was more uncomfortable than painful. It certainly wasn't sexually fulfilling. It was like having a really difficult crap in reverse.

Tufty was quick and grateful and I wondered what all the fuss was about. Yes, it hurt a bit, but it was just a sordid, weak little hurt that was entirely compatible with the absurdity of human nature. I wasn't particularly shocked by it and after a while it almost seemed normal, if not particularly enjoyable. They say you can get used to anything. It's sad that so much anguish, lust and subsequent gratification are all down to the simple friction of protoplasm between two nervous systems. Lust is a powerful deceiver, but why moralise over an instinct?

It's all right now and everything's cool. I've come to live with myself, even though I'm not sure what I am. I failed as an angry young man and I'm certainly not cut out to be an old poof. Once Tufty had got over the novelty of having me around he stopped trying to seduce me. He could and can have me any time, but our relationship has changed. I guess I was, as Roxanne might have said, "a dud fuck" in that department, but I'm always here to give him a willing ear and hold him when he has an anxiety attacks or cries out at night.

It's turned out that I've got more control than Tufty. I'm no longer fazed by my own sense of failure, whereas Tufty hasn't grasped that everything can be contained in a formula. In the end, success and failure amount to the same thing. They're both, as Kipling observed, imposters. We all do our 'stretch' in one form or another, until it's time to take our leave, graveward. We die and that's it. You don't buy life: you rent it. Nothing really matters. Nobody really wins or loses. The human race is no more important than mildew on a crab apple; no more permanent than leaves on a tree. Tufty still has too much faith in the system and hasn't worked out what's going on yet. I tend not to think of things in terms of success or failure anymore, so much as the scale of tragedy. God! After my catalogue of catastrophes

I'd gladly settle for humble failure. I'd wear it proudly, like a crown! It would be a welcome relief after being such a complete disaster zone.

Of the others, I don't hear much. It's too far to visit really. I get the odd letter from time to time but I'm not very good at writing back, so most people have given up on me. I suppose it's my way of dissociating myself from the past. The only thing I heard of any real interest was that Michelle of all people lost her job soon after I was convicted. I assume the two incidents were unconnected but Michelle was so devastated about being out of work that she took to the bottle and is now, so I'm told, on the game! It was about time she did something right. I never had any doubts about where her true talents lay.

    I never heard from Christine Hale, which seemed callous even by her standards, although 'callous' is probably the wrong word. In the end I decided it wasn't so much her, as the magnificence of her indifference towards me that I found so beguiling. The Curse seems to have more or less blown itself out, so perhaps it's just as well not to rock the boat. I don't know what it was, but Christine never quite forgave me for something I must have done all those years ago. Maybe she sensed, erroneously as it happens, that underneath it all I didn't think that she was quite good enough. And now perhaps she finds it galling that despite everything, one day I will get my complete physical freedom back, whereas she never will. The Curse, it would appear, has slightly backfired on her.

    Crystal Frost got married, which was what she wanted, to a restaurateur as it happened, and the remaining *dramatis personae* have just disappeared into the labyrinth of time. And what became of all those Radon boxes remains, for me, a mystery to this day.

Tufty's still good at making sure the warders don't bother us and we keep very much to ourselves most of the time. We're like a couple of chimpanzees peering out of a cage, clutching at each other occasionally for comfort. I go about my duties quite conscientiously. I'm almost a monk, really. There are no temptations apart from the odd cup of 'boiler maker's delight on a Saturday night before going to the TV room. I'm more or less straight. I'm in charge of the library now (power at last!), so Tufty and I have plenty to talk about. I go to chapel. Tufty put me onto that. It's funny how, by being a nonperson in society's eyes, I've found the dignity to act like a normal human being. Mr Nice Guy. Or so I hope.

    There's no question about my good behaviour clause. I'm a model prisoner; I often go to the chaplain's office for a chat and a cuppa. And I haven't felt a rage coming on for over a year. In that respect I think I've more or less made it through my breakdown or whatever the fuck it was. I admit it was no excuse for doing what I did, but most of us have some sort of freak-out during a lifetime.

I suppose I quite like it here, away from the everyday hassles of the outside world. Don't get me wrong. It's not the Wandsworth Hilton, but it's OK. I don't suppose I'll ever get used to the smell of excrement and Ajax. It's a bit of a coprophagic nightmare in that respect, and the constant noise gets me down sometimes. There's always a door being slammed or someone shouting and the people, to be honest, are a bit rough.

It won't go on for ever, of course. I'll be up for parole in another ten years or so, and I'll be nearly fifty by then. Tufty's due to be up for it at about the same time. He'll be in his mid-sixties, with not so much left of his life to start over. We've agreed that we'll have to let go of each other once we're out. What works in prison seldom works outside. Anyway, I've come to the conclusion that relationships are like J-cloths: they're not really meant to last. Friendships are just a means to an end. To what end I'm still not one hundred per cent sure.

I don't know what I'll do when I get out. I hope The Curse will have run its course or at least leave me alone. Anyway I've got a feeling that my powers of metaphysical defence are now greater than those of The Curse's paranormal attack. If not I'll just have to live with it as best I can.

I think I'll give marriage a miss. Who wants to be stuck with a depreciating asset for the rest of their lives? Besides I lack the necessary optimism to breed. Children are so awful and ungrateful these days, I can't understand why people have them. But on the other hand I certainly can't be a swinging young bachelor again and I'm a complete flop, literally, as a 'jessie'. The latter neither aroused me nor surprised me, but it did lead me to wonder if I'd be better off as a woman. It might make sense. Explains the drugs in India and why Fenella Fellon took to me. Now I know why small children burst into tears if I so much as look at them and why dogs start barking at me from across the street for no apparent reason. Or why I'm always the last person strangers choose to sit next to on the bus. They know. It's instinctive; they know something's not right. It's not surprising I've got it wrong all these years and upset so many people. I'm a woman in a man's body: a bitch rather than a misogynist. My chauvinism was merely the idiot child of my envy; my preoccupation with menstruation merely an appreciation of life itself.

On the practical side, I'm no good to any potential employer. I've had it in that respect. Who wants to employ a murderer and an ex-con? I don't want to be a suit or another strap-hanging loser in the service sector again anyway. I'm too grown up for an office now. I don't want somebody hovering around, watching me do some banal bottom-feeding job all day. I wouldn't mind doing something menial or arty, though. Like making ornamental balsawood elephants, perhaps. Why not? There aren't any real ones left. Or do something that no one else wants to do, like working night shifts. I'm too lazy and out of touch to start my own business or go out and get a qualification. Yech! Why bother? Life's too short. What I'd really like to be, with the odd state handout, is a housewife. I like housework and I don't think I'd mind being cooped up all day. Not after this place. Anything for a quiet life. Give me a room with a telly and a microwave and I'll be happy to while away the hours till it's time to take my place with the silent majority. I'll just sit in a room till it's time to lie in a box.

So I think I'll have a sex change when I get out of here, if I'm accepted for the operation. If that doesn't finish my parents off, nothing will. I might have to go to Brazil or somewhere where the doctors don't ask too many questions. I've still got the money to pay for it in my deposit account which Freddie, mercifully, talked me out of sending to Roxanne's parents in Cape Town. These slash 'n' burn ops don't come cheap. I know it sounds like slightly strong medicine for the job in hand, but I think it's the only way. Why not? The chances of my finding any normal sort of conjugal union after I get out of here out seem more and more remote as time goes by. Heck, it's only a routine sex change I'm looking for. I expect with the advances being made in genetic engineering, people will be able to change species one day. Perhaps there'll come a day when a person can wake up in the morning and say, "Ah, it must be Tuesday. I think I'll turn into an owl." I might as well give it a go and see what happens. What a laugh, eh? And I'm going to treat myself to the biggest pair of tits in the world! I'll get rid of all those nasty male hormones and excess testosterone that made me have all those rages and do all the silly things I used to do. Perhaps then I'll calm down a bit; stop murdering people for a start. Maybe even learn to say "cunt" not quite so often.

I don't suppose I'll ever lose my physical desire for women. I'll see how the hormone treatment makes me feel. Besides, I've come to the conclusion that underneath it all I prefer female company, even if I'm a bit out of practice. I feel more at home with them. Men aren't my scene - they're too rough and revolting. They do nothing for me and I'm not going to go through life in a state of anal discomfort just so that any passing stranger can get his kicks off my gnarled rectum and expose me to that fucking disease. I hope to God they find a proper cure. I bet the Japanese will have the last laugh and come up with something. Or the Koreans! I don't care who it is, but the sooner the better; I'm fed up with this living with the alien nonsense and dementedly checking for melanomas the whole time.

No, what I think I'll do after the op is become a lesbian and go the full circle. One way to get Fenella Fellon. I'll have the benefit of both worlds.

Can't catch STDs off a dildo, can you? Or a broom handle. Love is many splintered. My metamorphosis will be the death of James Mallet, murder by castration, and the birth of Jane Mallet, spinster and dyke to the gentry, complete with a black belt in flower arranging. The ultimate in penile reform! I'll be a bit past it by then and won't exactly be auditioning to be a Bond girl, but a friend, oddly enough of my parents had a sex change at the tender age of seventy. He turned up to his daughter's wedding with little grey curls and a handbag, wearing a cerise frock with a daring hemline for the occasion. Apparently, he goes to his old regimental do's in a similar manner and people, oddly enough, accept him for what he is. He was a highly decorated soldier, after all. Now he's a highly decorous lady too.

So that's it. That's the rub. For all the thrashing about and spleen in the past, I've never found the contentment that I have now. The climb was hard but the view was worth it. All that frigging around, trying to be the biggest pair of trousers in the world was, in fact, a sham. For all the supposed privileges I was born with, the cap didn't fit. Is it any wonder that I found it difficult being an alpha male? I wasn't an alpha anything. It took this Dante's inferno where I now live to convince me that I could only achieve peace with myself by myself, away from outside interference and preconceptions of what I should and shouldn't be; to live each day as a personal triumph, regardless of its outcome. And it's provided a welcome refuge. It's as though the ghosts of all the suffering that has gone on here over the decades have provided an impenetrable barrier against the outside world. Which happily seems to include The Curse, if, let's face it, such a thing ever existed.

I think I'll turn in now and listen on my Walkperson to The Beadle's 'Happy Toad' tape I was given by my last visitor.

"You should see Styrofoam Sam... she's so good looking she looks like a man."

Yeah. Yeah. Yeah.

Goodnight.

www.ingramcontent.com/pod-product-compliance
Lightning Source LLC
Chambersburg PA
CBHW051644260626
47170CB00004B/1333